KAMUNAGARA

REBIRTH OF THE DEMONSLAYER

VOLUME ONE

NEW YORK, NEW YORK

Translation & Adaptation: Yuki Urakawa

Retouch and Lettering: Junemoon Studios

Design: Anime Works

Managing Editor: Frank Pannone

Publisher: John Sirabella

Special thanks to Clara Latham and Chet Brier

Media Blasters Press
Office of Publication
519 8th Avenue, 14th Floor
New York, New York 10018

ISBN: 1-58655-540-5

Printed in Canada

MEDIA BLASTERS PRESS
WWW.MEDIA-BLASTERS.COM

Anime Works

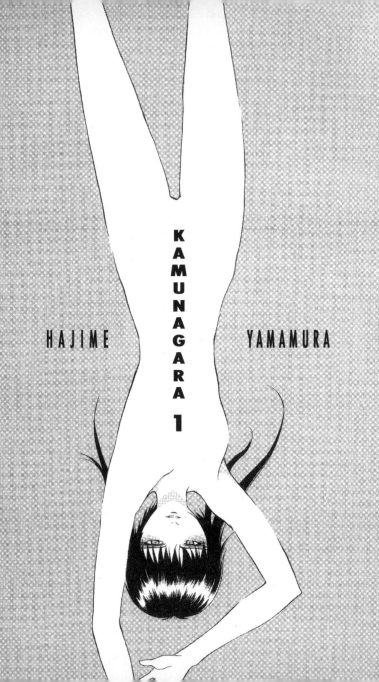

KAMUNAGARA 1

HAJIME   YAMAMURA

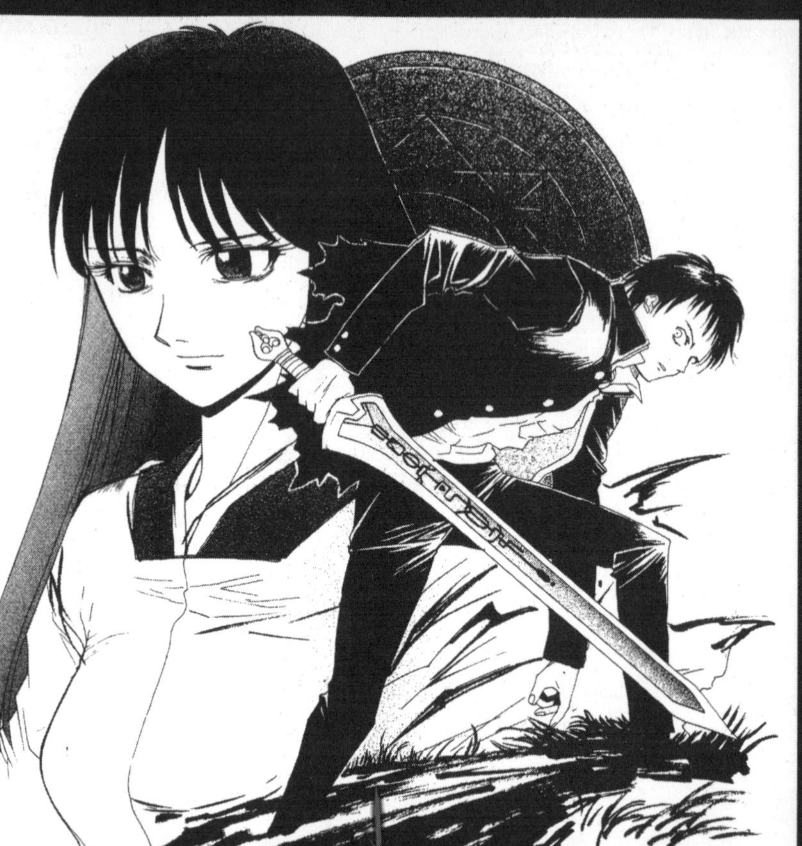

KAMUNAGARA

REBIRTH OF THE DEMONSLAYER

VOLUME ONE

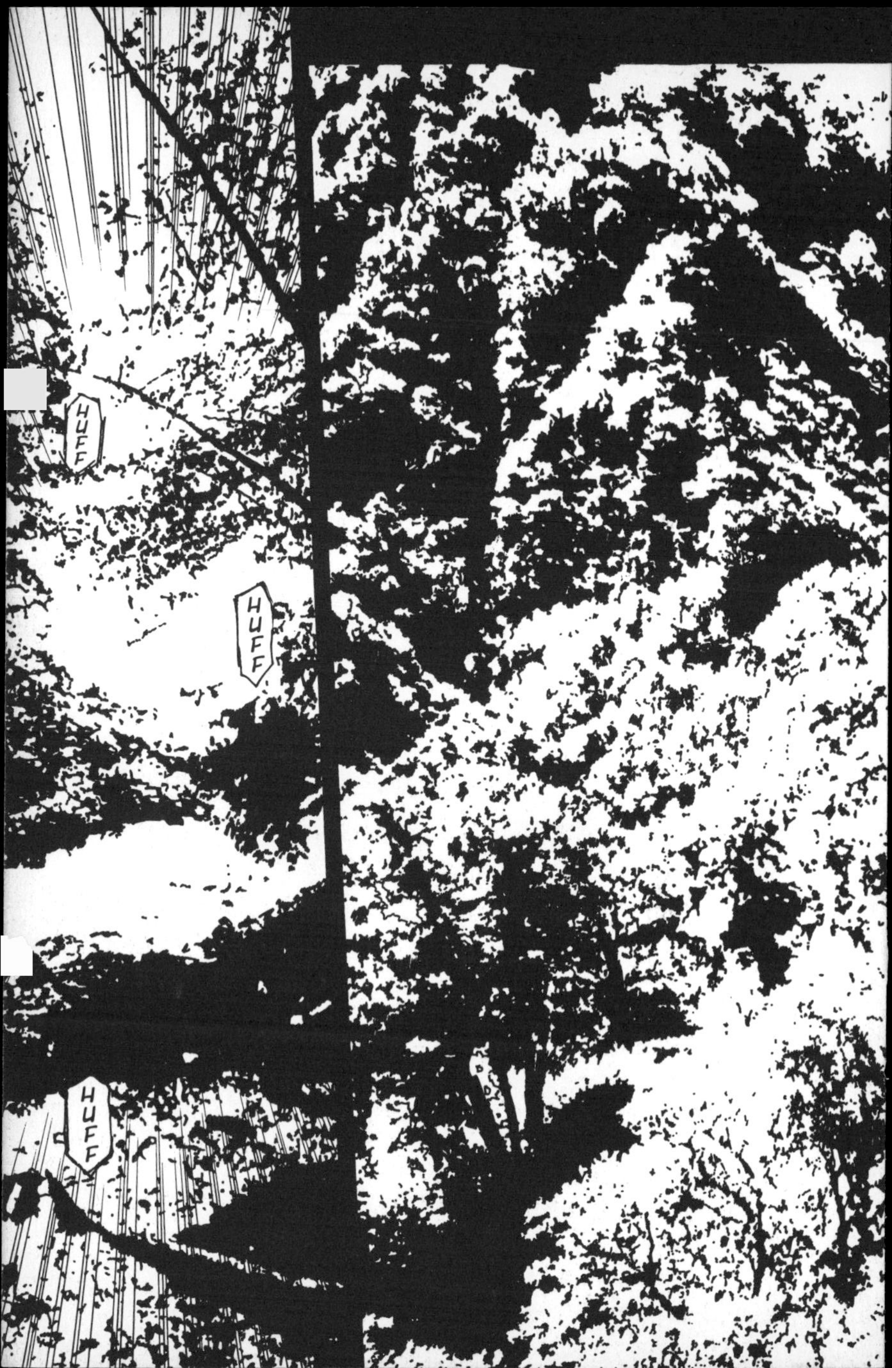
HUFF
HUFF
HUFF

#1. 見知らぬ記憶
Memories Unknown

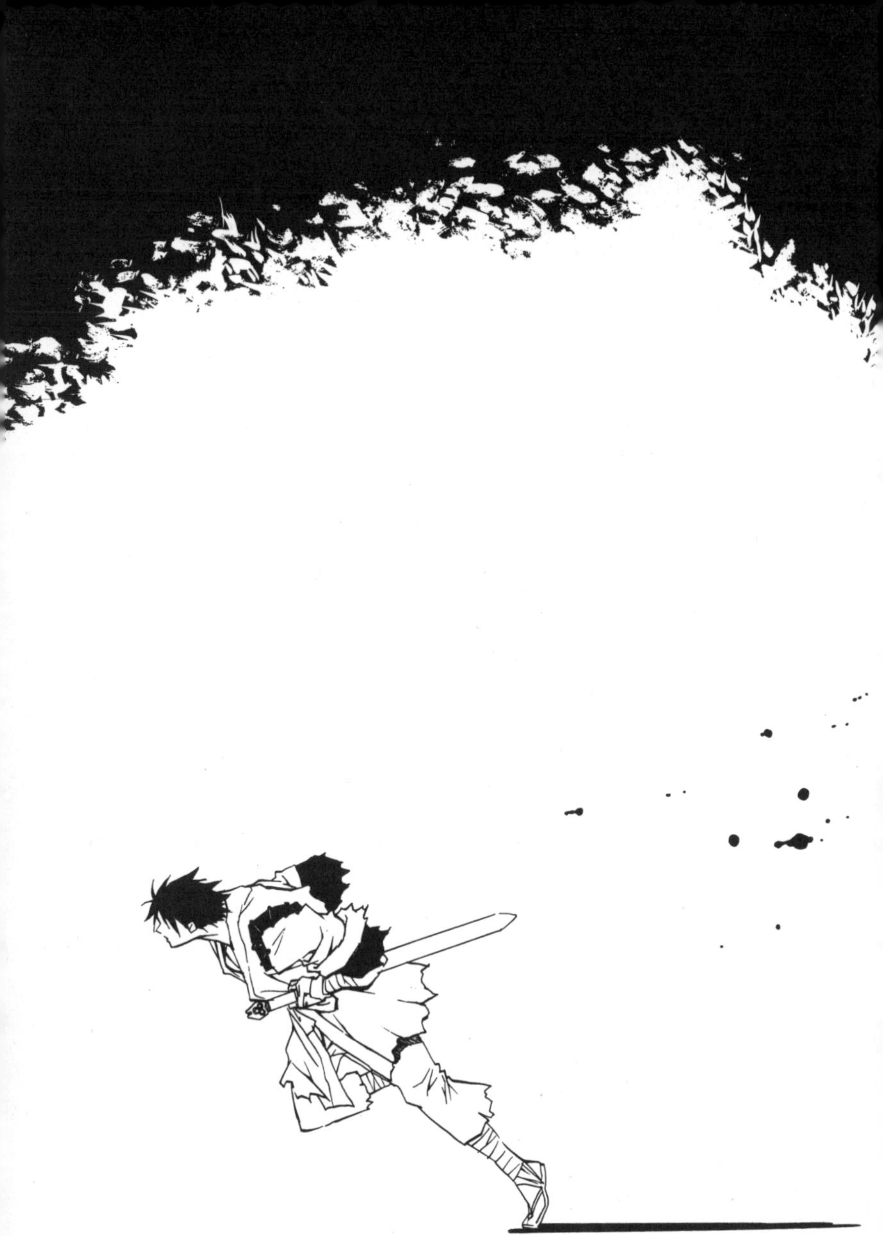

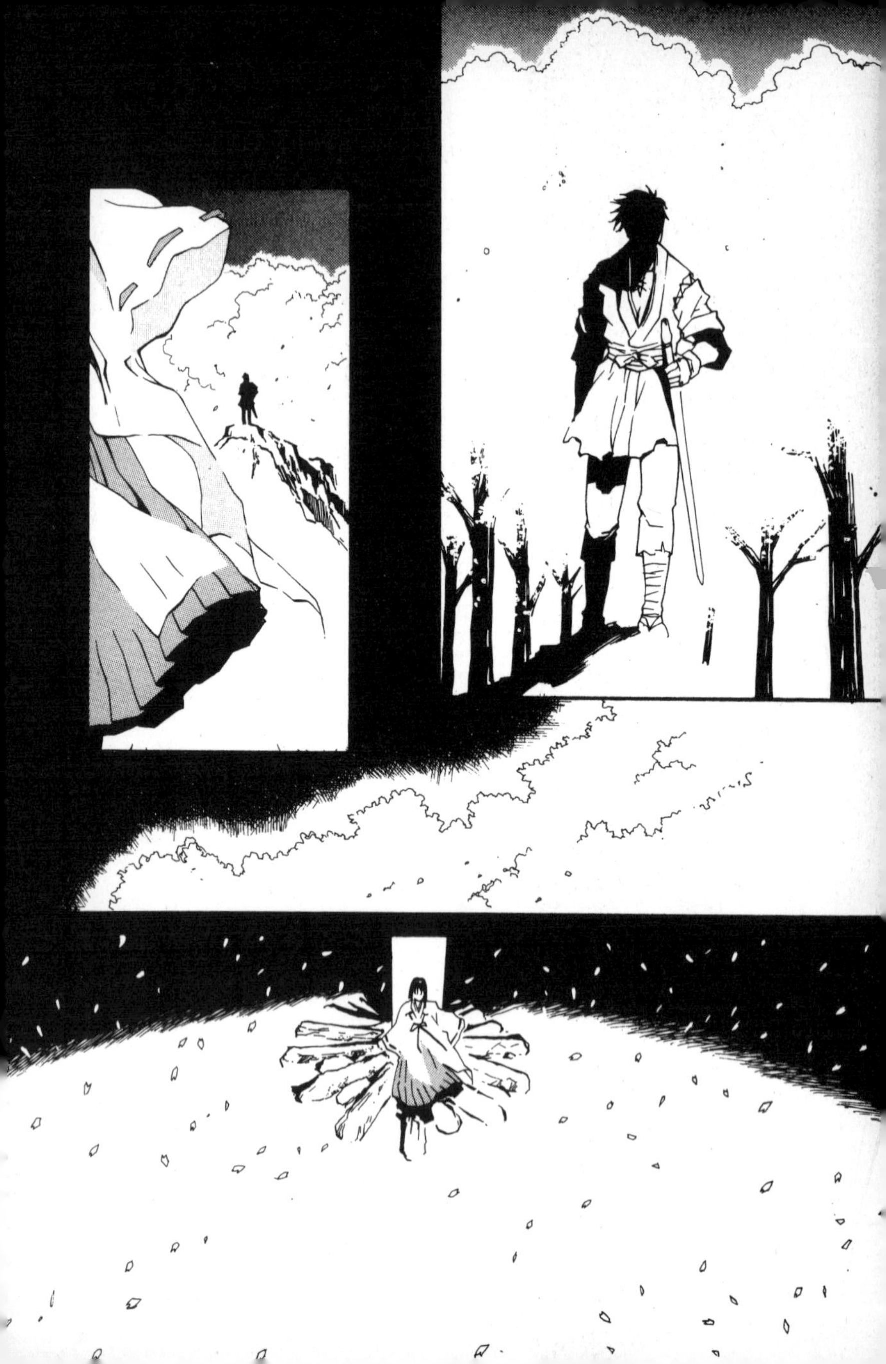

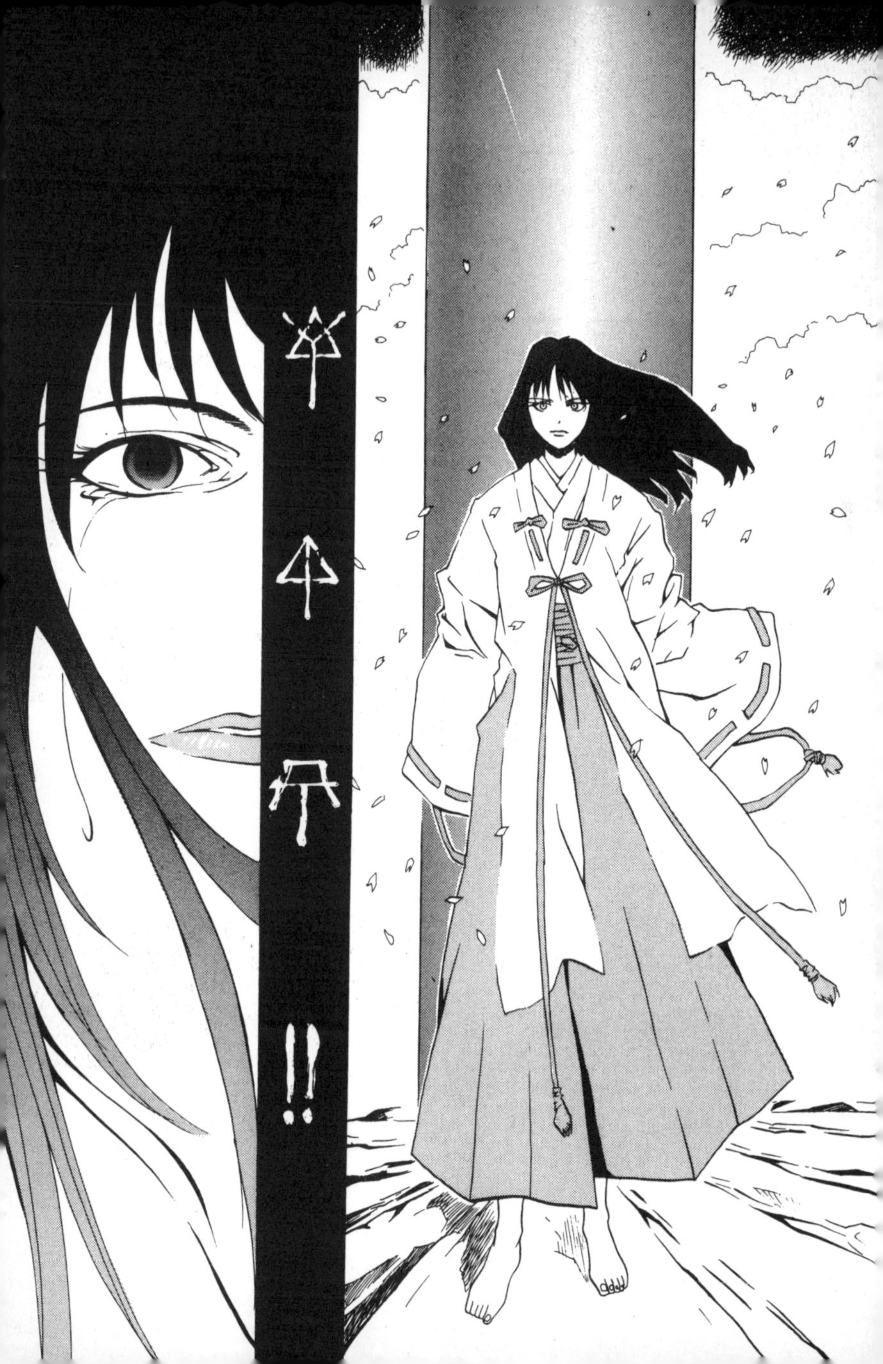

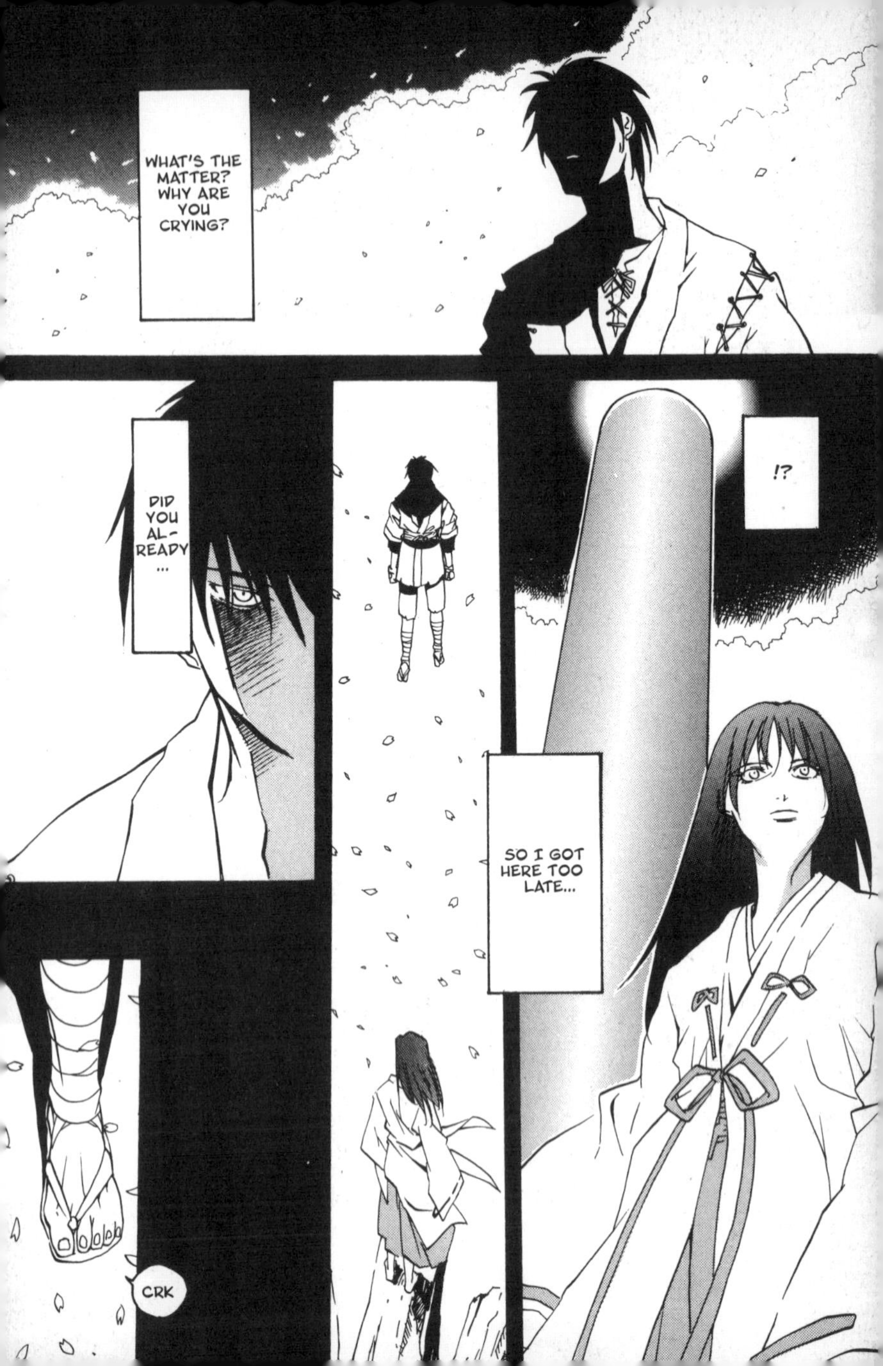

WHAT'S THE MATTER? WHY ARE YOU CRYING?
!?
SO I GOT HERE TOO LATE...
DID YOU AL-READY ...
CRK

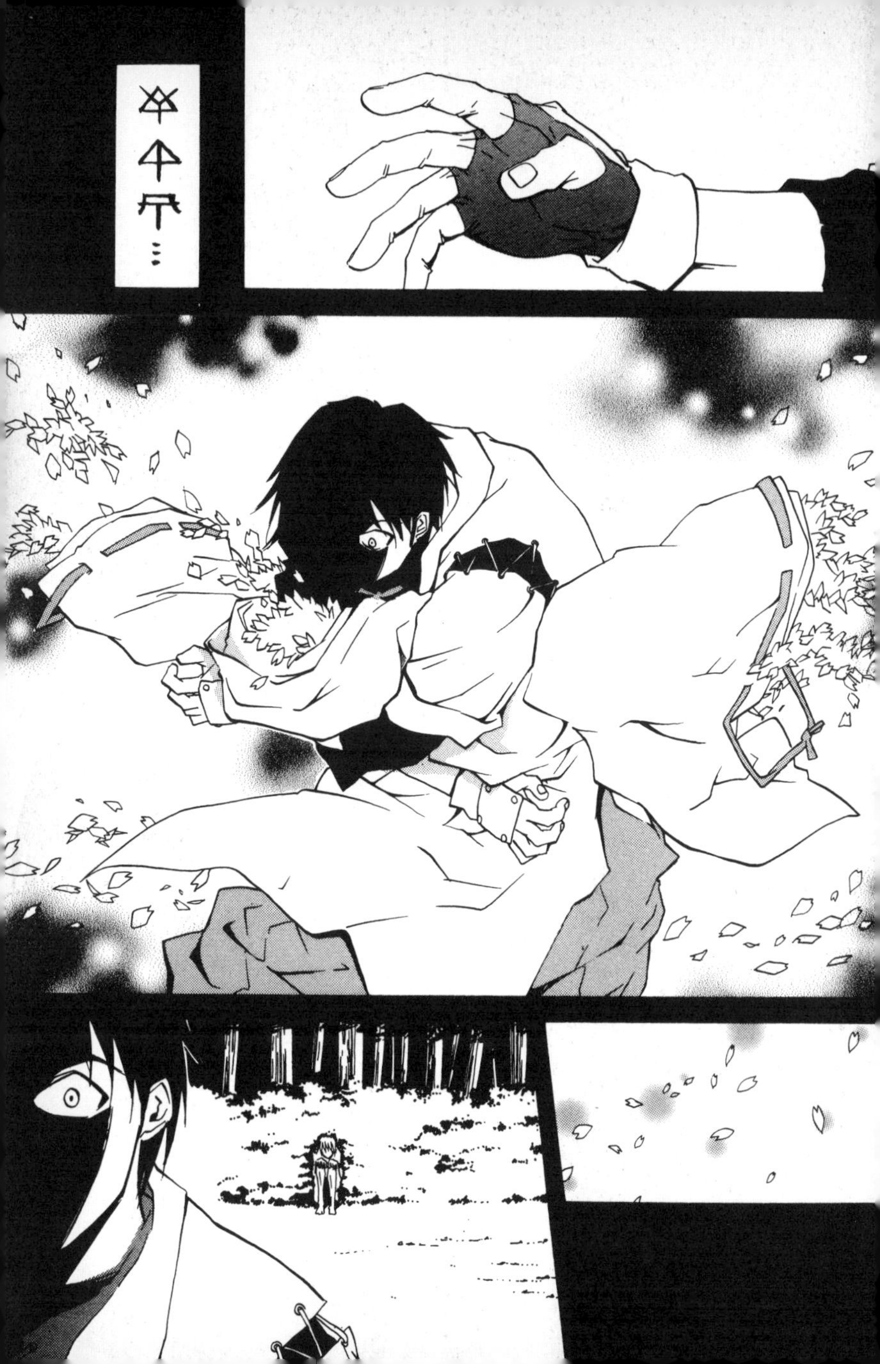

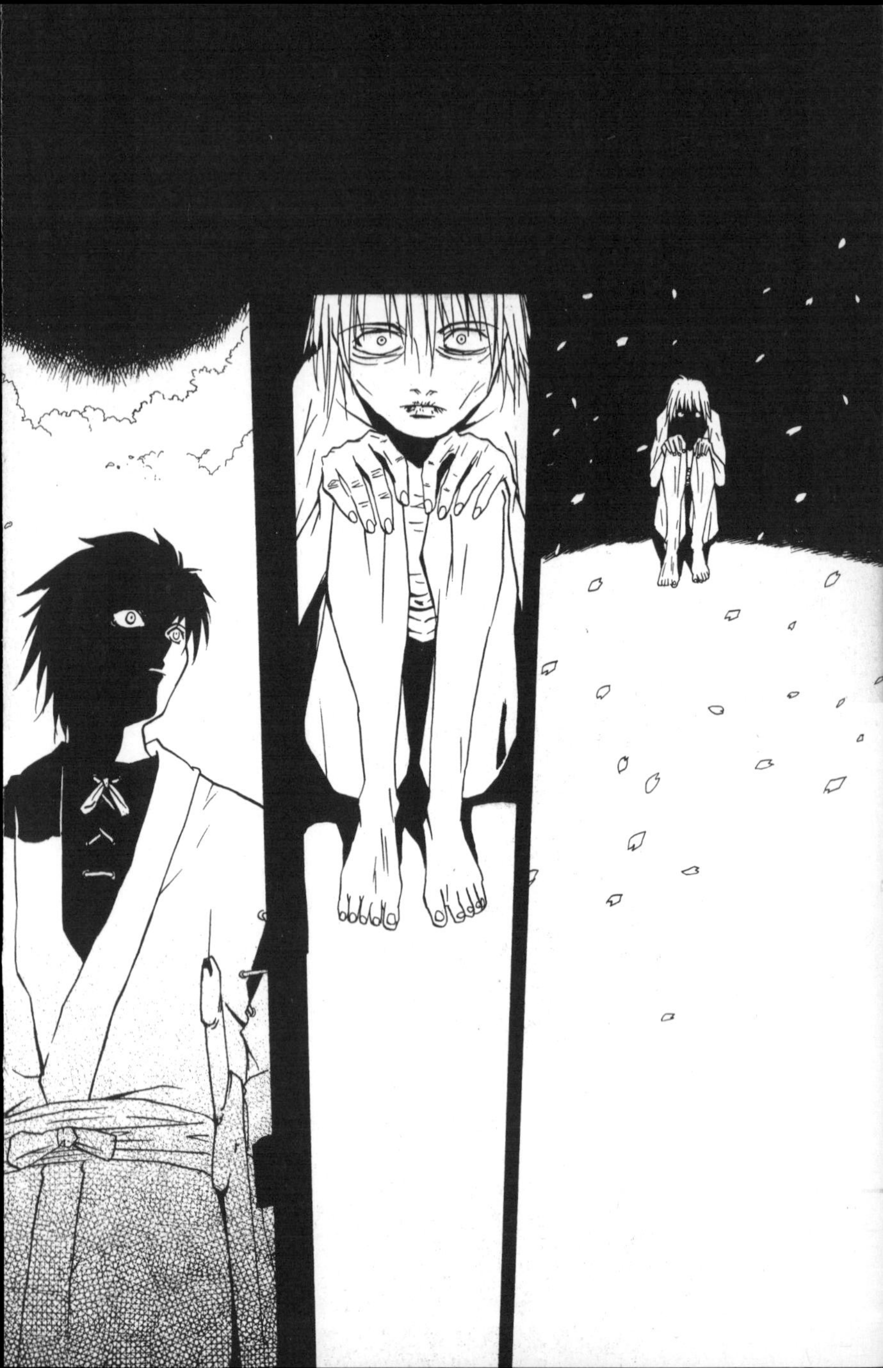

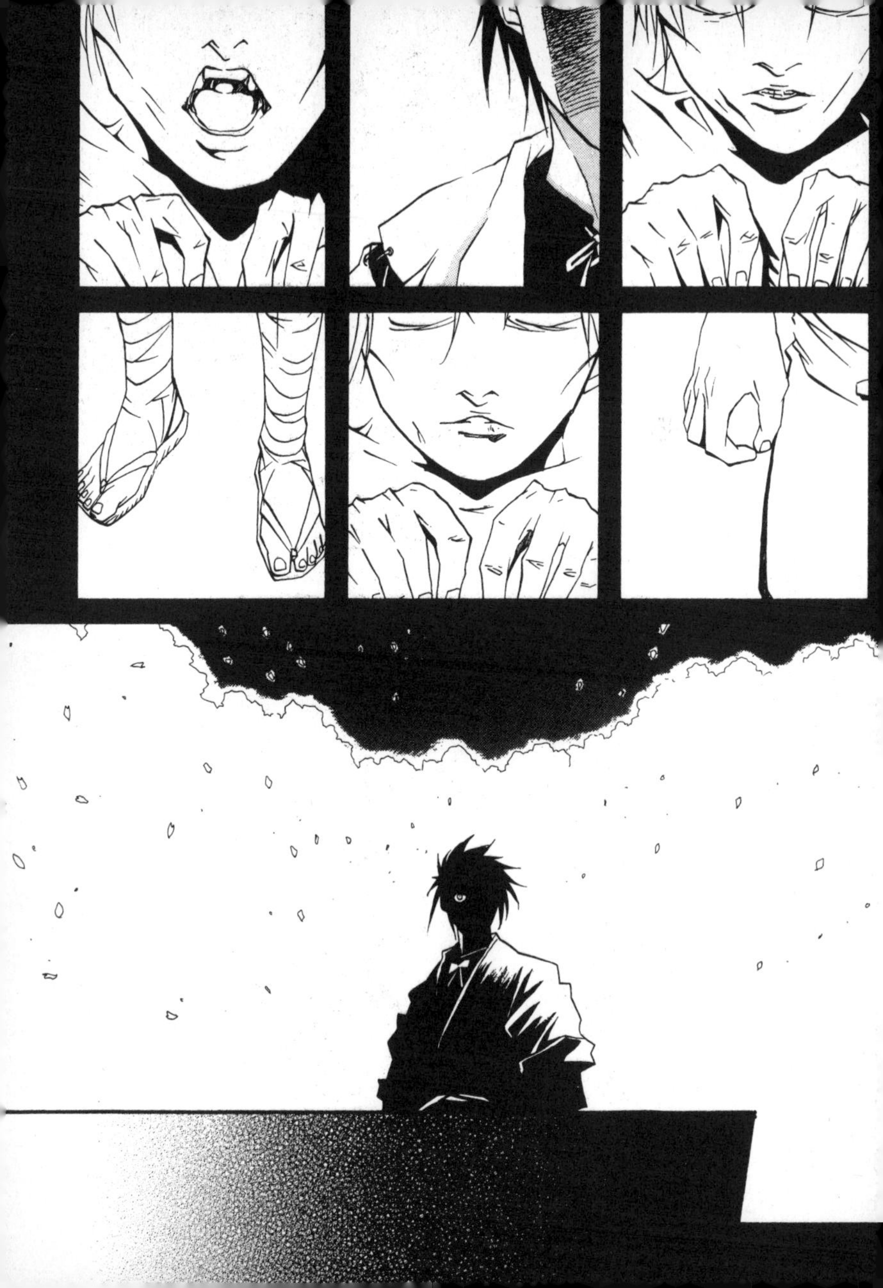

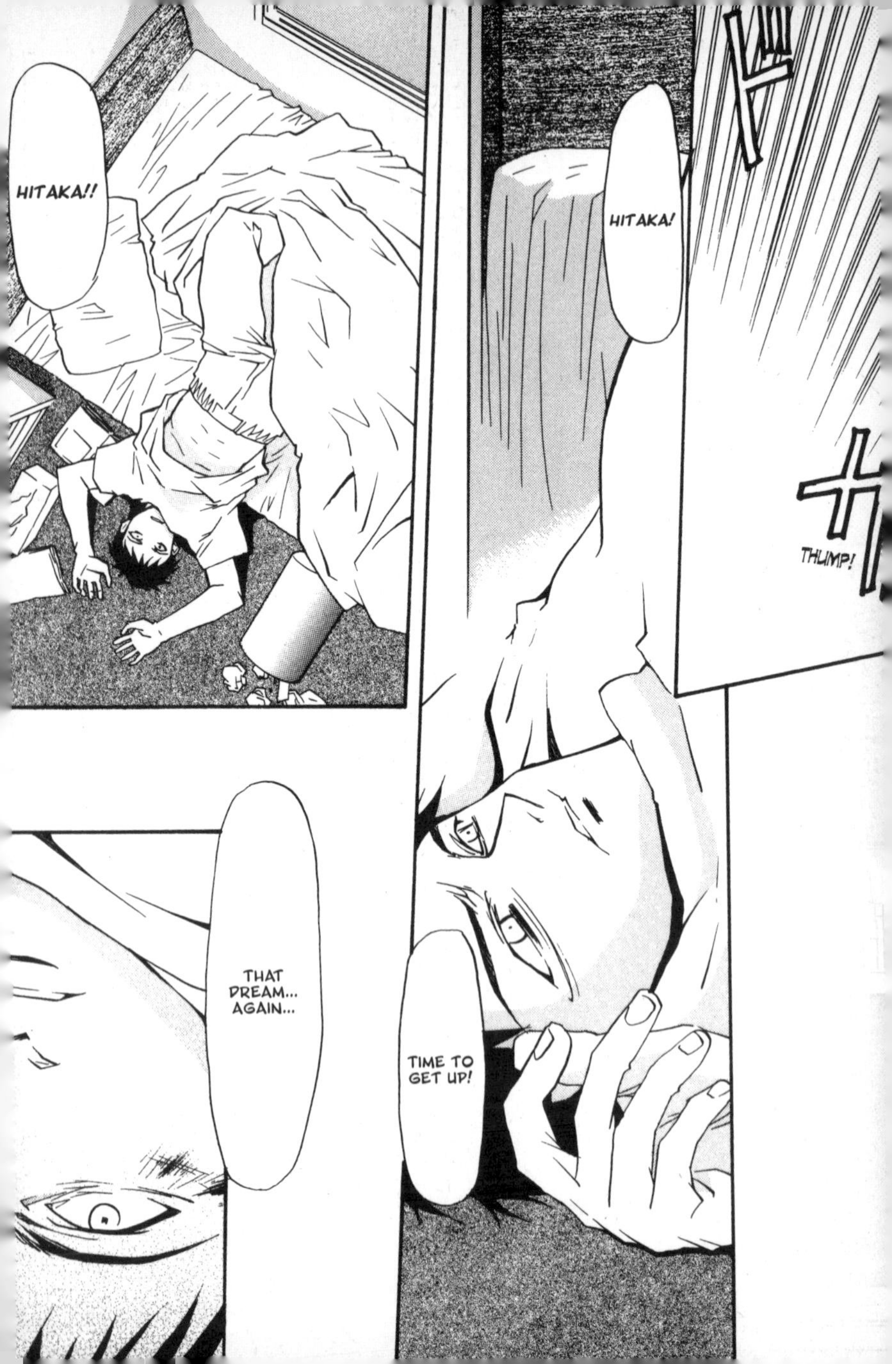
THUMP!
HITAKA!
TIME TO GET UP!
HITAKA!!
THAT DREAM... AGAIN...

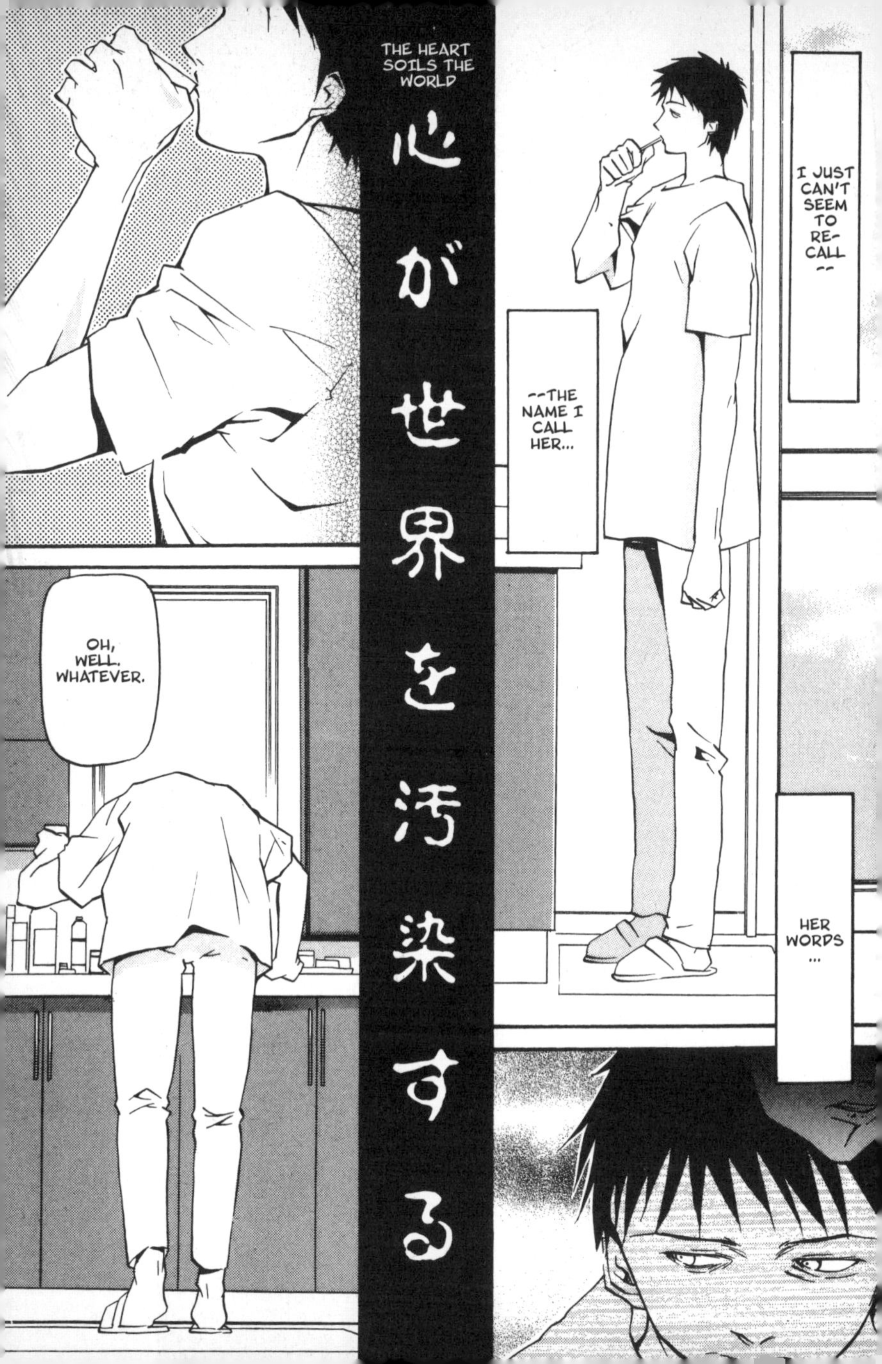
I JUST CAN'T SEEM TO RE-CALL --
--THE NAME I CALL HER...
HER WORDS ...
THE HEART SOILS THE WORLD
心が世界を汚染する
OH, WELL. WHATEVER.

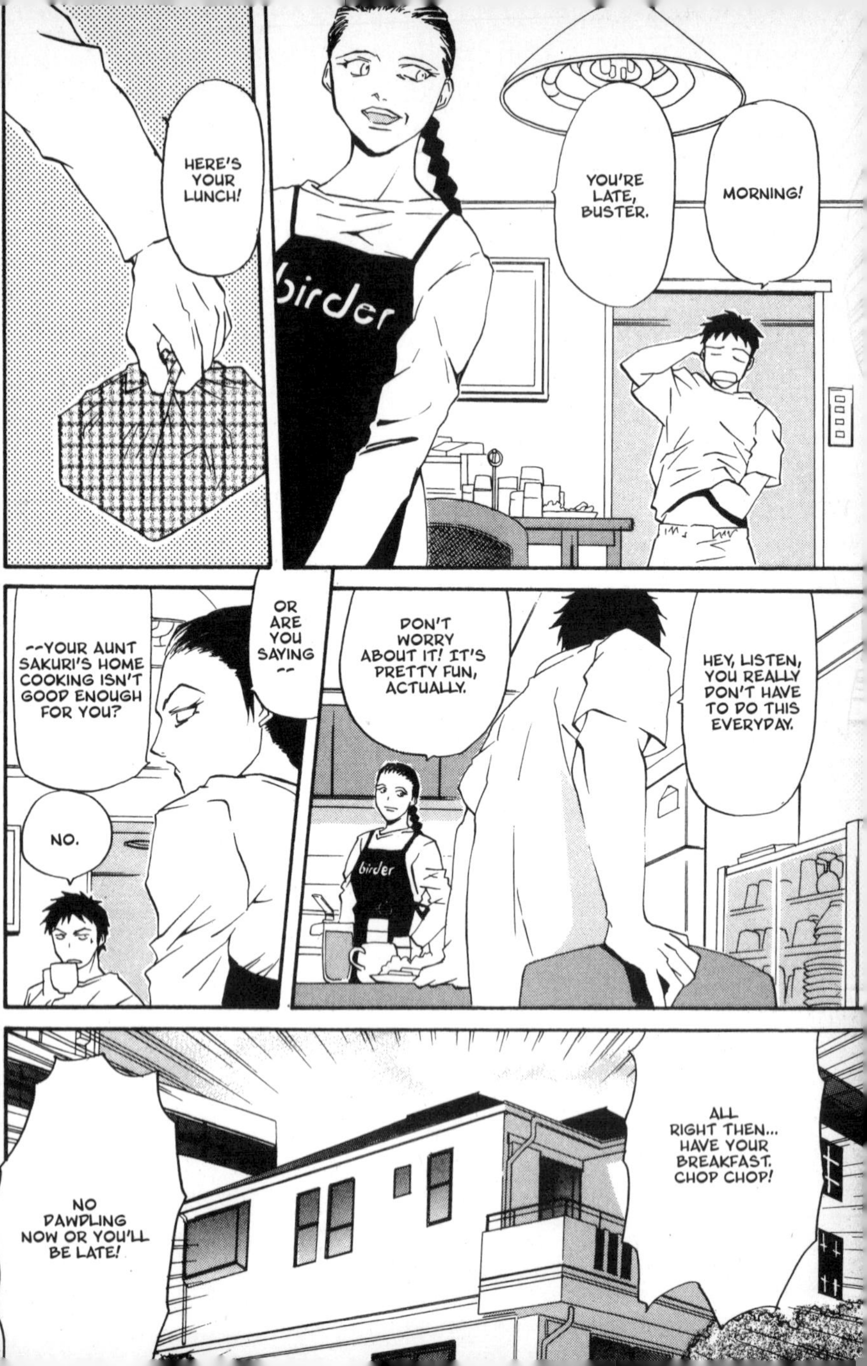
MORNING!
YOU'RE LATE, BUSTER.
birder
HERE'S YOUR LUNCH!
HEY, LISTEN, YOU REALLY DON'T HAVE TO DO THIS EVERYDAY.
DON'T WORRY ABOUT IT! IT'S PRETTY FUN, ACTUALLY.
birder
OR ARE YOU SAYING --
--YOUR AUNT SAKURI'S HOME COOKING ISN'T GOOD ENOUGH FOR YOU?
NO.
ALL RIGHT THEN... HAVE YOUR BREAKFAST. CHOP CHOP!
NO DAWDLING NOW OR YOU'LL BE LATE!

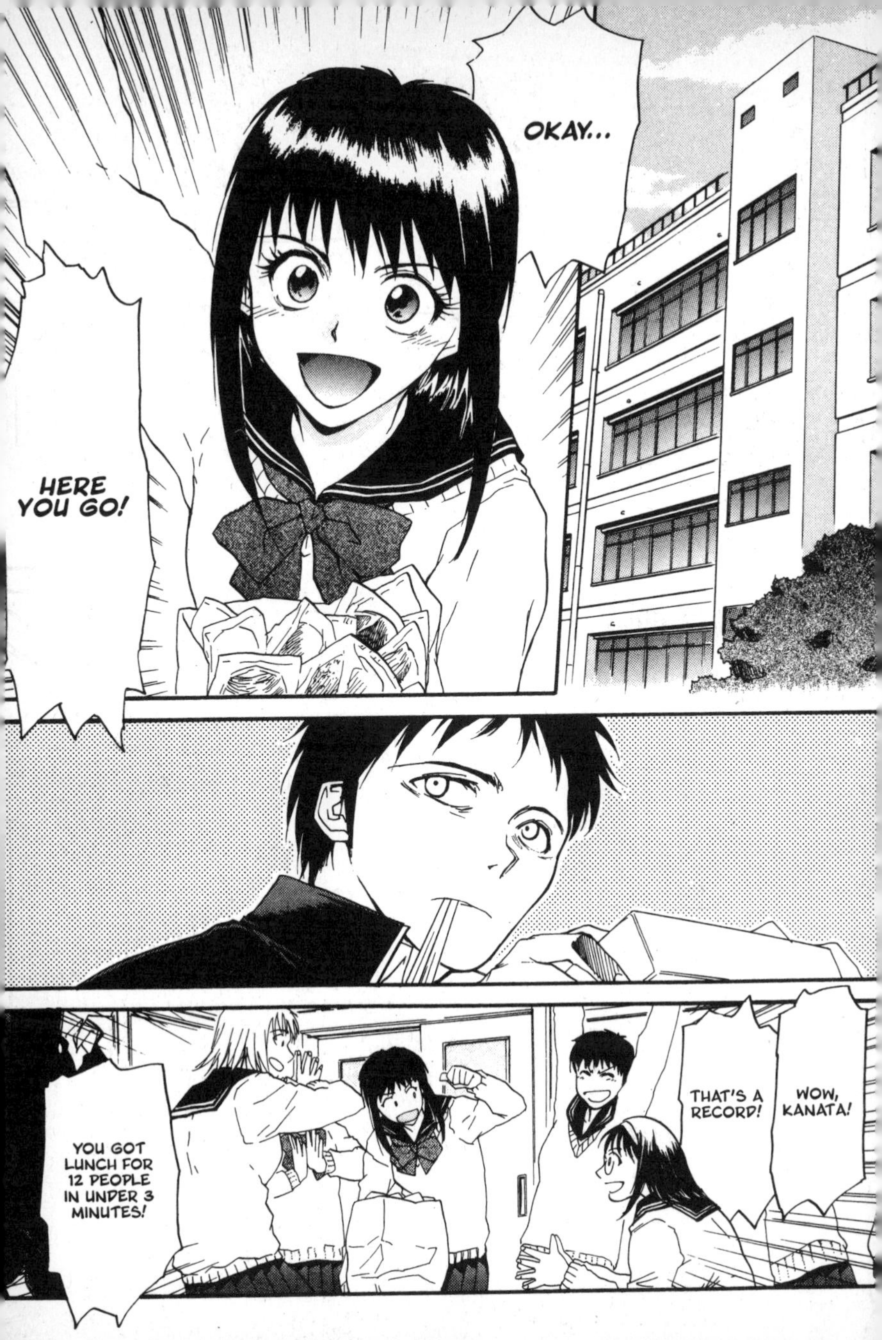
OKAY...
HERE YOU GO!
WOW, KANATA!
THAT'S A RECORD!
YOU GOT LUNCH FOR 12 PEOPLE IN UNDER 3 MINUTES!

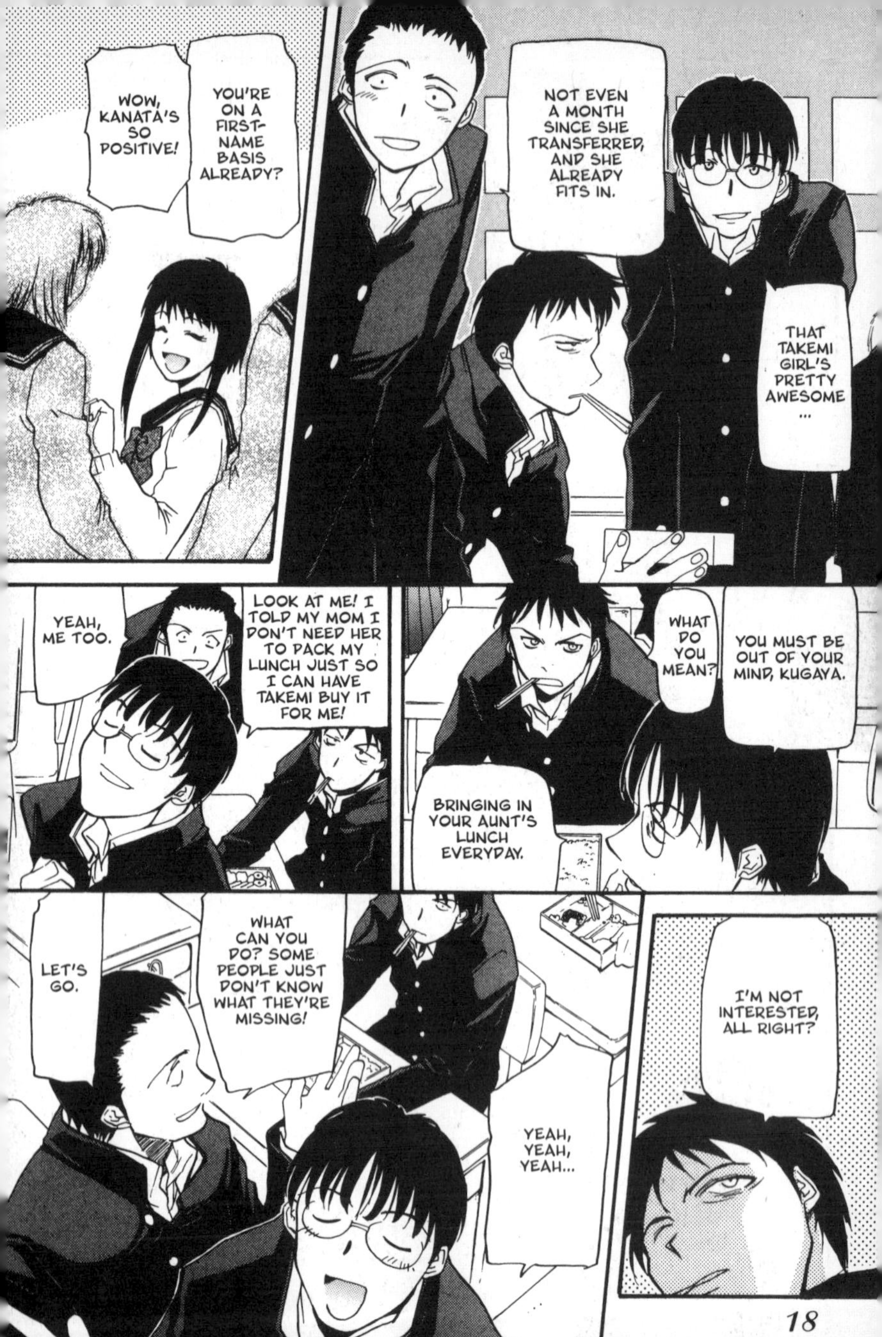
THAT TAKEMI GIRL'S PRETTY AWESOME...
NOT EVEN A MONTH SINCE SHE TRANSFERRED, AND SHE ALREADY FITS IN.
YOU'RE ON A FIRST-NAME BASIS ALREADY?
WOW, KANATA'S SO POSITIVE!
YOU MUST BE OUT OF YOUR MIND, KUGAYA.
WHAT DO YOU MEAN?
BRINGING IN YOUR AUNT'S LUNCH EVERYDAY.
LOOK AT ME! I TOLD MY MOM I DON'T NEED HER TO PACK MY LUNCH JUST SO I CAN HAVE TAKEMI BUY IT FOR ME!
YEAH, ME TOO.
I'M NOT INTERESTED, ALL RIGHT?
WHAT CAN YOU DO? SOME PEOPLE JUST DON'T KNOW WHAT THEY'RE MISSING!
YEAH, YEAH, YEAH...
LET'S GO.

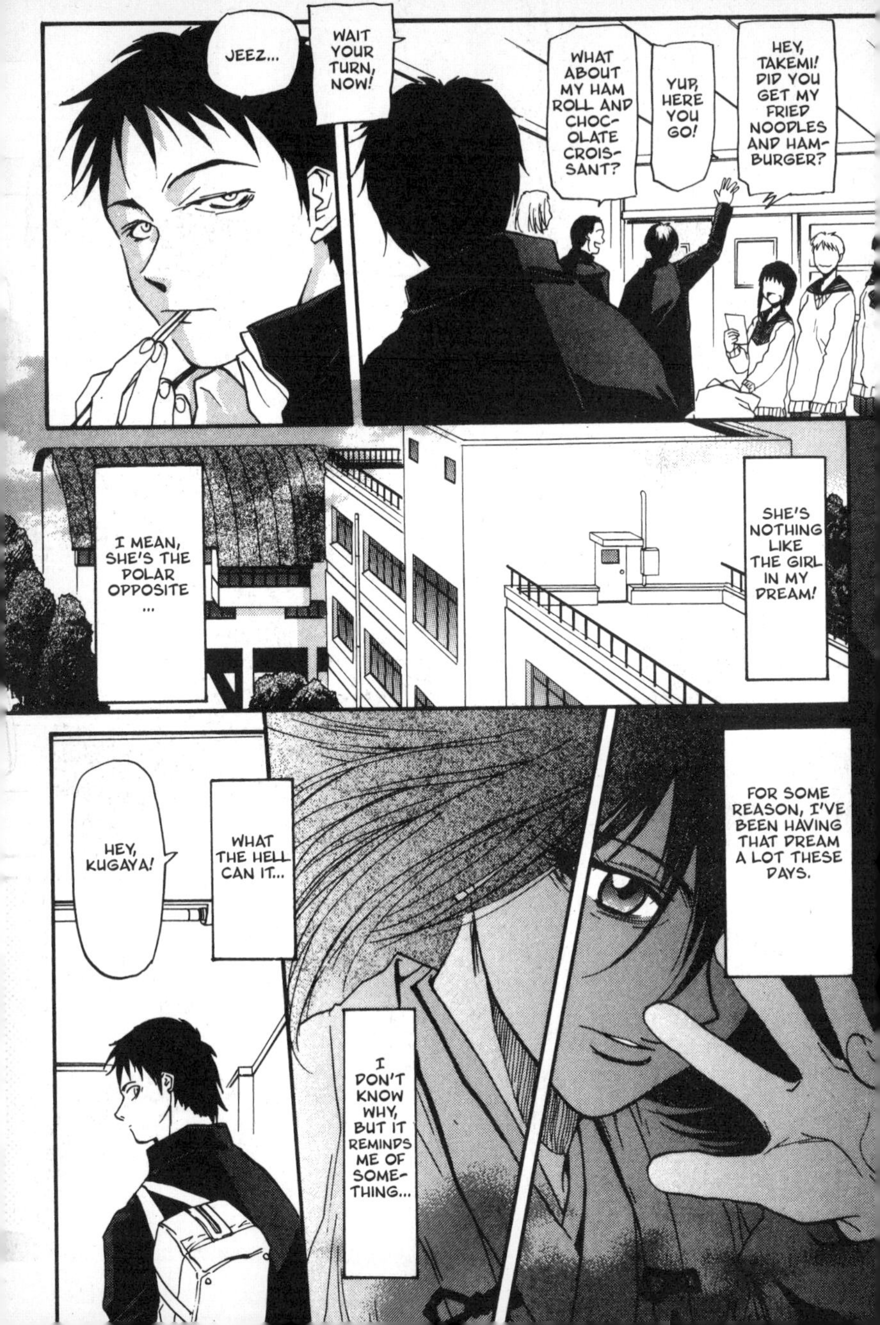
HEY, TAKEMI! DID YOU GET MY FRIED NOODLES AND HAM-BURGER?
YUP, HERE YOU GO!
WHAT ABOUT MY HAM ROLL AND CHOC-OLATE CROIS-SANT?
WAIT YOUR TURN, NOW!
JEEZ...
SHE'S NOTHING LIKE THE GIRL IN MY DREAM!
I MEAN, SHE'S THE POLAR OPPOSITE ...
FOR SOME REASON, I'VE BEEN HAVING THAT DREAM A LOT THESE DAYS.
I DON'T KNOW WHY, BUT IT REMINDS ME OF SOME-THING...
WHAT THE HELL CAN IT...
HEY, KUGAYA!

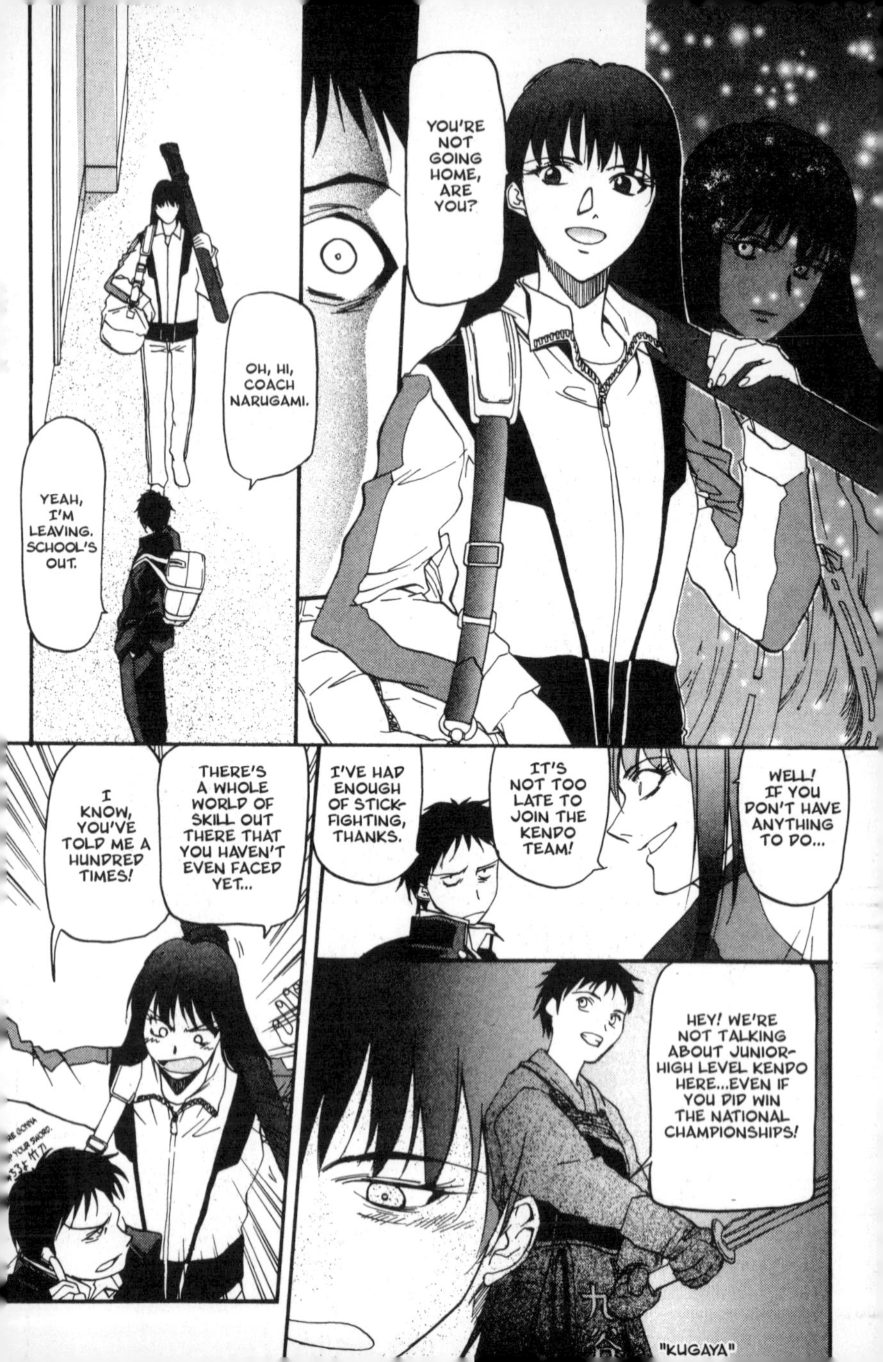
YOU'RE NOT GOING HOME, ARE YOU?
OH, HI, COACH NARUGAMI.
YEAH, I'M LEAVING. SCHOOL'S OUT.
WELL! IF YOU DON'T HAVE ANYTHING TO DO...
IT'S NOT TOO LATE TO JOIN THE KENDO TEAM!
I'VE HAD ENOUGH OF STICK-FIGHTING, THANKS.
HEY! WE'RE NOT TALKING ABOUT JUNIOR-HIGH LEVEL KENDO HERE...EVEN IF YOU DID WIN THE NATIONAL CHAMPIONSHIPS!
"KUGAYA"
THERE'S A WHOLE WORLD OF SKILL OUT THERE THAT YOU HAVEN'T EVEN FACED YET...
I KNOW, YOU'VE TOLD ME A HUNDRED TIMES!

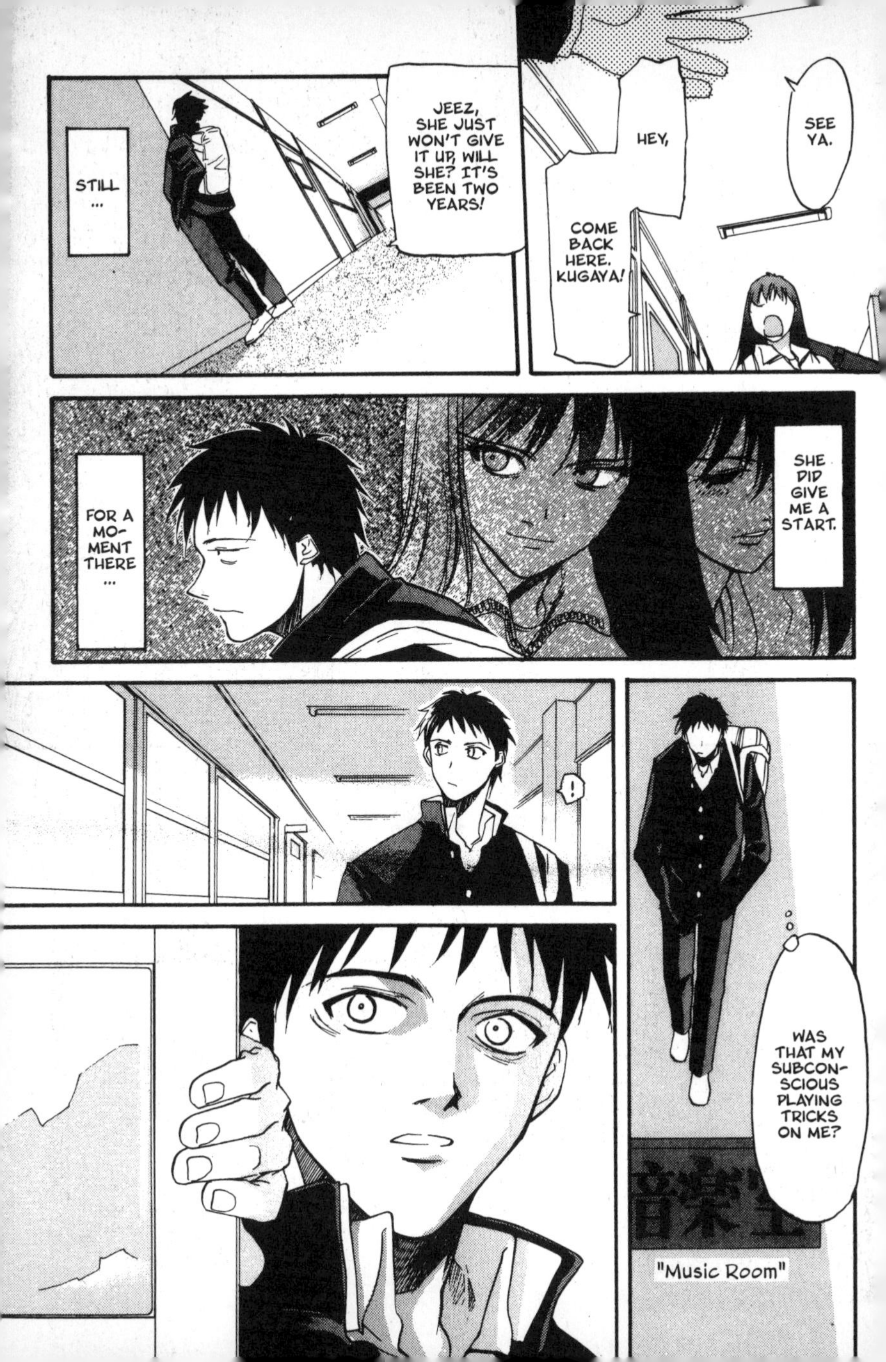
SEE YA.
HEY,
COME BACK HERE. KUGAYA!
JEEZ, SHE JUST WON'T GIVE IT UP, WILL SHE? IT'S BEEN TWO YEARS!
STILL ...
SHE DID GIVE ME A START.
FOR A MO-MENT THERE ...
WAS THAT MY SUBCON-SCIOUS PLAYING TRICKS ON ME?
音楽室
"Music Room"
!

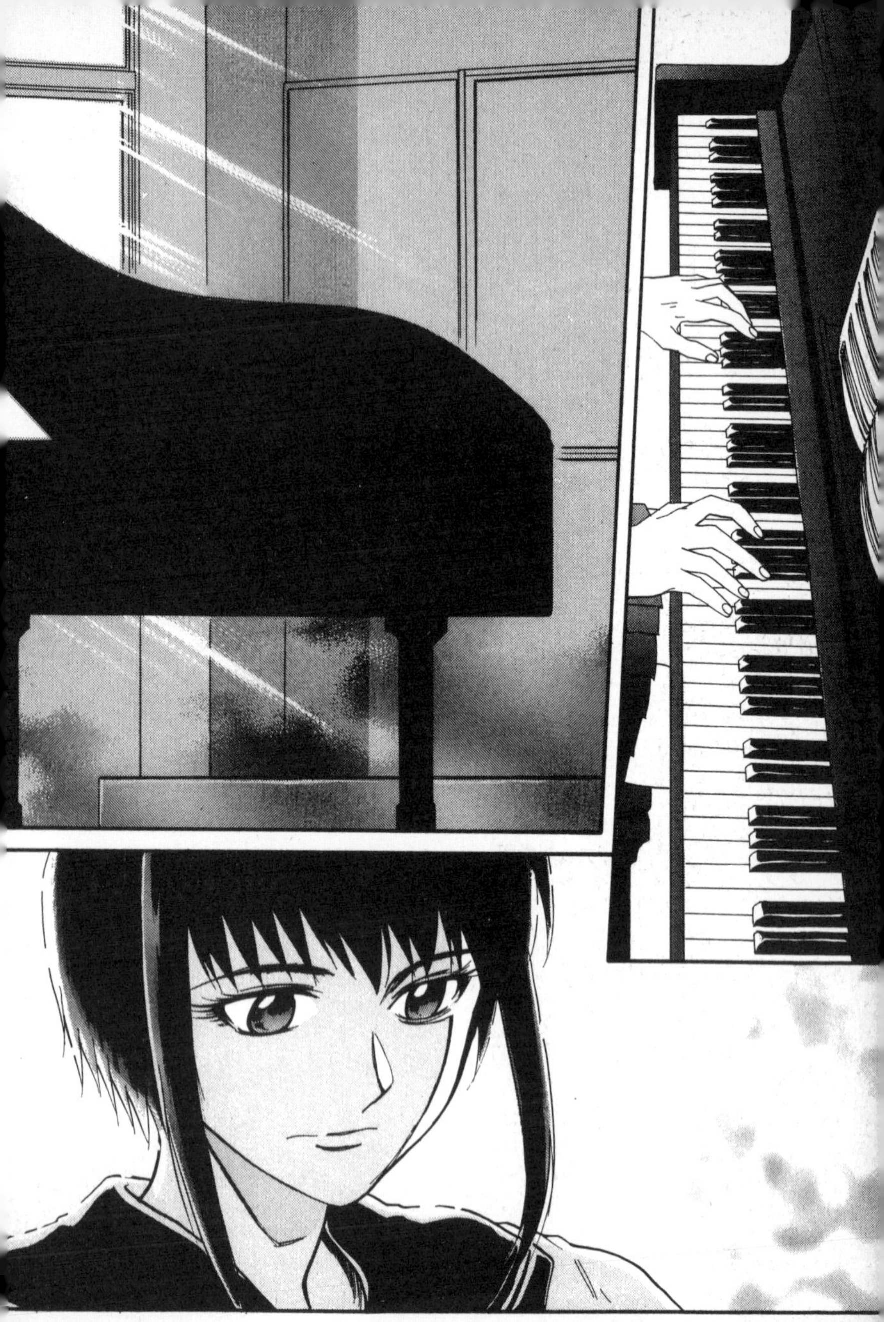

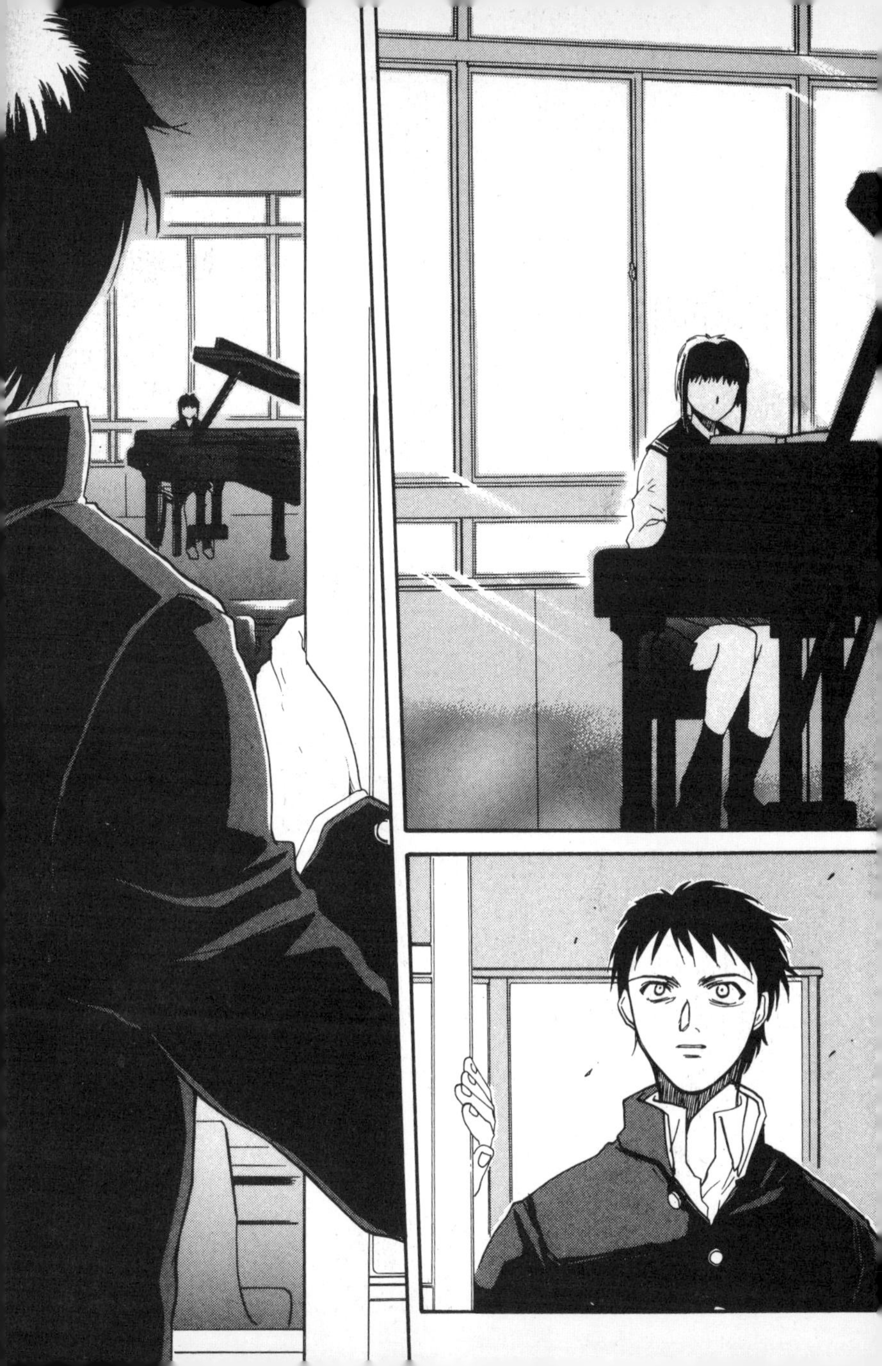

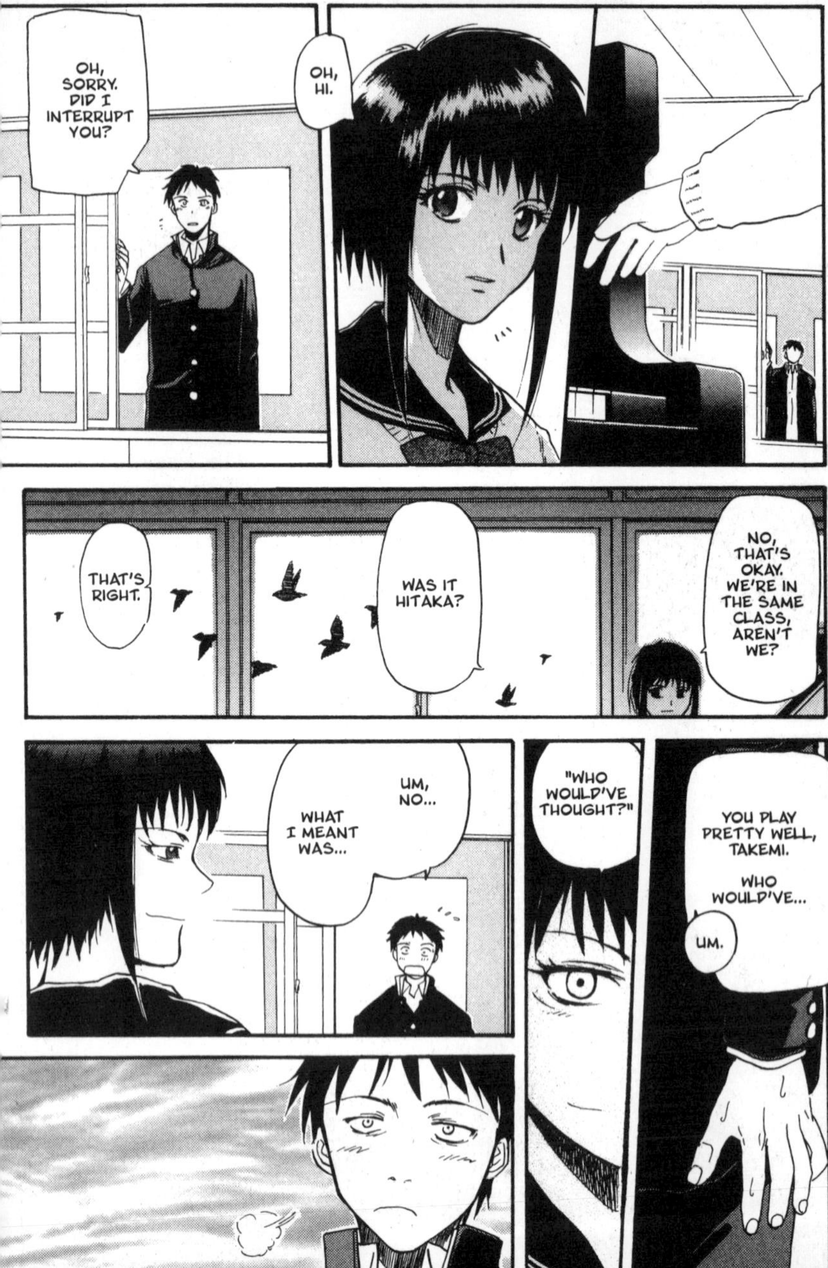
OH, HI.
OH, SORRY. DID I INTERRUPT YOU?
NO, THAT'S OKAY. WE'RE IN THE SAME CLASS, AREN'T WE?
WAS IT HITAKA?
THAT'S RIGHT.
YOU PLAY PRETTY WELL, TAKEMI.
WHO WOULD'VE...
UM.
"WHO WOULD'VE THOUGHT?"
UM, NO...
WHAT I MEANT WAS...

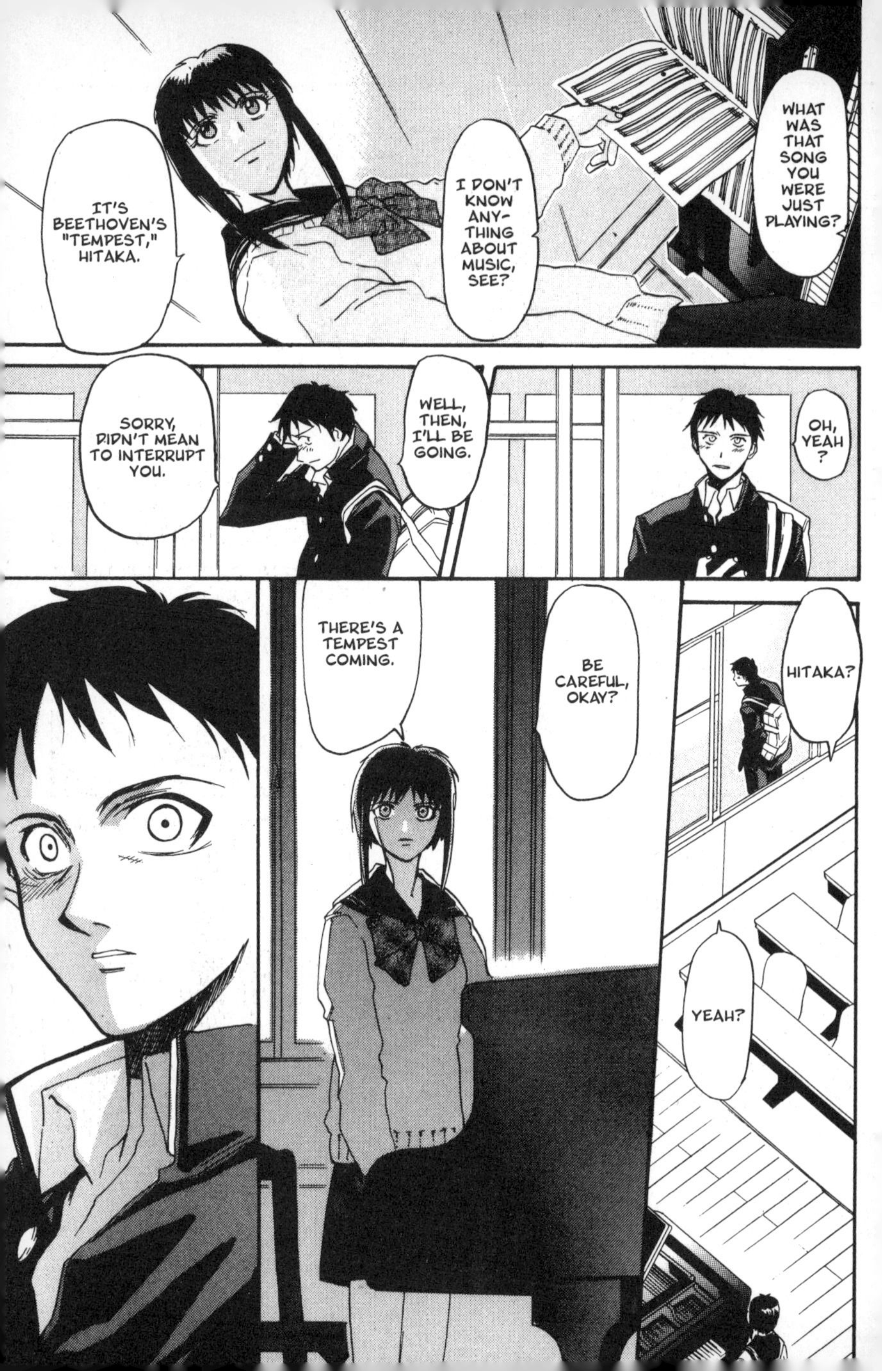
WHAT WAS THAT SONG YOU WERE JUST PLAYING?
I DON'T KNOW ANY-THING ABOUT MUSIC, SEE?
IT'S BEETHOVEN'S "TEMPEST," HITAKA.
OH, YEAH?
WELL, THEN, I'LL BE GOING.
SORRY, DIDN'T MEAN TO INTERRUPT YOU.
HITAKA?
YEAH?
BE CAREFUL, OKAY?
THERE'S A TEMPEST COMING.

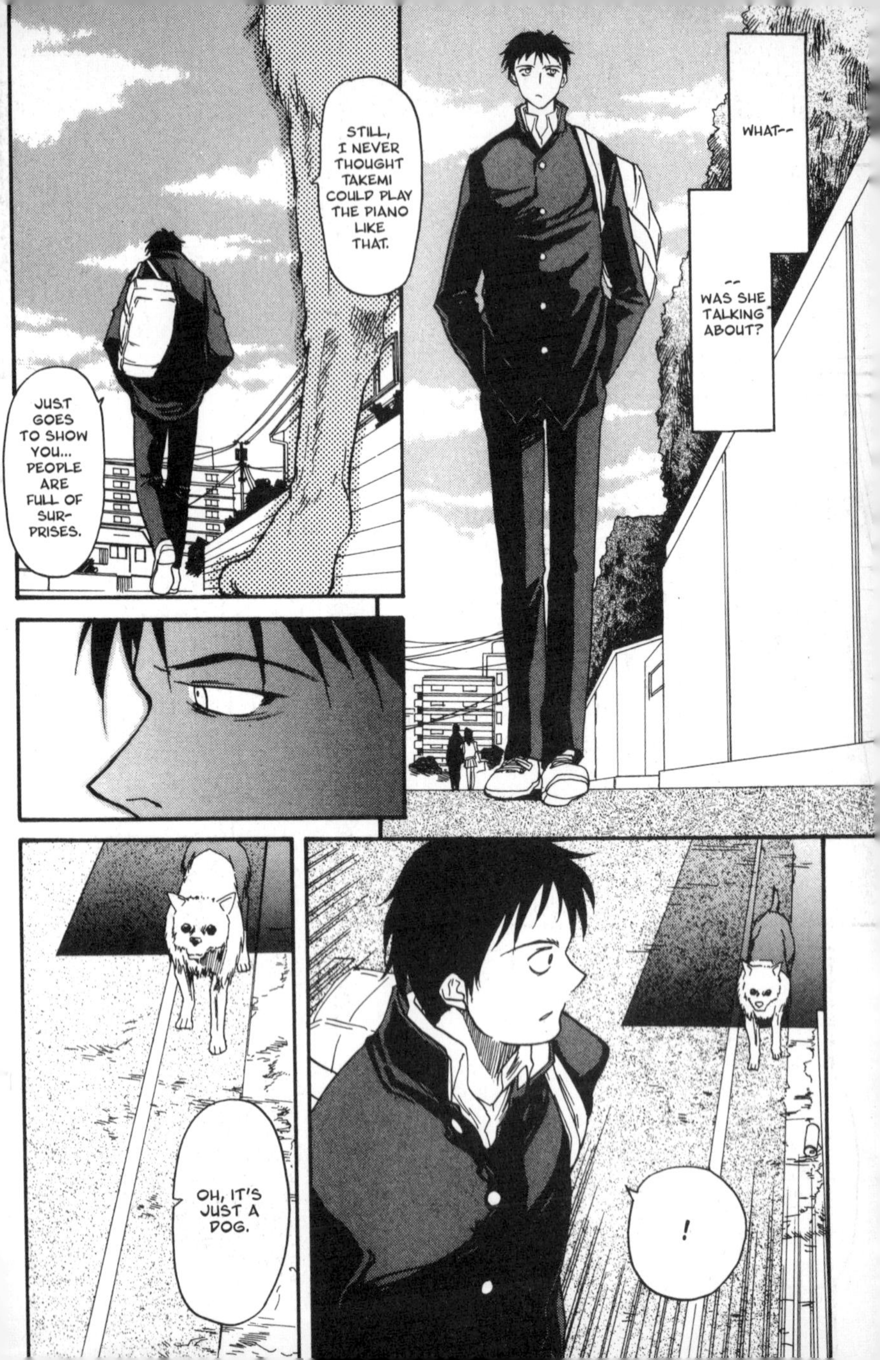
WHAT--
--WAS SHE TALKING ABOUT?
STILL, I NEVER THOUGHT TAKEMI COULD PLAY THE PIANO LIKE THAT.
JUST GOES TO SHOW YOU... PEOPLE ARE FULL OF SURPRISES.
!
OH, IT'S JUST A DOG.

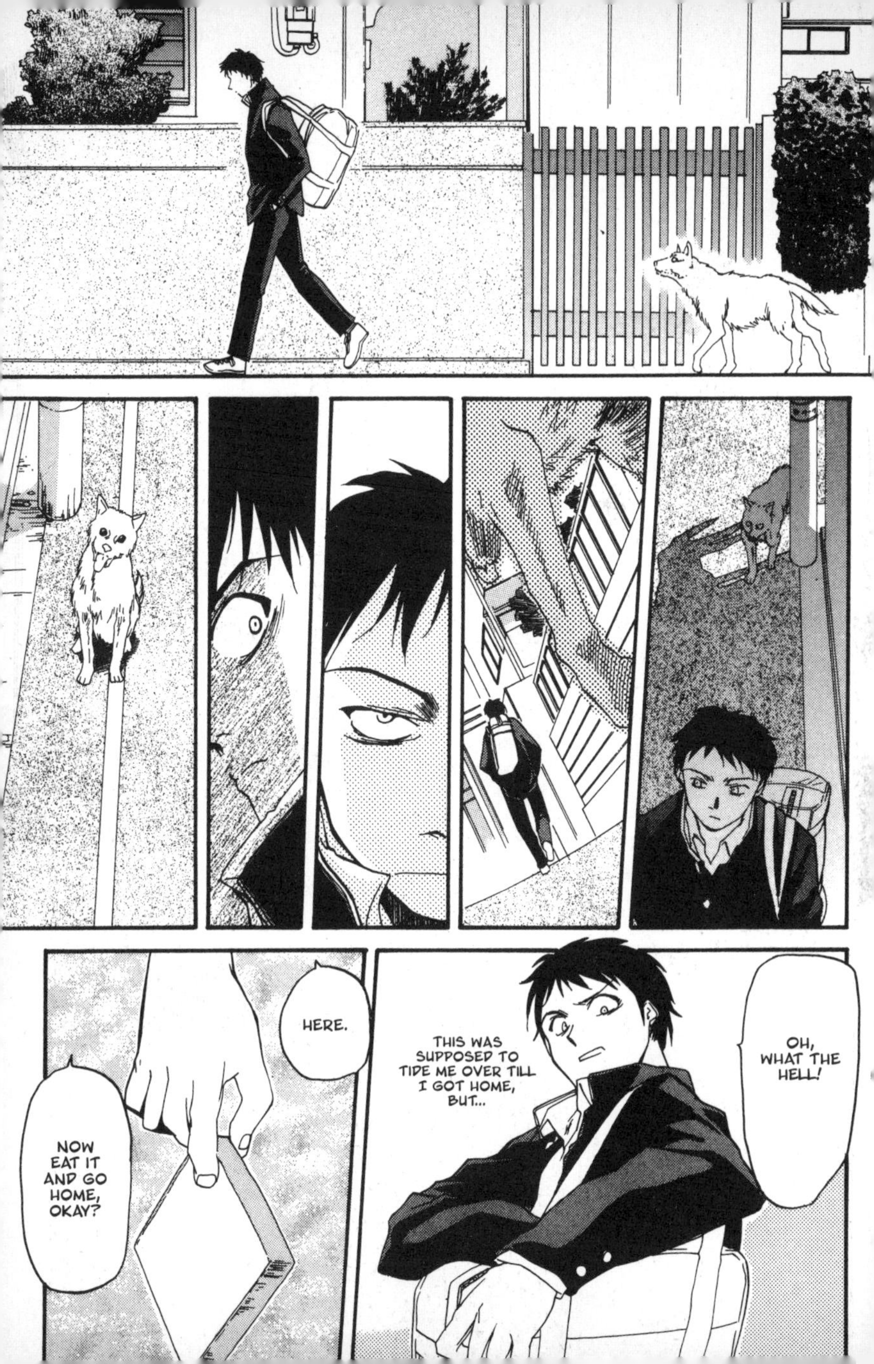
OH, WHAT THE HELL!
THIS WAS SUPPOSED TO TIDE ME OVER TILL I GOT HOME, BUT...
HERE.
NOW EAT IT AND GO HOME, OKAY?

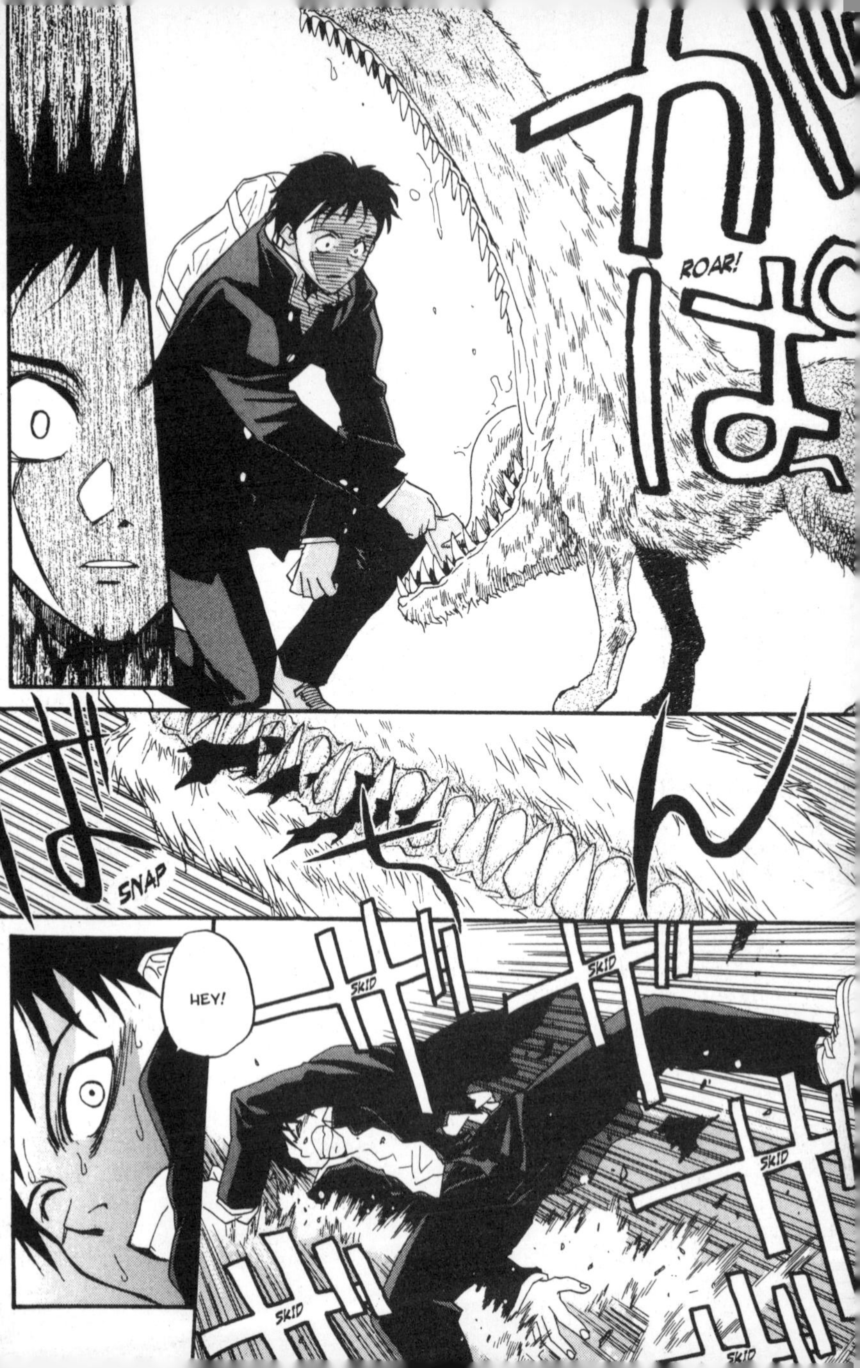
ROAR!
SNAP
SKID
SKID
HEY!
SKID
SKID
SKID

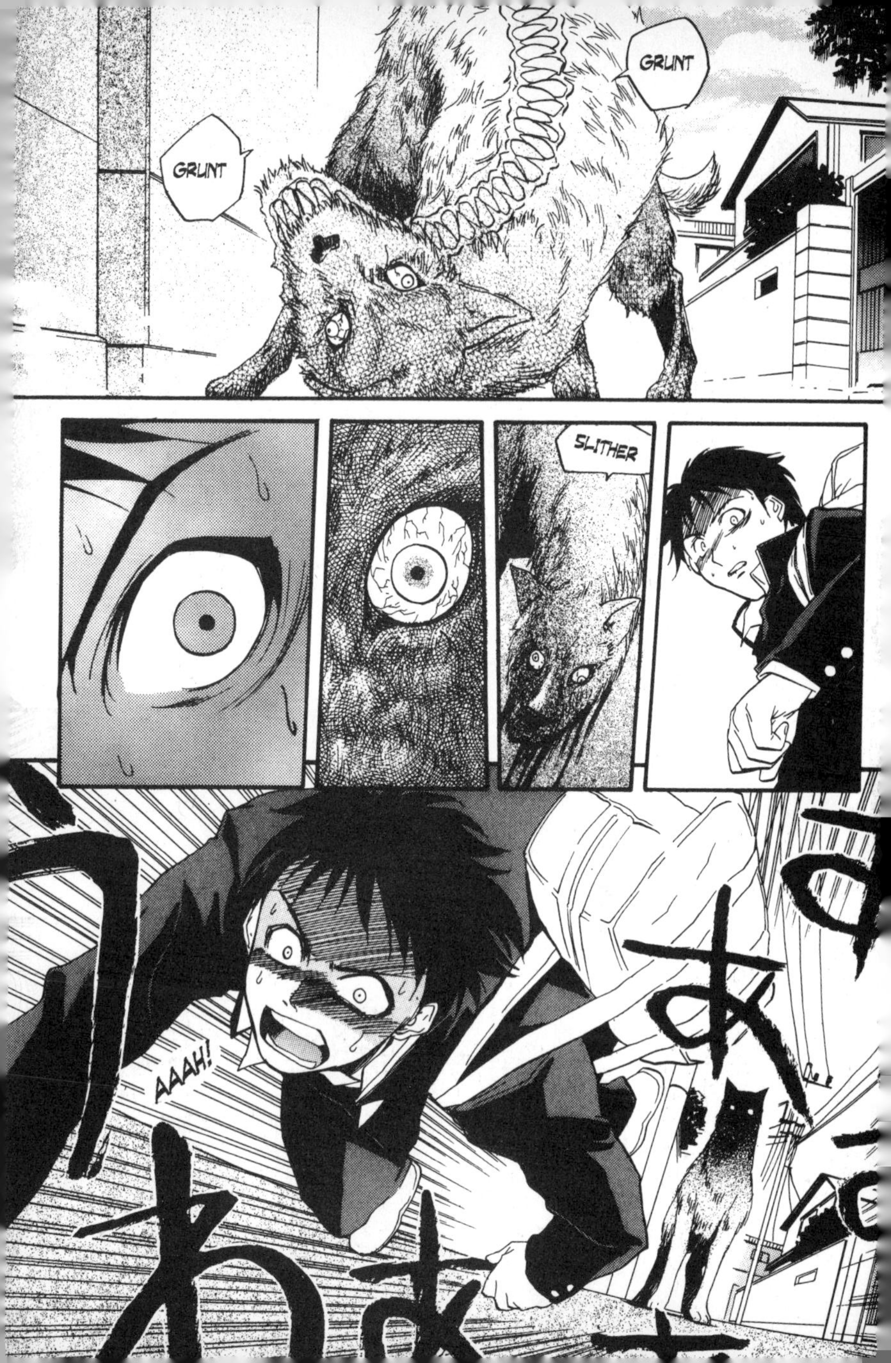
GRUNT
GRUNT
SLITHER
AAAH!

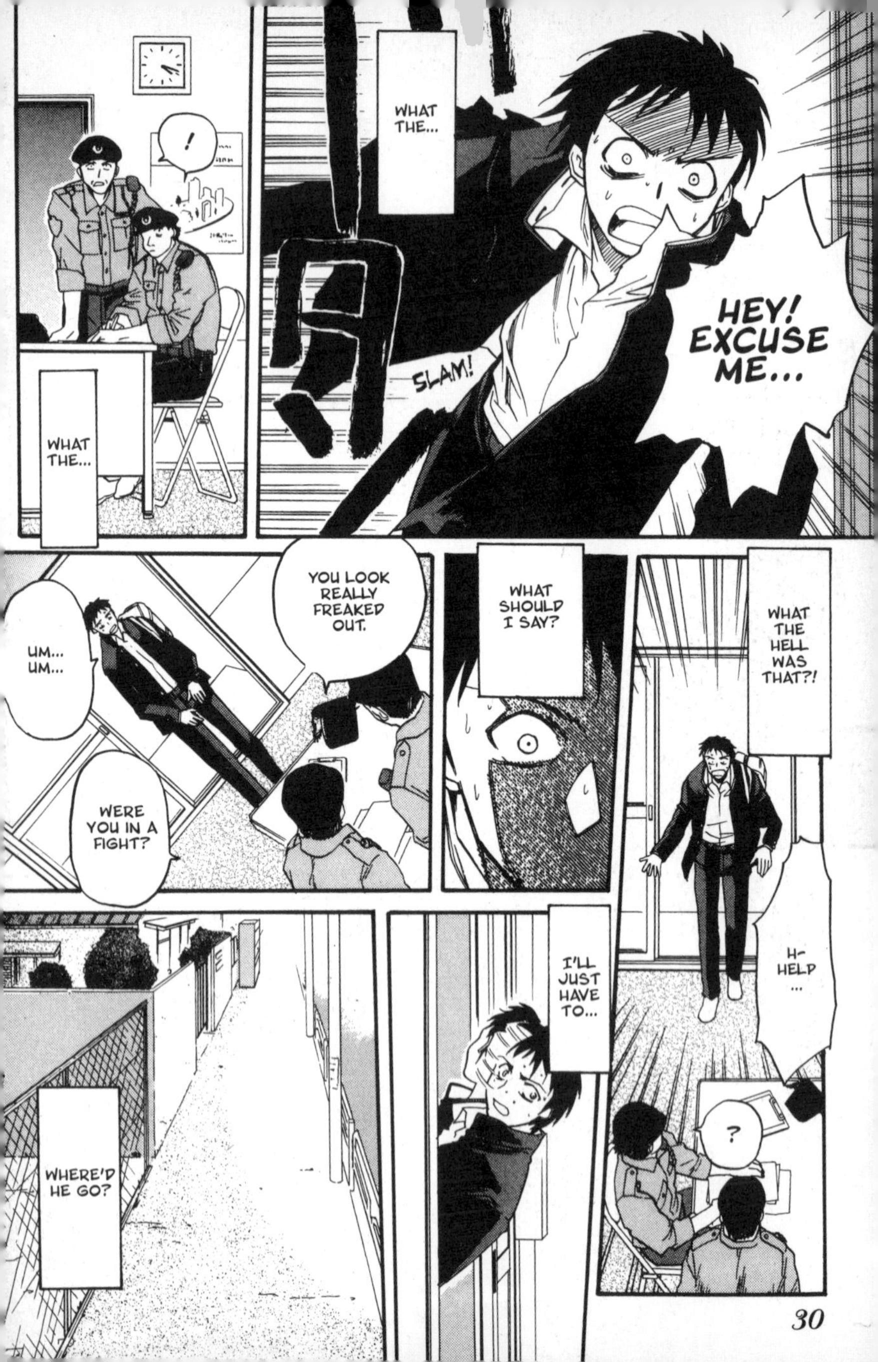

WHAT THE...
HEY! EXCUSE ME...
SLAM!
!
WHAT THE...
WHAT THE HELL WAS THAT?!
H- HELP ...
?
WHAT SHOULD I SAY?
YOU LOOK REALLY FREAKED OUT.
UM... UM...
WERE YOU IN A FIGHT?
I'LL JUST HAVE TO...
WHERE'D HE GO?

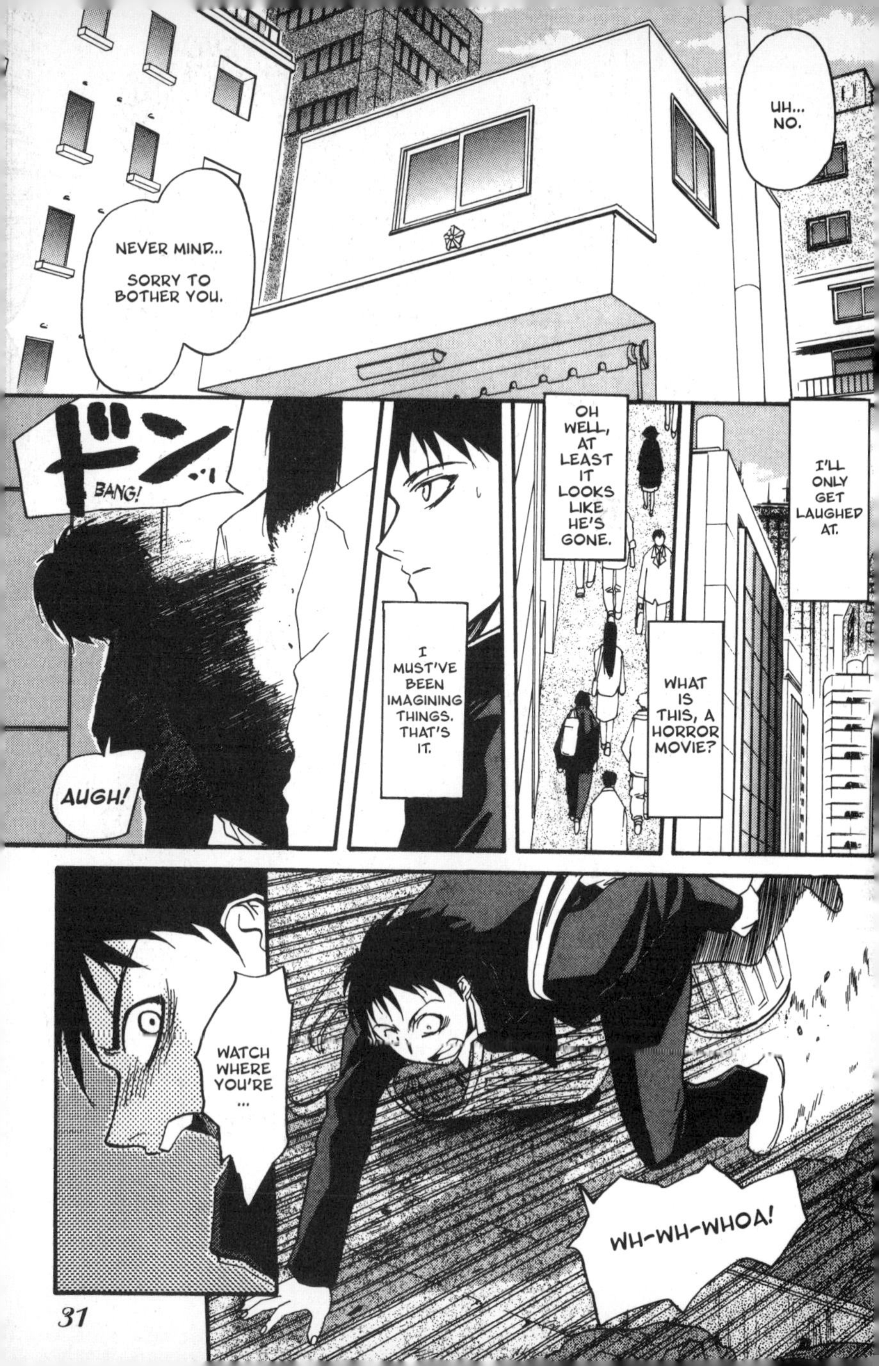
UH... NO.
NEVER MIND...
SORRY TO BOTHER YOU.
I'LL ONLY GET LAUGHED AT.
WHAT IS THIS, A HORROR MOVIE?
OH WELL, AT LEAST IT LOOKS LIKE HE'S GONE.
I MUST'VE BEEN IMAGINING THINGS. THAT'S IT.
ドン
BANG!
AUGH!
WH-WH-WHOA!
WATCH WHERE YOU'RE ...

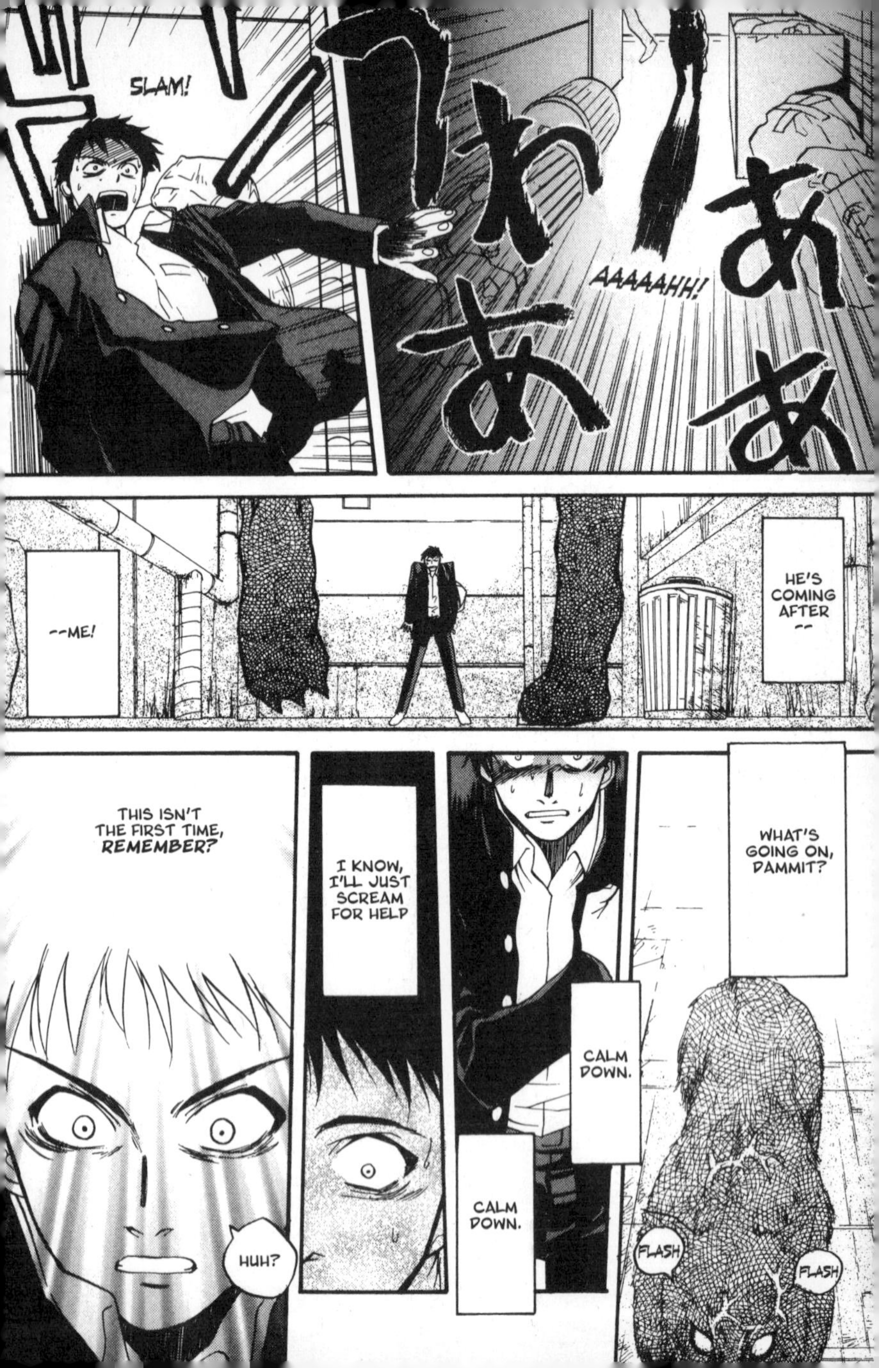
SLAM!
わあ
ああ
AAAAAHH!
HE'S COMING AFTER --
--ME!
WHAT'S GOING ON, DAMMIT?
FLASH
FLASH
CALM DOWN.
CALM DOWN.
I KNOW, I'LL JUST SCREAM FOR HELP
THIS ISN'T THE FIRST TIME, **REMEMBER?**
HUH?

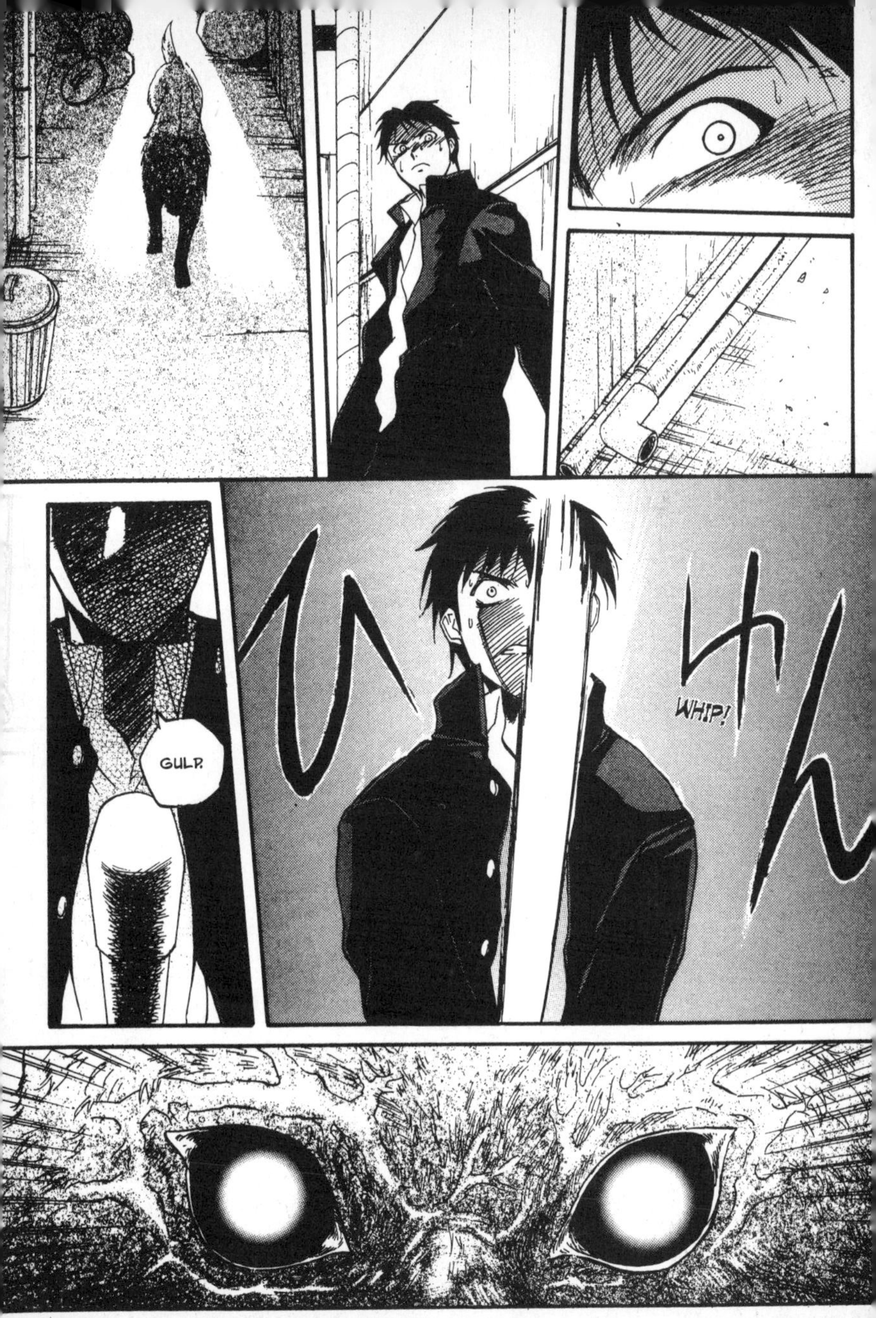
WHIP!
GULP.

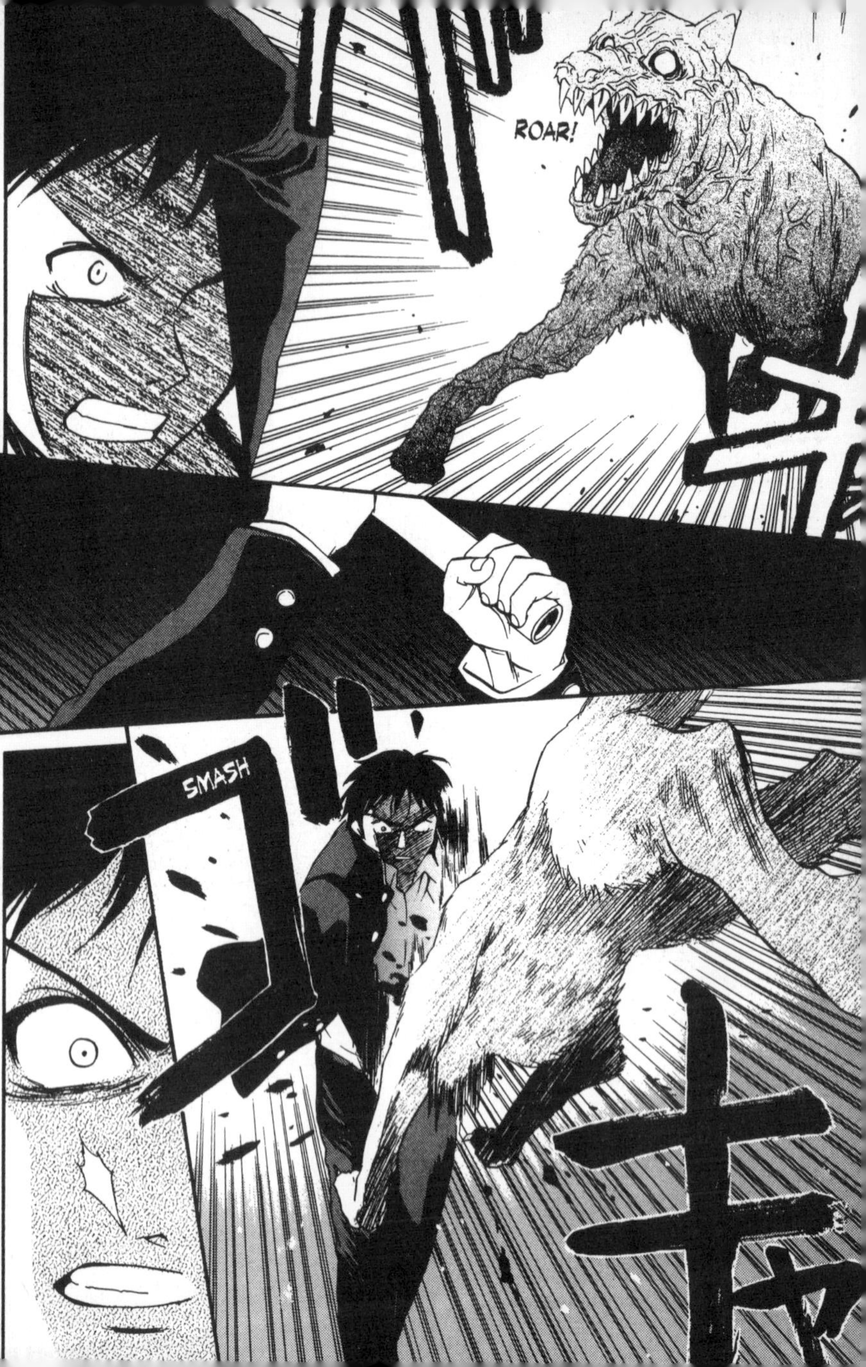
ROAR!
SMASH

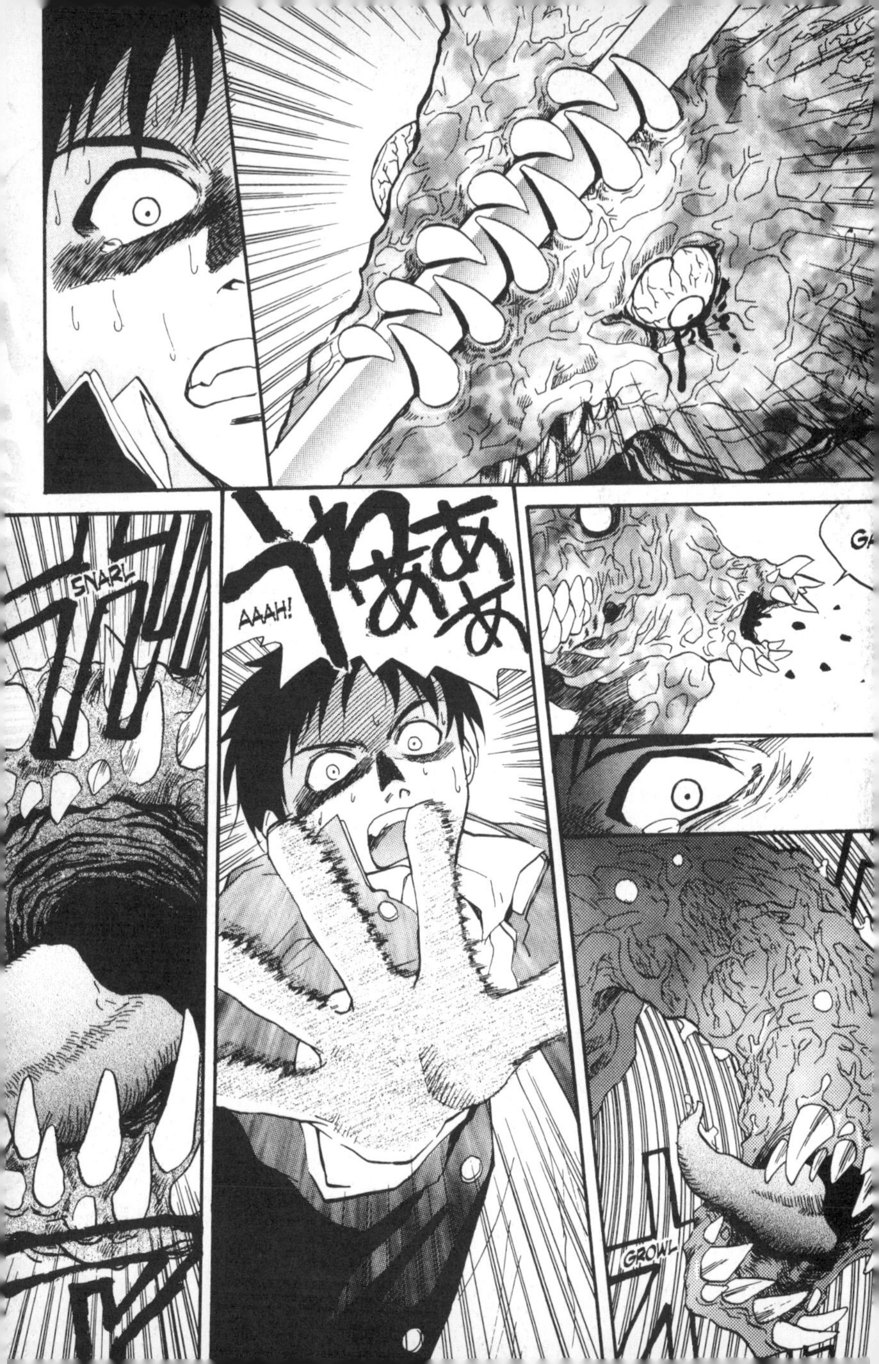
GA
うわあああ
AAAH!
SNARL
GROWL

HISSS
DRIP
DRIP
DRIP
DRIP
DRIP

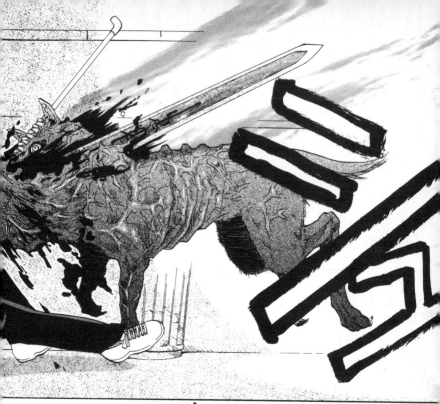

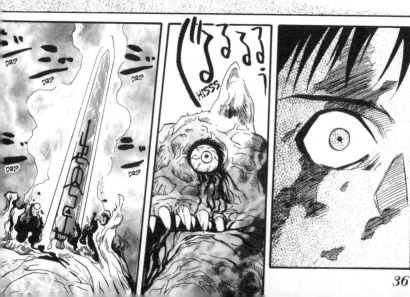

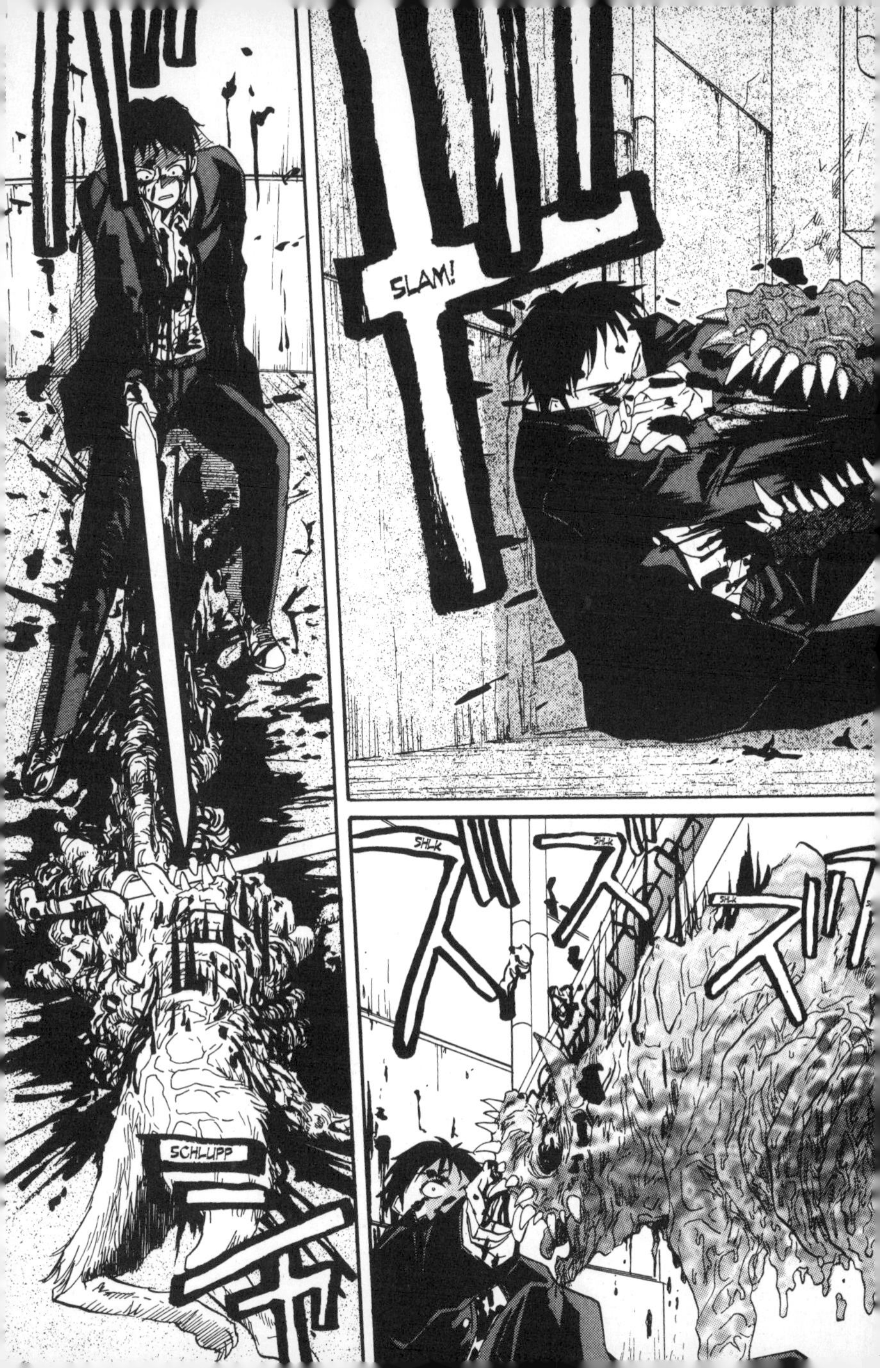
SLAM!
SHLK
SHLK
SHLK
SCHLUPP

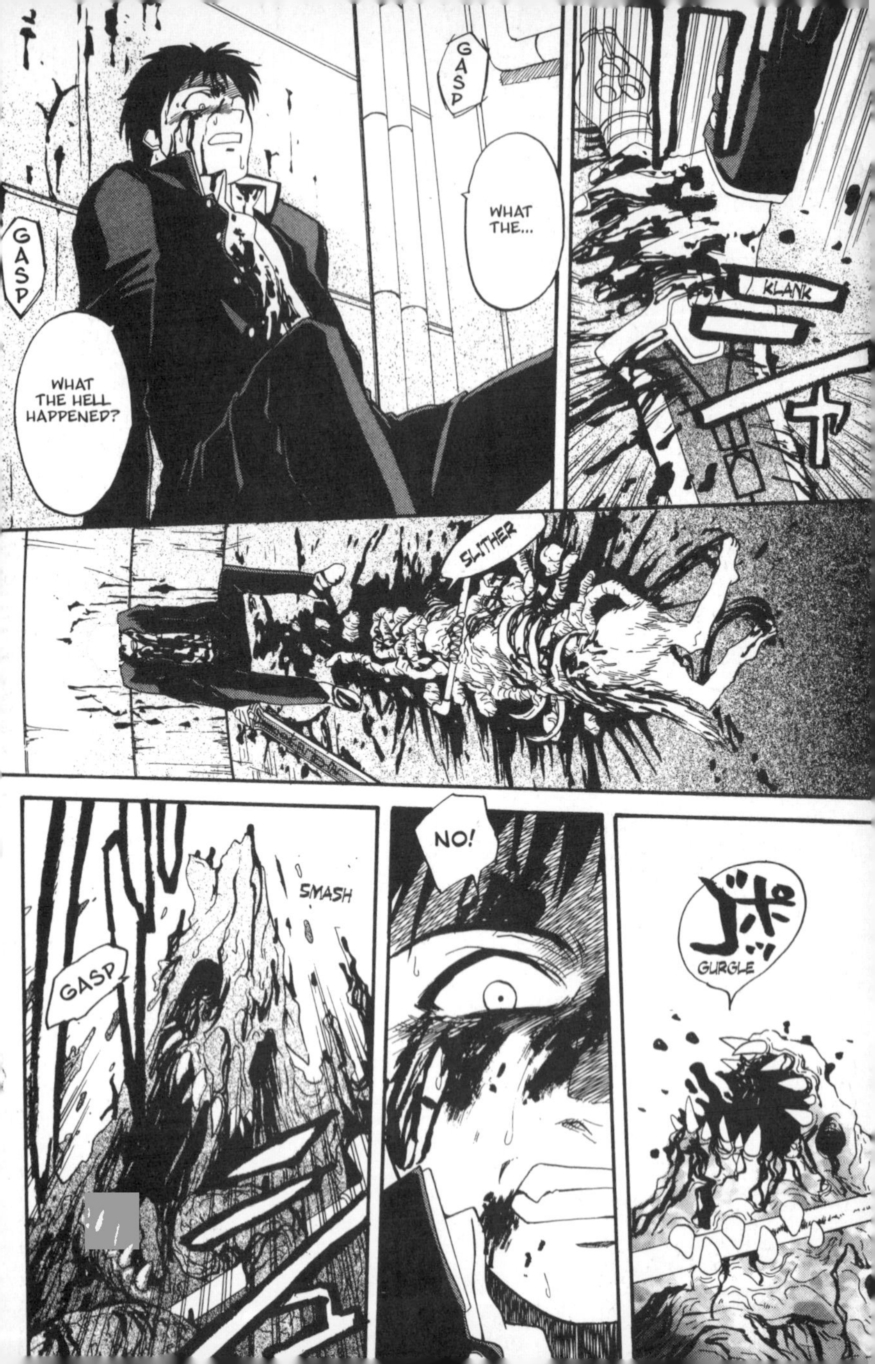
KLANK
GASP
WHAT THE...
GASP
WHAT THE HELL HAPPENED?
SLITHER
ゴポッ
GURGLE
NO!
SMASH
GASP

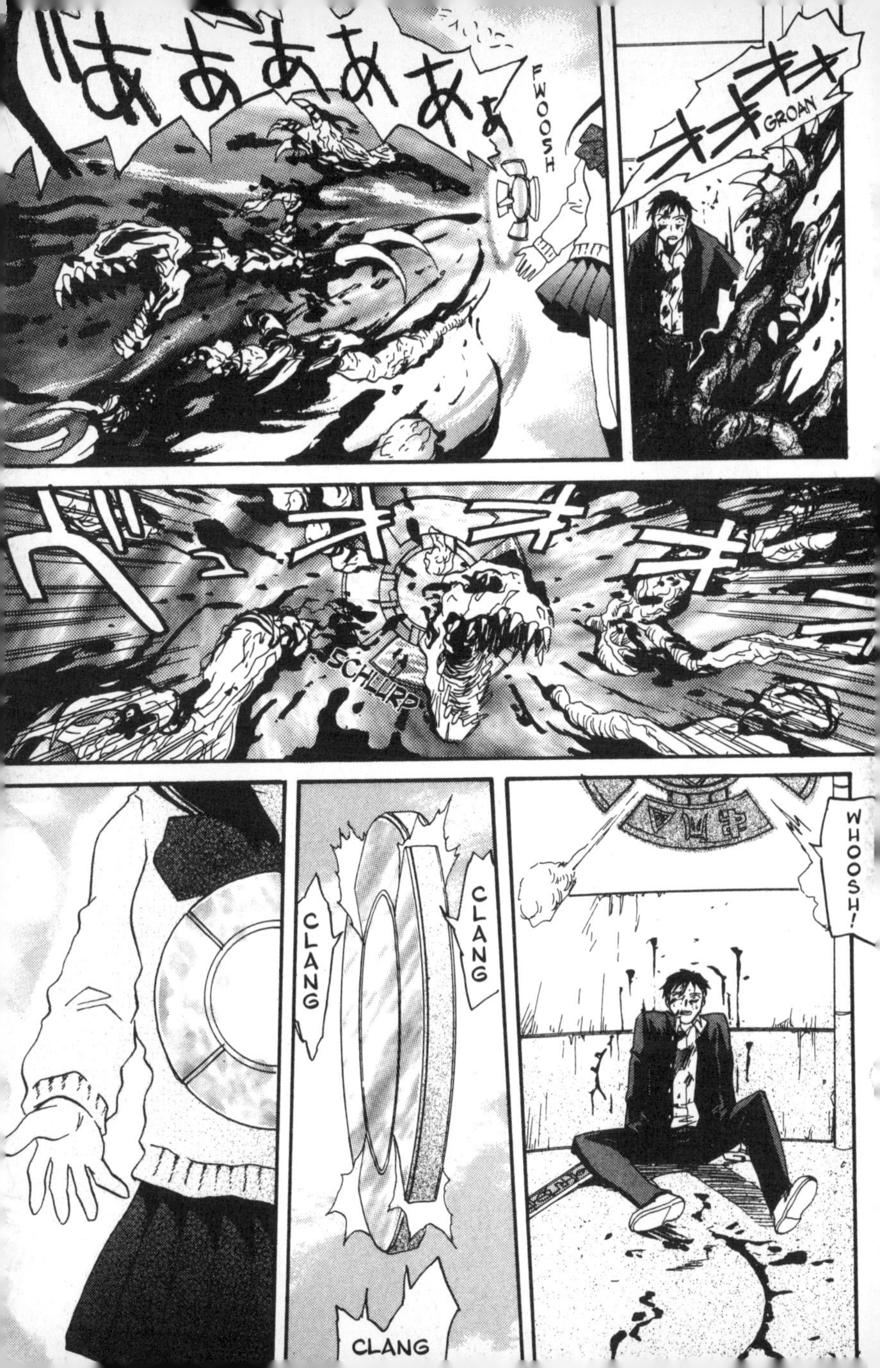
キキキキ
GROAN
はあああああぁ
FWOOSH
SCHLURP
WHOOSH!
CLANG
CLANG
CLANG

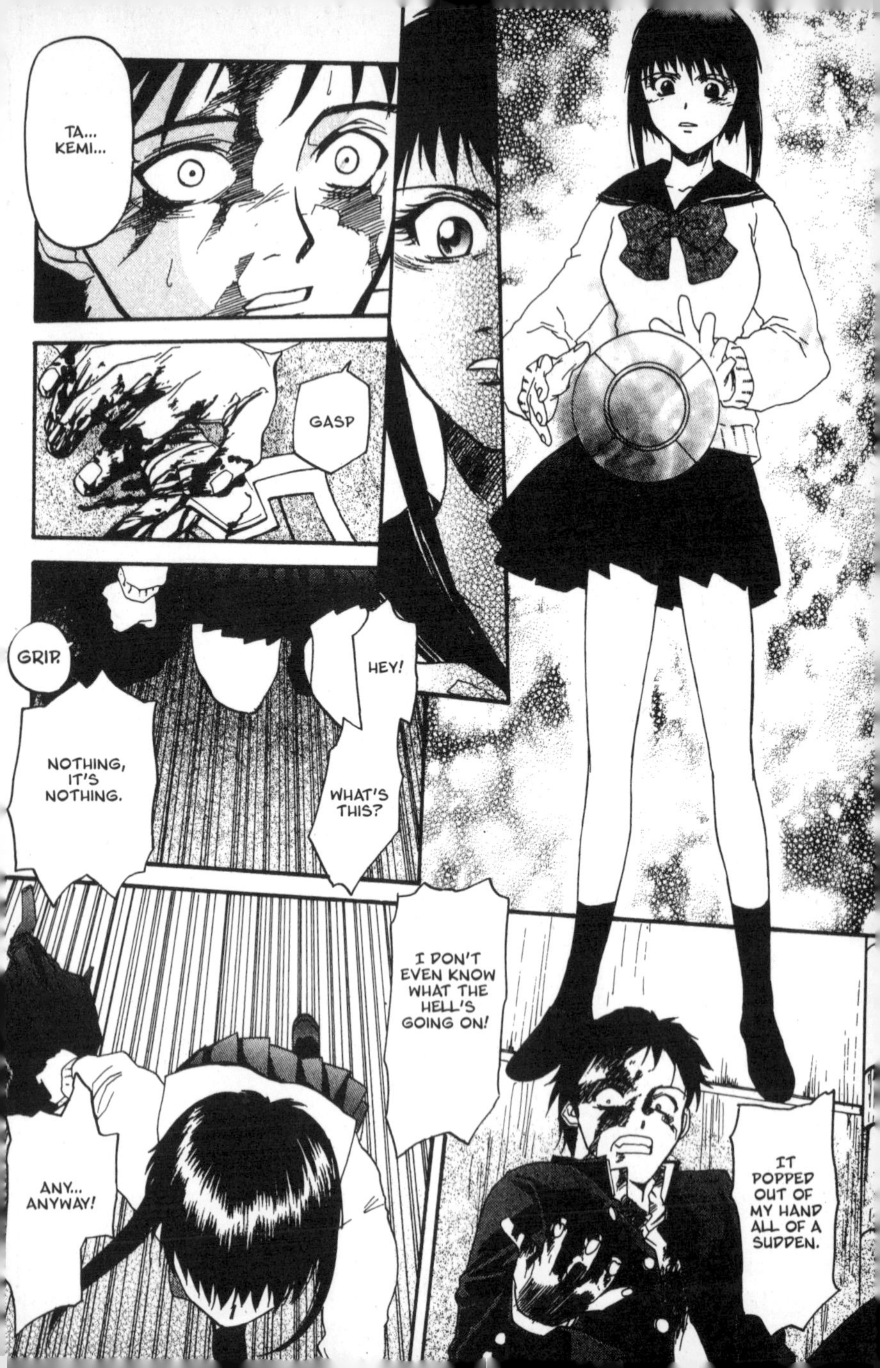

TA... KEMI...
GASP
HEY!
WHAT'S THIS?
GRIP.
NOTHING, IT'S NOTHING.
IT POPPED OUT OF MY HAND ALL OF A SUDDEN.
I DON'T EVEN KNOW WHAT THE HELL'S GOING ON!
ANY... ANYWAY!

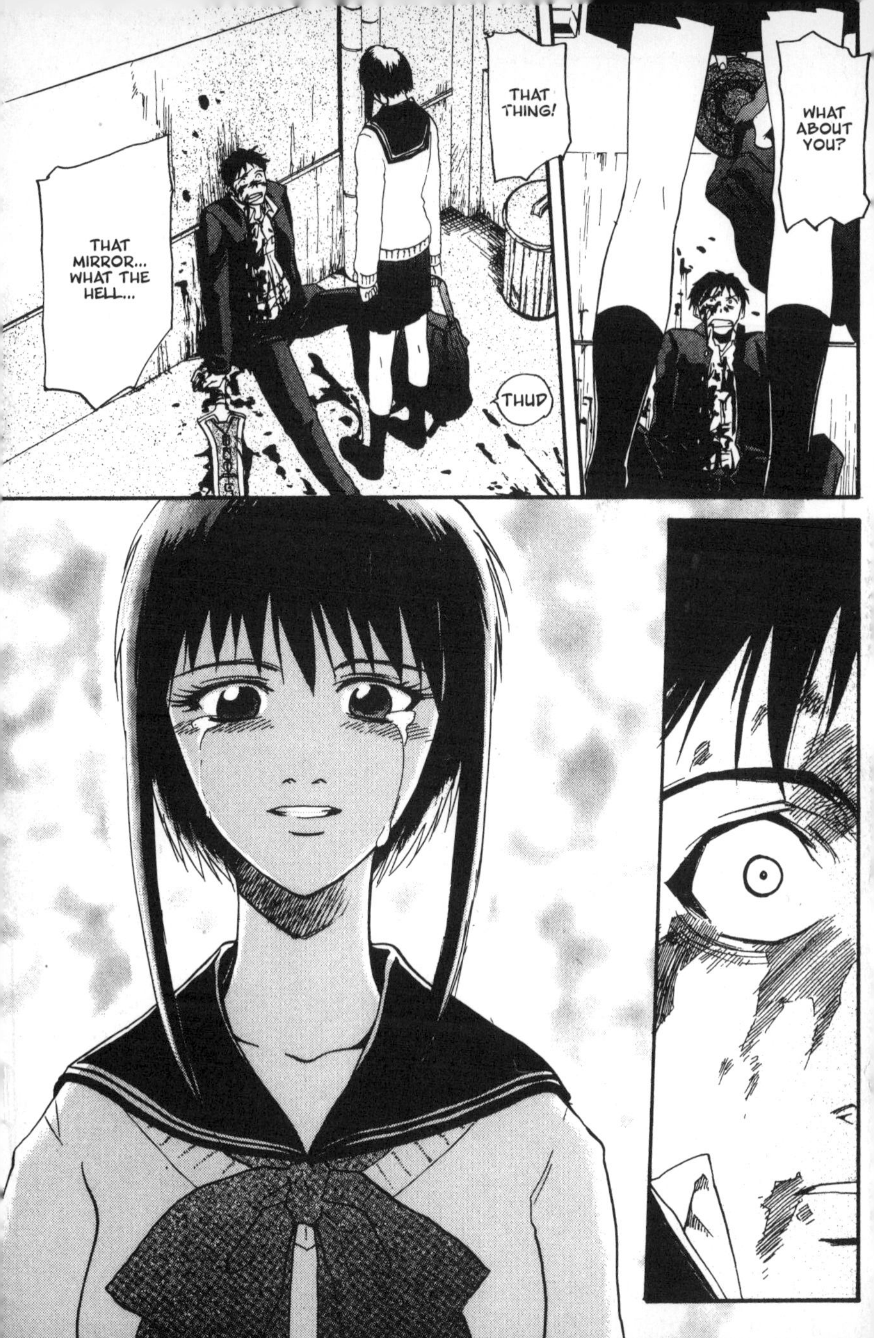
WHAT ABOUT YOU?
THAT THING!
THAT MIRROR... WHAT THE HELL...
THUD

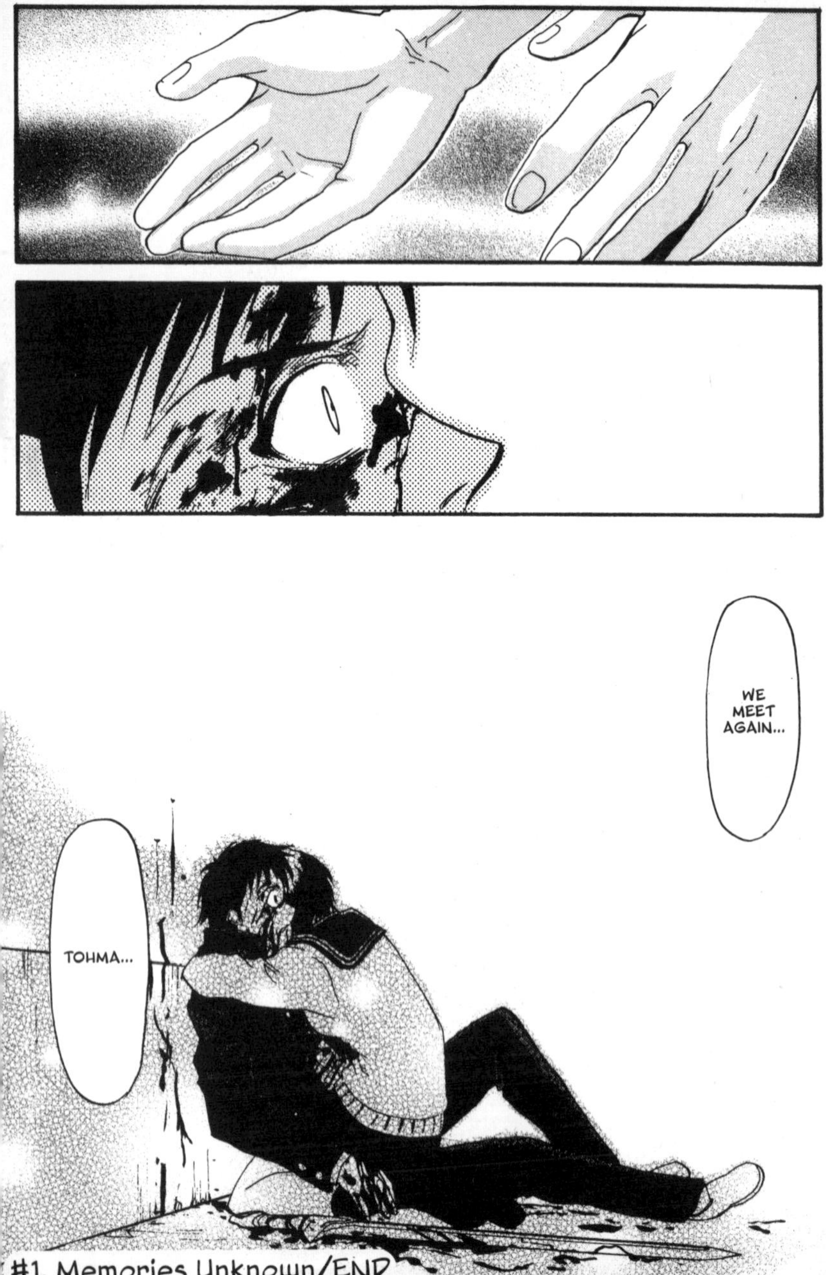
WE MEET AGAIN...
TOHMA...
#1. Memories Unknown/END

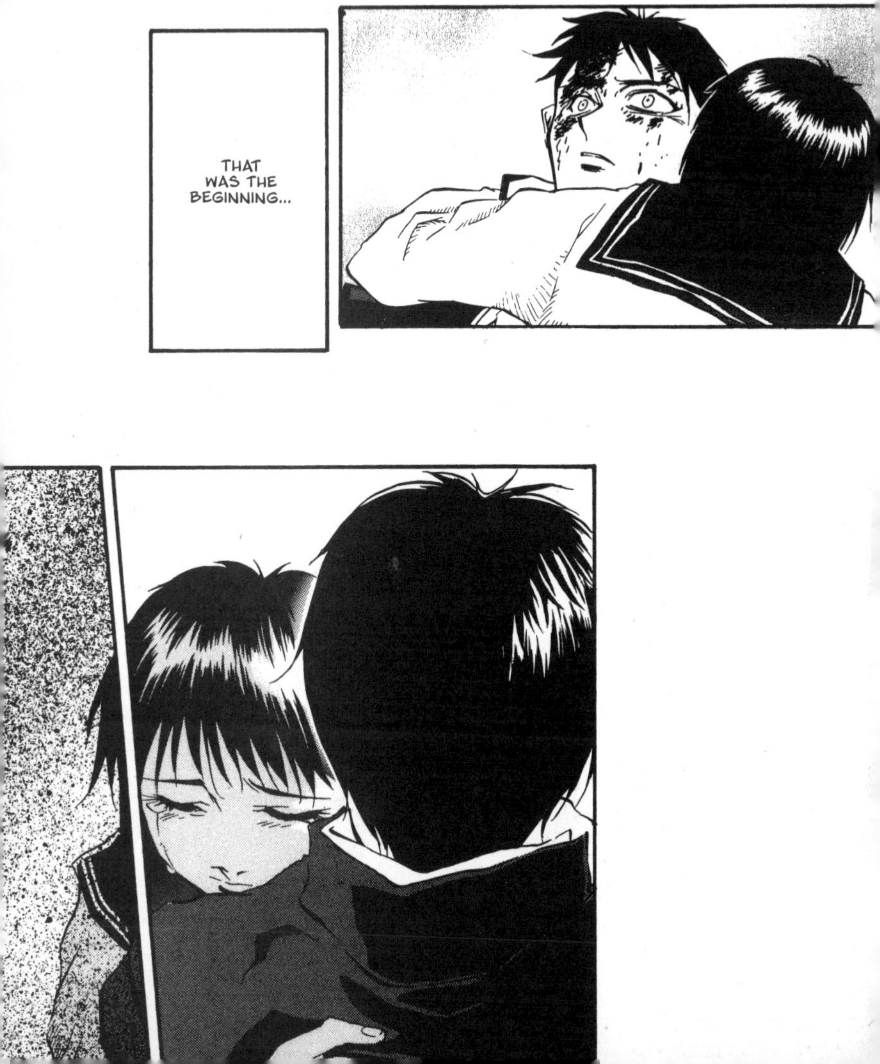
THAT WAS THE BEGINNING...

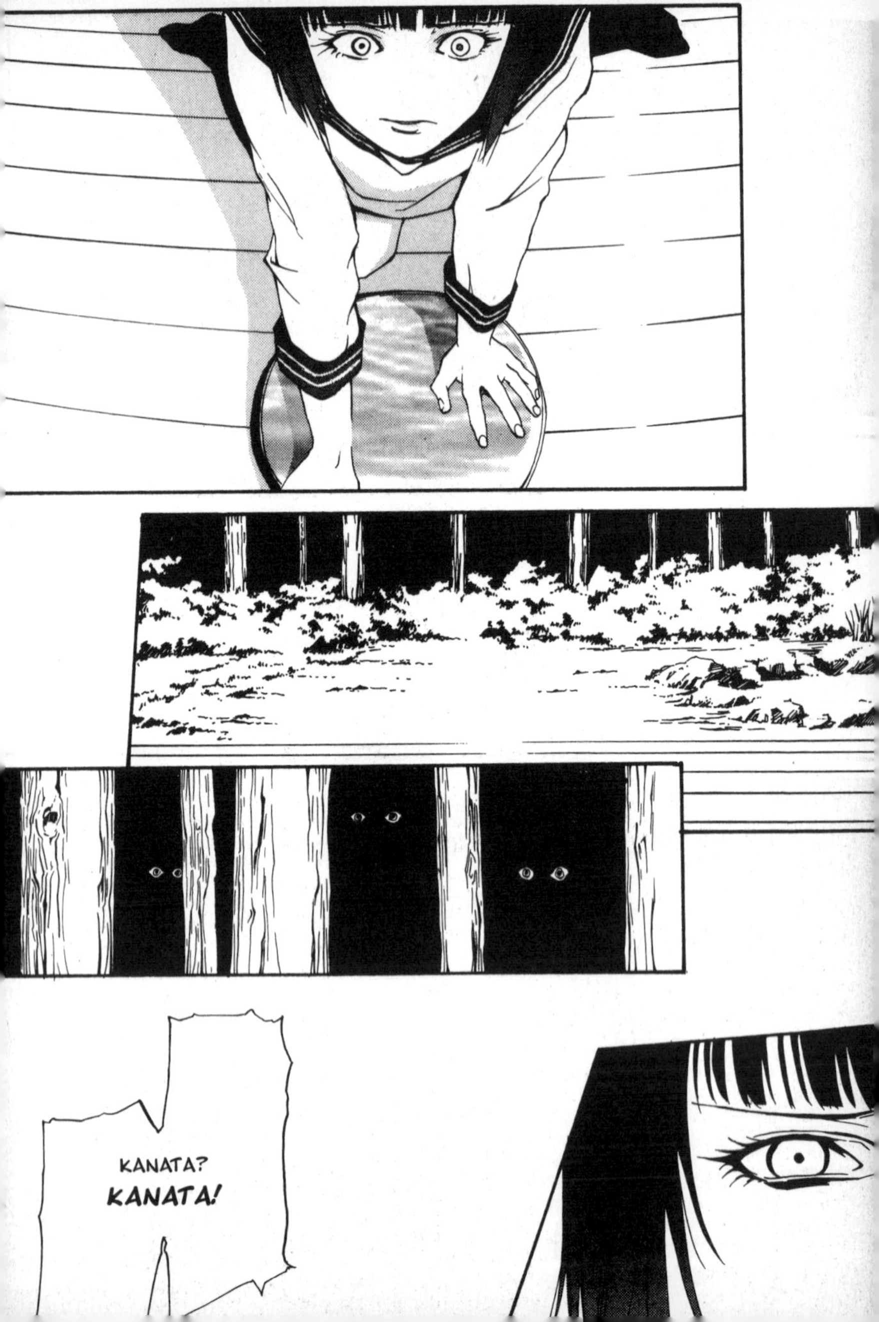
KANATA?
KANATA!

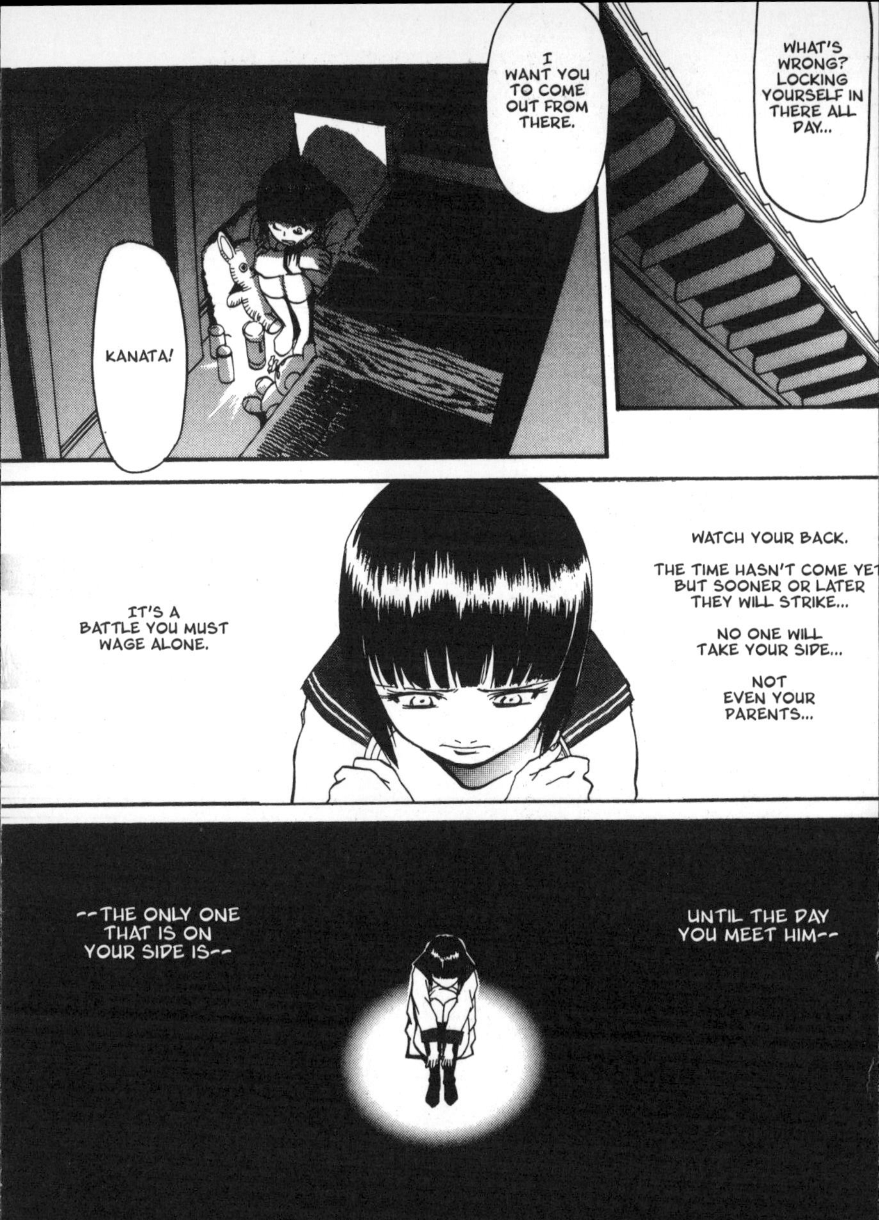
WHAT'S WRONG? LOCKING YOURSELF IN THERE ALL DAY...
I WANT YOU TO COME OUT FROM THERE.
KANATA!
WATCH YOUR BACK.
THE TIME HASN'T COME YET
BUT SOONER OR LATER THEY WILL STRIKE...
NO ONE WILL TAKE YOUR SIDE...
NOT EVEN YOUR PARENTS...
IT'S A BATTLE YOU MUST WAGE ALONE.
UNTIL THE DAY YOU MEET HIM--
--THE ONLY ONE THAT IS ON YOUR SIDE IS--

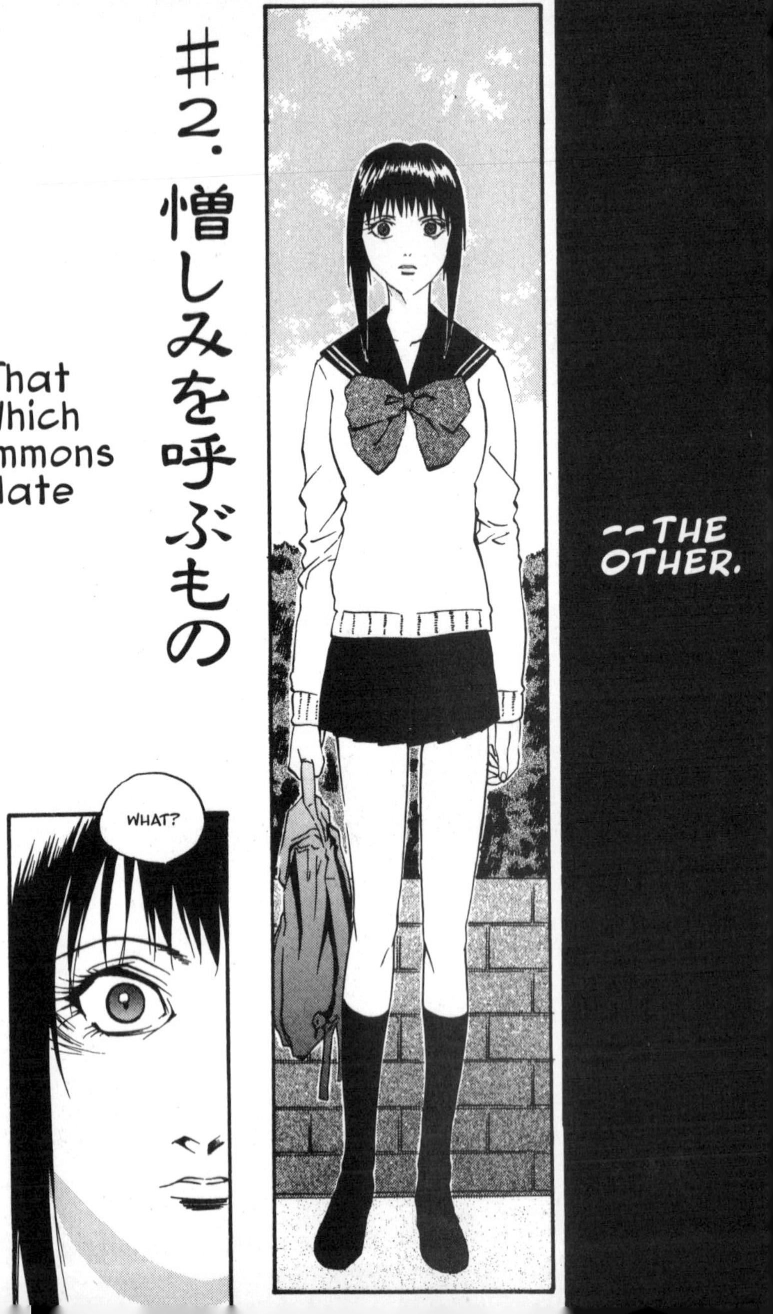
--THE OTHER.
#2. 憎しみを呼ぶもの
That Which Summons Hate
WHAT?

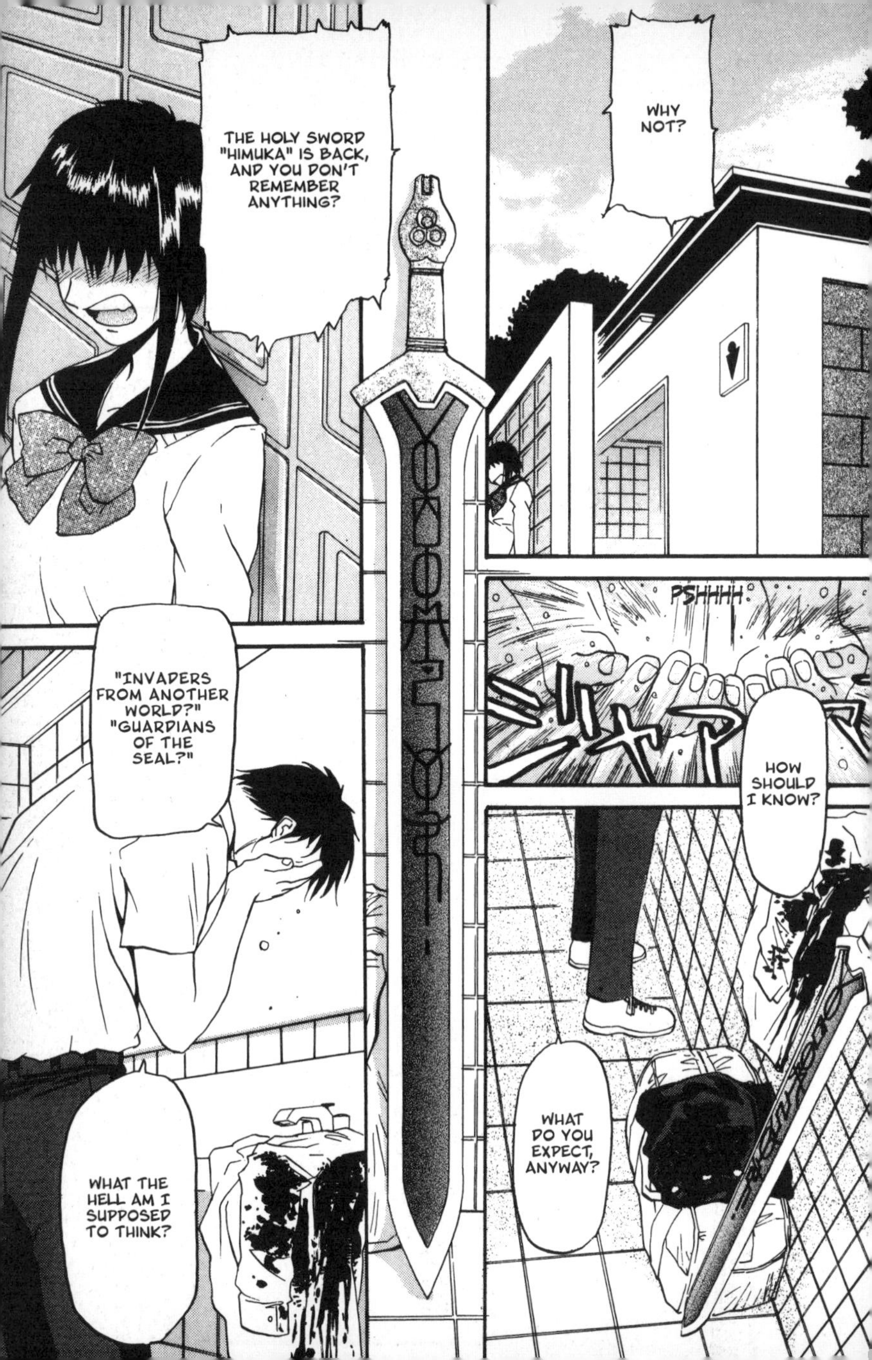
WHY NOT?
THE HOLY SWORD "HIMUKA" IS BACK, AND YOU DON'T REMEMBER ANYTHING?
PSHHHH
HOW SHOULD I KNOW?
WHAT DO YOU EXPECT, ANYWAY?
"INVADERS FROM ANOTHER WORLD?" "GUARDIANS OF THE SEAL?"
WHAT THE HELL AM I SUPPOSED TO THINK?

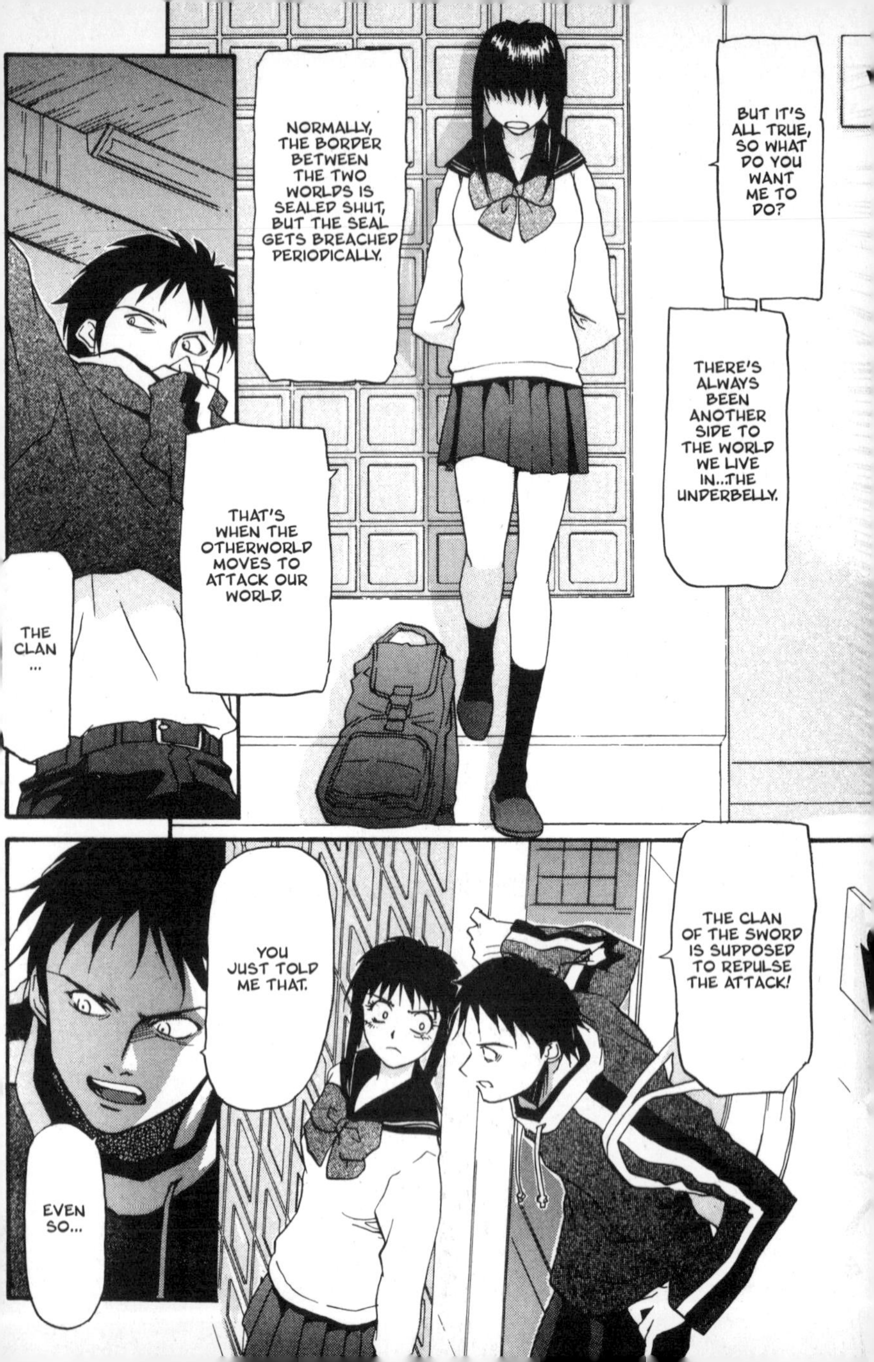
BUT IT'S ALL TRUE, SO WHAT DO YOU WANT ME TO DO?
THERE'S ALWAYS BEEN ANOTHER SIDE TO THE WORLD WE LIVE IN...THE UNDERBELLY.
NORMALLY, THE BORDER BETWEEN THE TWO WORLDS IS SEALED SHUT, BUT THE SEAL GETS BREACHED PERIODICALLY.
THAT'S WHEN THE OTHERWORLD MOVES TO ATTACK OUR WORLD.
THE CLAN ...
THE CLAN OF THE SWORD IS SUPPOSED TO REPULSE THE ATTACK!
YOU JUST TOLD ME THAT.
EVEN SO...

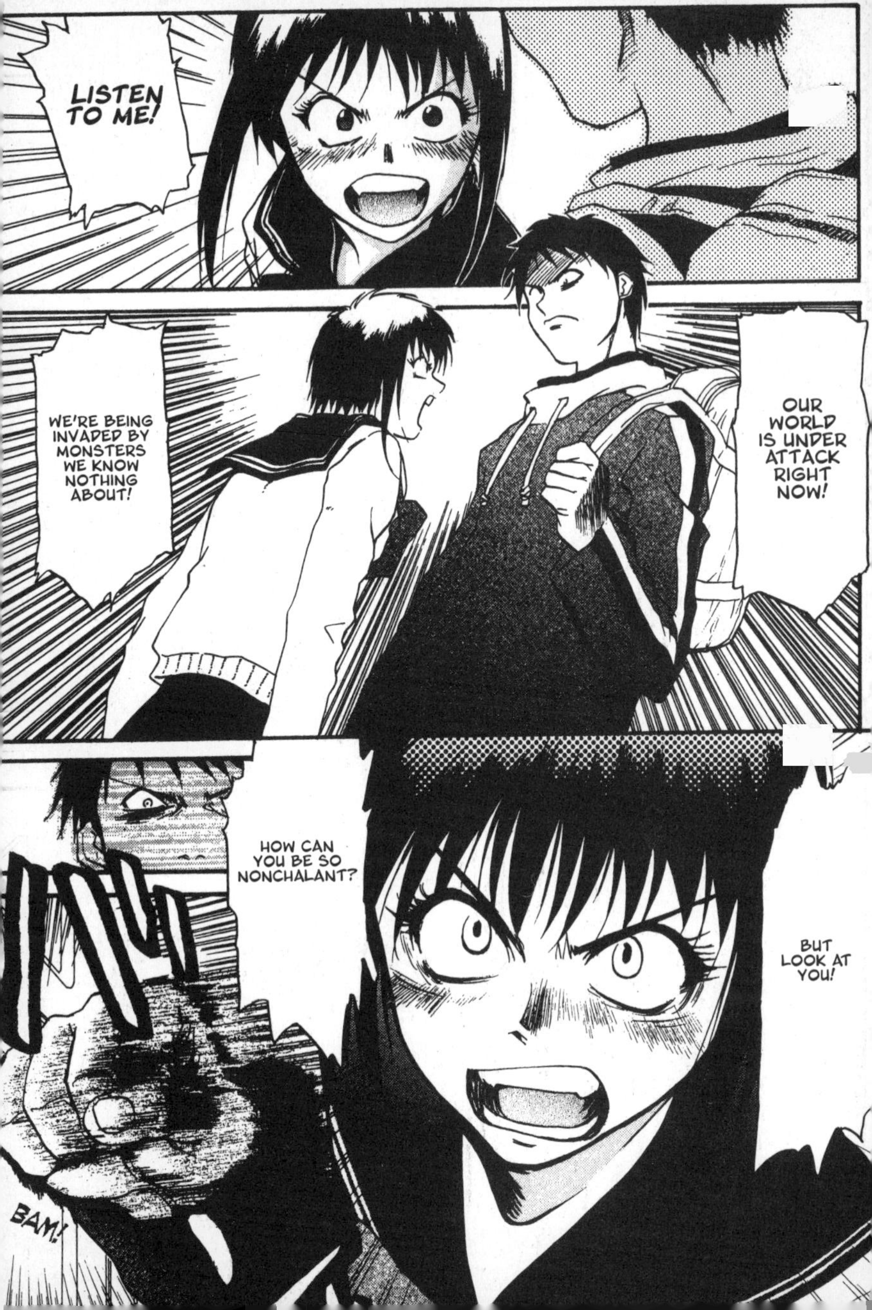
LISTEN TO ME!
OUR WORLD IS UNDER ATTACK RIGHT NOW!
WE'RE BEING INVADED BY MONSTERS WE KNOW NOTHING ABOUT!
BUT LOOK AT YOU!
HOW CAN YOU BE SO NONCHALANT?
BAM!

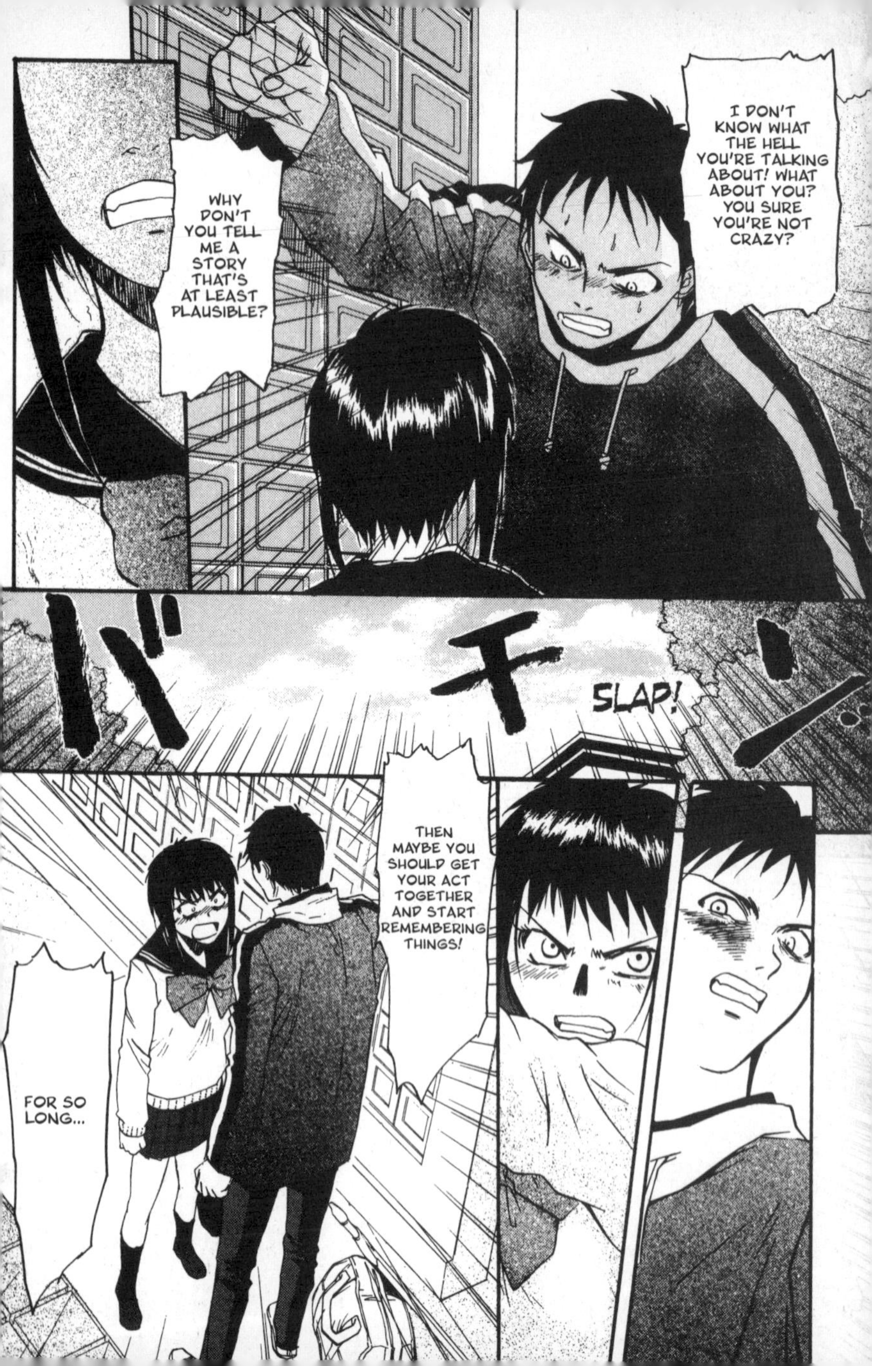
I DON'T KNOW WHAT THE HELL YOU'RE TALKING ABOUT! WHAT ABOUT YOU? YOU SURE YOU'RE NOT CRAZY?
WHY DON'T YOU TELL ME A STORY THAT'S AT LEAST PLAUSIBLE?
SLAP!
THEN MAYBE YOU SHOULD GET YOUR ACT TOGETHER AND START REMEMBERING THINGS!
FOR SO LONG...

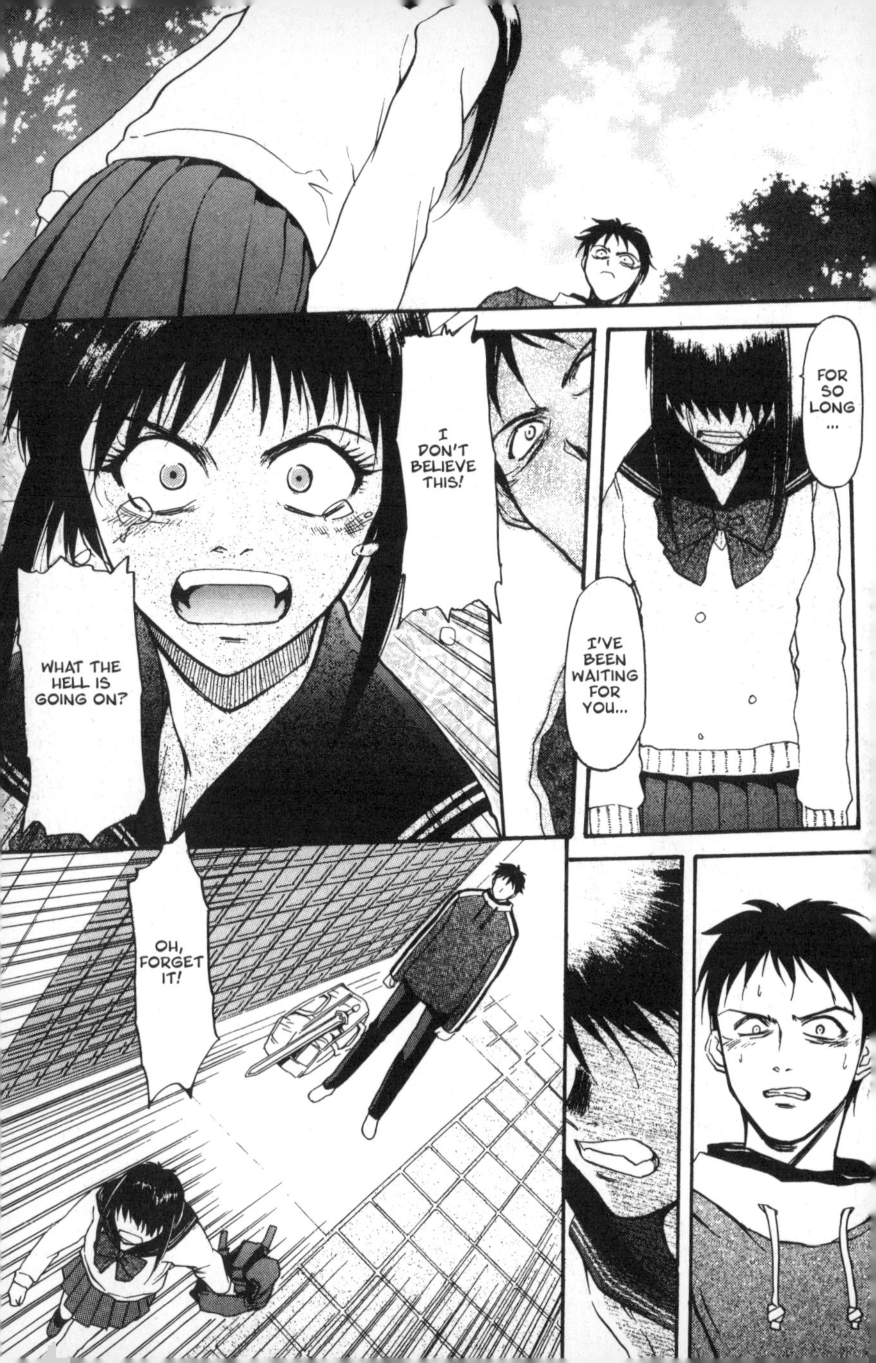
FOR SO LONG...
I'VE BEEN WAITING FOR YOU...
I DON'T BELIEVE THIS!
WHAT THE HELL IS GOING ON?
OH, FORGET IT!

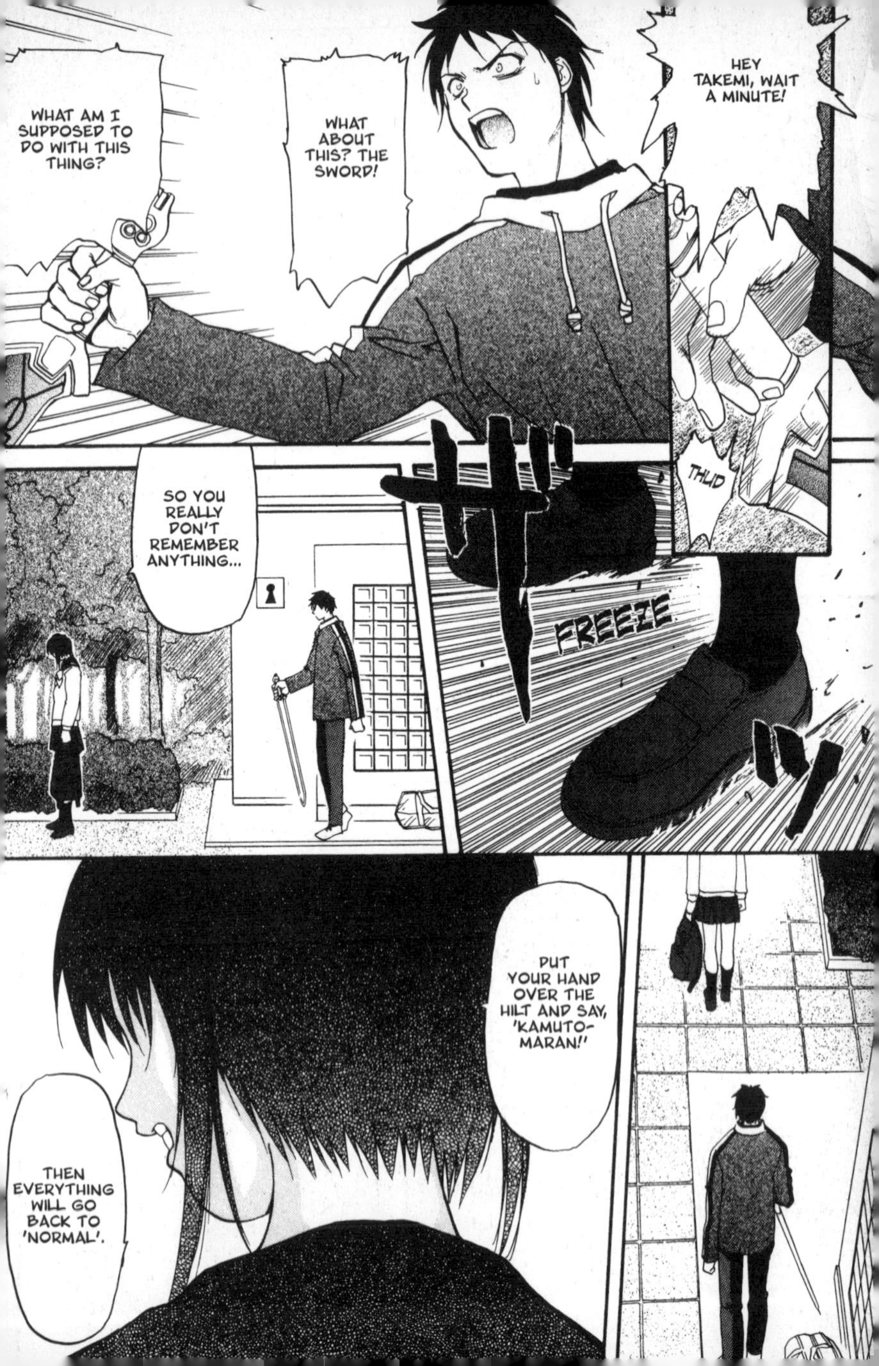
HEY TAKEMI, WAIT A MINUTE!
WHAT ABOUT THIS? THE SWORD!
WHAT AM I SUPPOSED TO DO WITH THIS THING?
THUD
FREEZE
SO YOU REALLY DON'T REMEMBER ANYTHING...
PUT YOUR HAND OVER THE HILT AND SAY, 'KAMUTO-MARAN!'
THEN EVERYTHING WILL GO BACK TO 'NORMAL'.

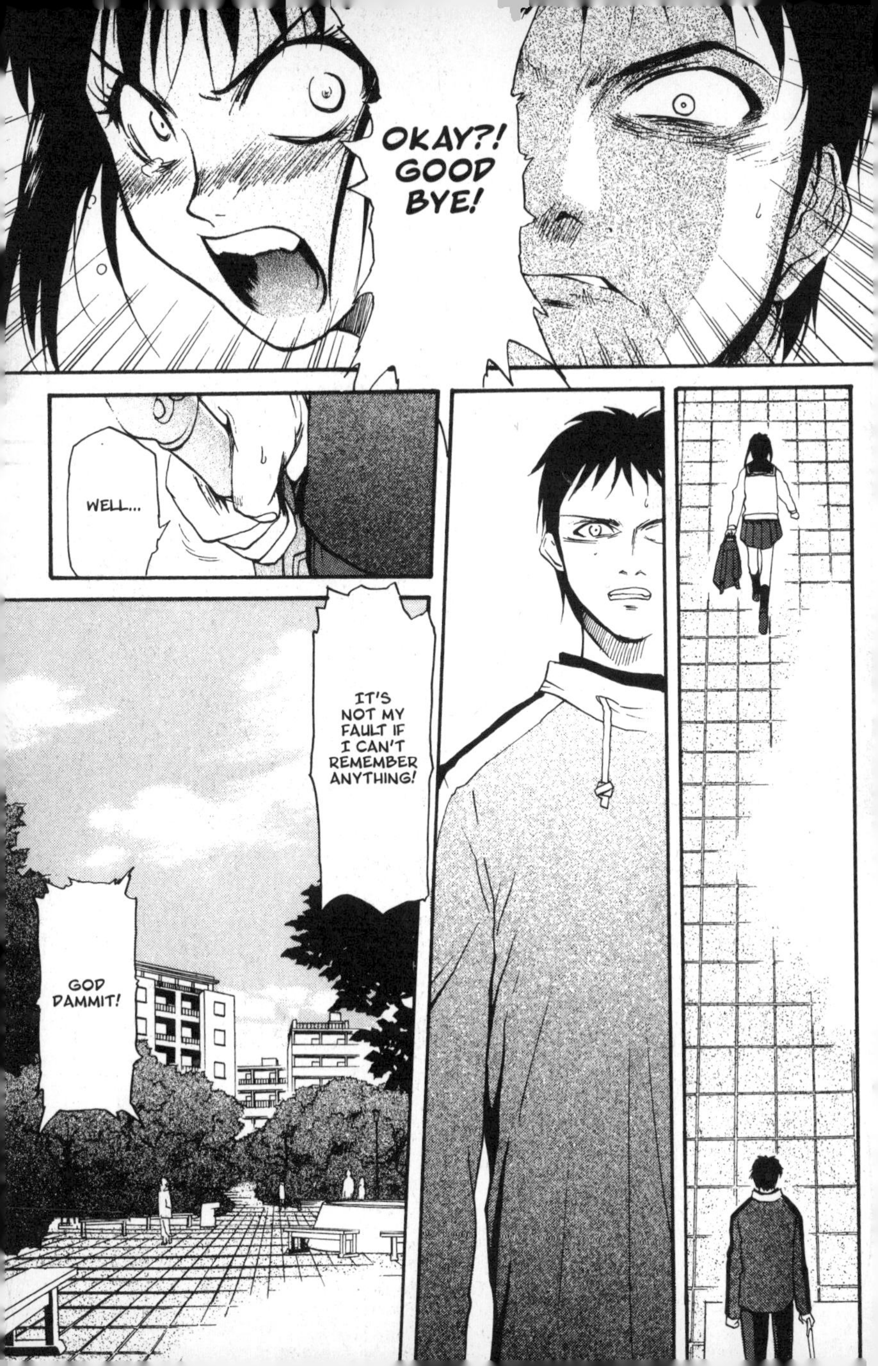
OKAY?! GOOD BYE!
WELL...
IT'S NOT MY FAULT IF I CAN'T REMEMBER ANYTHING!
GOD DAMMIT!

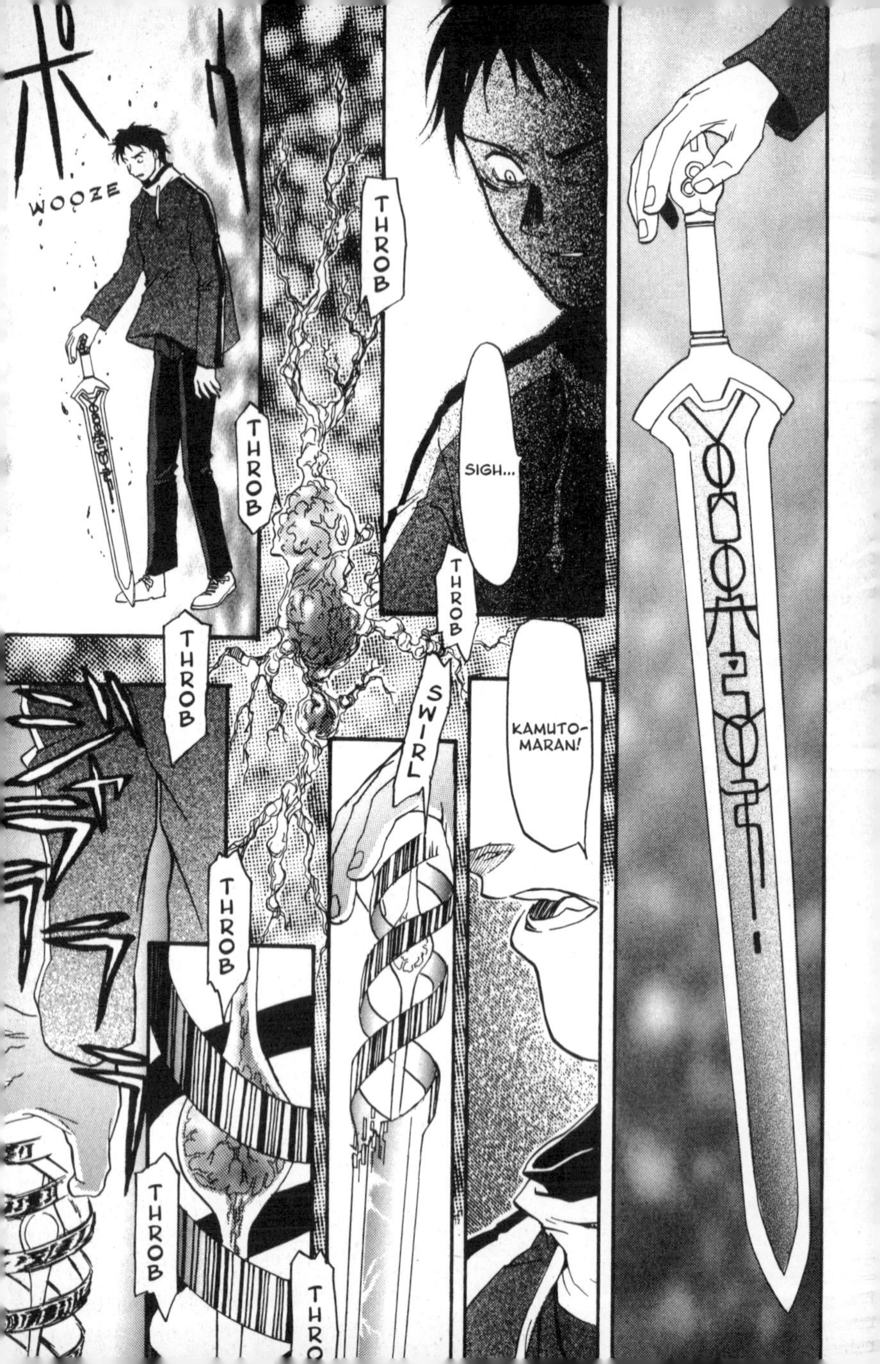
SIGH...
THROB
KAMUTO-MARAN!
SWIRL
THRO
THROB
THROB
WOOZE
THROB
THROB
THROB

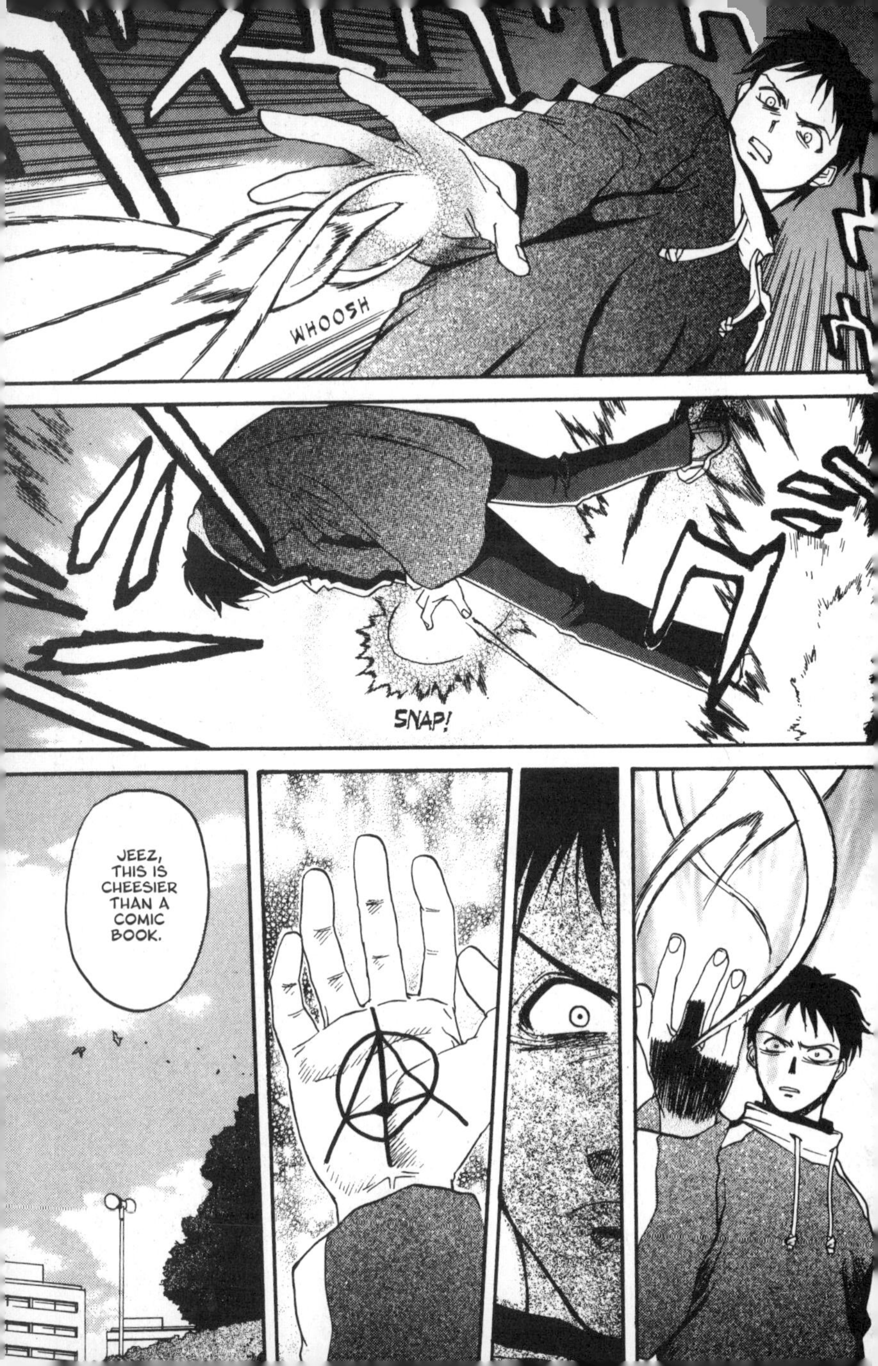
WHOOSH
SNAP!
JEEZ, THIS IS CHEESIER THAN A COMIC BOOK.

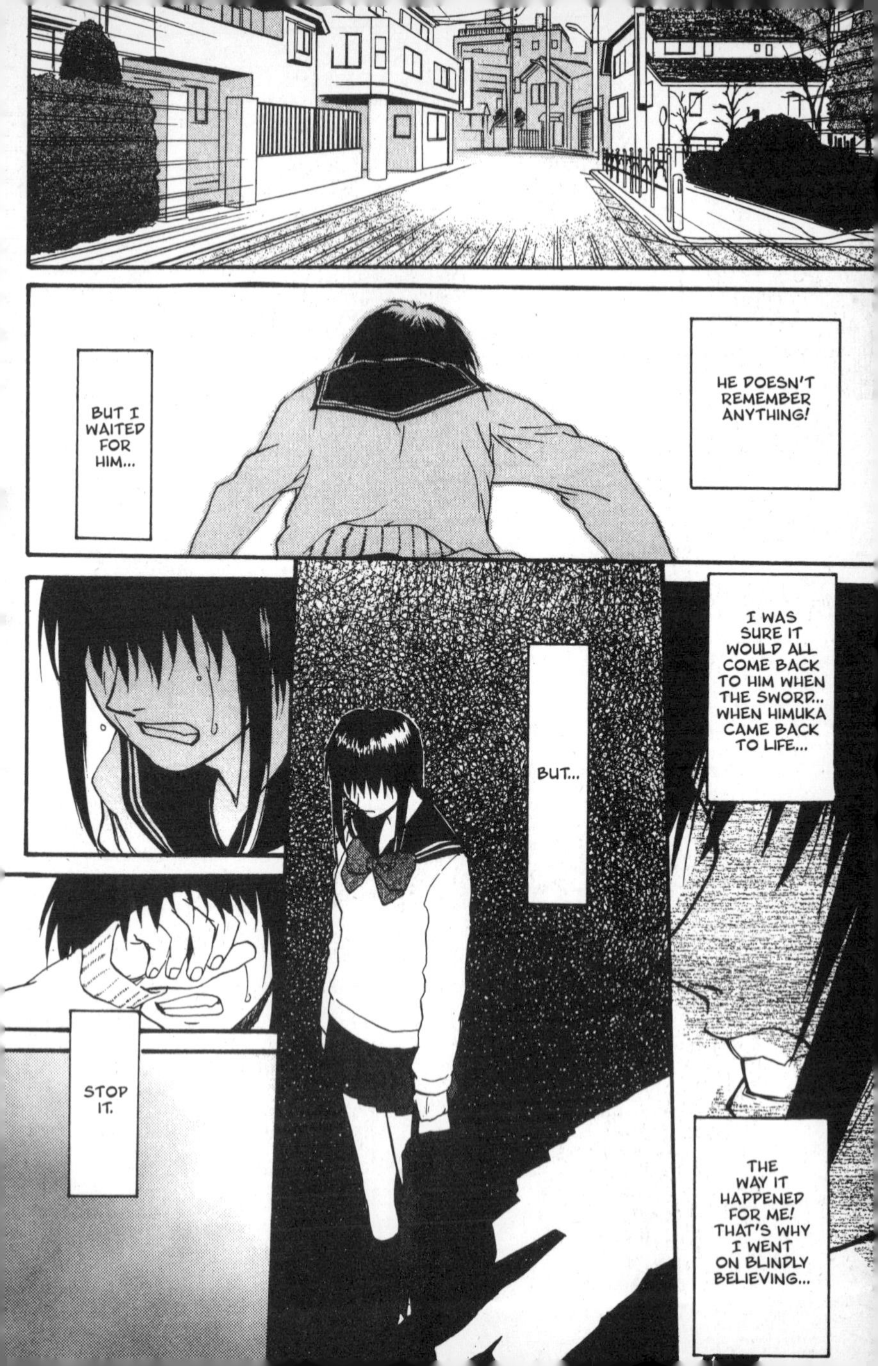
HE DOESN'T REMEMBER ANYTHING!
BUT I WAITED FOR HIM...
I WAS SURE IT WOULD ALL COME BACK TO HIM WHEN THE SWORD.. WHEN HIMUKA CAME BACK TO LIFE...
THE WAY IT HAPPENED FOR ME! THAT'S WHY I WENT ON BLINDLY BELIEVING...
BUT...
STOP IT.

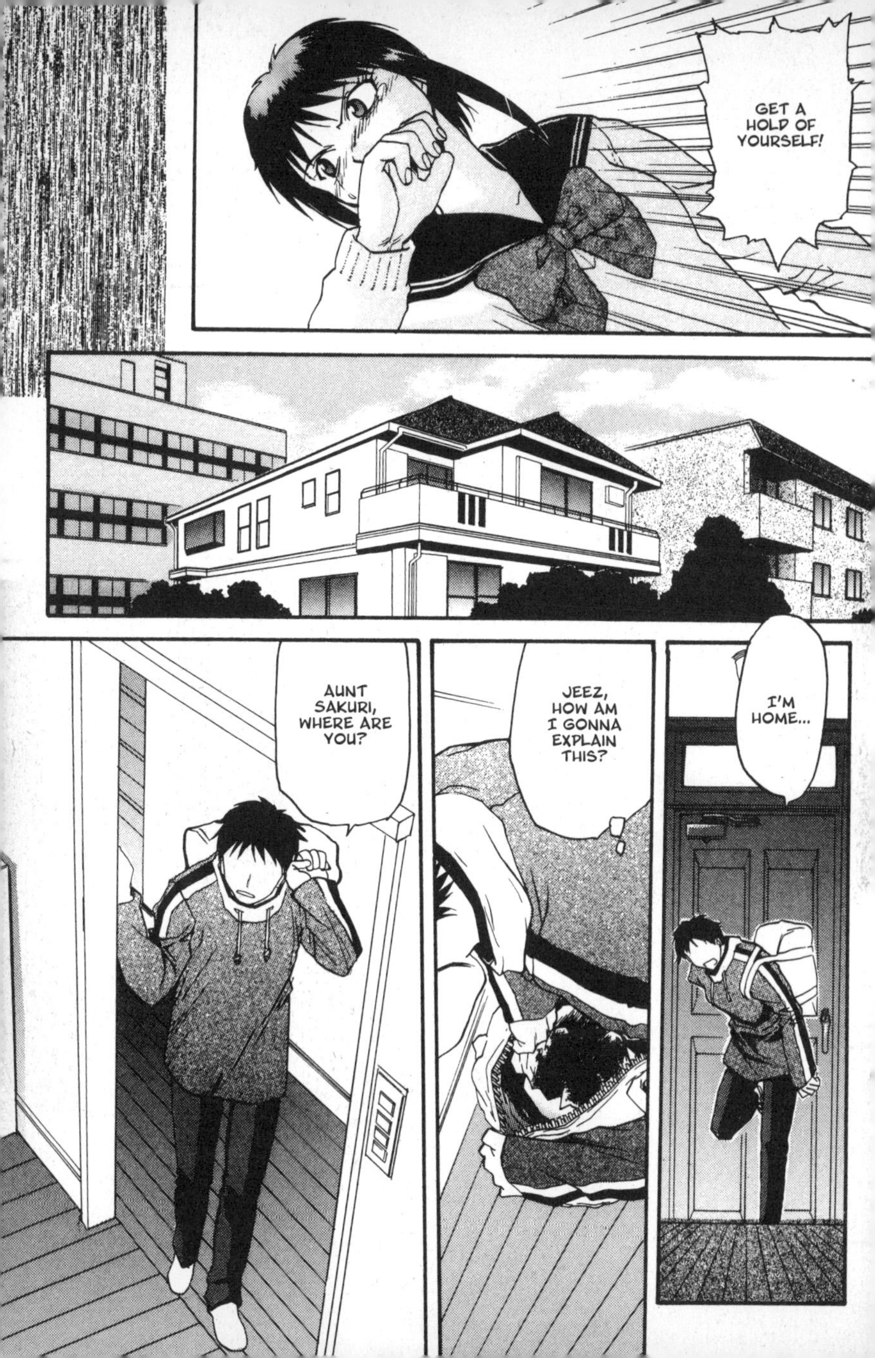
GET A HOLD OF YOURSELF!
I'M HOME...
JEEZ, HOW AM I GONNA EXPLAIN THIS?
AUNT SAKURI, WHERE ARE YOU?

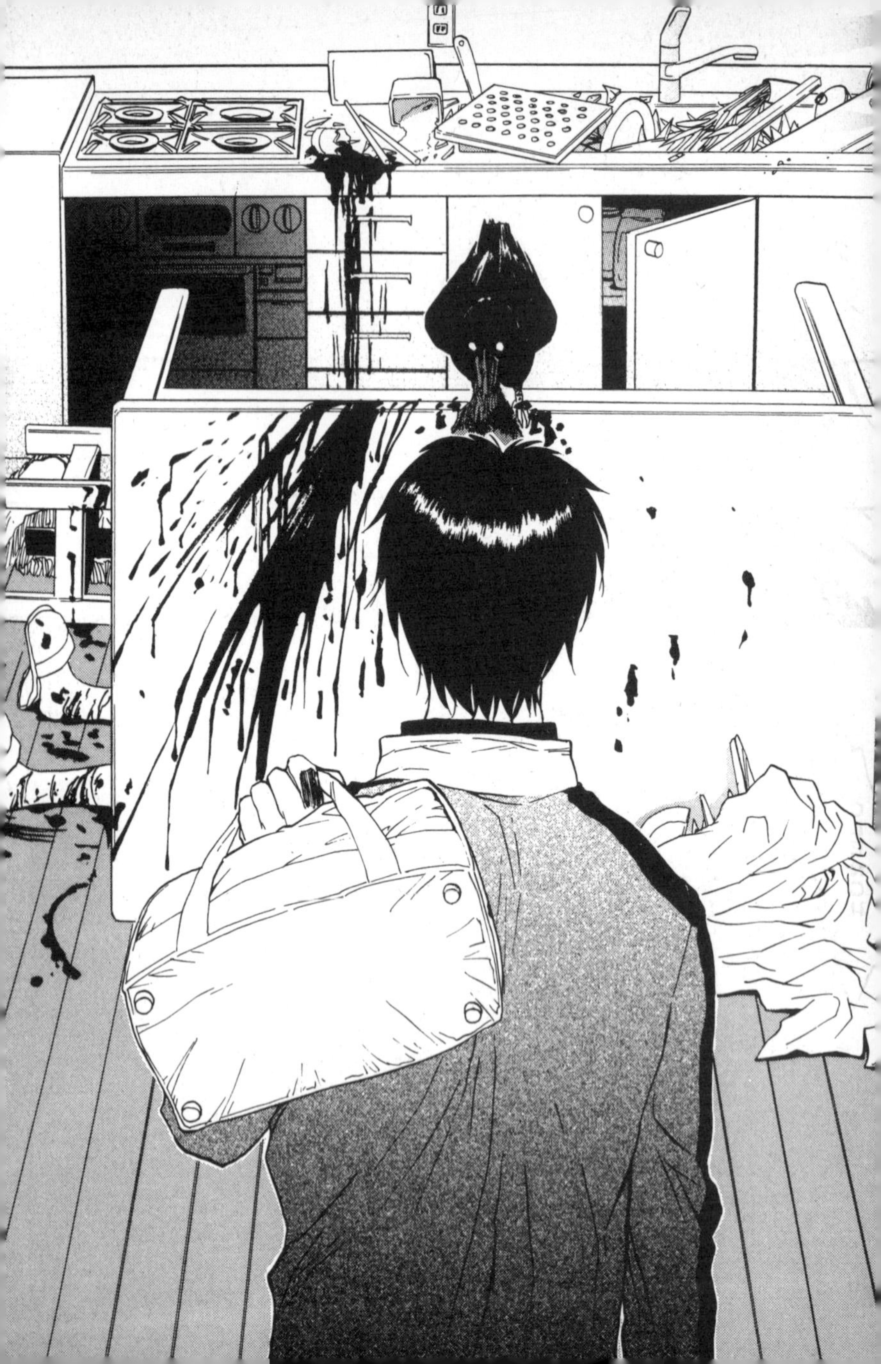

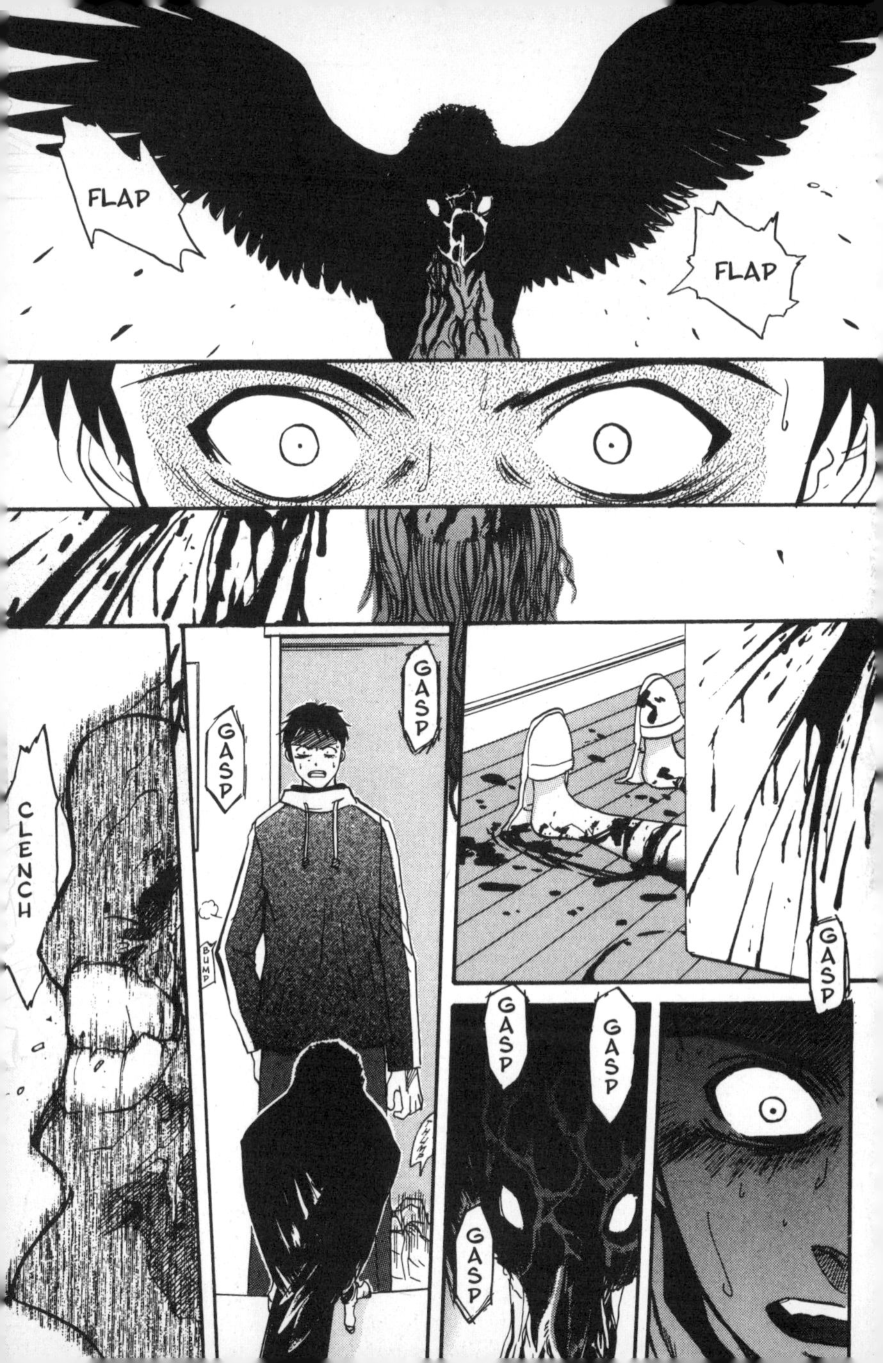

FLAP
FLAP
GASP
GASP
GASP
GASP
GASP
GASP
BUMP
CLENCH

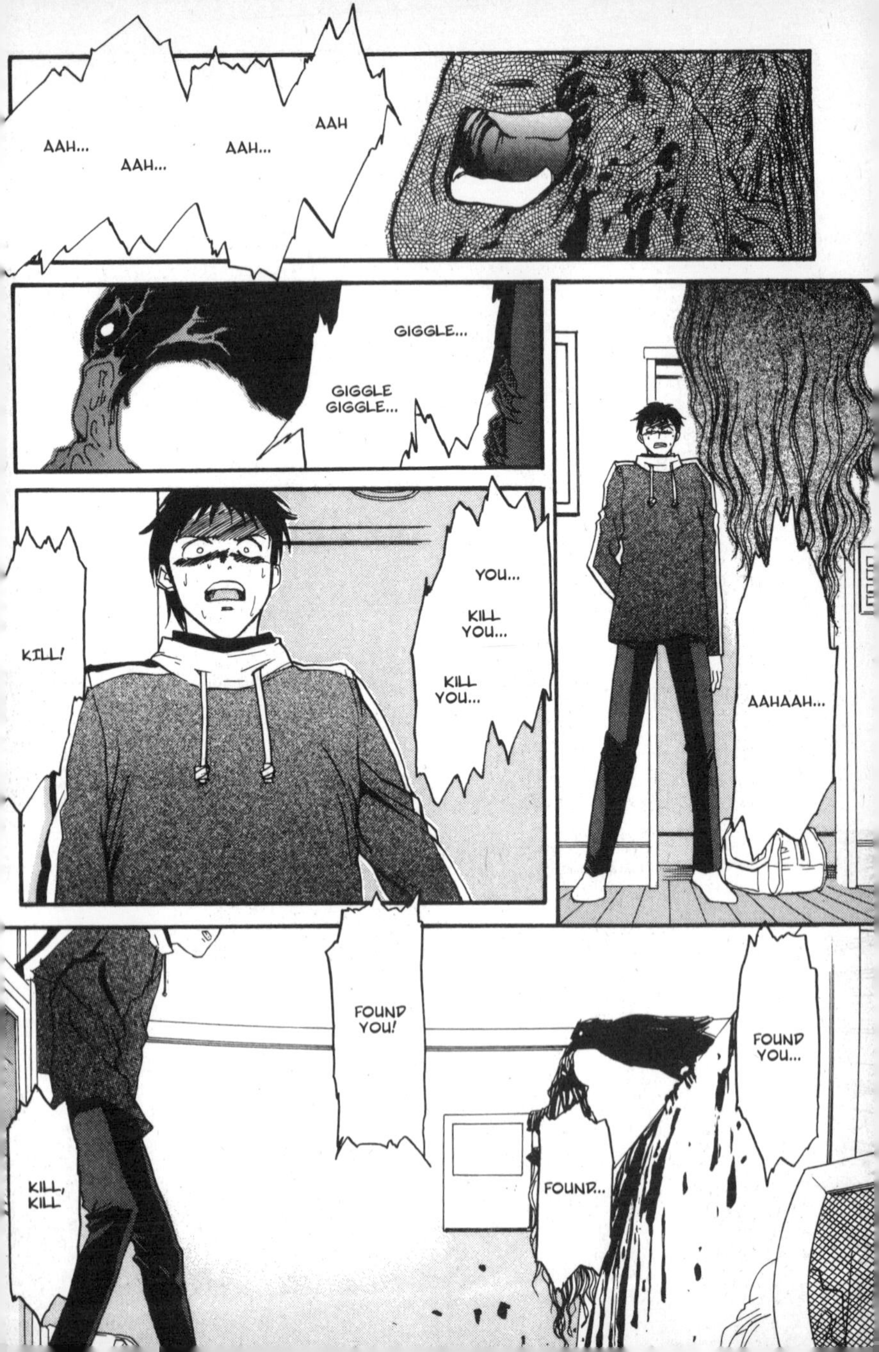
AAH... AAH... AAH... AAH
AAHAAH...
GIGGLE...
GIGGLE GIGGLE...
YOU... KILL YOU... KILL YOU...
KILL!
FOUND YOU...
FOUND...
FOUND YOU!
KILL, KILL

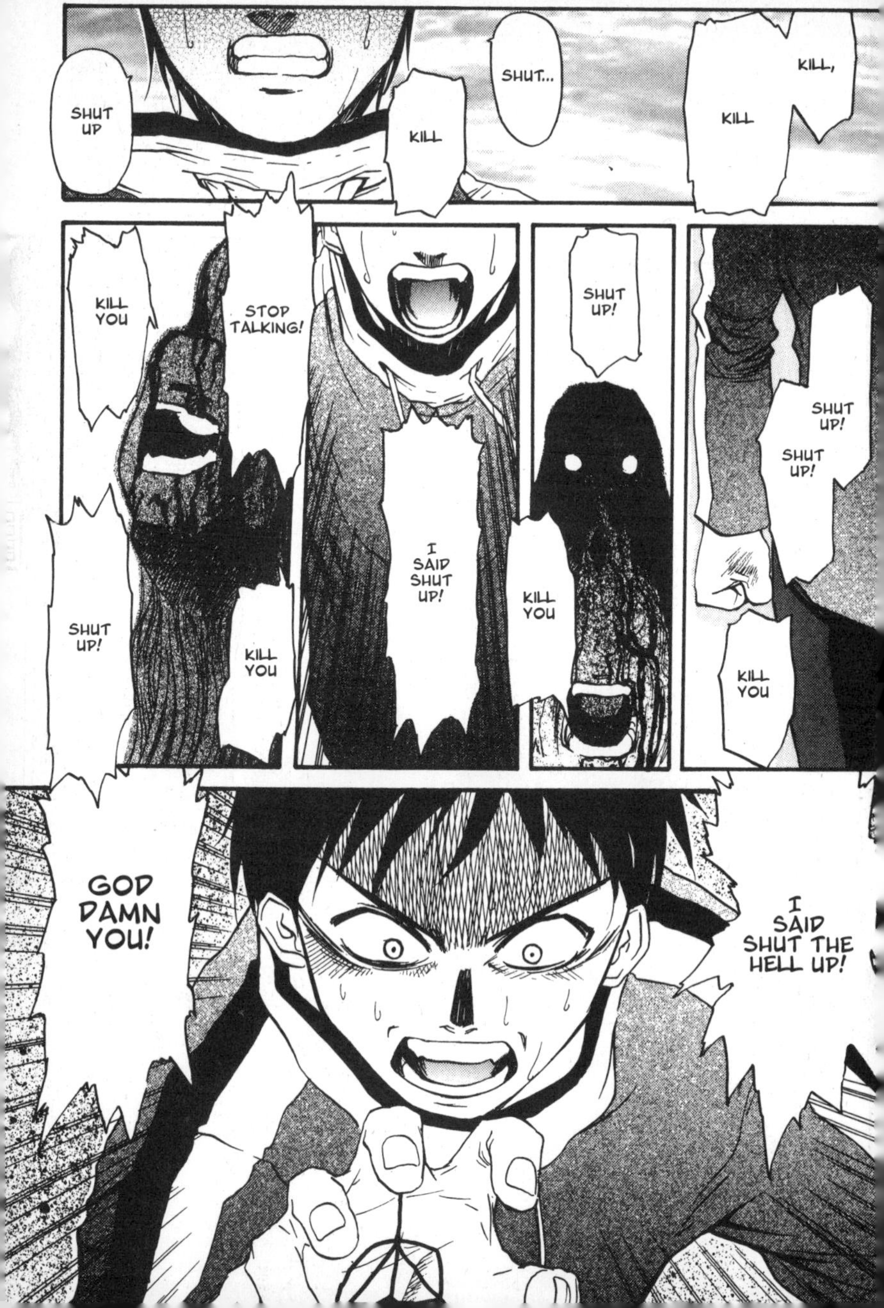
KILL,
KILL
SHUT...
KILL
SHUT UP
SHUT UP!
SHUT UP!
KILL YOU
SHUT UP!
KILL YOU
I SAID SHUT UP!
STOP TALKING!
KILL YOU
KILL YOU
SHUT UP!
I SAID SHUT THE HELL UP!
GOD DAMN YOU!

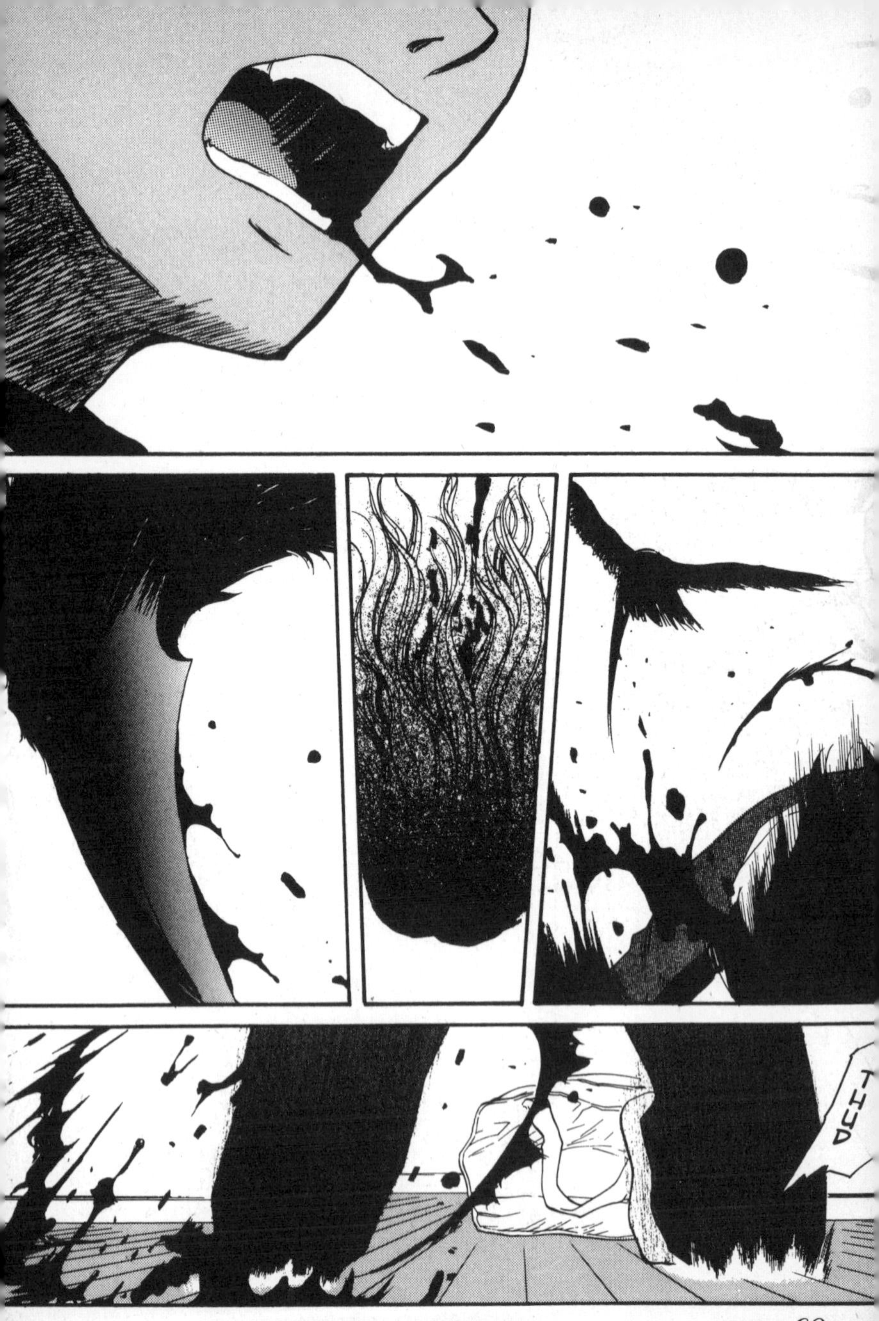
THUD

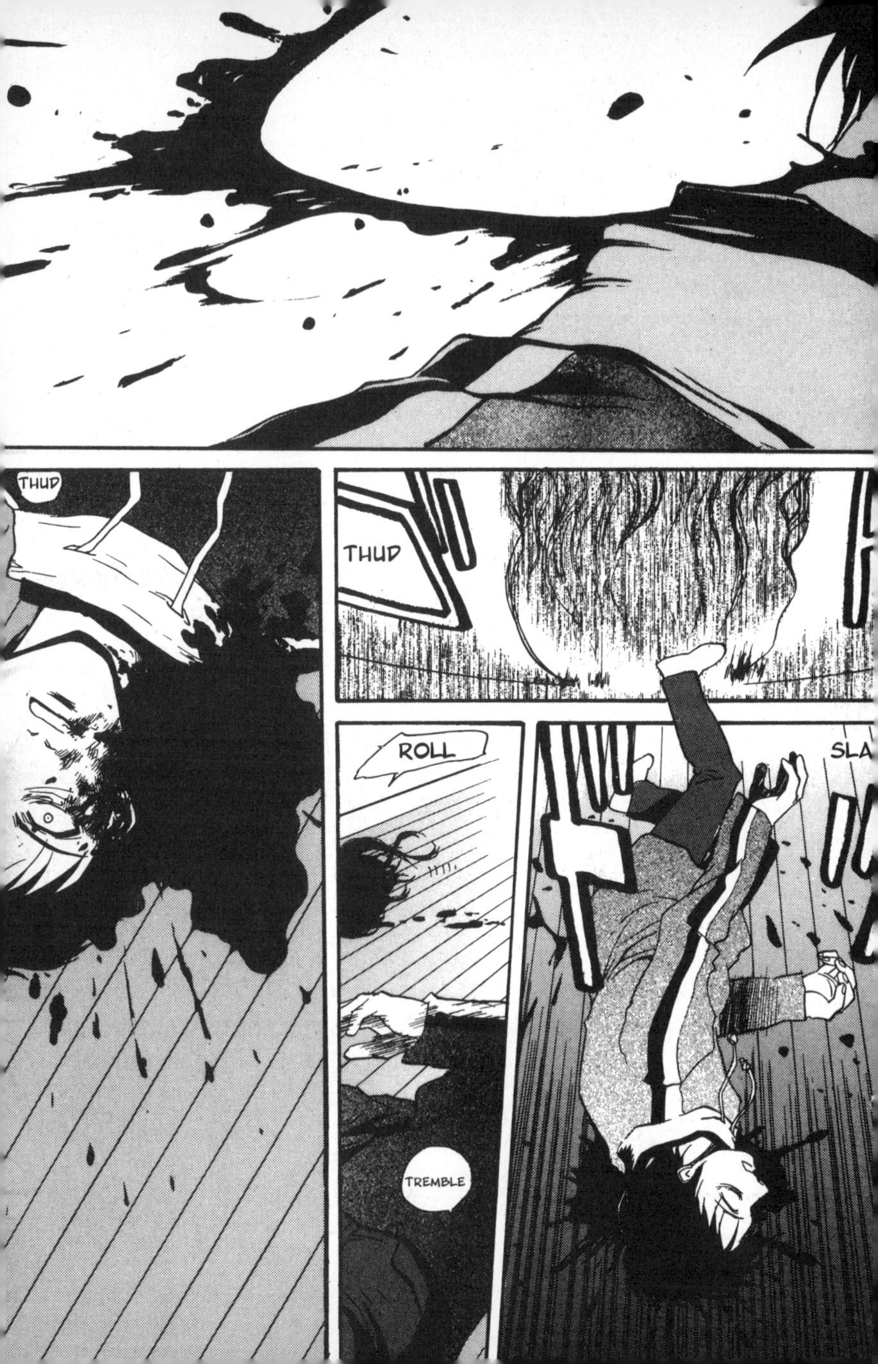
THUD
SLA
ROLL
TREMBLE
THUD

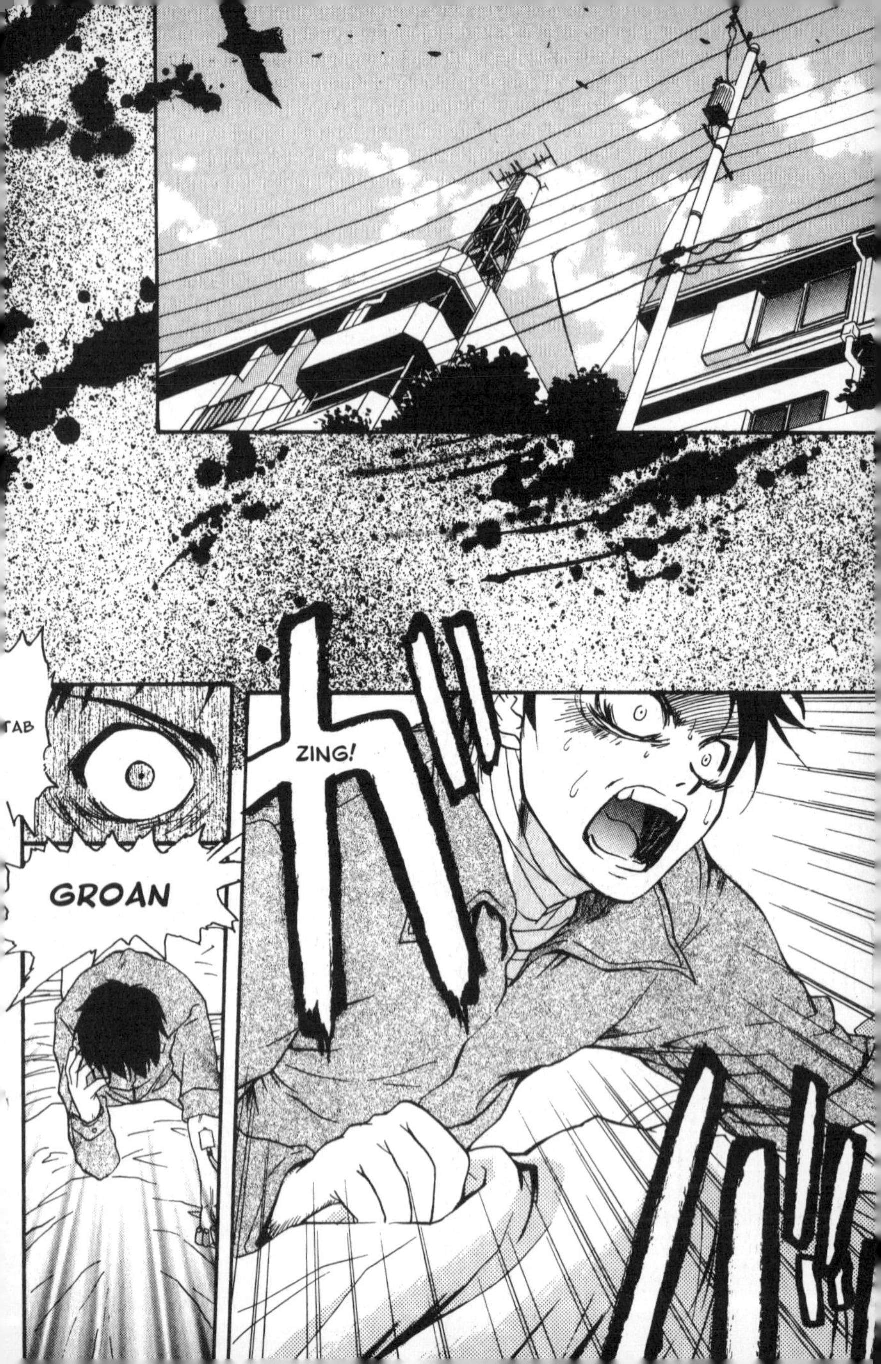
ZING!
TAB
GROAN

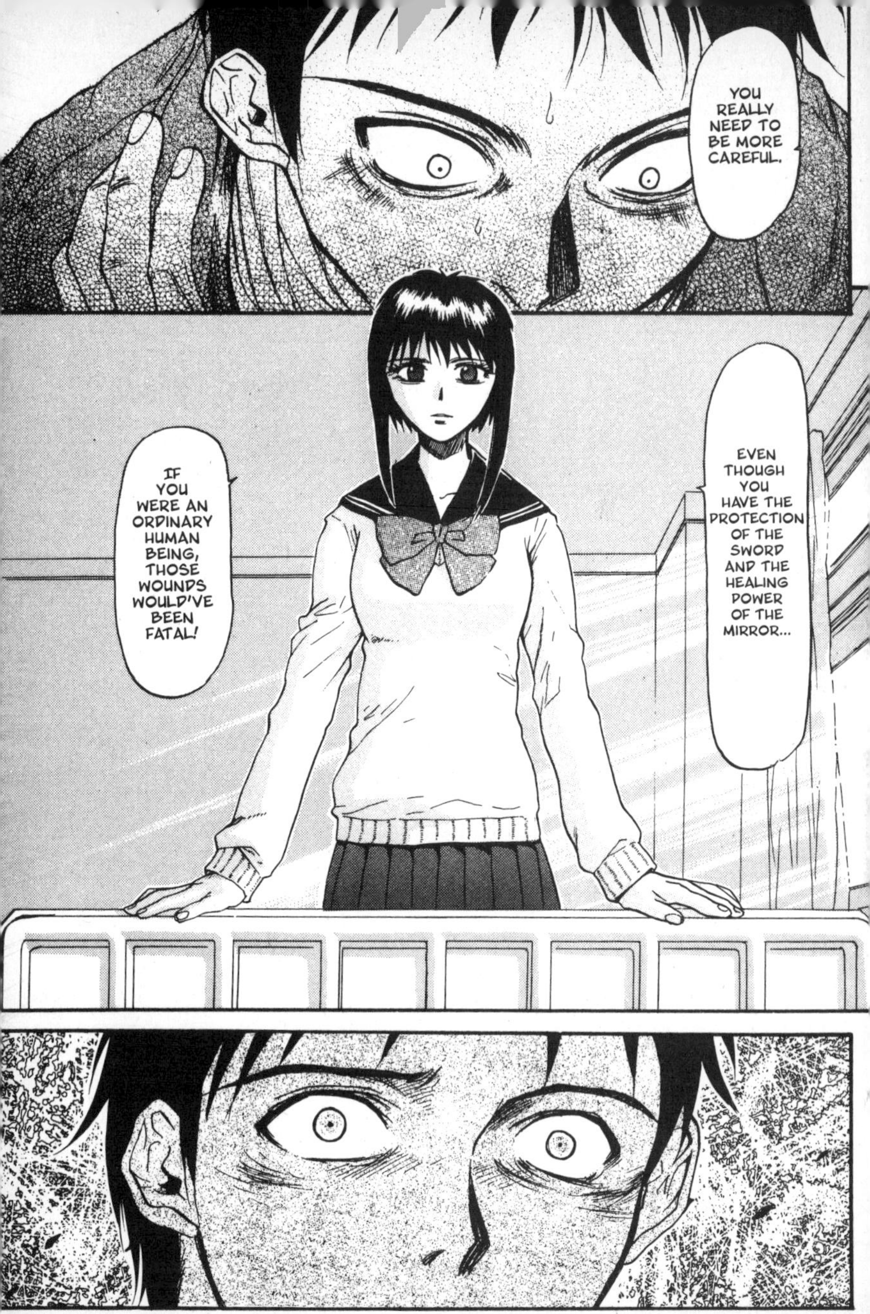
YOU REALLY NEED TO BE MORE CAREFUL.
EVEN THOUGH YOU HAVE THE PROTECTION OF THE SWORD AND THE HEALING POWER OF THE MIRROR...
IF YOU WERE AN ORDINARY HUMAN BEING, THOSE WOUNDS WOULD'VE BEEN FATAL!

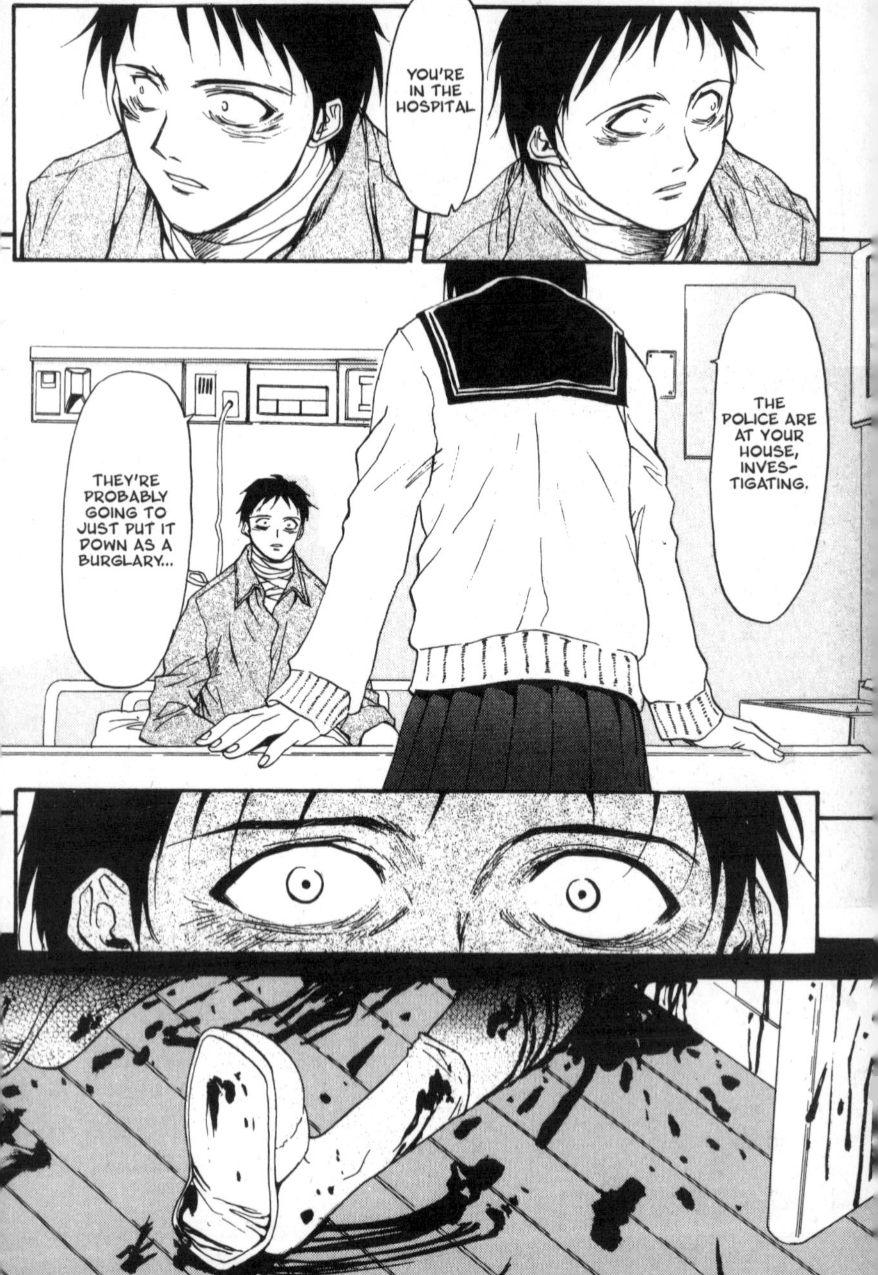
YOU'RE IN THE HOSPITAL
THE POLICE ARE AT YOUR HOUSE, INVES-TIGATING.
THEY'RE PROBABLY GOING TO JUST PUT IT DOWN AS A BURGLARY...

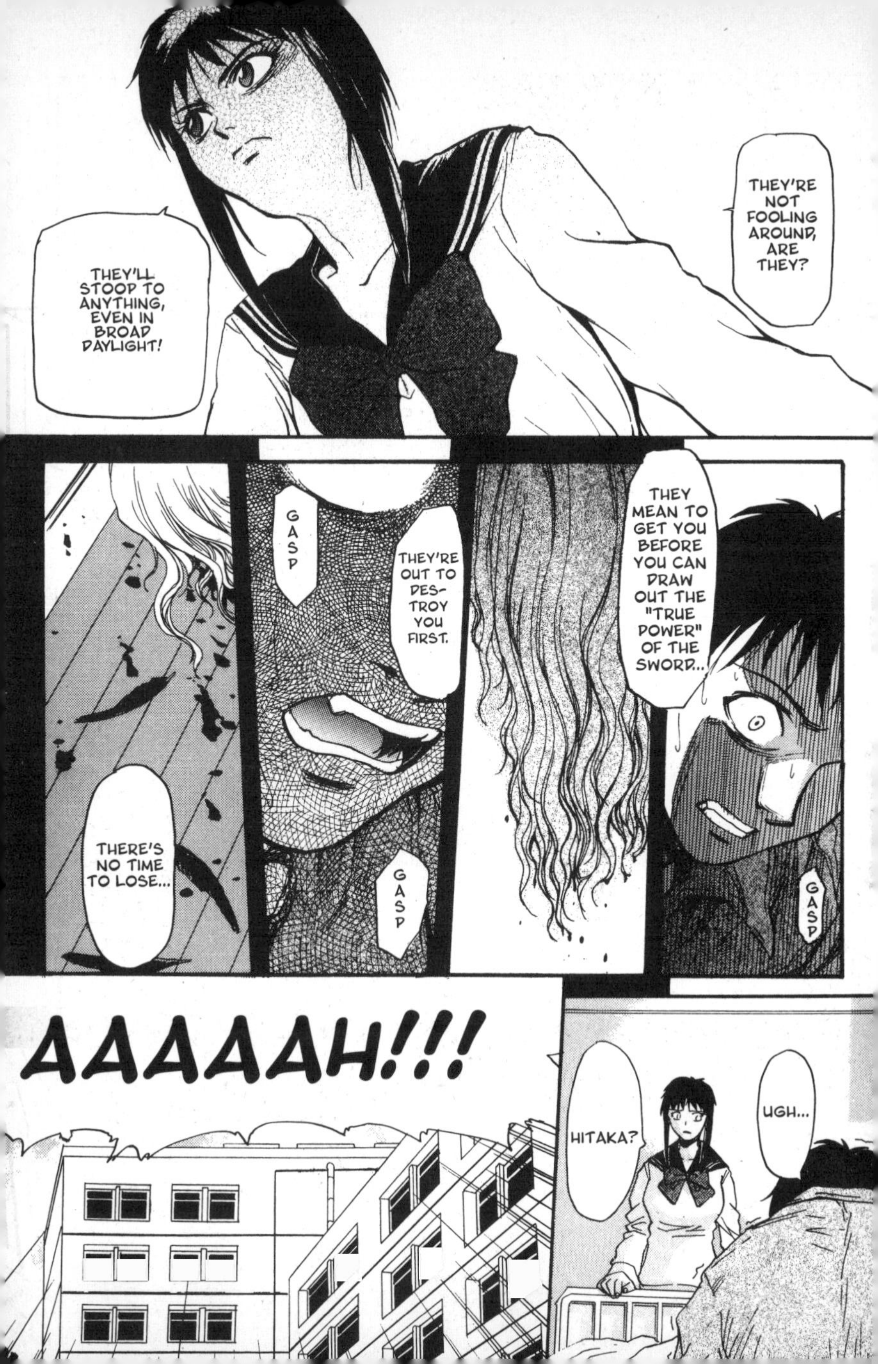
THEY'RE NOT FOOLING AROUND, ARE THEY?
THEY'LL STOOP TO ANYTHING, EVEN IN BROAD DAYLIGHT!
THEY MEAN TO GET YOU BEFORE YOU CAN DRAW OUT THE "TRUE POWER" OF THE SWORD...
GASP
GASP
THEY'RE OUT TO DES-TROY YOU FIRST.
GASP
THERE'S NO TIME TO LOSE...
UGH...
HITAKA?
AAAAAH!!!

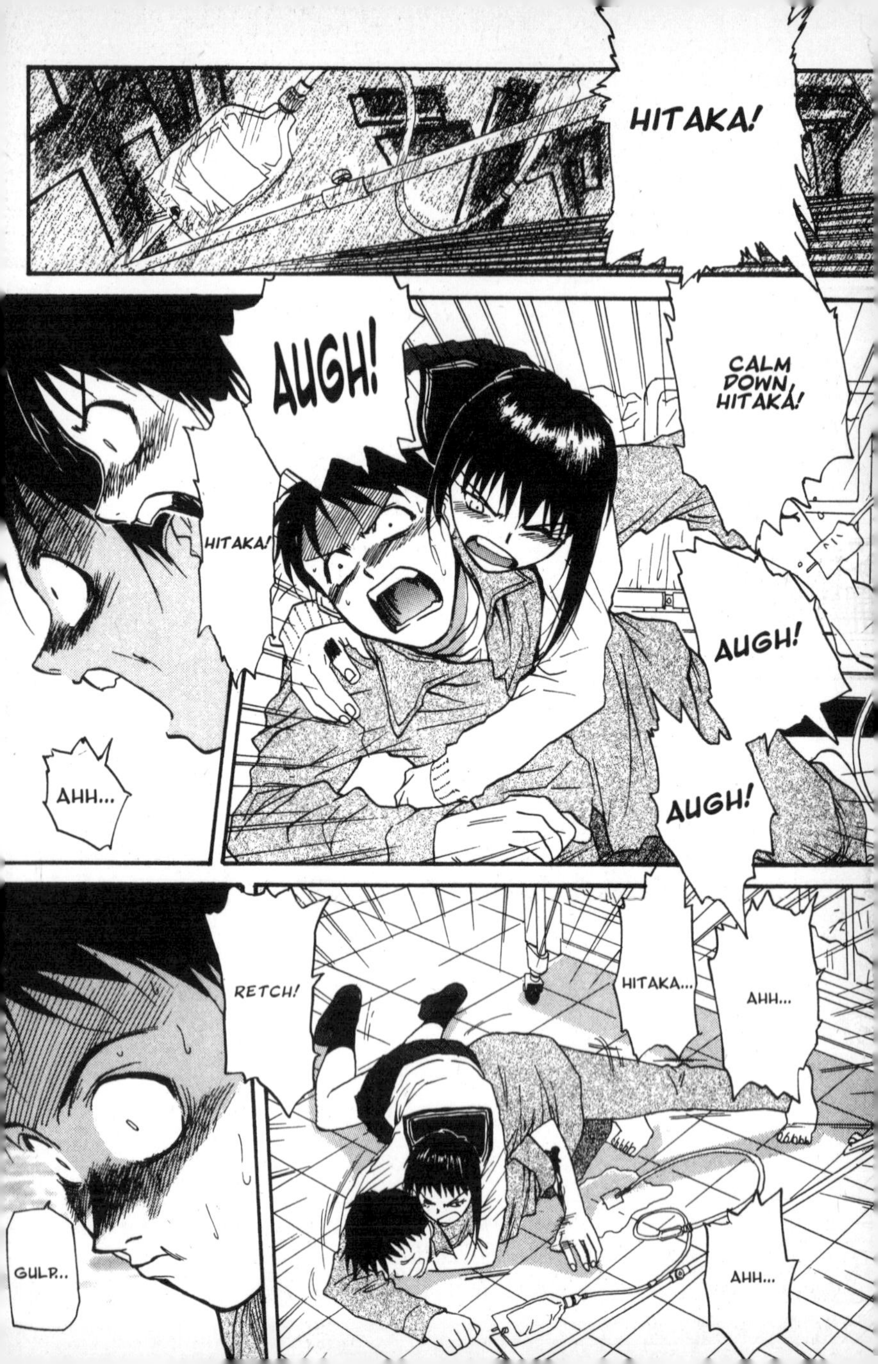
HITAKA!
CALM DOWN, HITAKA!
AUGH!
HITAKA!
AUGH!
AUGH!
AHH...
AHH...
HITAKA...
RETCH!
AHH...
GULP...

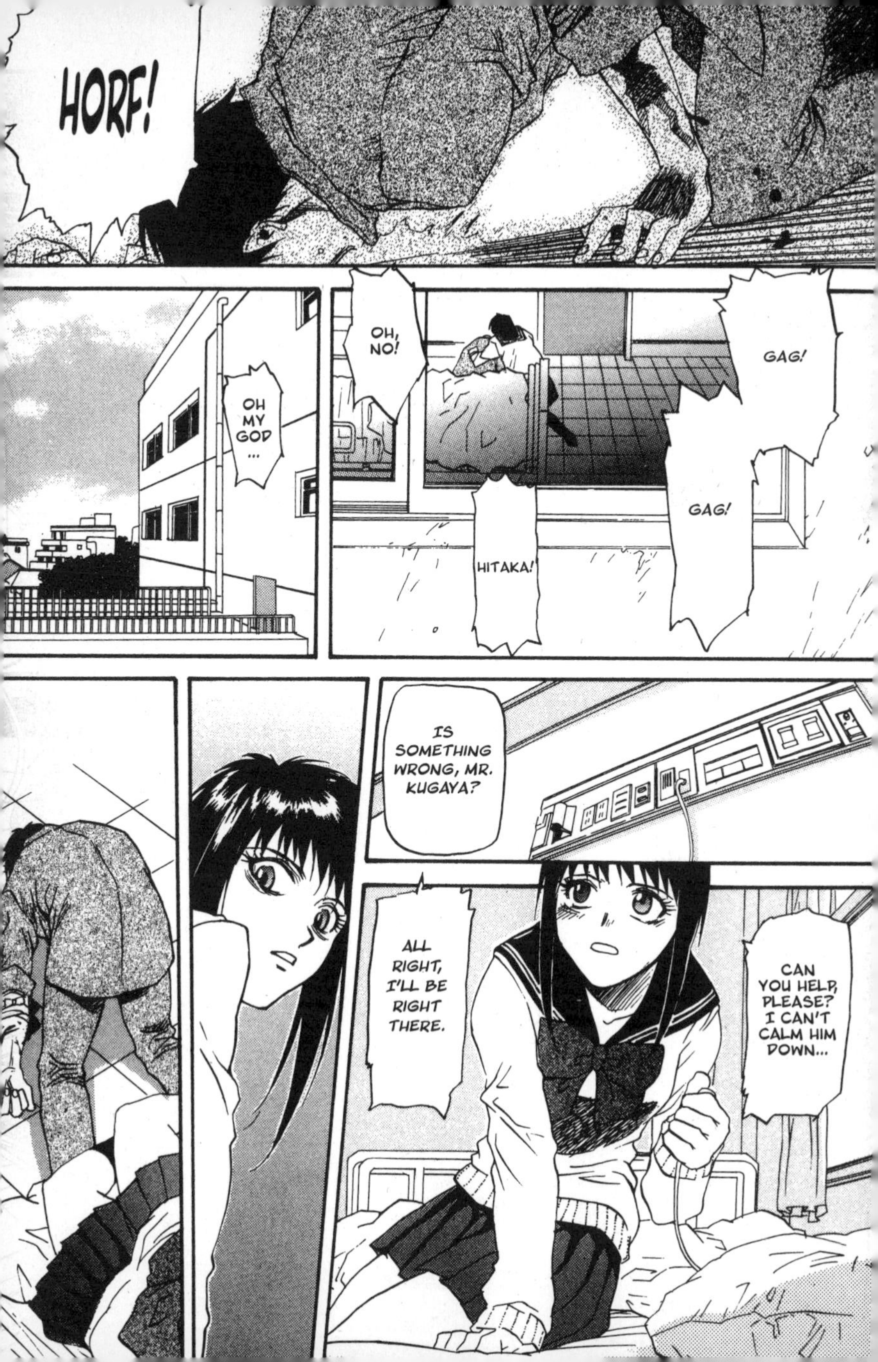
HORF!
GAG!
OH, NO!
GAG!
HITAKA!
OH MY GOD ...
IS SOMETHING WRONG, MR. KUGAYA?
CAN YOU HELP, PLEASE? I CAN'T CALM HIM DOWN...
ALL RIGHT, I'LL BE RIGHT THERE.

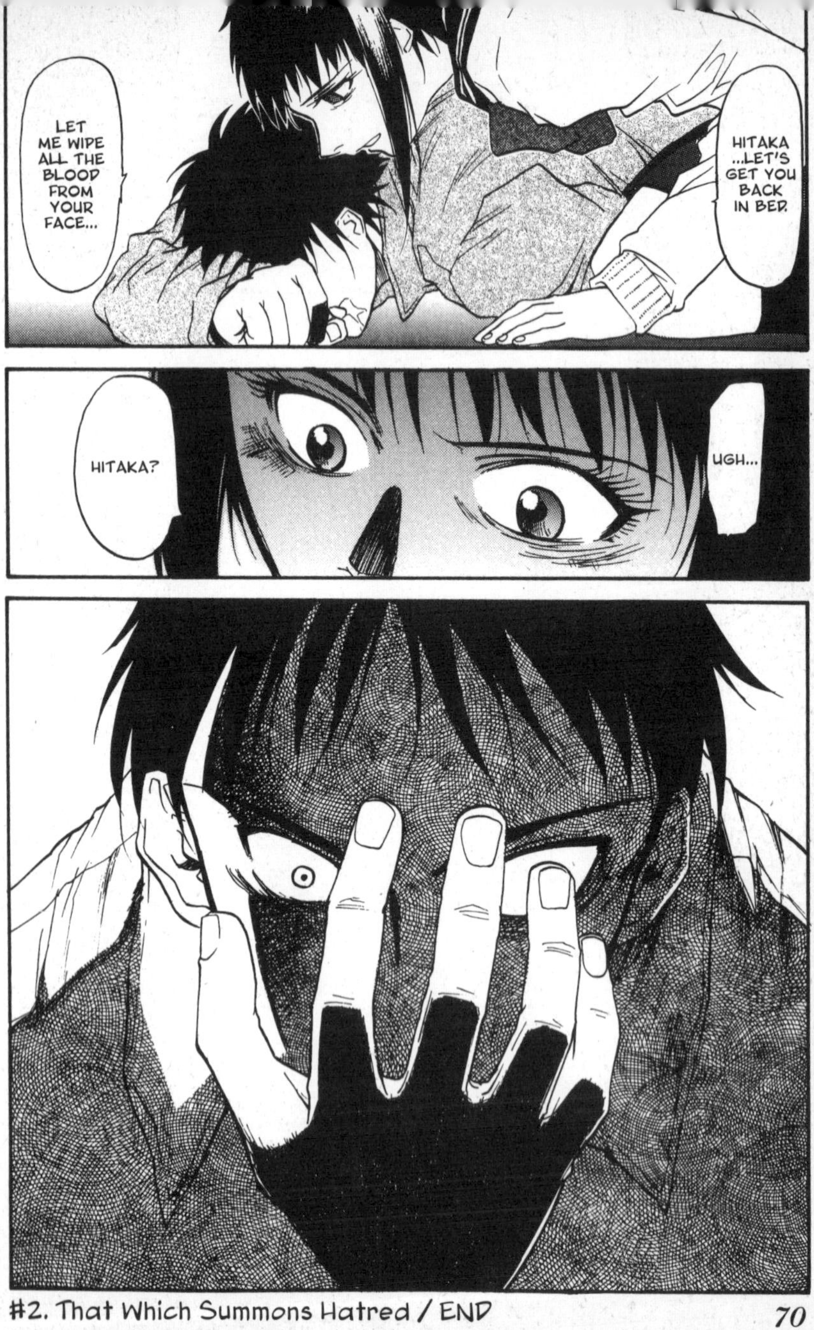
HITAKA ...LET'S GET YOU BACK IN BED.
LET ME WIPE ALL THE BLOOD FROM YOUR FACE...
UGH...
HITAKA?

#2. That Which Summons Hatred / END

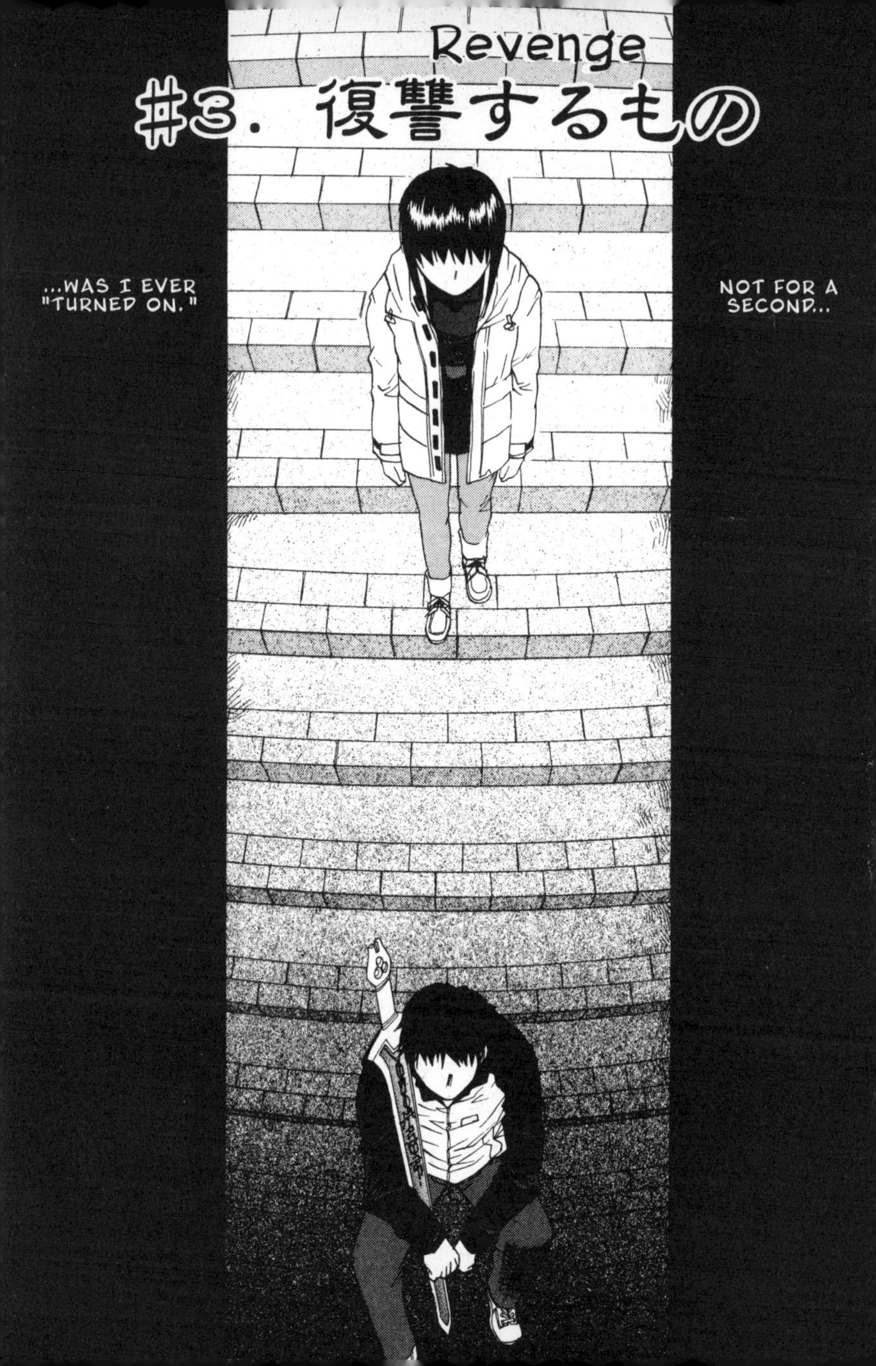
Revenge
#3. 復讐するもの
NOT FOR A SECOND...
...WAS I EVER "TURNED ON."

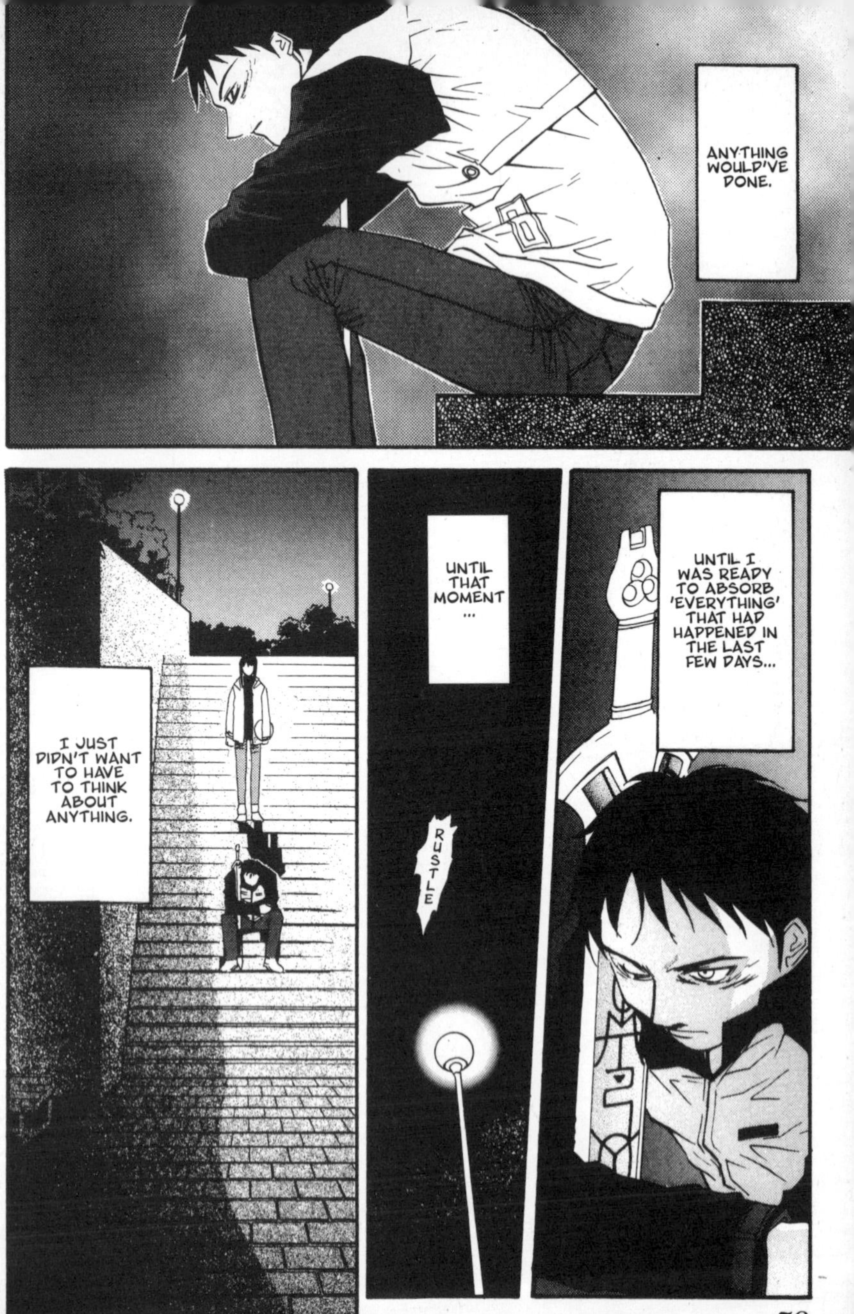
ANYTHING WOULD'VE DONE.
UNTIL I WAS READY TO ABSORB 'EVERYTHING' THAT HAD HAPPENED IN THE LAST FEW DAYS...
UNTIL THAT MOMENT ...
RUSTLE
I JUST DIDN'T WANT TO HAVE TO THINK ABOUT ANYTHING.

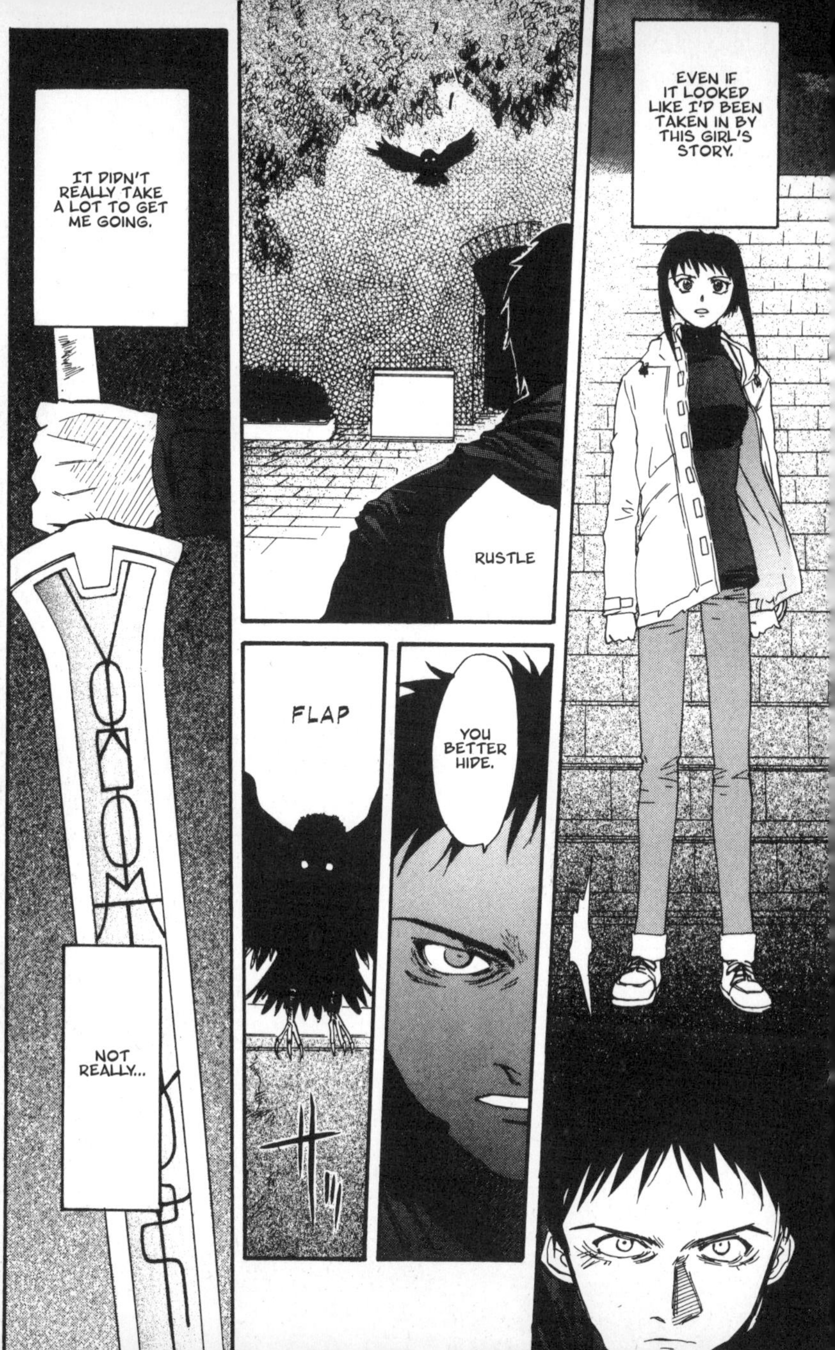
EVEN IF IT LOOKED LIKE I'D BEEN TAKEN IN BY THIS GIRL'S STORY.
RUSTLE
YOU BETTER HIDE.
FLAP
IT DIDN'T REALLY TAKE A LOT TO GET ME GOING.
NOT REALLY...

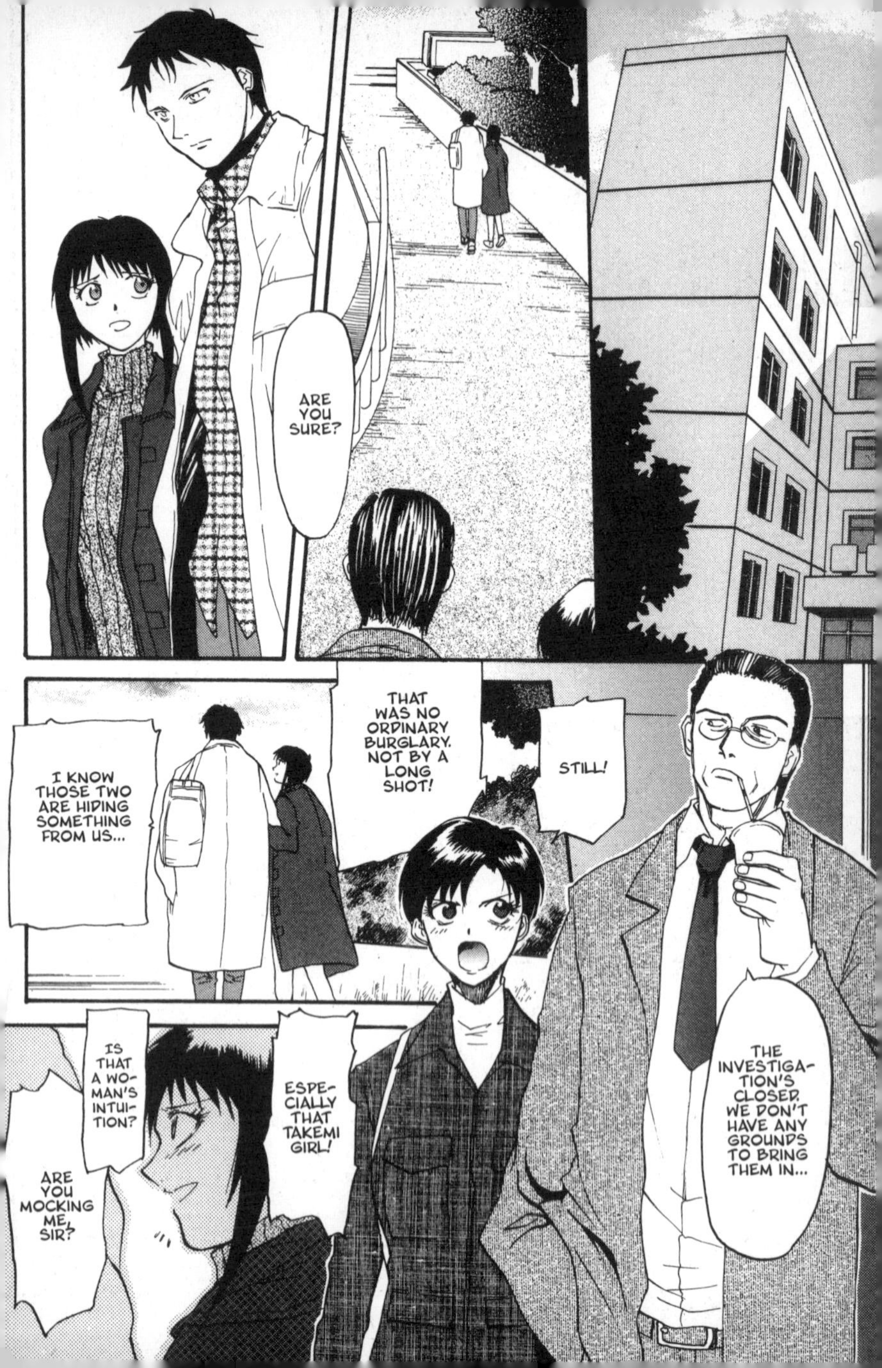
ARE YOU SURE?
THE INVESTIGATION'S CLOSED. WE DON'T HAVE ANY GROUNDS TO BRING THEM IN...
STILL!
THAT WAS NO ORDINARY BURGLARY. NOT BY A LONG SHOT!
I KNOW THOSE TWO ARE HIDING SOMETHING FROM US...
ESPECIALLY THAT TAKEMI GIRL!
IS THAT A WOMAN'S INTUITION?
ARE YOU MOCKING ME, SIR?

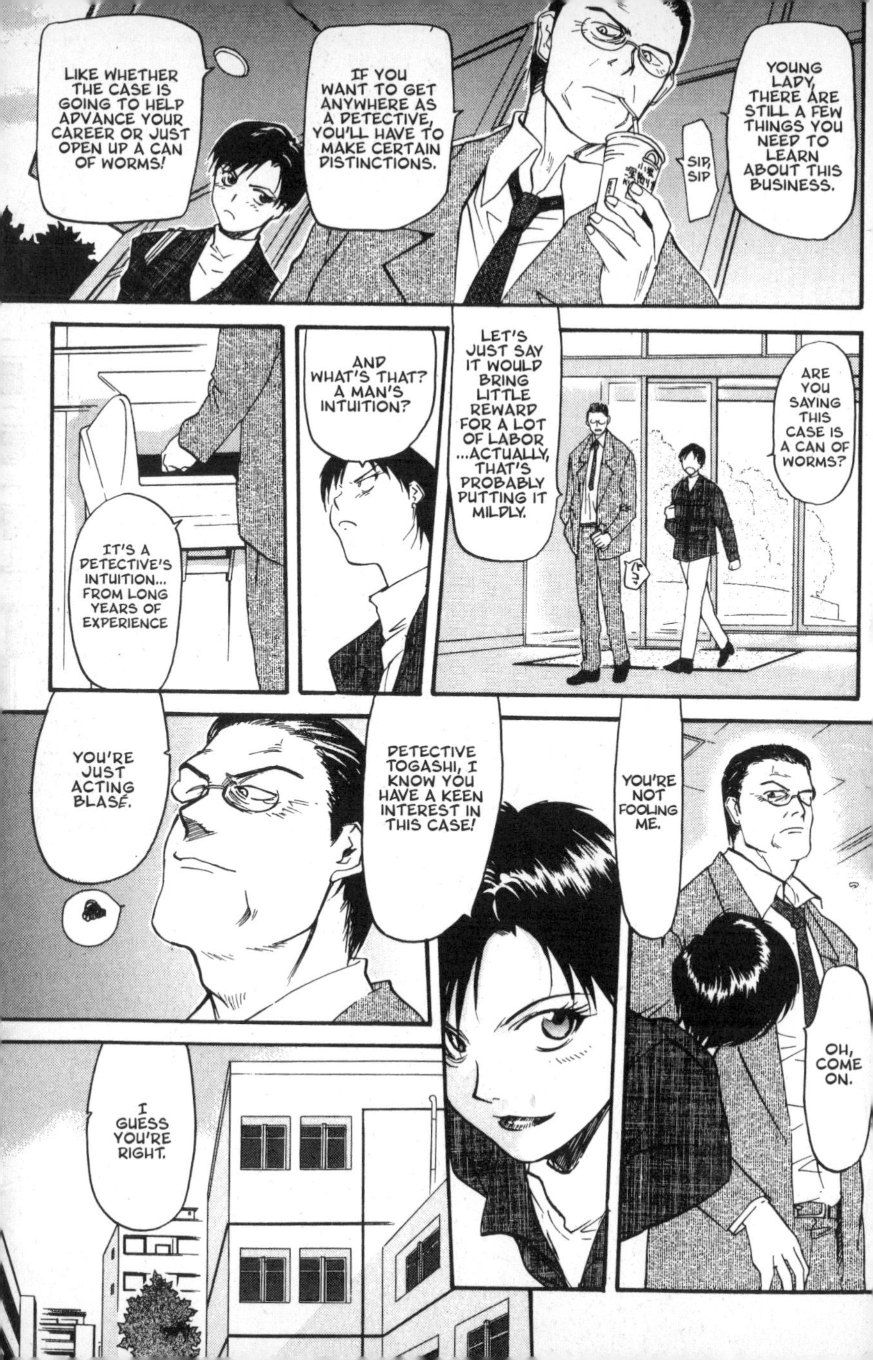
YOUNG LADY, THERE ARE STILL A FEW THINGS YOU NEED TO LEARN ABOUT THIS BUSINESS.
SIP, SIP
IF YOU WANT TO GET ANYWHERE AS A DETECTIVE, YOU'LL HAVE TO MAKE CERTAIN DISTINCTIONS.
LIKE WHETHER THE CASE IS GOING TO HELP ADVANCE YOUR CAREER OR JUST OPEN UP A CAN OF WORMS!
ARE YOU SAYING THIS CASE IS A CAN OF WORMS?
LET'S JUST SAY IT WOULD BRING LITTLE REWARD FOR A LOT OF LABOR ...ACTUALLY, THAT'S PROBABLY PUTTING IT MILDLY.
AND WHAT'S THAT? A MAN'S INTUITION?
IT'S A DETECTIVE'S INTUITION... FROM LONG YEARS OF EXPERIENCE
DETECTIVE TOGASHI, I KNOW YOU HAVE A KEEN INTEREST IN THIS CASE!
YOU'RE NOT FOOLING ME.
OH, COME ON.
YOU'RE JUST ACTING BLASÉ.
I GUESS YOU'RE RIGHT.

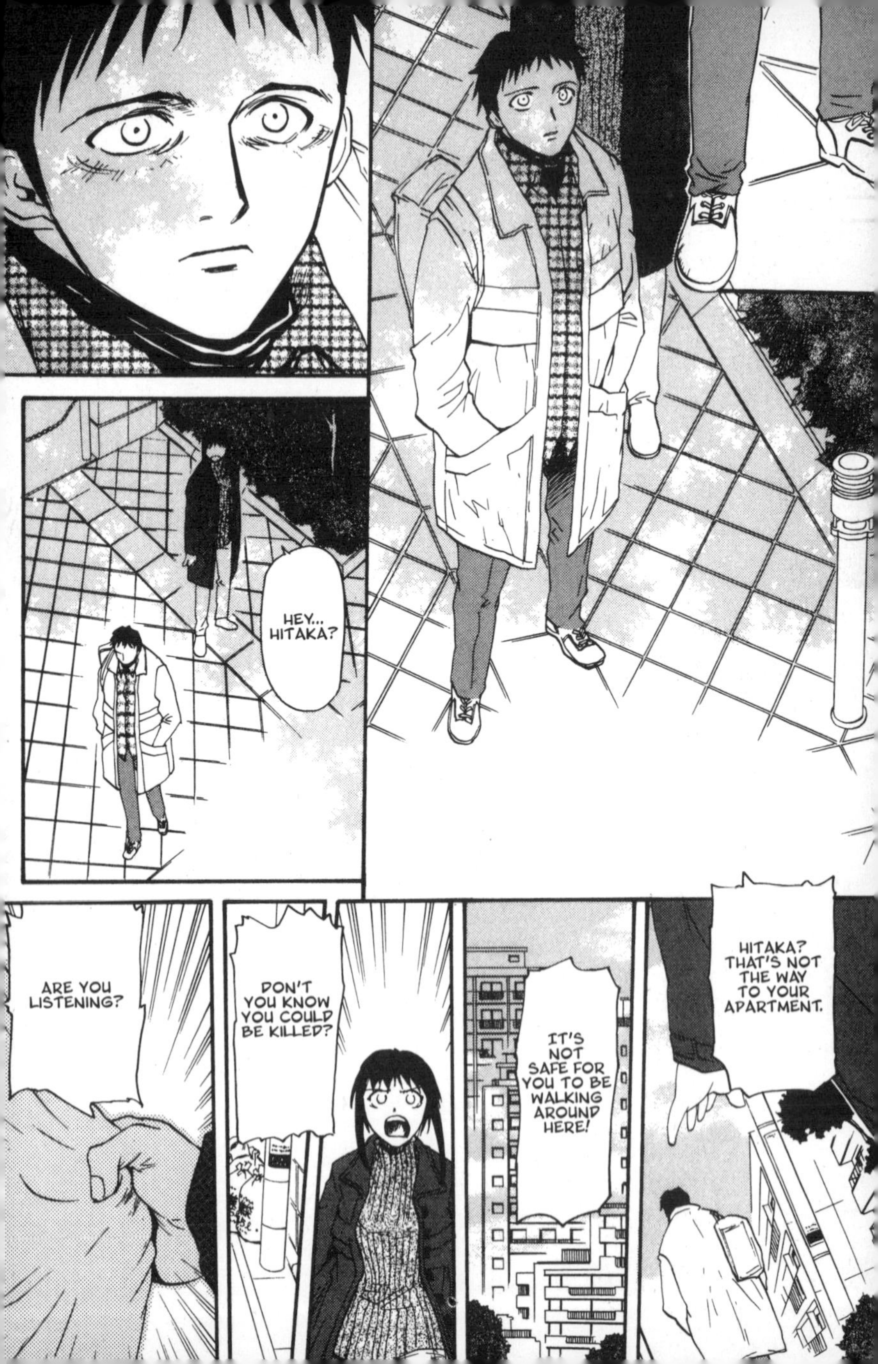
HEY... HITAKA?
HITAKA? THAT'S NOT THE WAY TO YOUR APARTMENT.
IT'S NOT SAFE FOR YOU TO BE WALKING AROUND HERE!
DON'T YOU KNOW YOU COULD BE KILLED?
ARE YOU LISTENING?

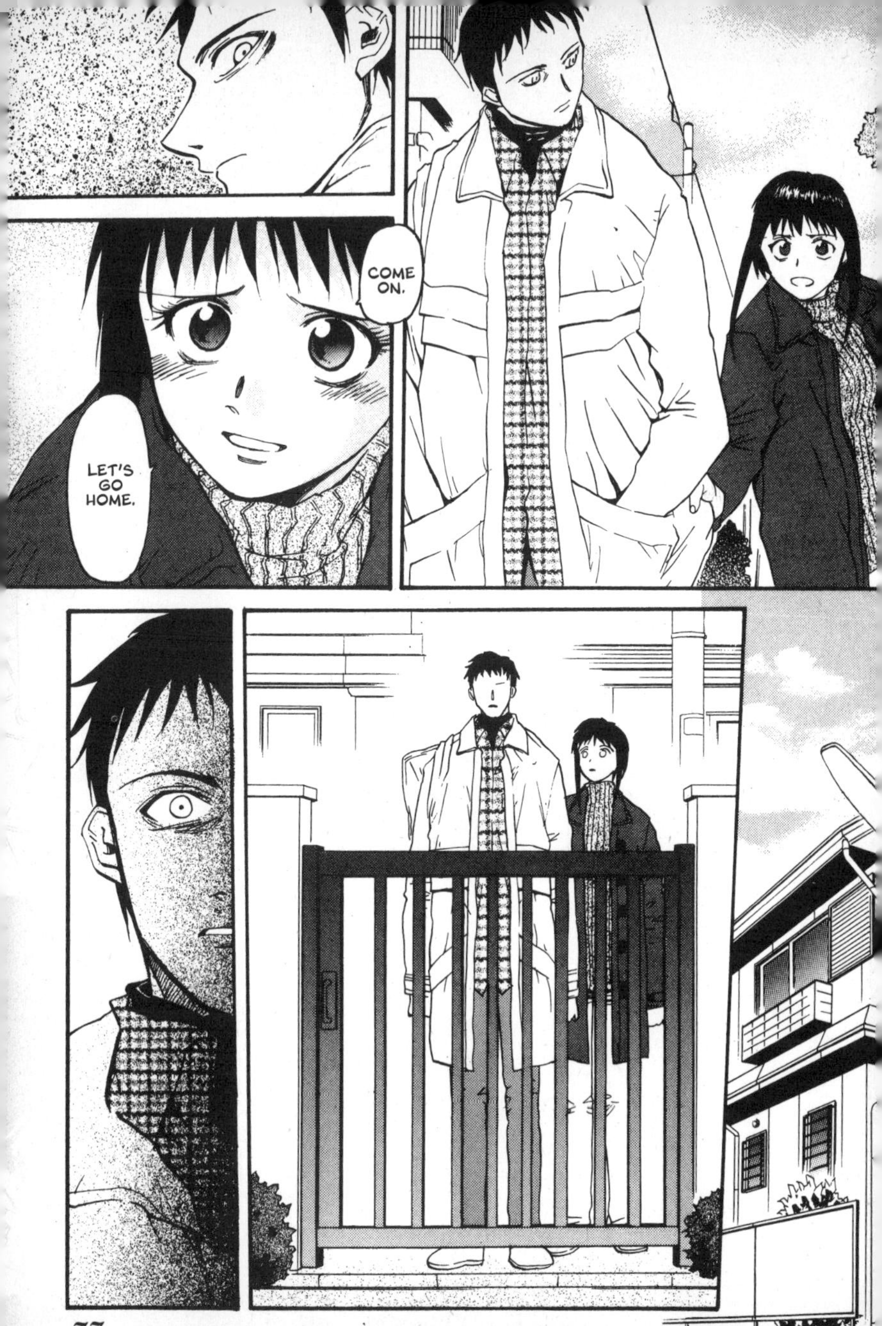
COME ON.
LET'S GO HOME.

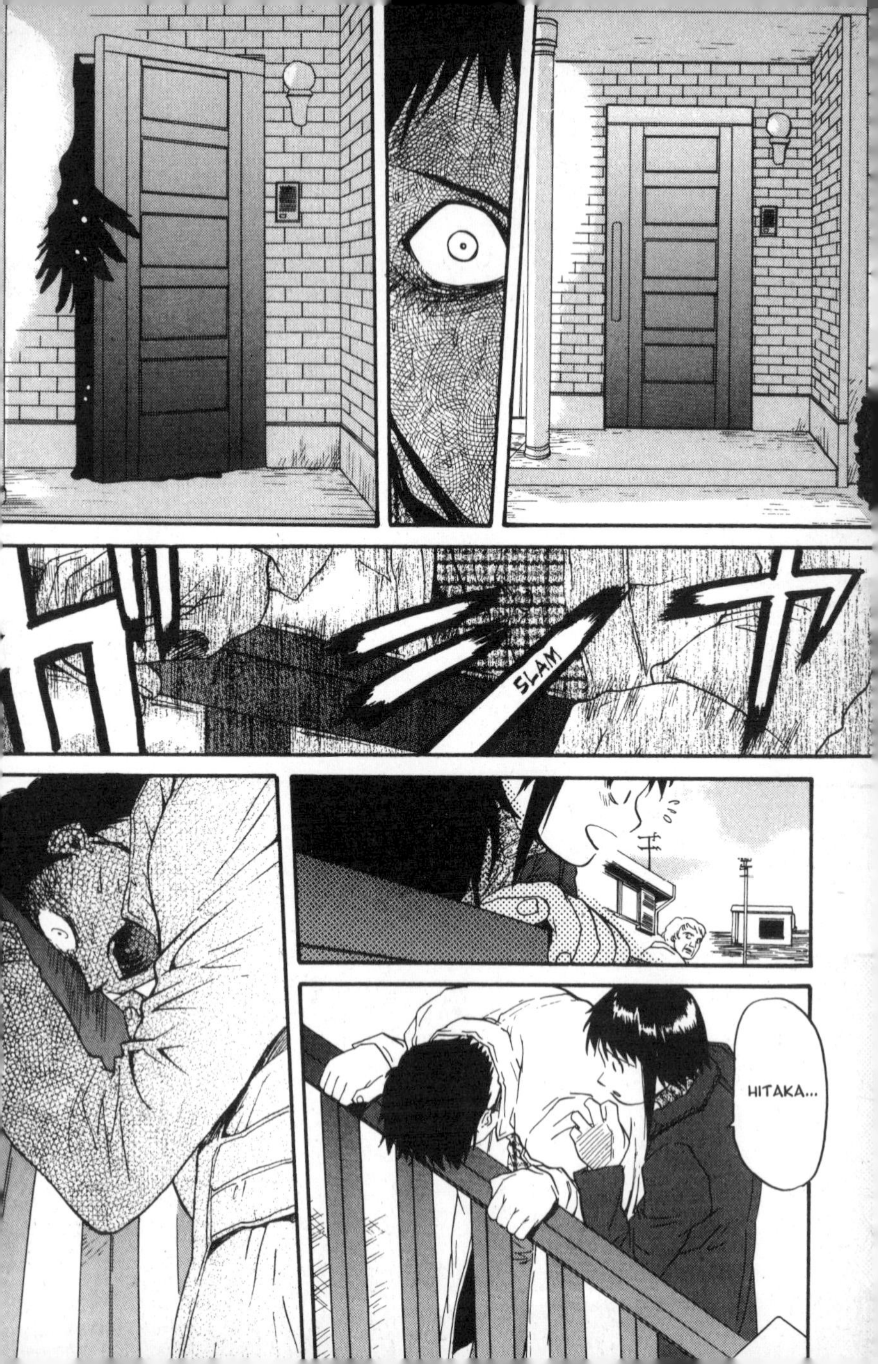
SLAM
HITAKA...

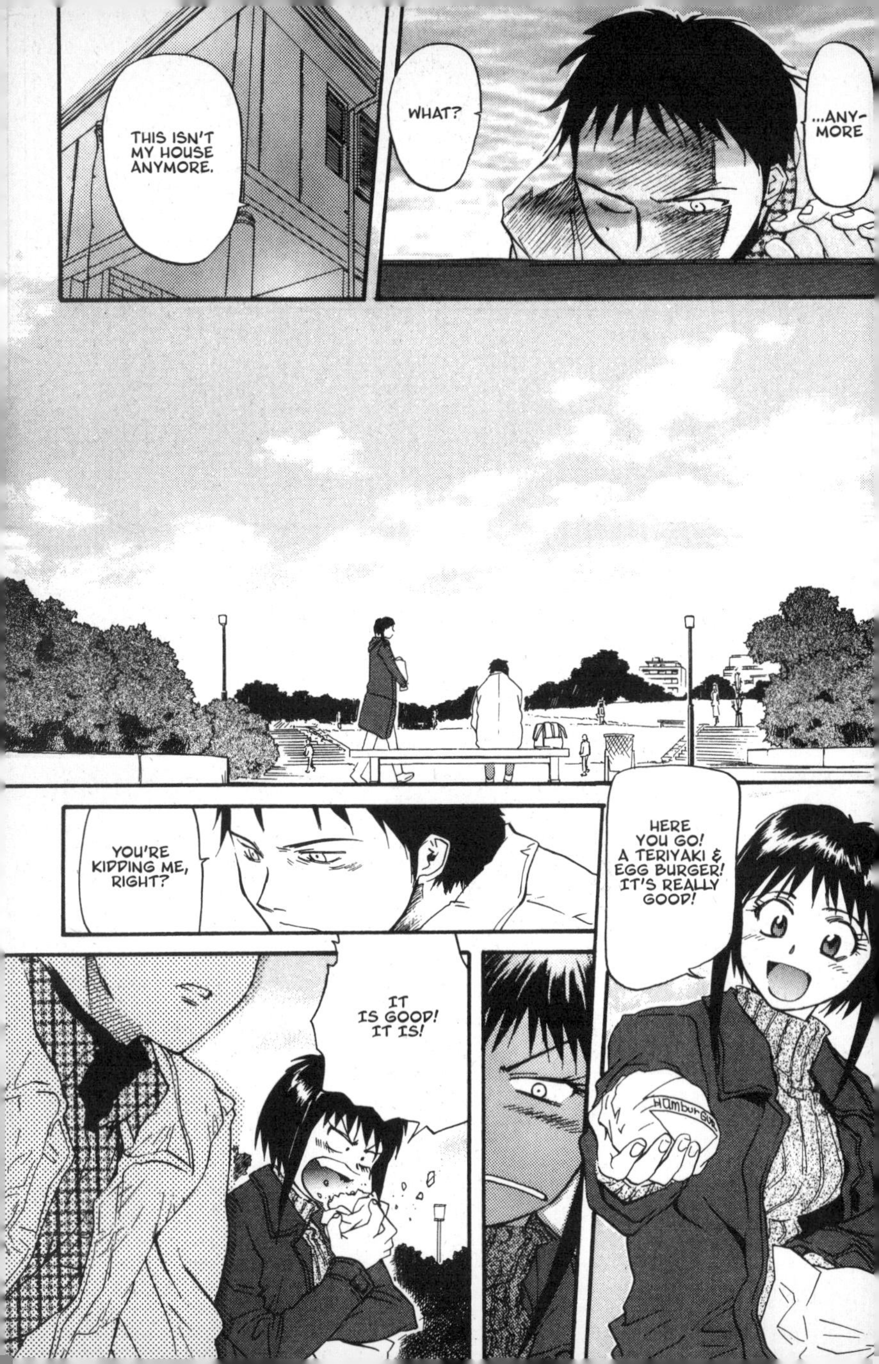

...ANY-
MORE
WHAT?
THIS ISN'T MY HOUSE ANYMORE.
HERE YOU GO! A TERIYAKI & EGG BURGER! IT'S REALLY GOOD!
YOU'RE KIDDING ME, RIGHT?
HAMBURGER
IT IS GOOD! IT IS!

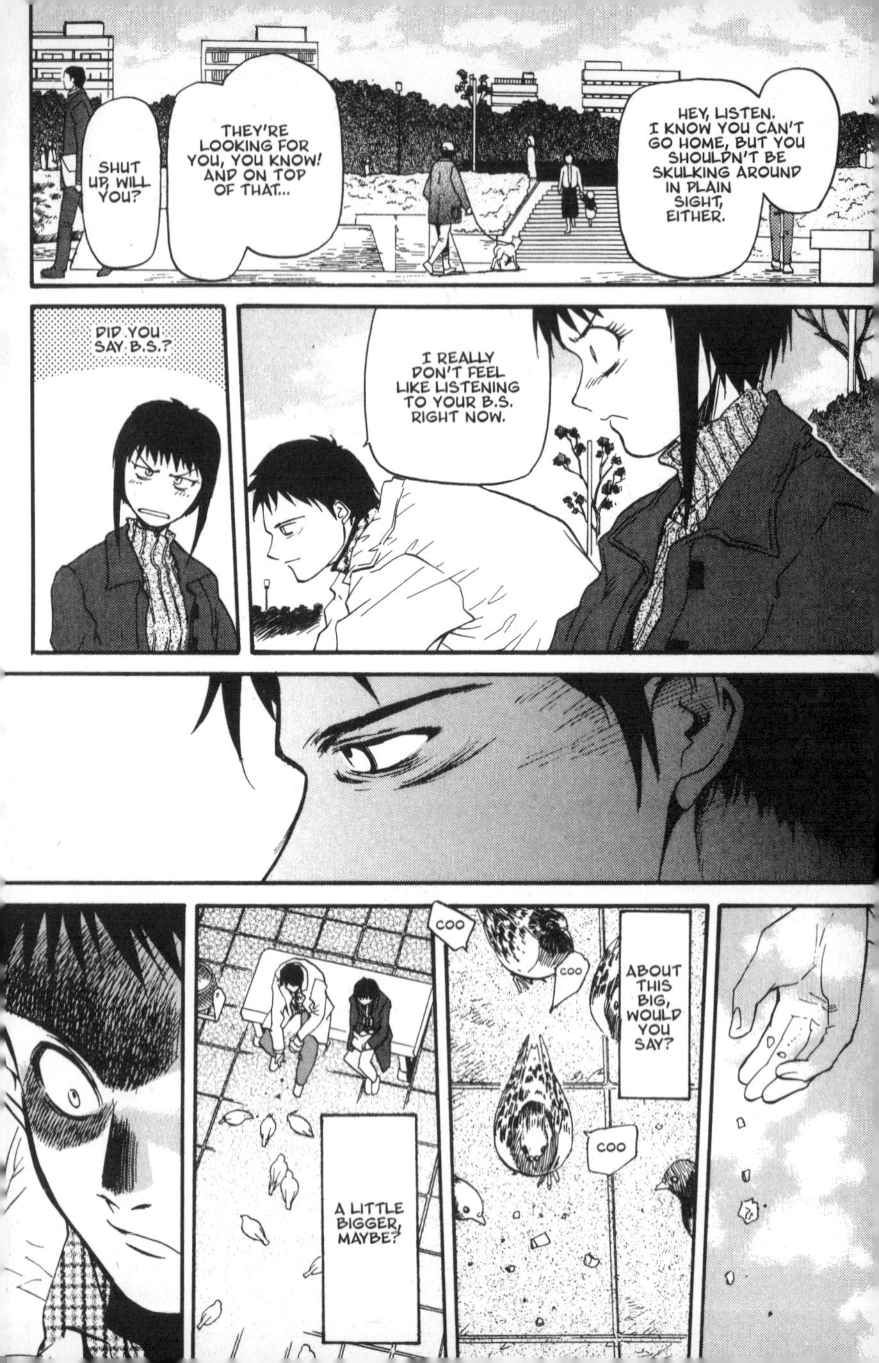
HEY, LISTEN. I KNOW YOU CAN'T GO HOME, BUT YOU SHOULDN'T BE SKULKING AROUND IN PLAIN SIGHT, EITHER.
THEY'RE LOOKING FOR YOU, YOU KNOW! AND ON TOP OF THAT...
SHUT UP, WILL YOU?
I REALLY DON'T FEEL LIKE LISTENING TO YOUR B.S. RIGHT NOW.
DID YOU SAY B.S.?
COO
COO
ABOUT THIS BIG, WOULD YOU SAY?
COO
A LITTLE BIGGER, MAYBE?

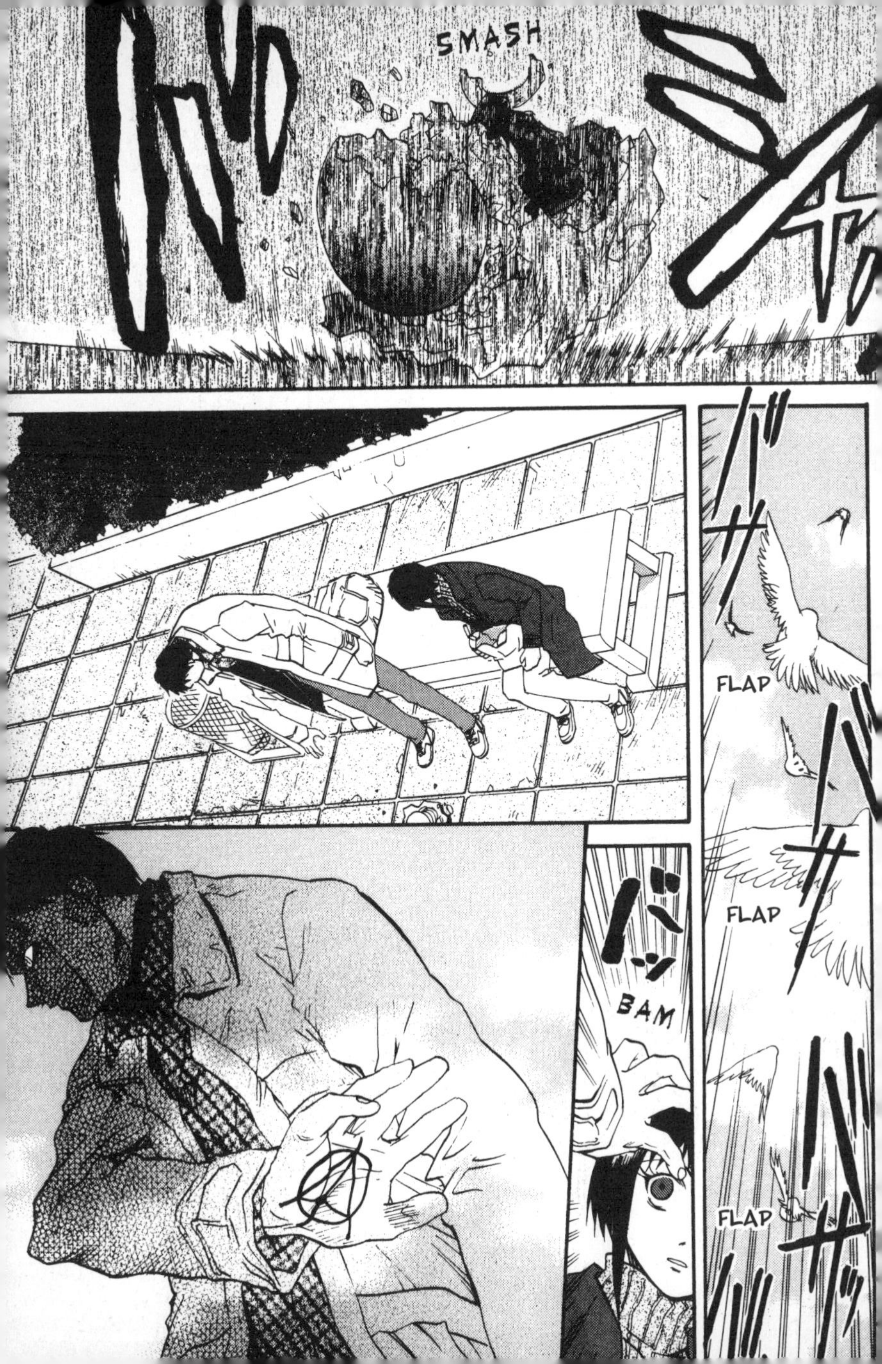
SMASH
FLAP
FLAP
FLAP
BAM

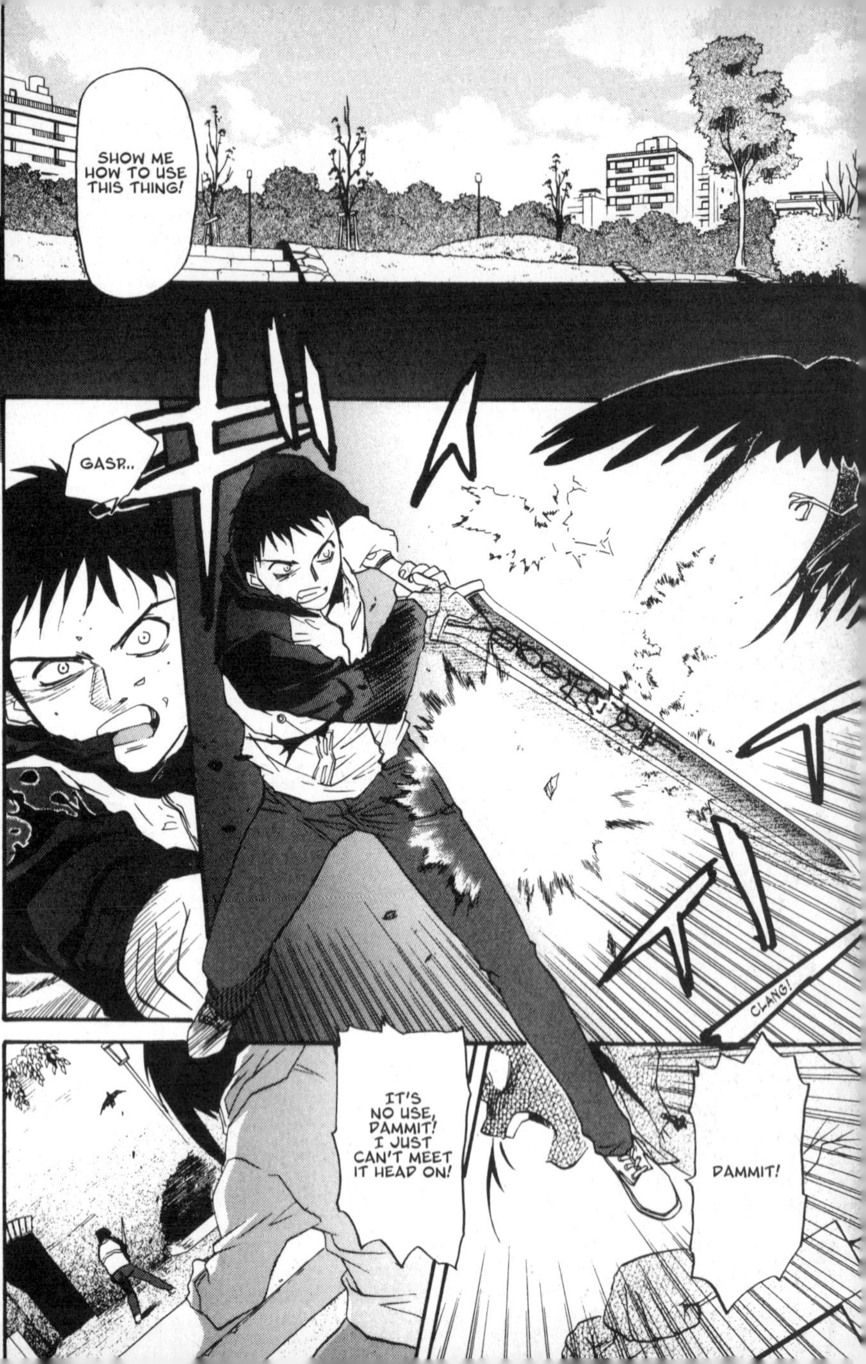
SHOW ME HOW TO USE THIS THING!
GASP...
CLANG!
DAMMIT!
IT'S NO USE, DAMMIT! I JUST CAN'T MEET IT HEAD ON!

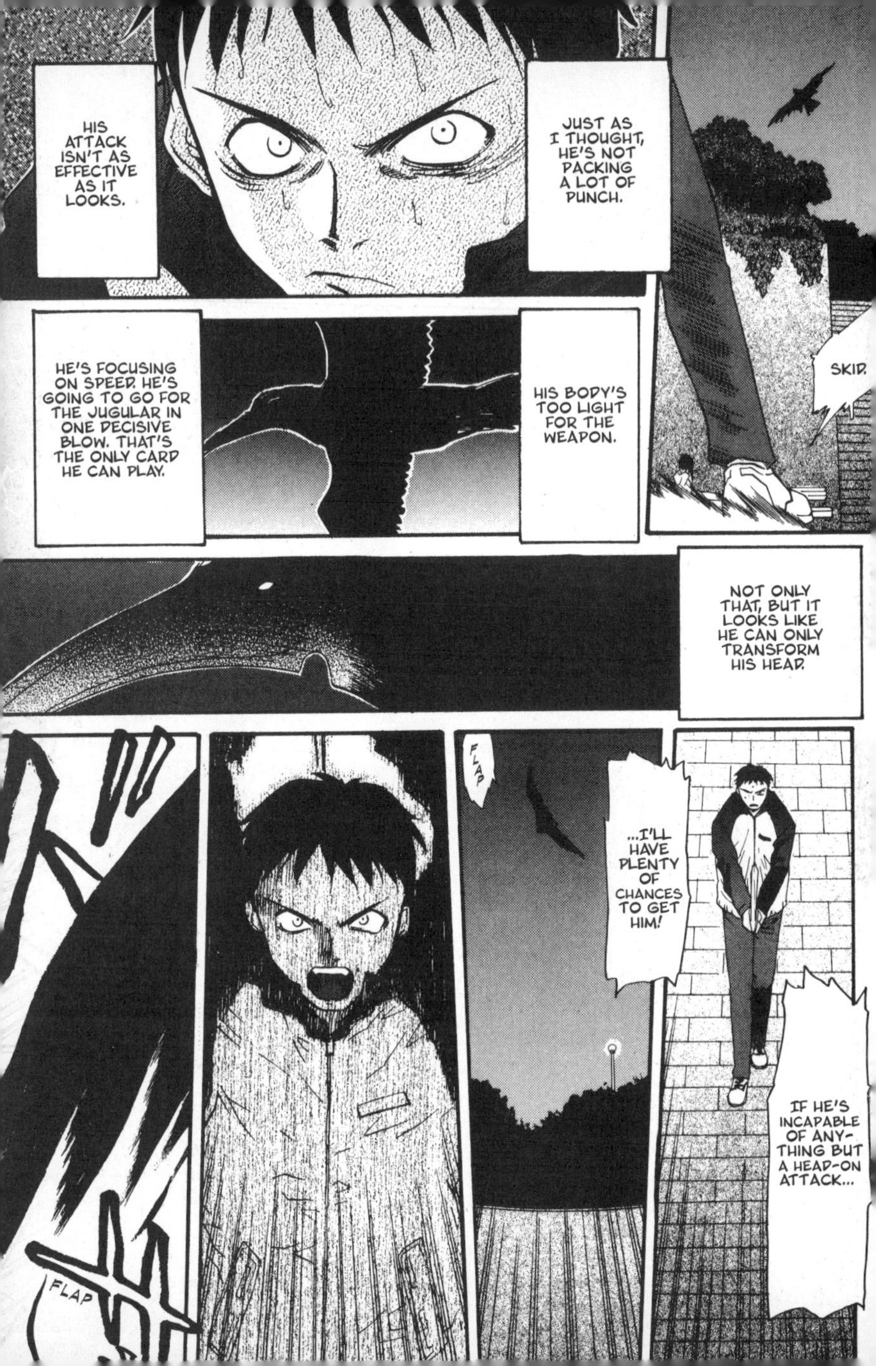
SKID.
JUST AS I THOUGHT, HE'S NOT PACKING A LOT OF PUNCH.
HIS ATTACK ISN'T AS EFFECTIVE AS IT LOOKS.
HIS BODY'S TOO LIGHT FOR THE WEAPON.
HE'S FOCUSING ON SPEED. HE'S GOING TO GO FOR THE JUGULAR IN ONE DECISIVE BLOW. THAT'S THE ONLY CARD HE CAN PLAY.
NOT ONLY THAT, BUT IT LOOKS LIKE HE CAN ONLY TRANSFORM HIS HEAD.
IF HE'S INCAPABLE OF ANYTHING BUT A HEAD-ON ATTACK...
...I'LL HAVE PLENTY OF CHANCES TO GET HIM!
FLAP
FLAP

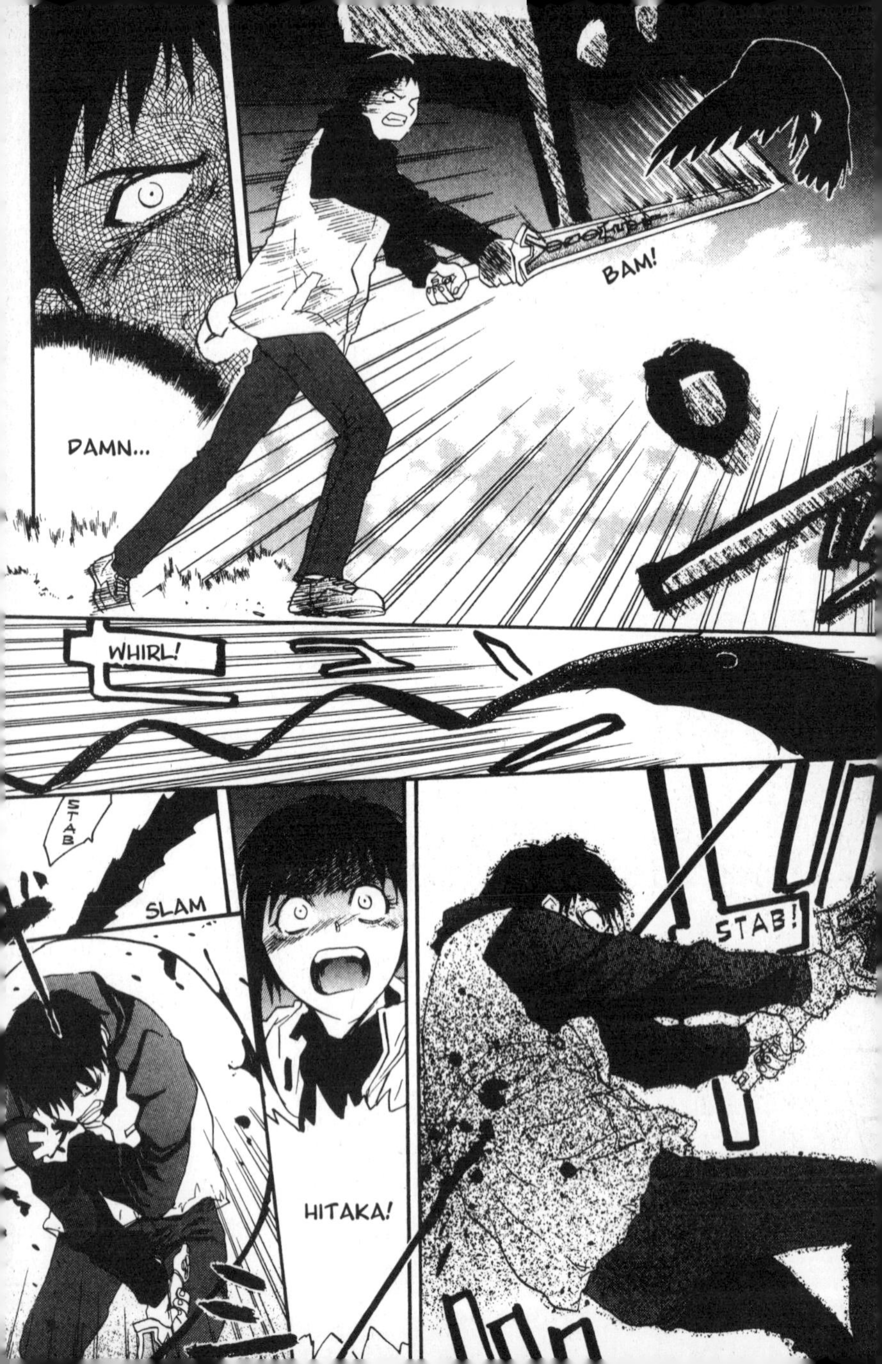
BAM!
DAMN...
WHIRL!
STAB!
HITAKA!
STAB
SLAM

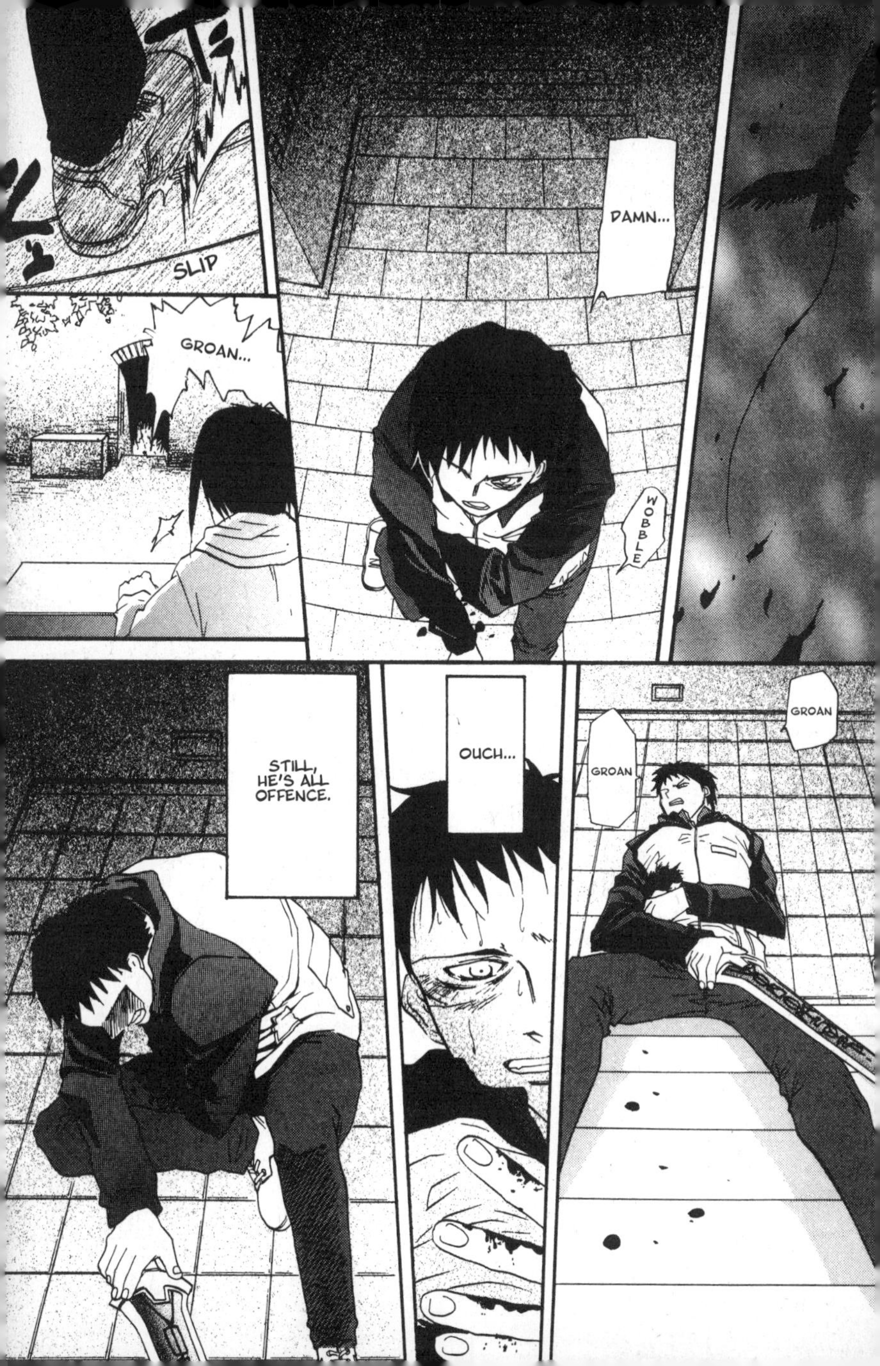

DAMN...
WOBBLE
SLIP
GROAN...
GROAN
GROAN
OUCH...
STILL, HE'S ALL OFFENCE.

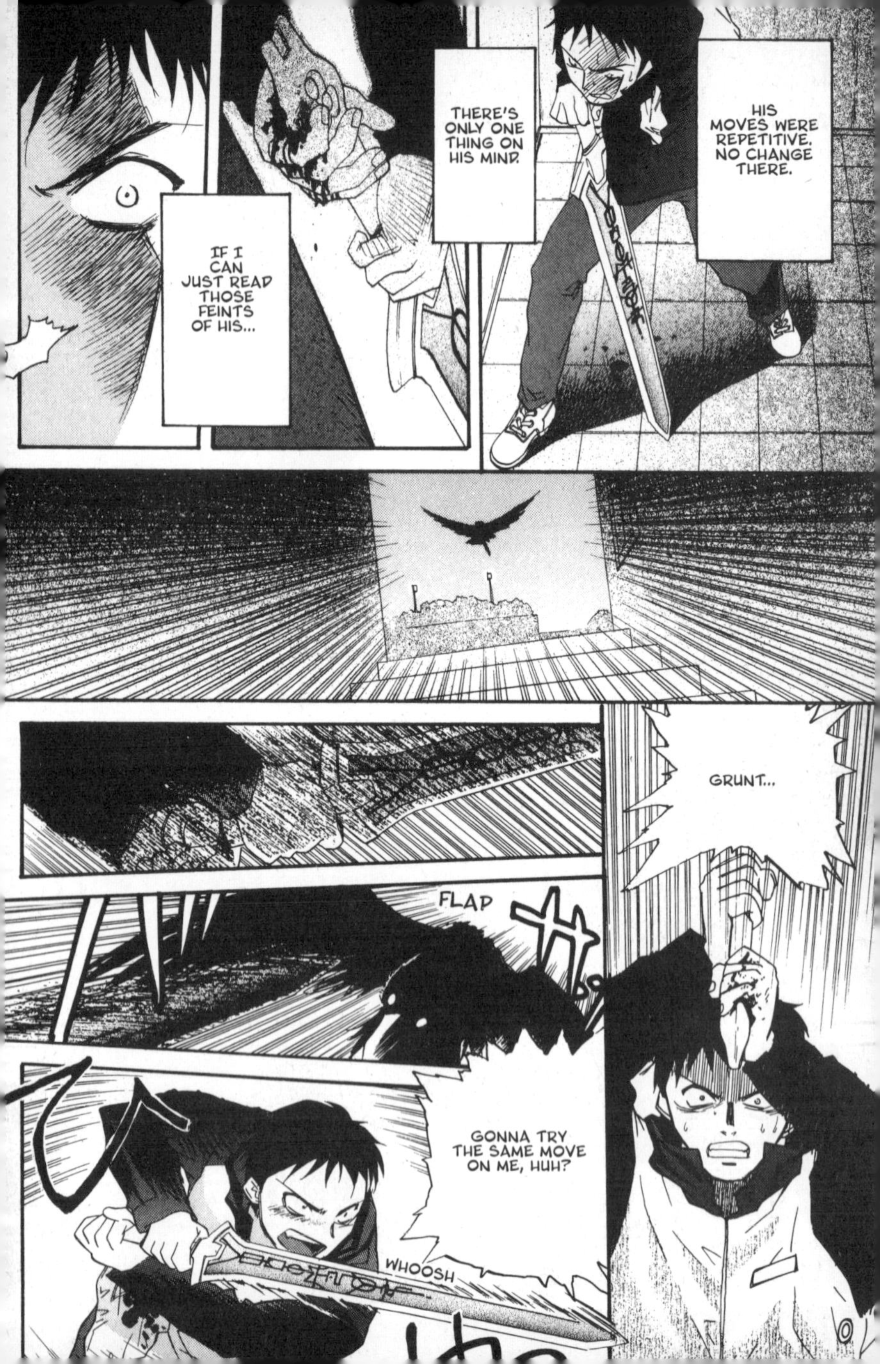
HIS MOVES WERE REPETITIVE. NO CHANGE THERE.
THERE'S ONLY ONE THING ON HIS MIND.
IF I CAN JUST READ THOSE FEINTS OF HIS...
GRUNT...
FLAP
GONNA TRY THE SAME MOVE ON ME, HUH?
WHOOSH

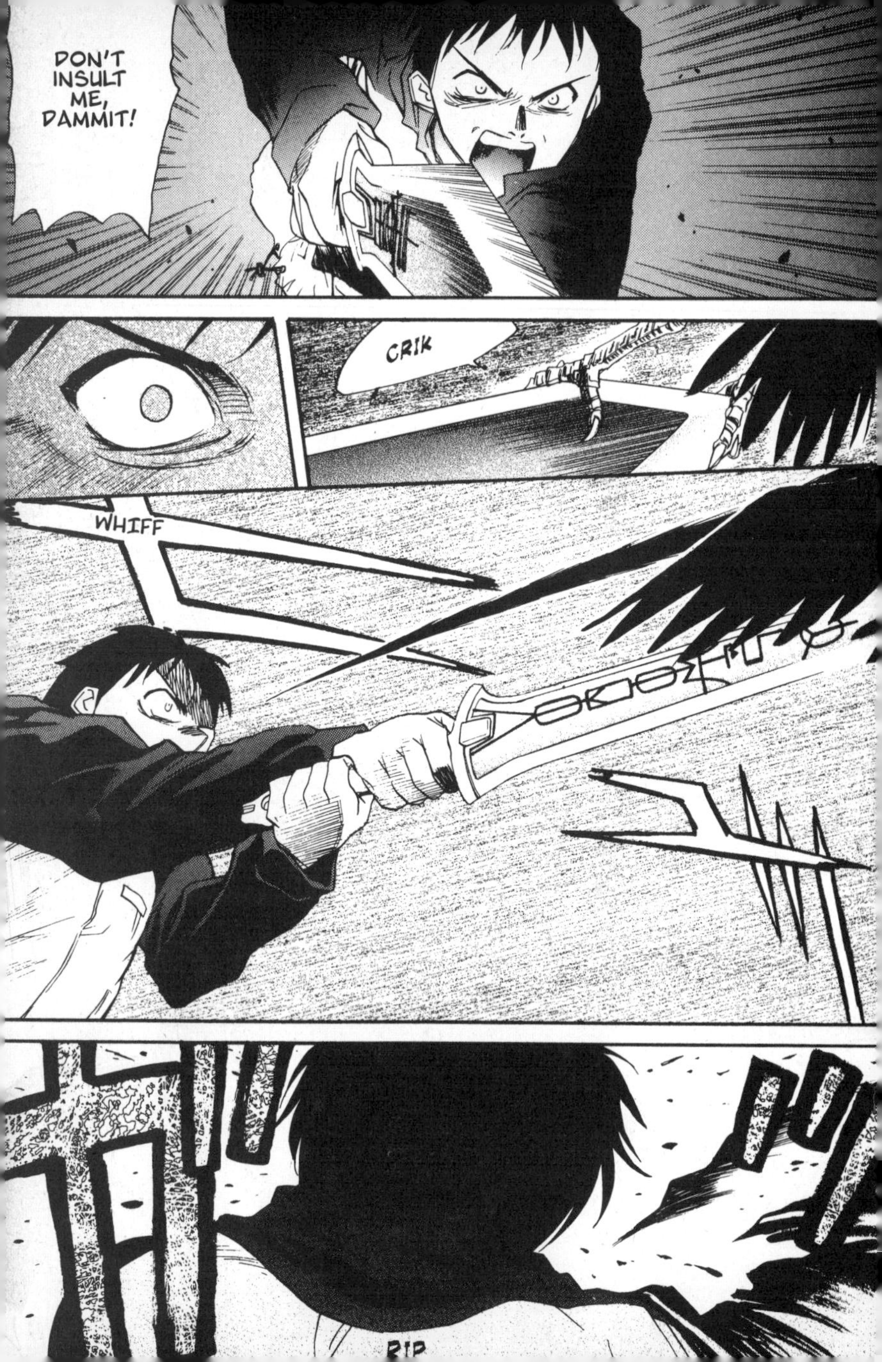
DON'T INSULT ME, DAMMIT!
CRIK
WHIFF
RIP

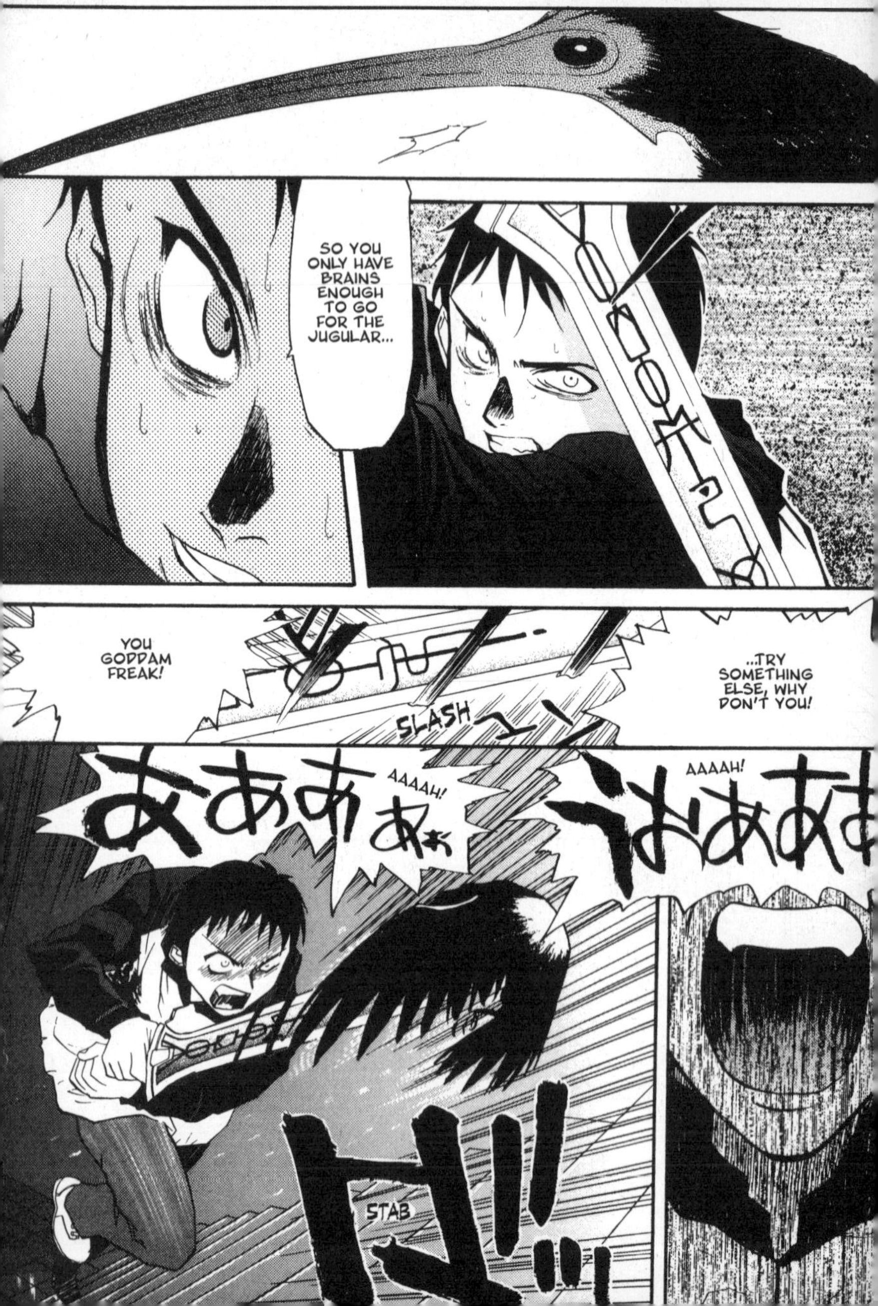
SO YOU ONLY HAVE BRAINS ENOUGH TO GO FOR THE JUGULAR...
...TRY SOMETHING ELSE, WHY DON'T YOU!
SLASH
YOU GODDAM FREAK!
AAAAH!
AAAAH!
STAB

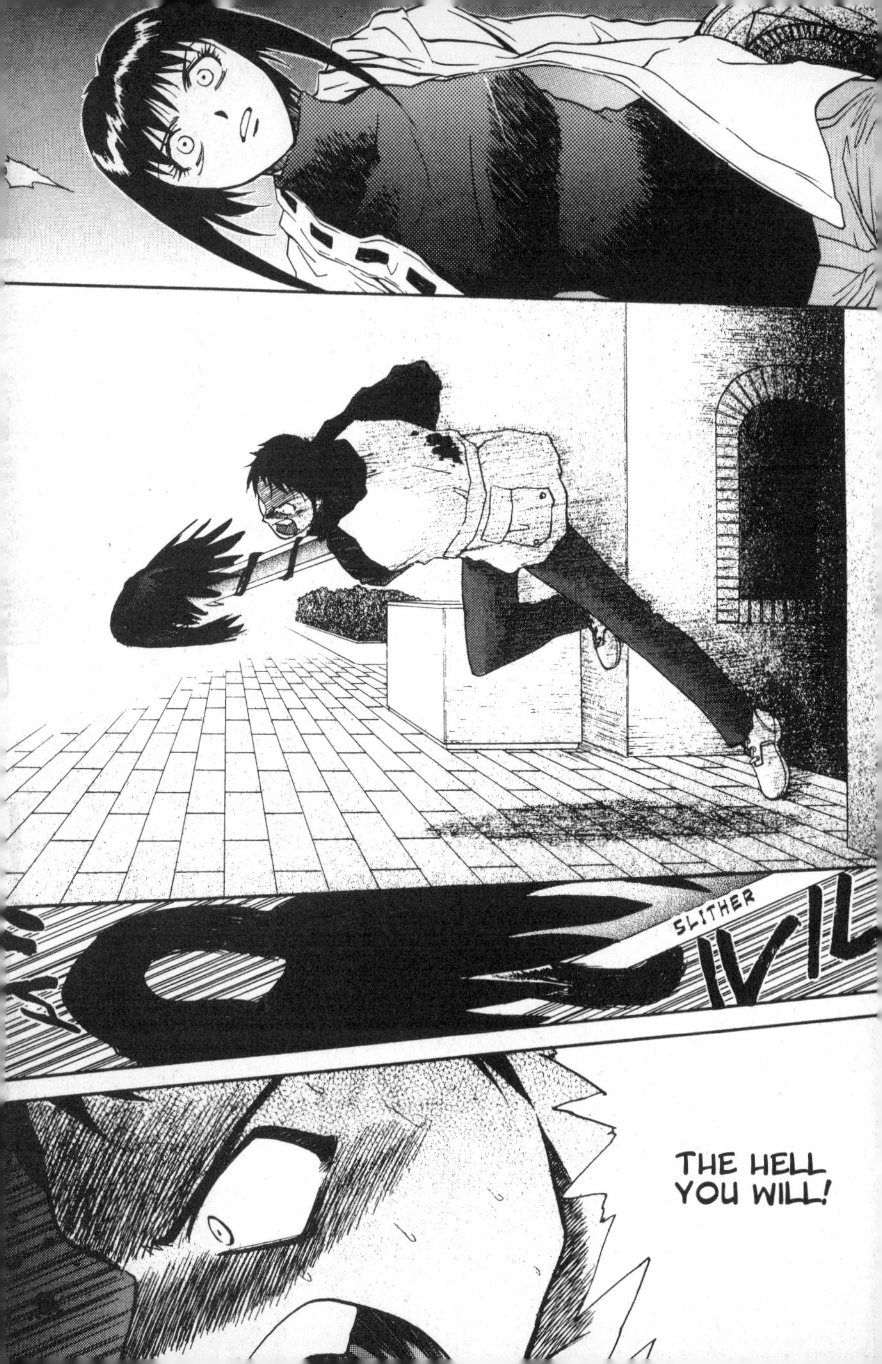
SLITHER
THE HELL YOU WILL!

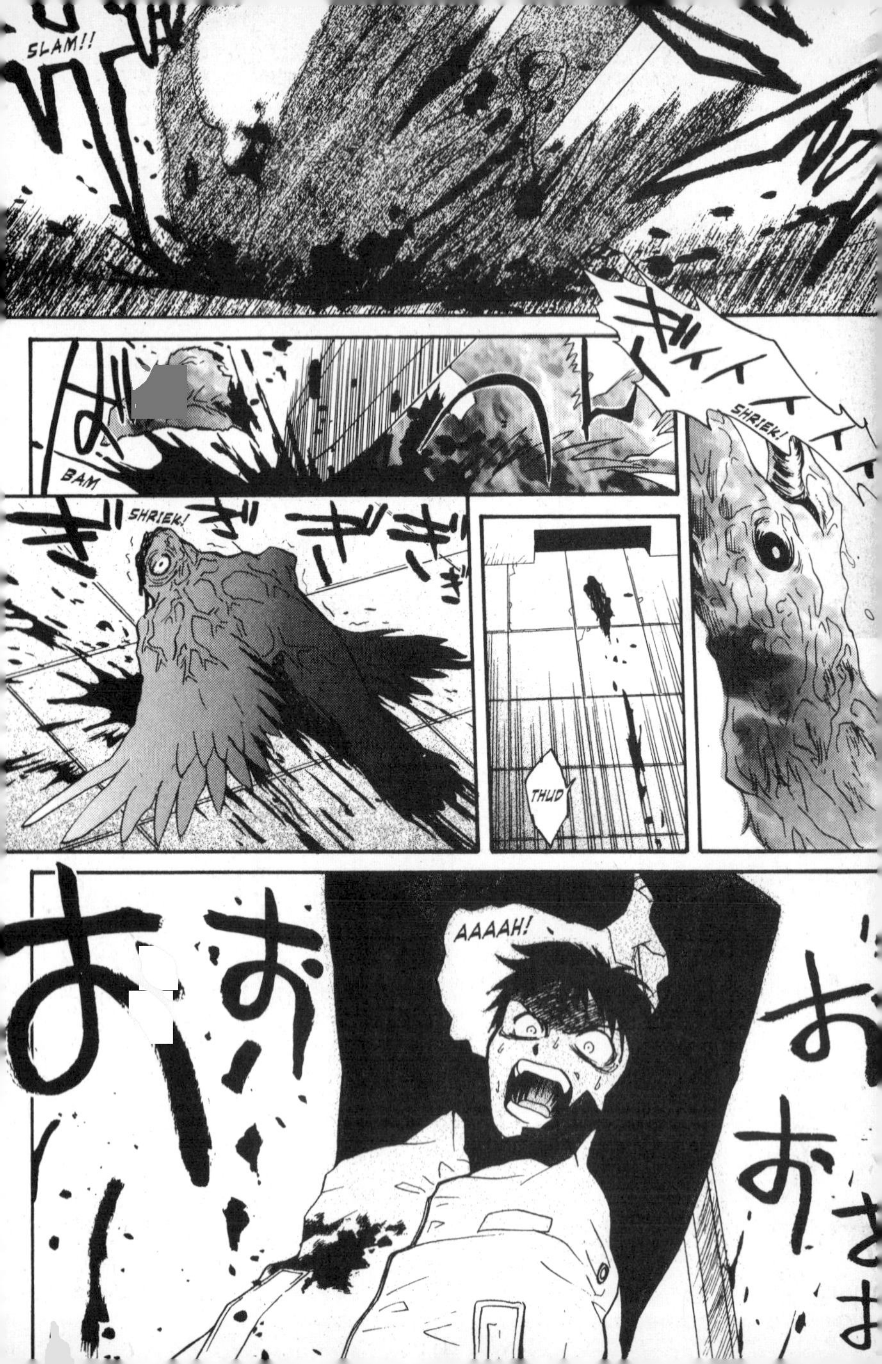
SLAM!!
SHRIEK!
BAM
THUD
SHRIEK!
AAAAH!

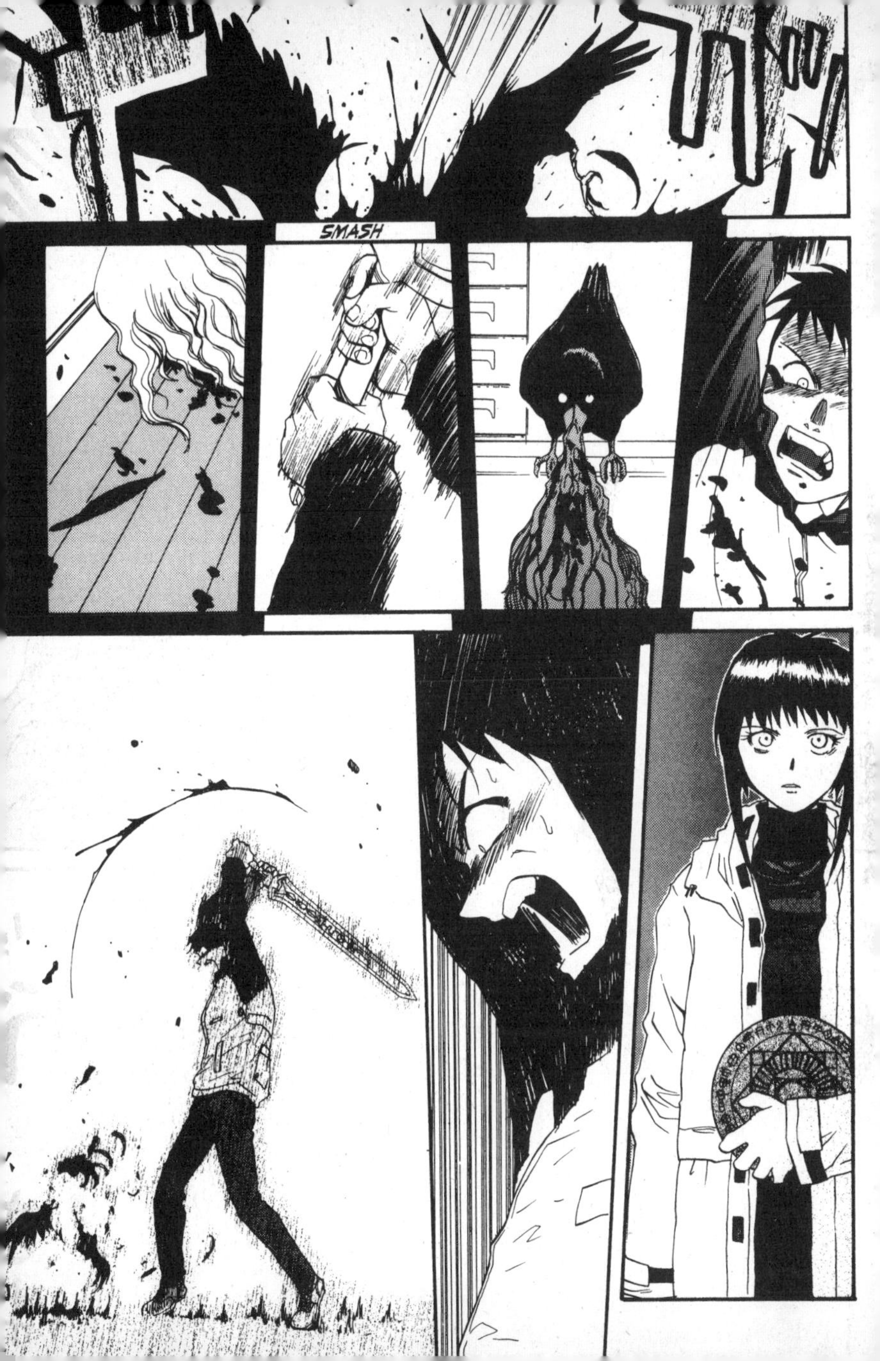
SMASH

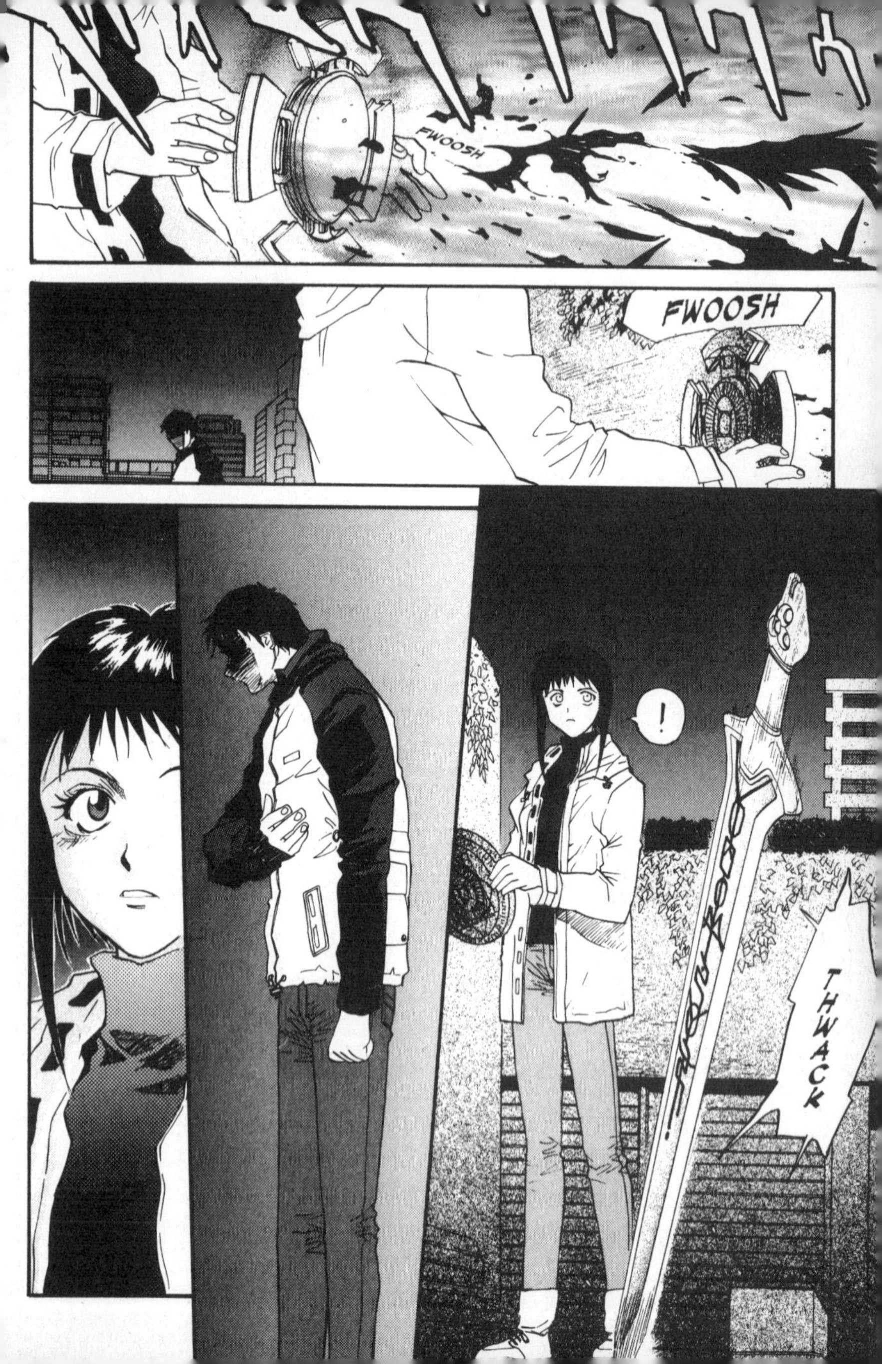
FWOOSH
FWOOSH
THWACK
!

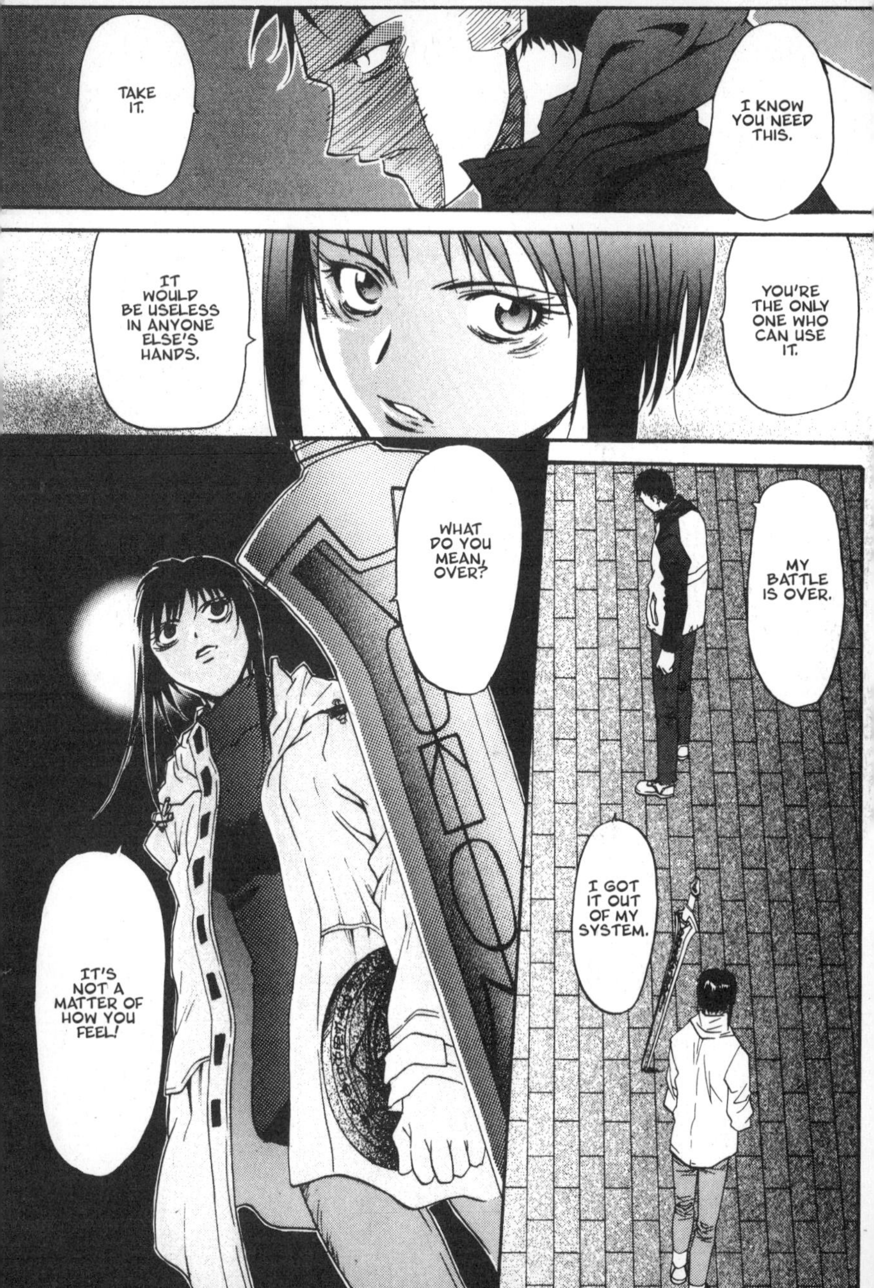

I KNOW YOU NEED THIS.
TAKE IT.
YOU'RE THE ONLY ONE WHO CAN USE IT.
IT WOULD BE USELESS IN ANYONE ELSE'S HANDS.
MY BATTLE IS OVER.
I GOT IT OUT OF MY SYSTEM.
WHAT DO YOU MEAN, OVER?
IT'S NOT A MATTER OF HOW YOU FEEL!

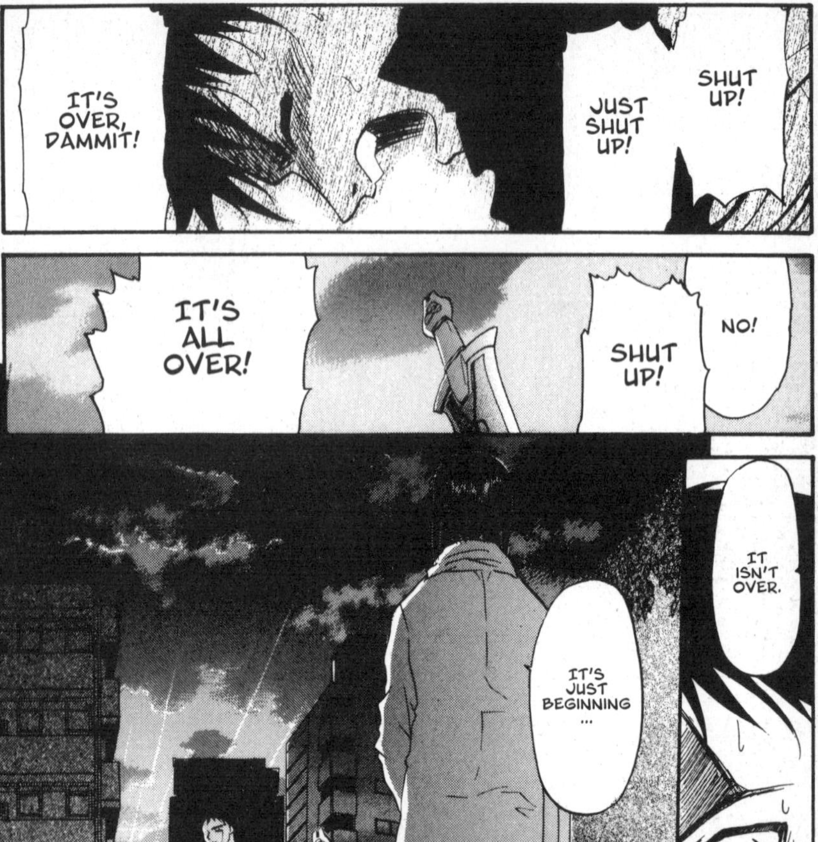
SHUT UP!
JUST SHUT UP!
IT'S OVER, DAMMIT!
NO!
SHUT UP!
IT'S ALL OVER!
IT ISN'T OVER.
IT'S JUST BEGINNING ...

#3. Revenge / END

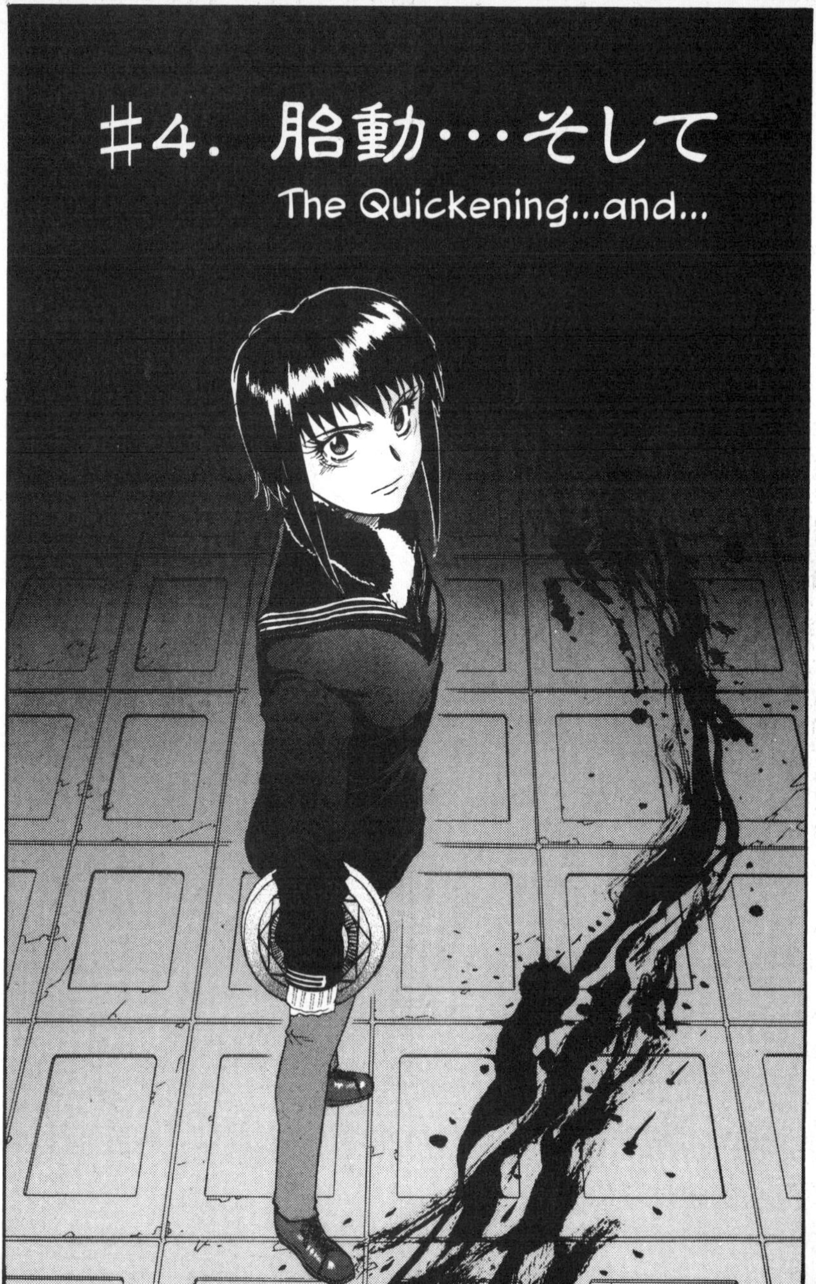
#4. 胎動・・・そして
The Quickening...and...

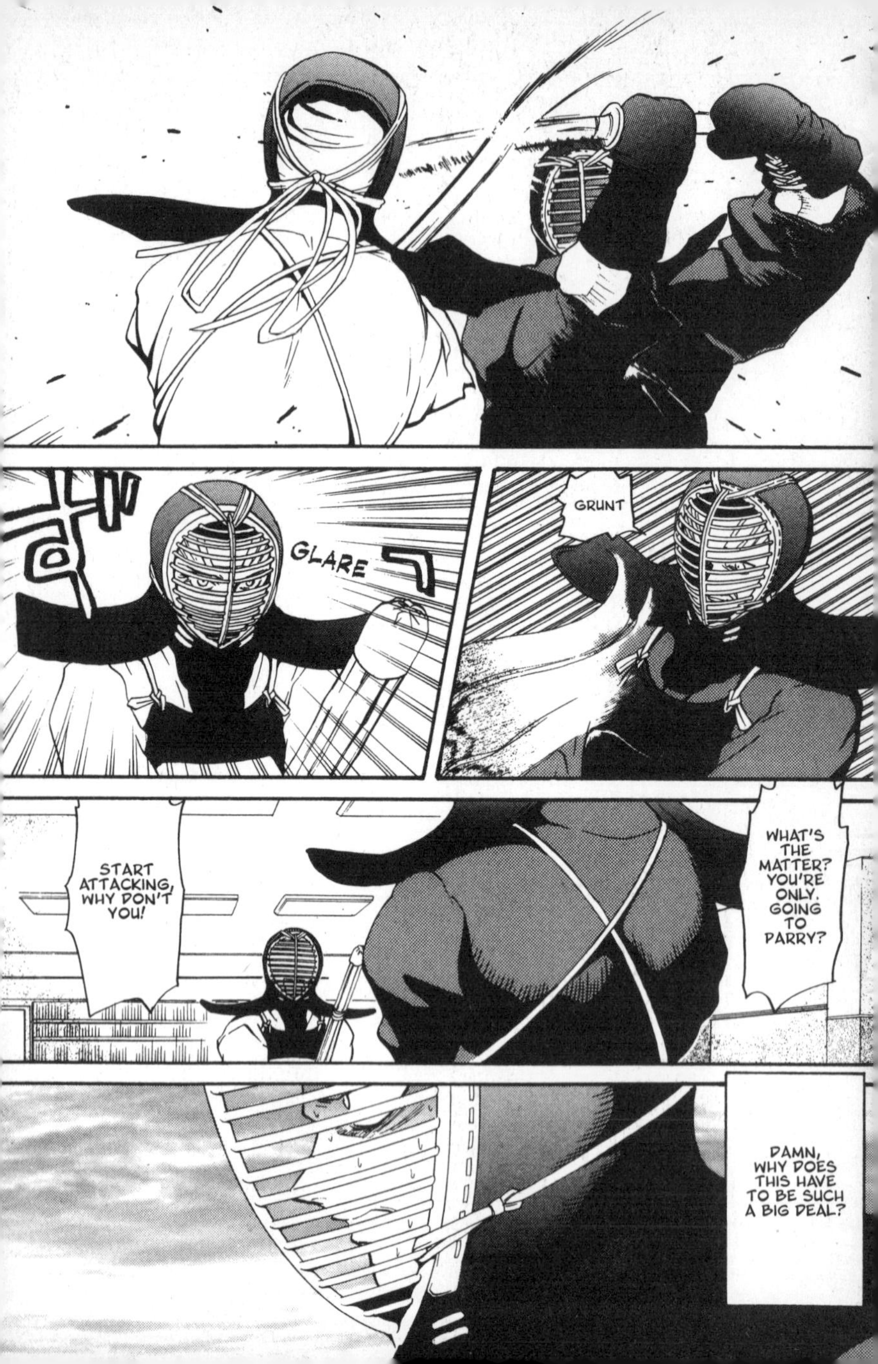
GRUNT
GLARE
WHAT'S THE MATTER? YOU'RE ONLY. GOING TO PARRY?
START ATTACKING, WHY DON'T YOU!
DAMN, WHY DOES THIS HAVE TO BE SUCH A BIG DEAL?

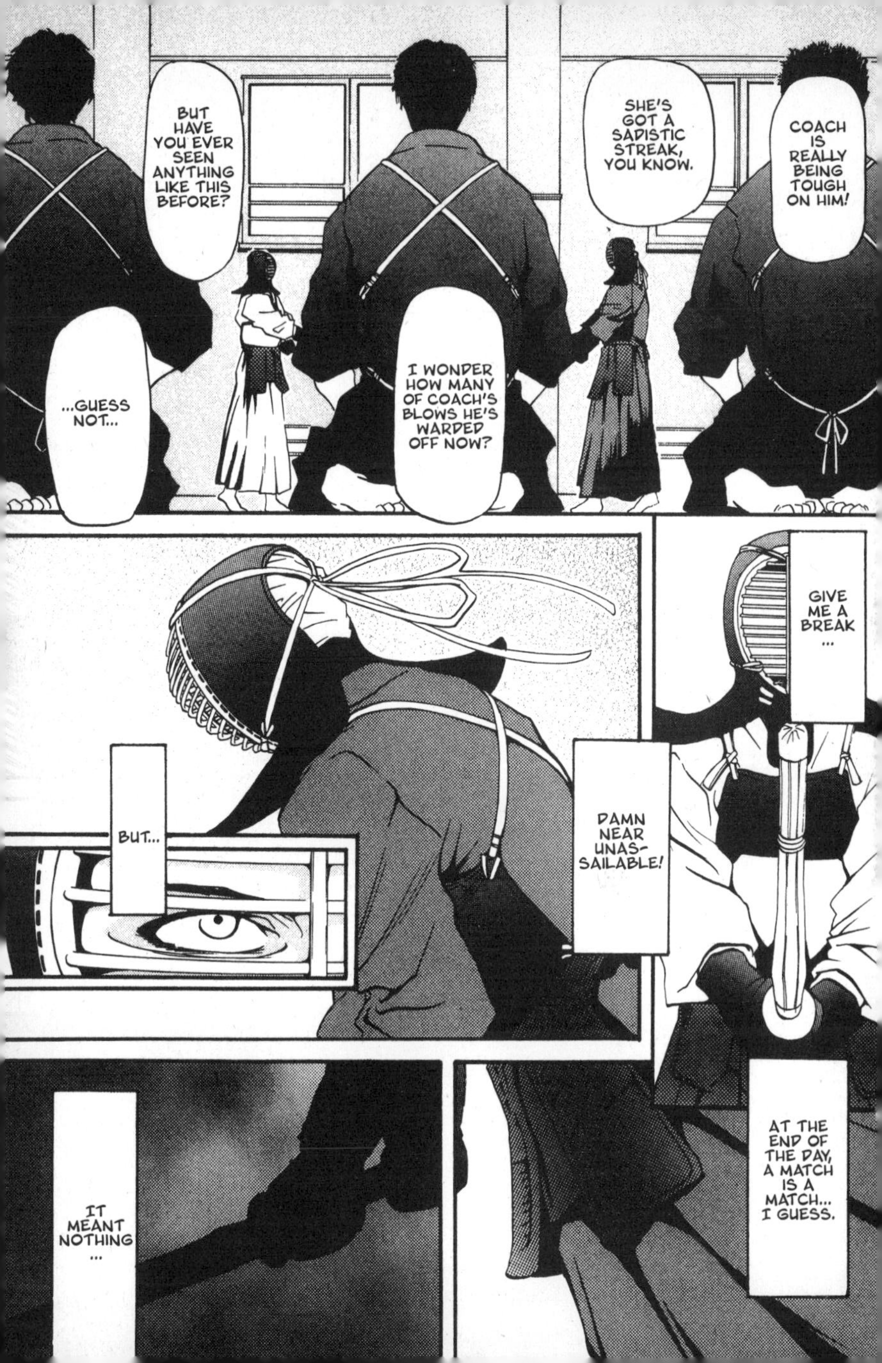
COACH IS REALLY BEING TOUGH ON HIM!
SHE'S GOT A SADISTIC STREAK, YOU KNOW.
BUT HAVE YOU EVER SEEN ANYTHING LIKE THIS BEFORE?
I WONDER HOW MANY OF COACH'S BLOWS HE'S WARDED OFF NOW?
...GUESS NOT...
GIVE ME A BREAK ...
DAMN NEAR UNAS-SAILABLE!
BUT...
AT THE END OF THE DAY, A MATCH IS A MATCH... I GUESS.
IT MEANT NOTHING ...

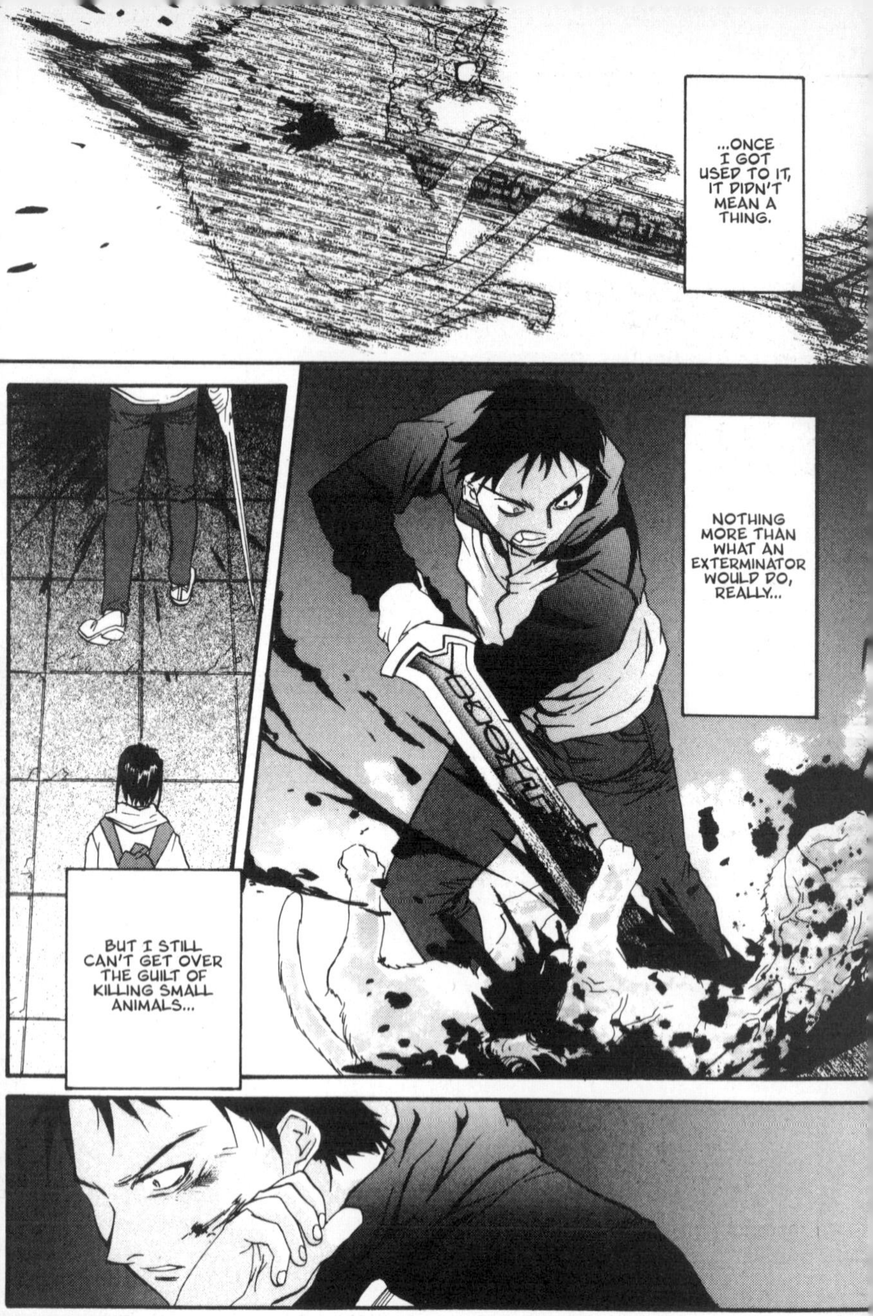
...ONCE I GOT USED TO IT, IT DIDN'T MEAN A THING.
NOTHING MORE THAN WHAT AN EXTERMINATOR WOULD DO, REALLY...
BUT I STILL CAN'T GET OVER THE GUILT OF KILLING SMALL ANIMALS...

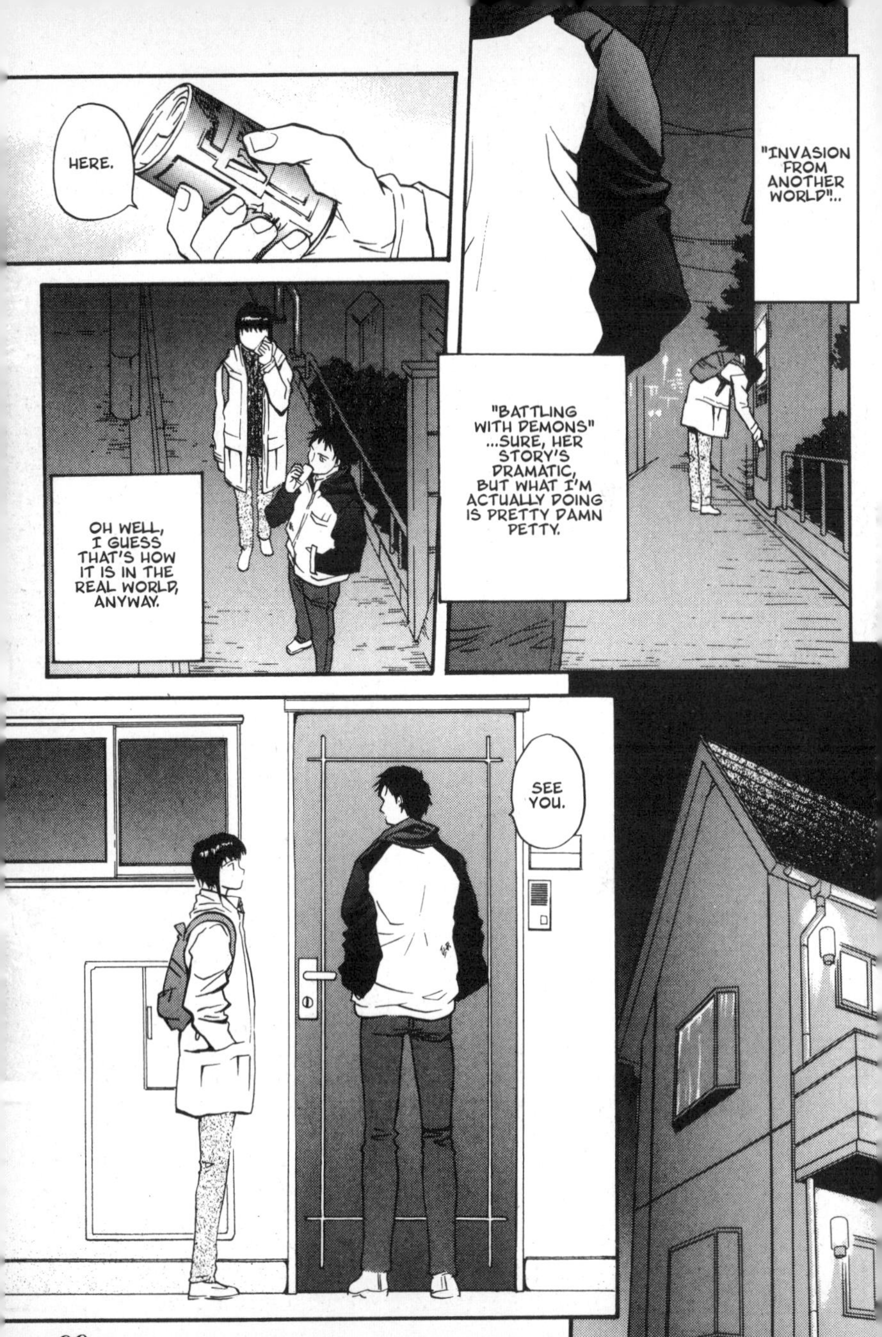
"INVASION FROM ANOTHER WORLD"...
"BATTLING WITH DEMONS" ...SURE, HER STORY'S DRAMATIC, BUT WHAT I'M ACTUALLY DOING IS PRETTY DAMN PETTY.
HERE.
OH WELL, I GUESS THAT'S HOW IT IS IN THE REAL WORLD, ANYWAY.
SEE YOU.

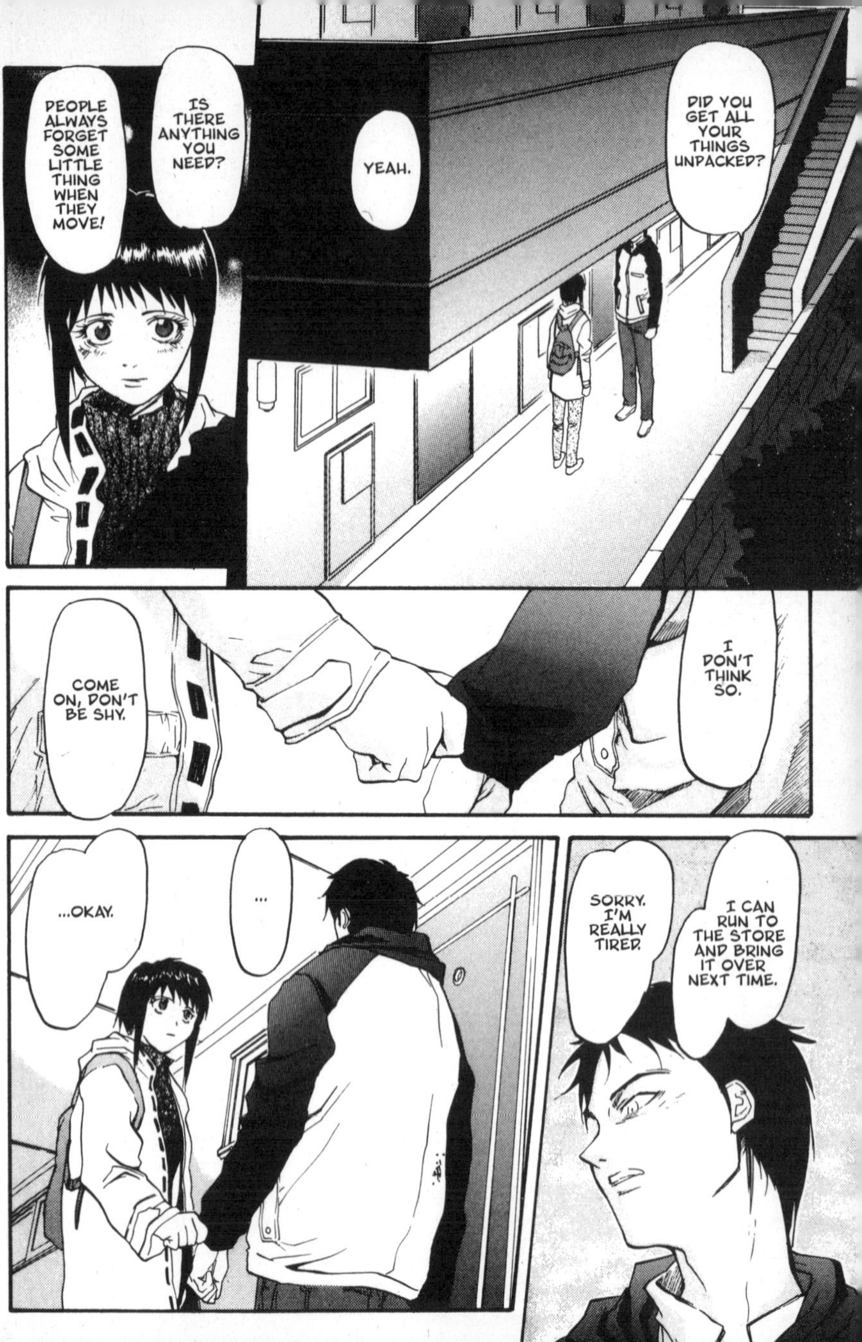
DID YOU GET ALL YOUR THINGS UNPACKED?
YEAH.
IS THERE ANYTHING YOU NEED?
PEOPLE ALWAYS FORGET SOME LITTLE THING WHEN THEY MOVE!
I DON'T THINK SO.
COME ON, DON'T BE SHY.
I CAN RUN TO THE STORE AND BRING IT OVER NEXT TIME.
SORRY. I'M REALLY TIRED.
...
...OKAY.

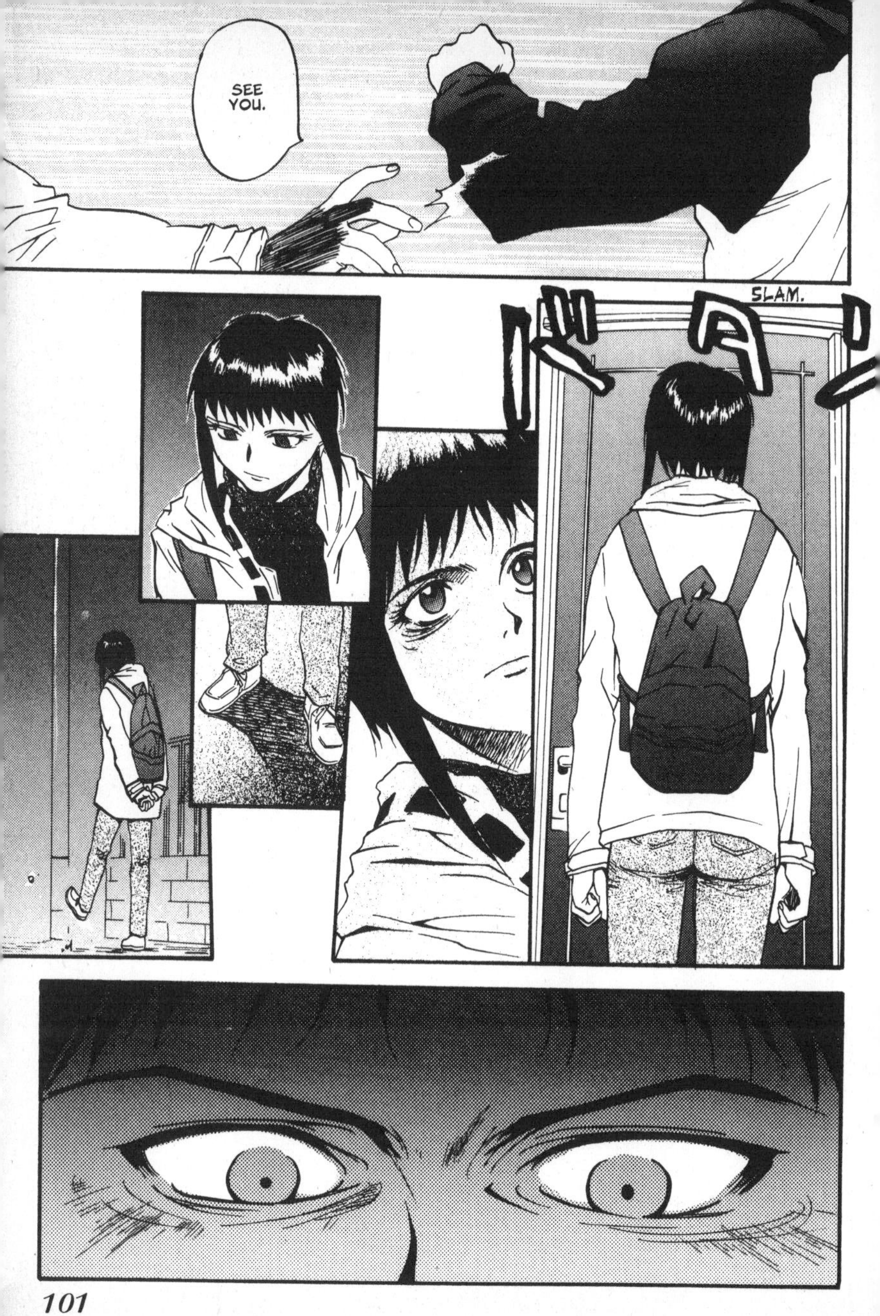
SEE YOU.
SLAM.

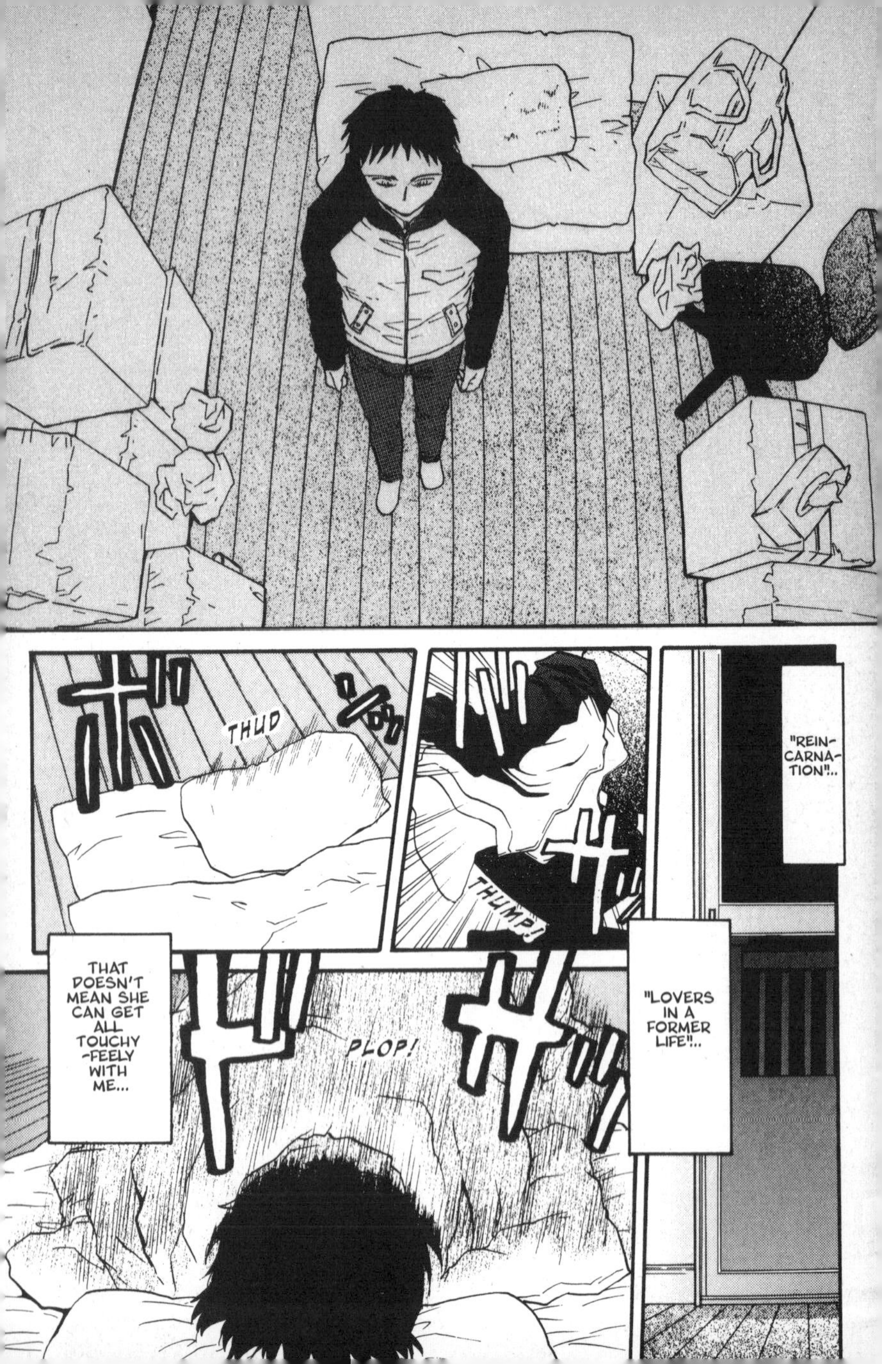
"REIN-CARNATION"..
"LOVERS IN A FORMER LIFE"..
THUMP!
THUD
PLOP!
THAT DOESN'T MEAN SHE CAN GET ALL TOUCHY-FEELY WITH ME...

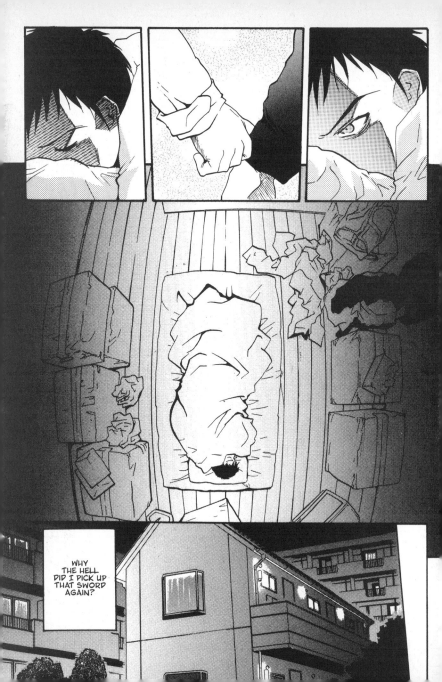

WHY THE HELL DID I PICK UP THAT SWORD AGAIN?

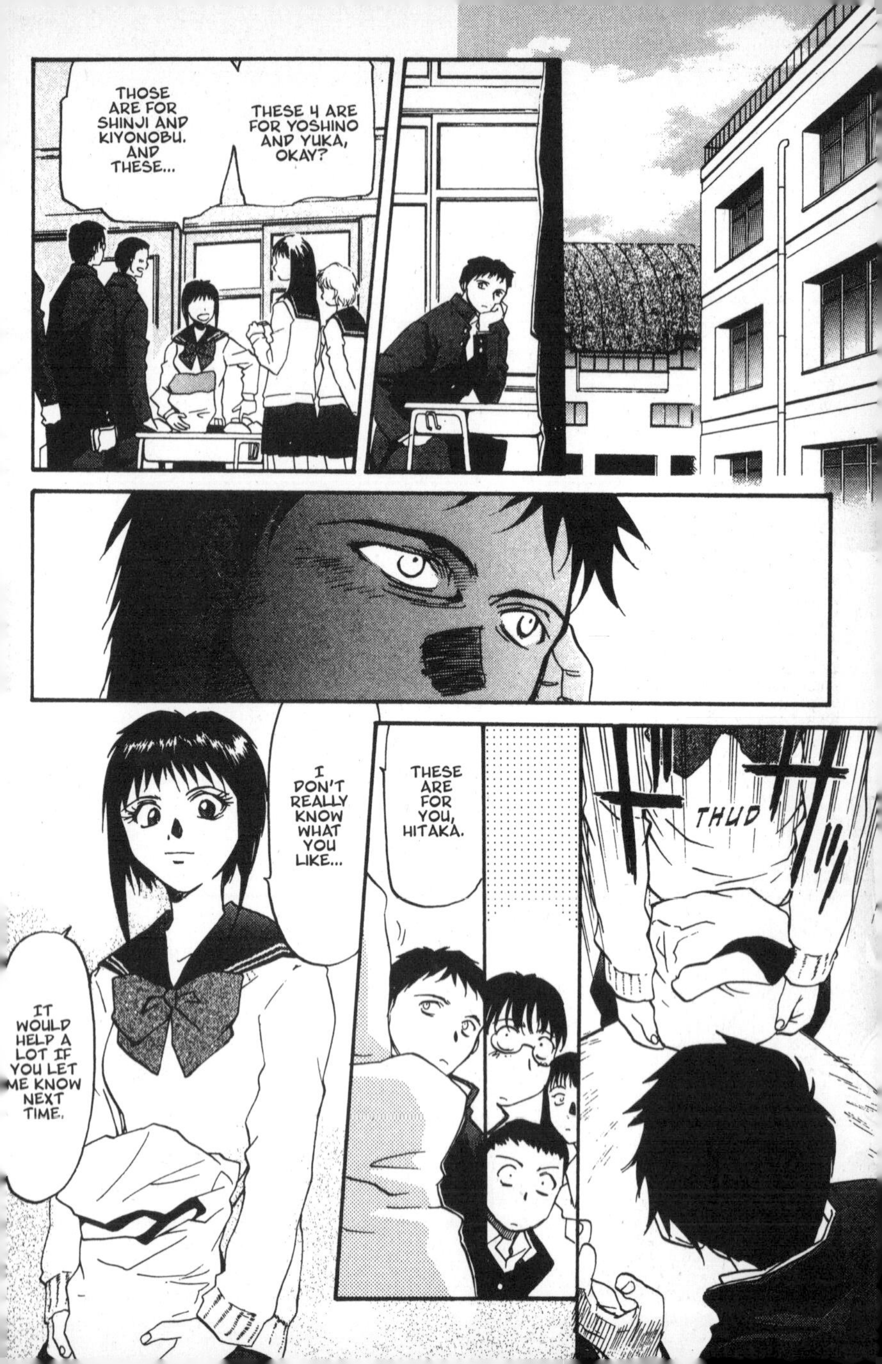
THESE 4 ARE FOR YOSHINO AND YUKA, OKAY?
THOSE ARE FOR SHINJI AND KIYONOBU. AND THESE...
THUD
THESE ARE FOR YOU, HITAKA.
I DON'T REALLY KNOW WHAT YOU LIKE...
IT WOULD HELP A LOT IF YOU LET ME KNOW NEXT TIME.

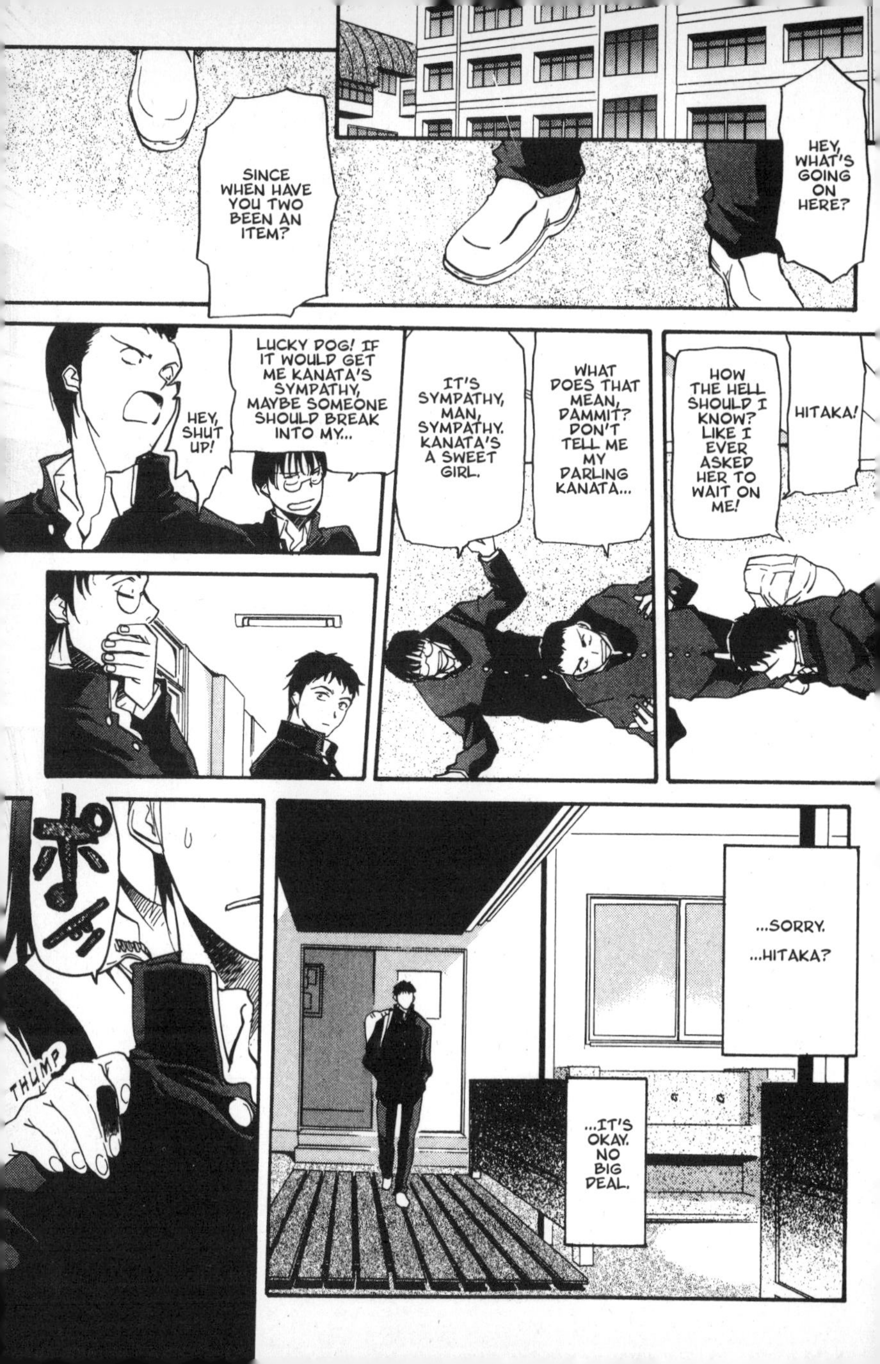
HEY, WHAT'S GOING ON HERE?
SINCE WHEN HAVE YOU TWO BEEN AN ITEM?
HITAKA!
HOW THE HELL SHOULD I KNOW? LIKE I EVER ASKED HER TO WAIT ON ME!
WHAT DOES THAT MEAN, DAMMIT? DON'T TELL ME MY DARLING KANATA...
IT'S SYMPATHY, MAN, SYMPATHY. KANATA'S A SWEET GIRL.
LUCKY DOG! IF IT WOULD GET ME KANATA'S SYMPATHY, MAYBE SOMEONE SHOULD BREAK INTO MY...
HEY, SHUT UP!
...SORRY.
...HITAKA?
...IT'S OKAY. NO BIG DEAL.
ポン
THUMP

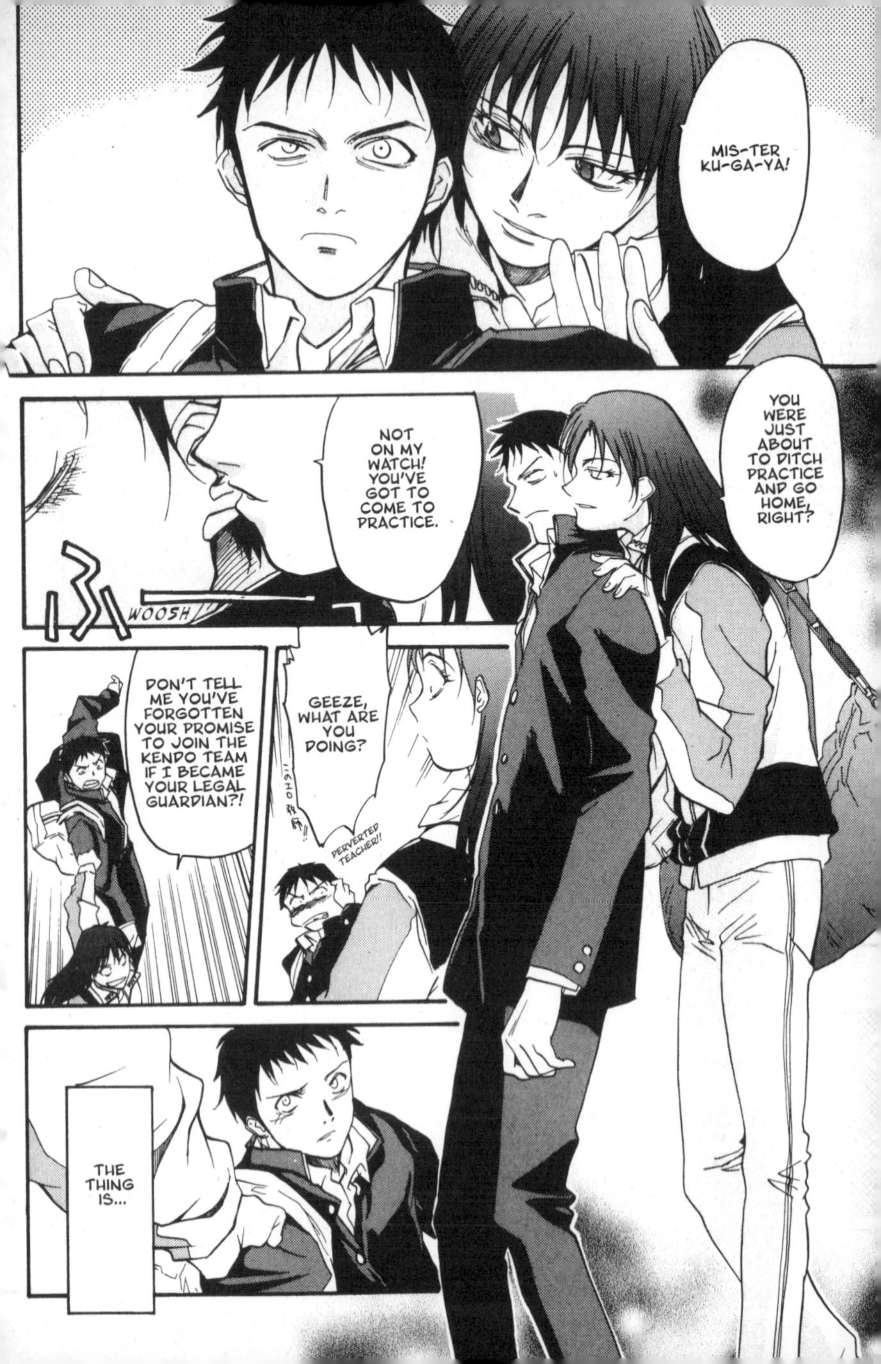
MIS-TER KU-GA-YA!
YOU WERE JUST ABOUT TO DITCH PRACTICE AND GO HOME, RIGHT?
NOT ON MY WATCH! YOU'VE GOT TO COME TO PRACTICE.
WOOSH
GEEZE, WHAT ARE YOU DOING?
PERVERTED TEACHER!!
DON'T TELL ME YOU'VE FORGOTTEN YOUR PROMISE TO JOIN THE KENDO TEAM IF I BECAME YOUR LEGAL GUARDIAN?!
THE THING IS...

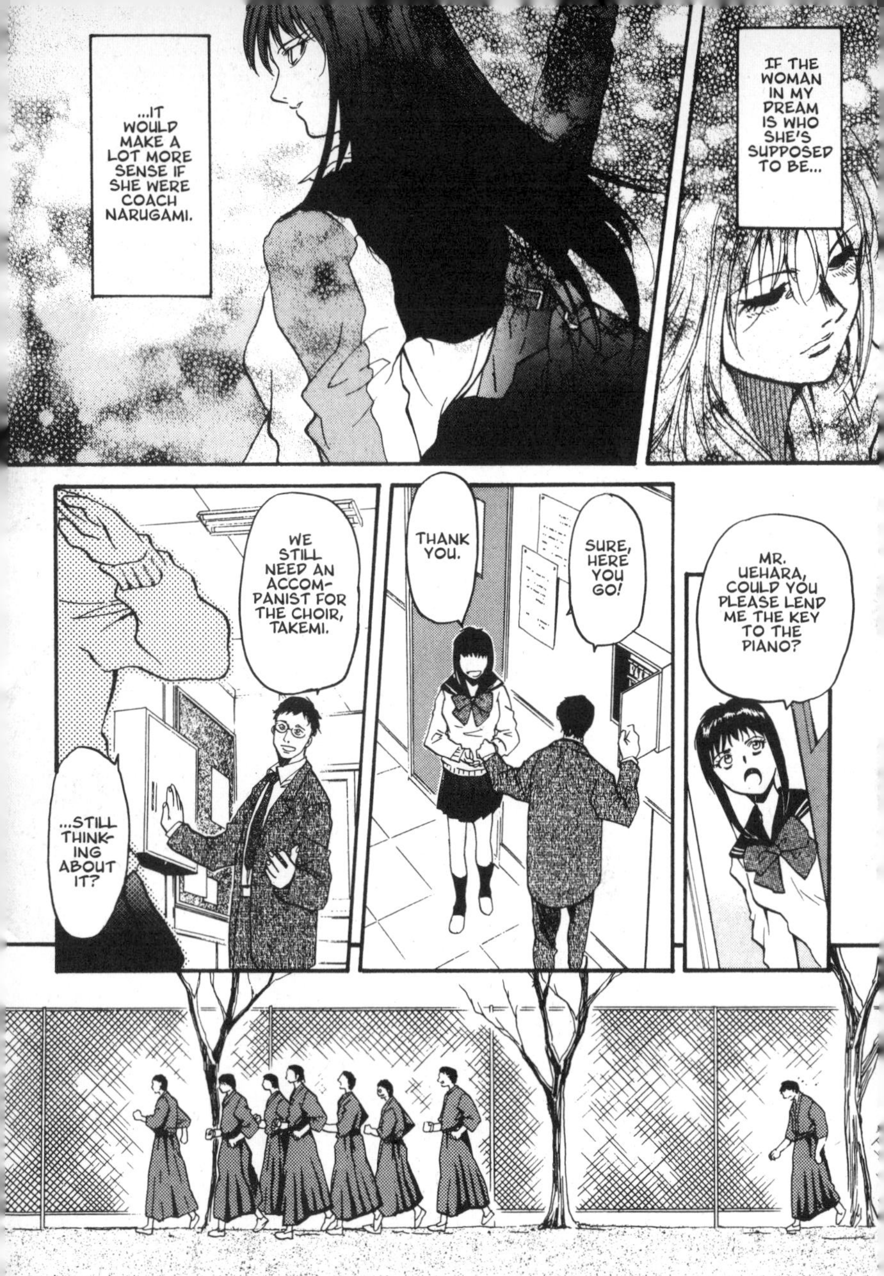
IF THE WOMAN IN MY DREAM IS WHO SHE'S SUPPOSED TO BE...
...IT WOULD MAKE A LOT MORE SENSE IF SHE WERE COACH NARUGAMI.
MR. UEHARA, COULD YOU PLEASE LEND ME THE KEY TO THE PIANO?
SURE, HERE YOU GO!
THANK YOU.
WE STILL NEED AN ACCOMPANIST FOR THE CHOIR, TAKEMI.
...STILL THINKING ABOUT IT?

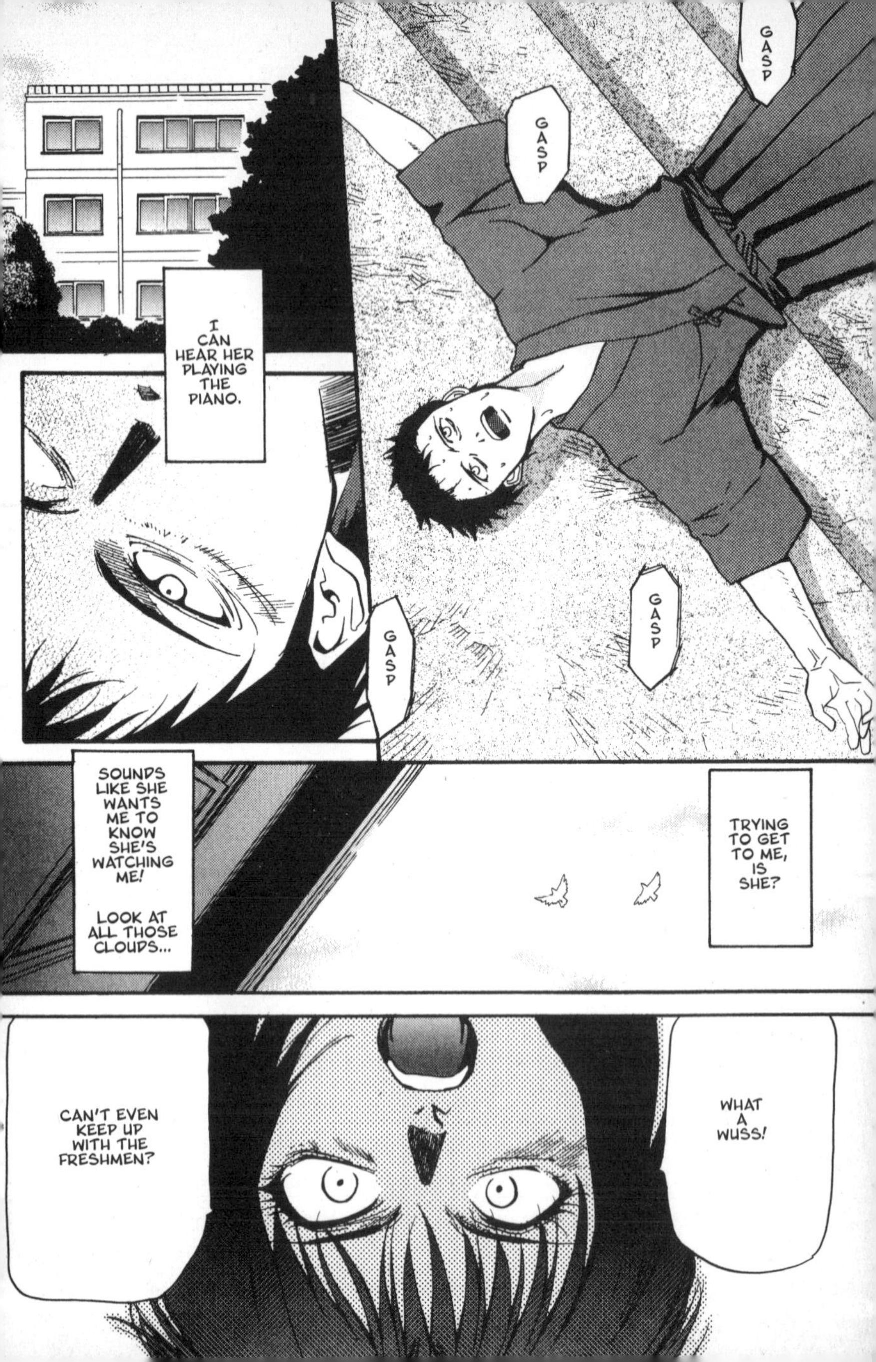
GASP
GASP
GASP
I CAN HEAR HER PLAYING THE PIANO.
GASP
TRYING TO GET TO ME, IS SHE?
SOUNDS LIKE SHE WANTS ME TO KNOW SHE'S WATCHING ME!
LOOK AT ALL THOSE CLOUDS...
WHAT A WUSS!
CAN'T EVEN KEEP UP WITH THE FRESHMEN?

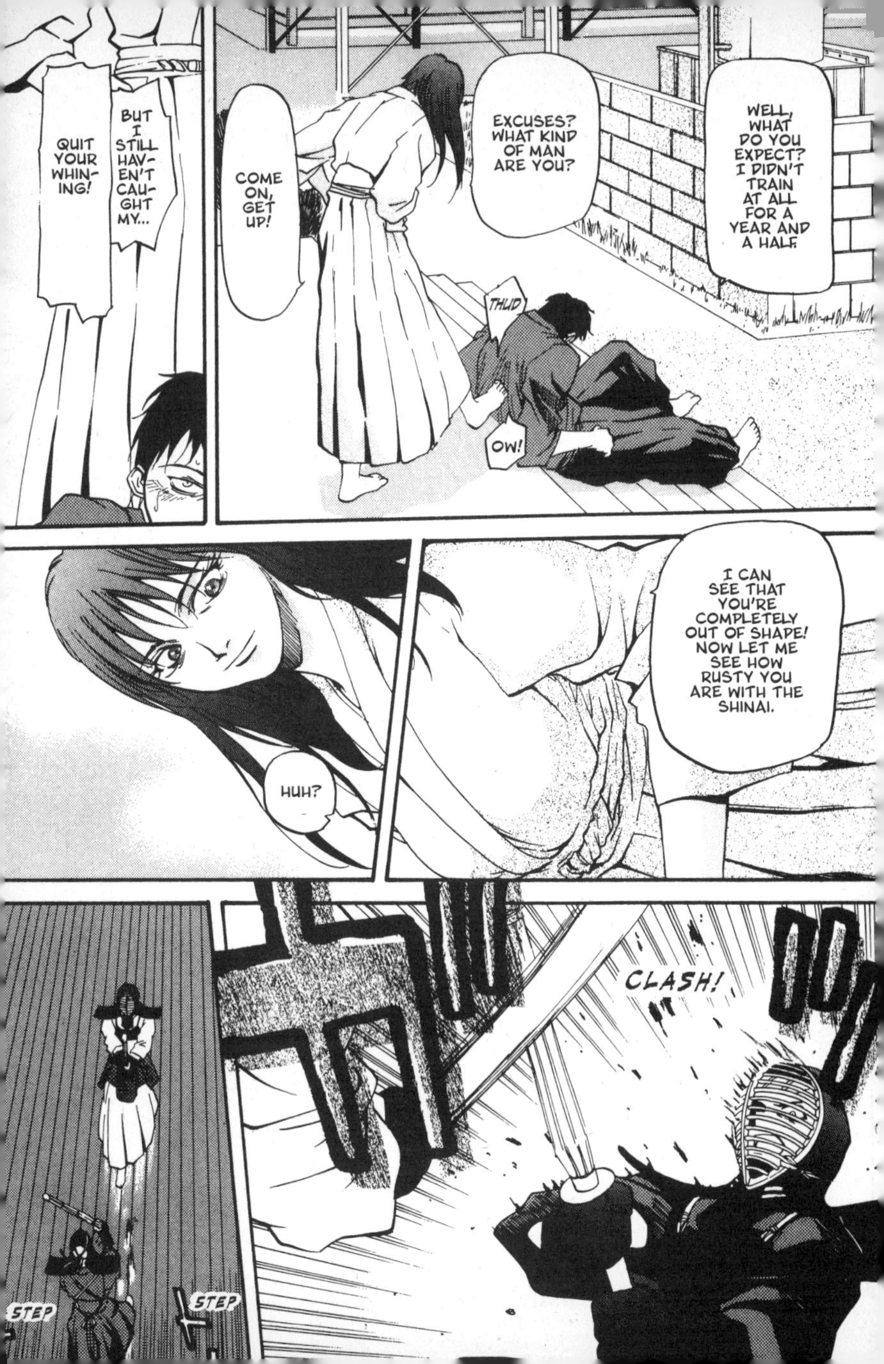
WELL, WHAT DO YOU EXPECT? I DIDN'T TRAIN AT ALL FOR A YEAR AND A HALF.
EXCUSES? WHAT KIND OF MAN ARE YOU?
COME ON, GET UP!
THUD
OW!
BUT I STILL HAV-EN'T CAU-GHT MY...
QUIT YOUR WHIN-ING!
I CAN SEE THAT YOU'RE COMPLETELY OUT OF SHAPE! NOW LET ME SEE HOW RUSTY YOU ARE WITH THE SHINAI.
HUH?
CLASH!
STEP
STEP

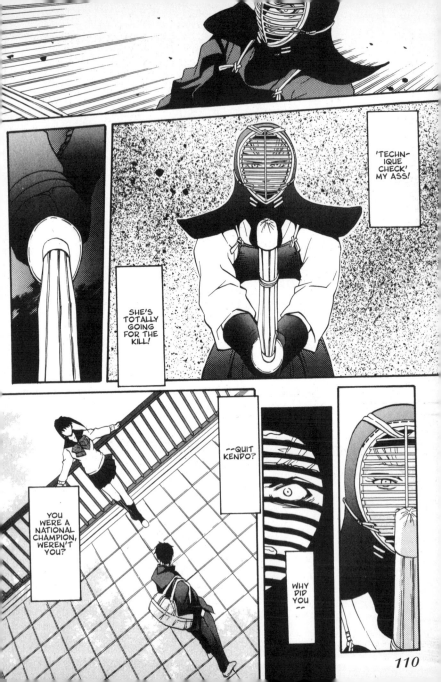

'TECHNIQUE CHECK' MY ASS!

SHE'S TOTALLY GOING FOR THE KILL!

--QUIT KENDO?

YOU WERE A NATIONAL CHAMPION, WEREN'T YOU?

WHY DID YOU--

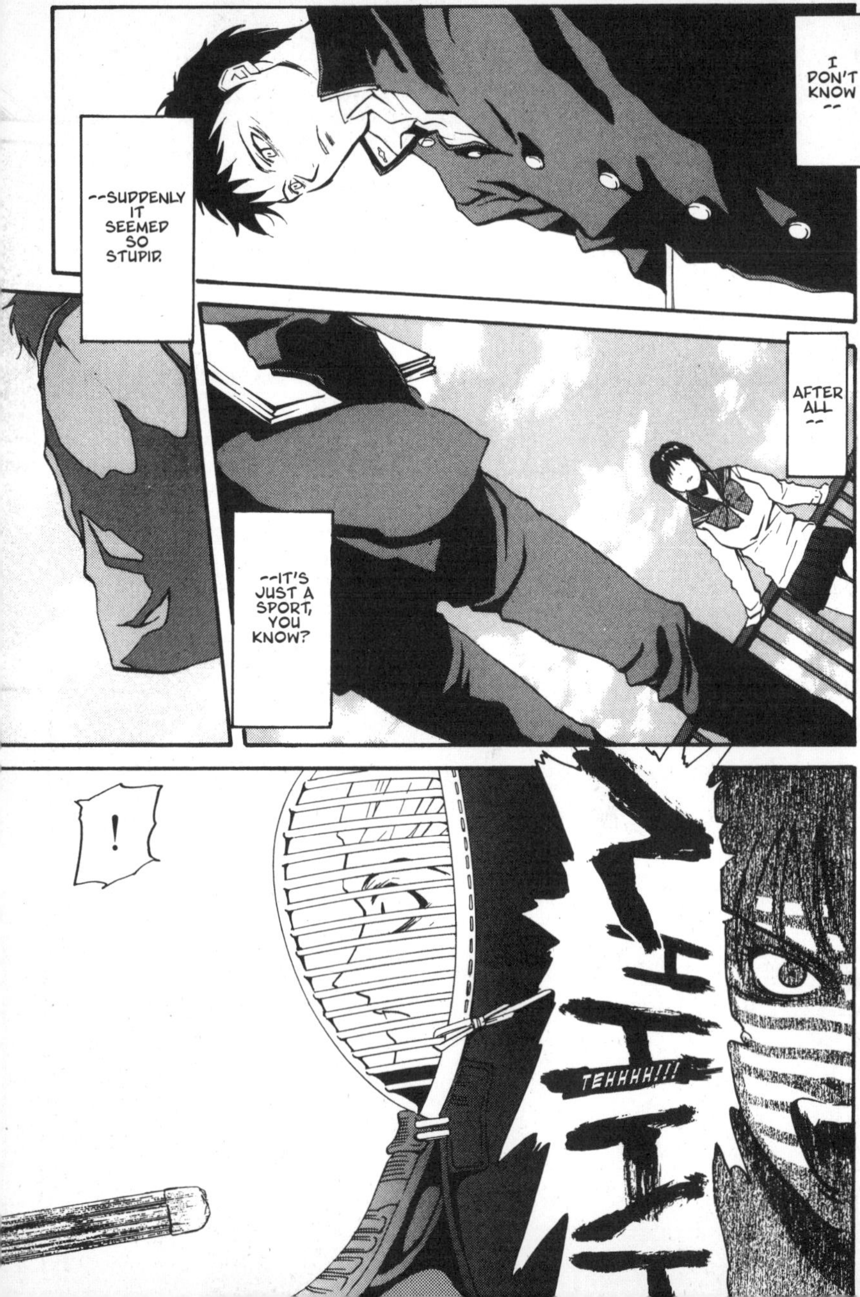
I DON'T KNOW --
--SUDDENLY IT SEEMED SO STUPID.
AFTER ALL --
--IT'S JUST A SPORT, YOU KNOW?
TEHHHH!!!
!

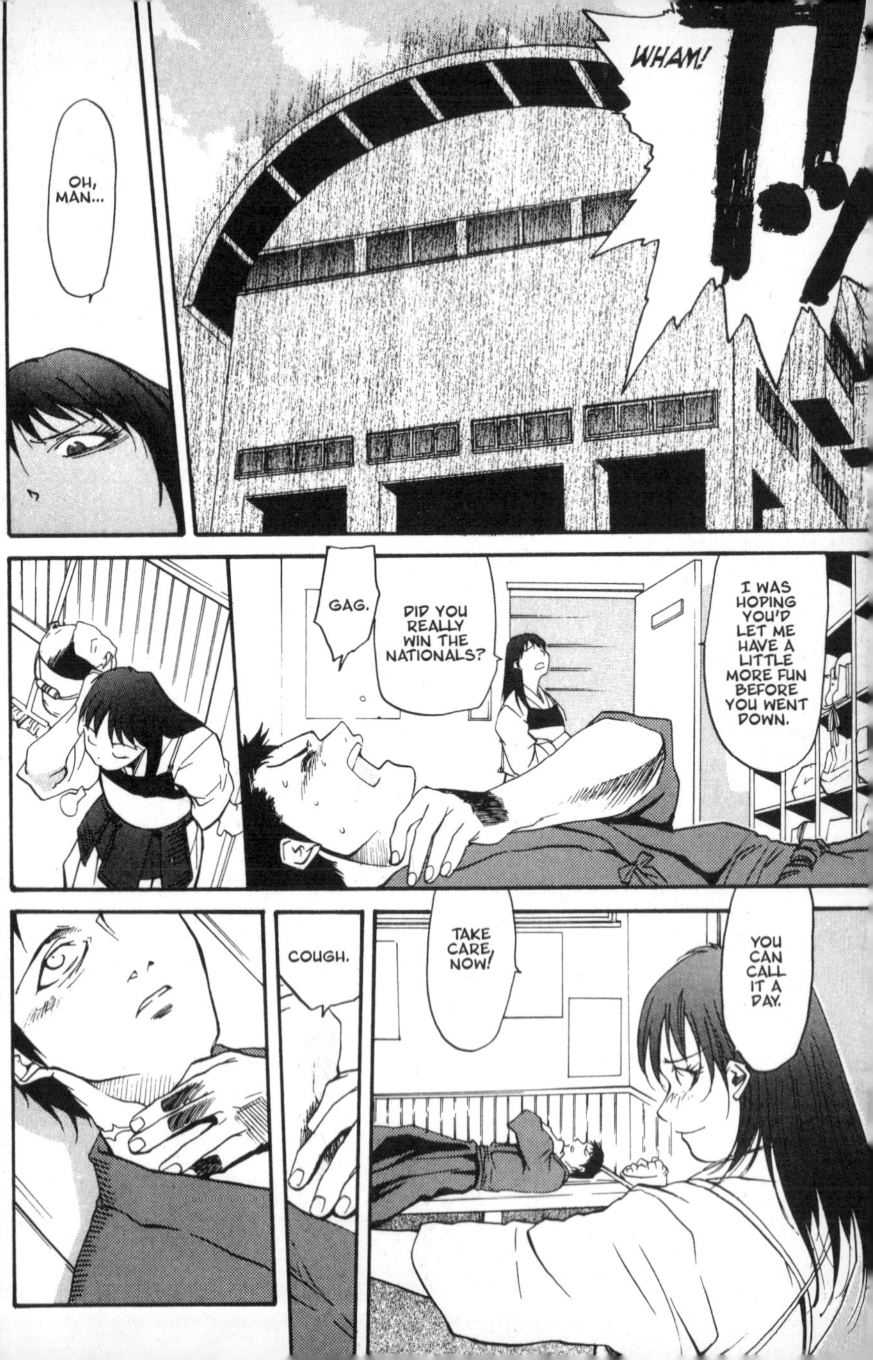
WHAM!
OH, MAN...
I WAS HOPING YOU'D LET ME HAVE A LITTLE MORE FUN BEFORE YOU WENT DOWN.
DID YOU REALLY WIN THE NATIONALS?
GAG.
YOU CAN CALL IT A DAY.
TAKE CARE, NOW!
COUGH.

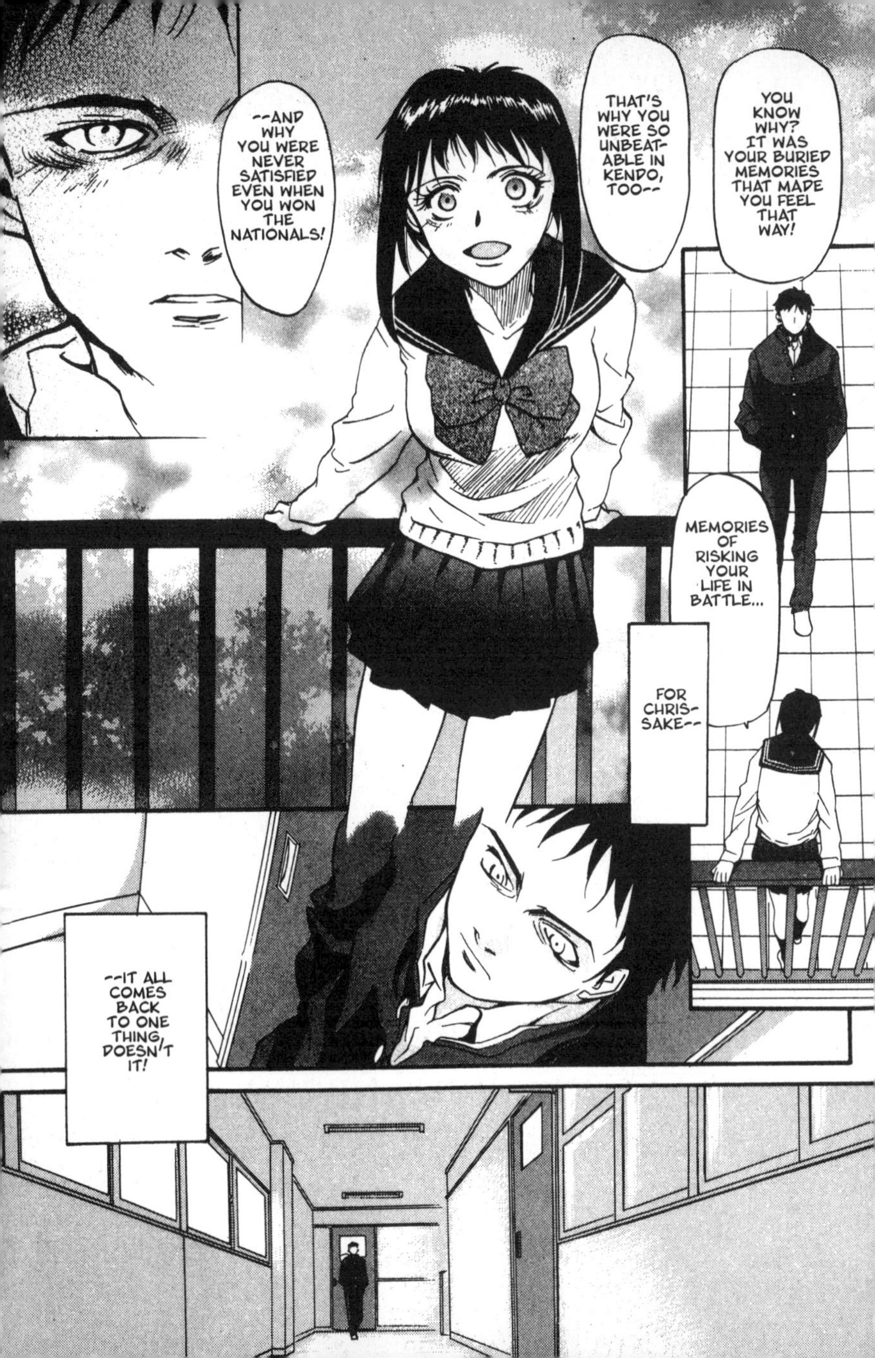
YOU KNOW WHY? IT WAS YOUR BURIED MEMORIES THAT MADE YOU FEEL THAT WAY!
THAT'S WHY YOU WERE SO UNBEAT-ABLE IN KENDO, TOO--
--AND WHY YOU WERE NEVER SATISFIED EVEN WHEN YOU WON THE NATIONALS!
MEMORIES OF RISKING YOUR LIFE IN BATTLE...
FOR CHRIS-SAKE--
--IT ALL COMES BACK TO ONE THING, DOESN'T IT!

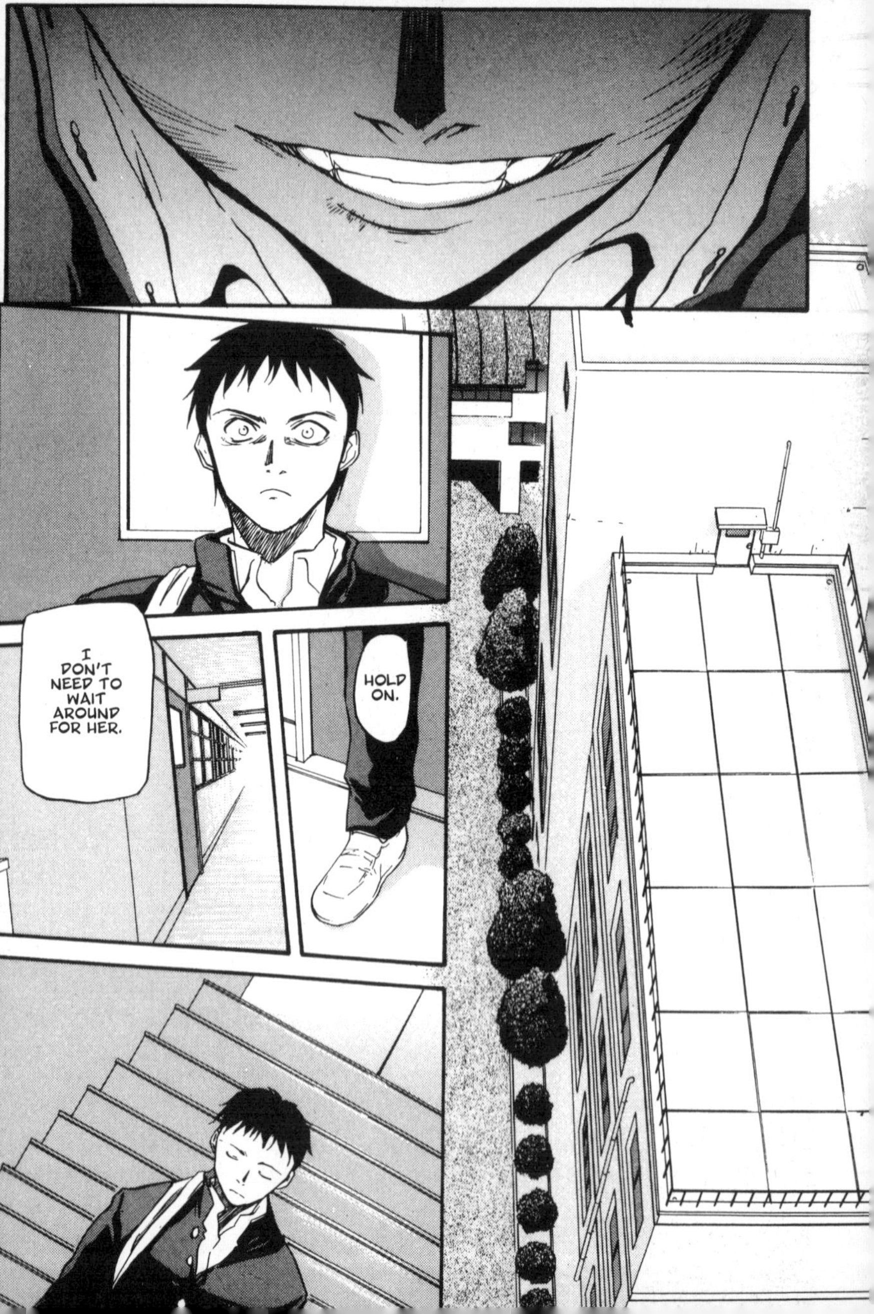
HOLD ON.
I DON'T NEED TO WAIT AROUND FOR HER.

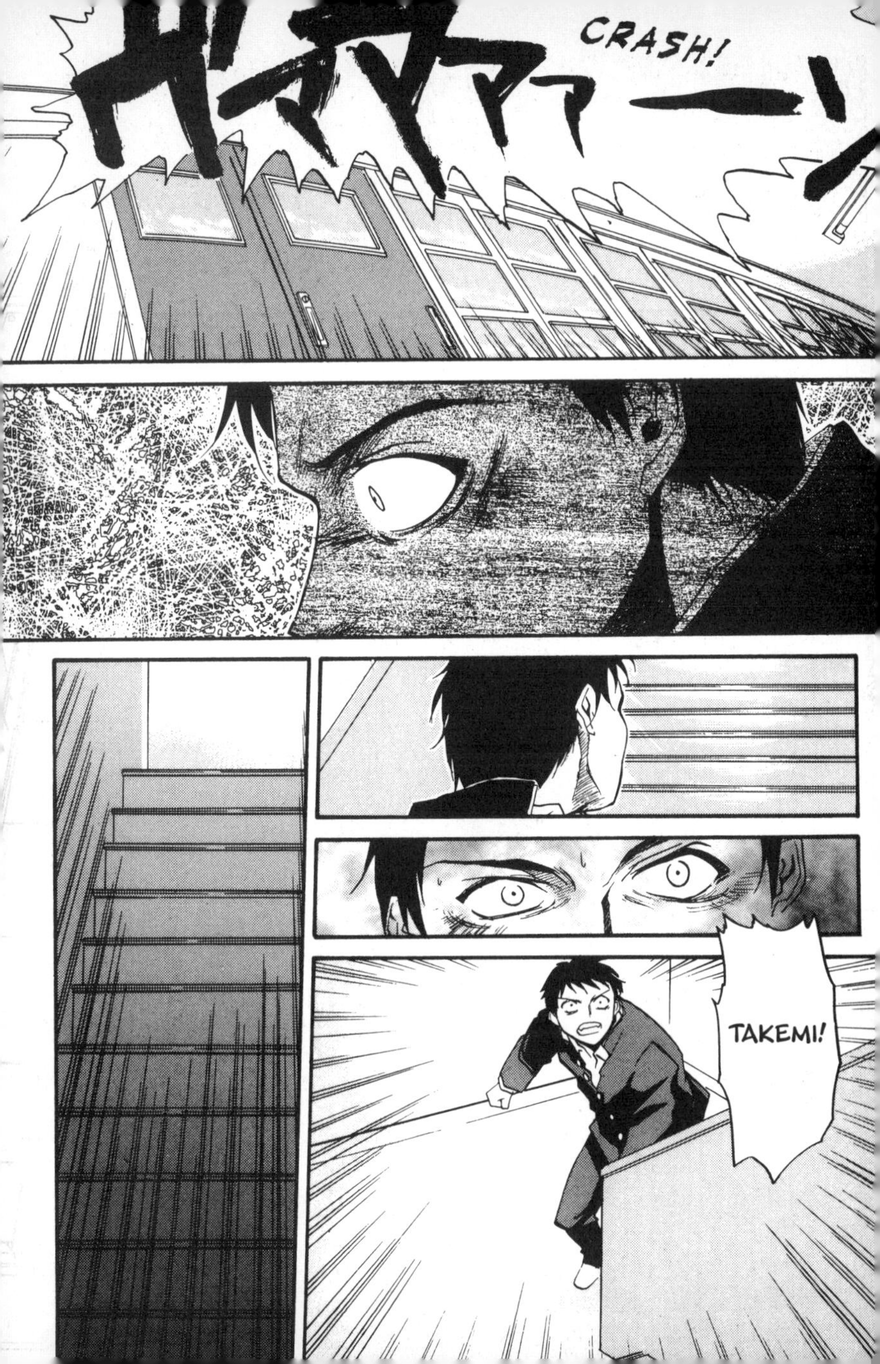
ガシャアアーーン
CRASH!
TAKEMI!

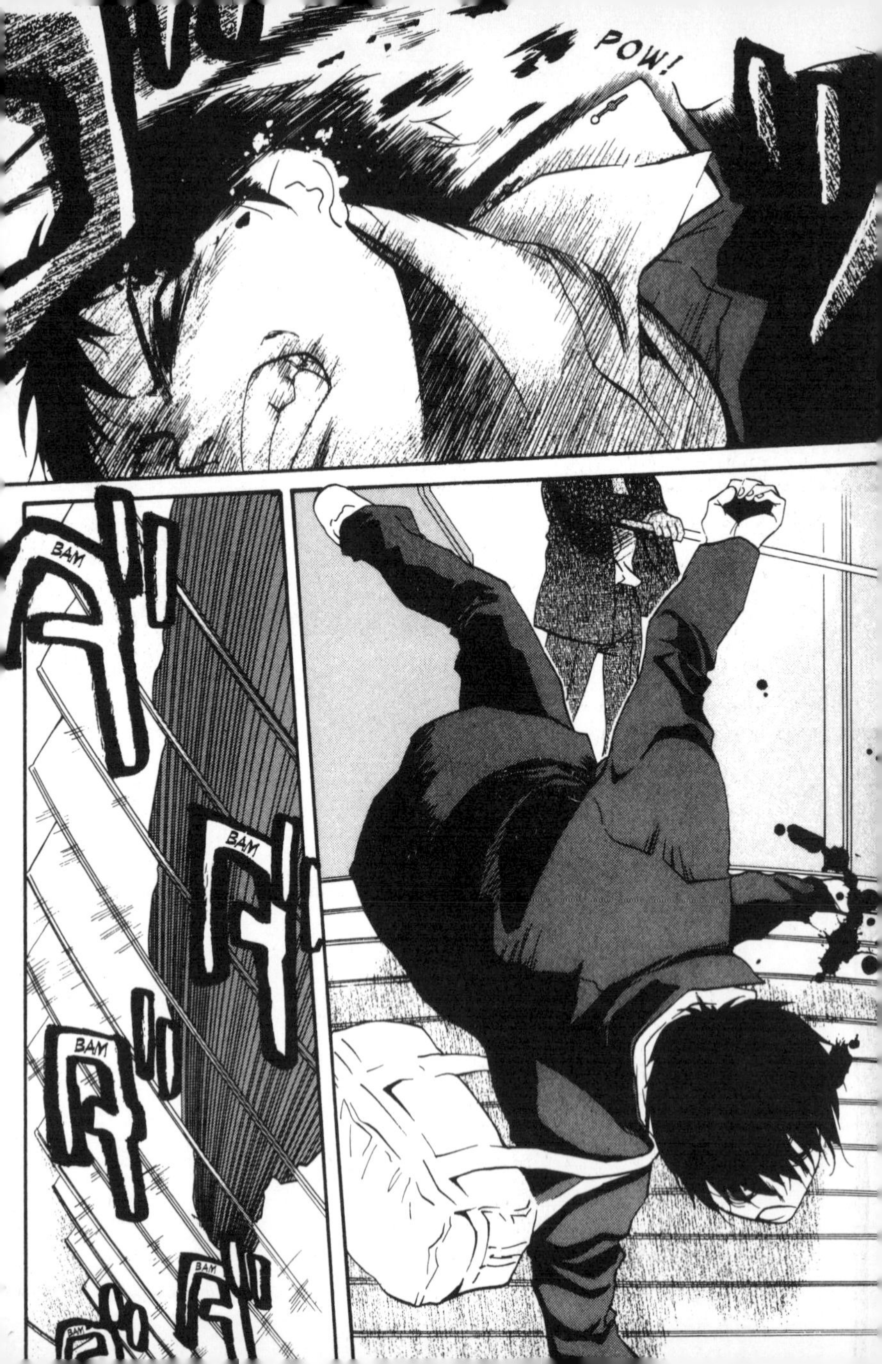
POW!
BAM
BAM
BAM
BAM
BAM

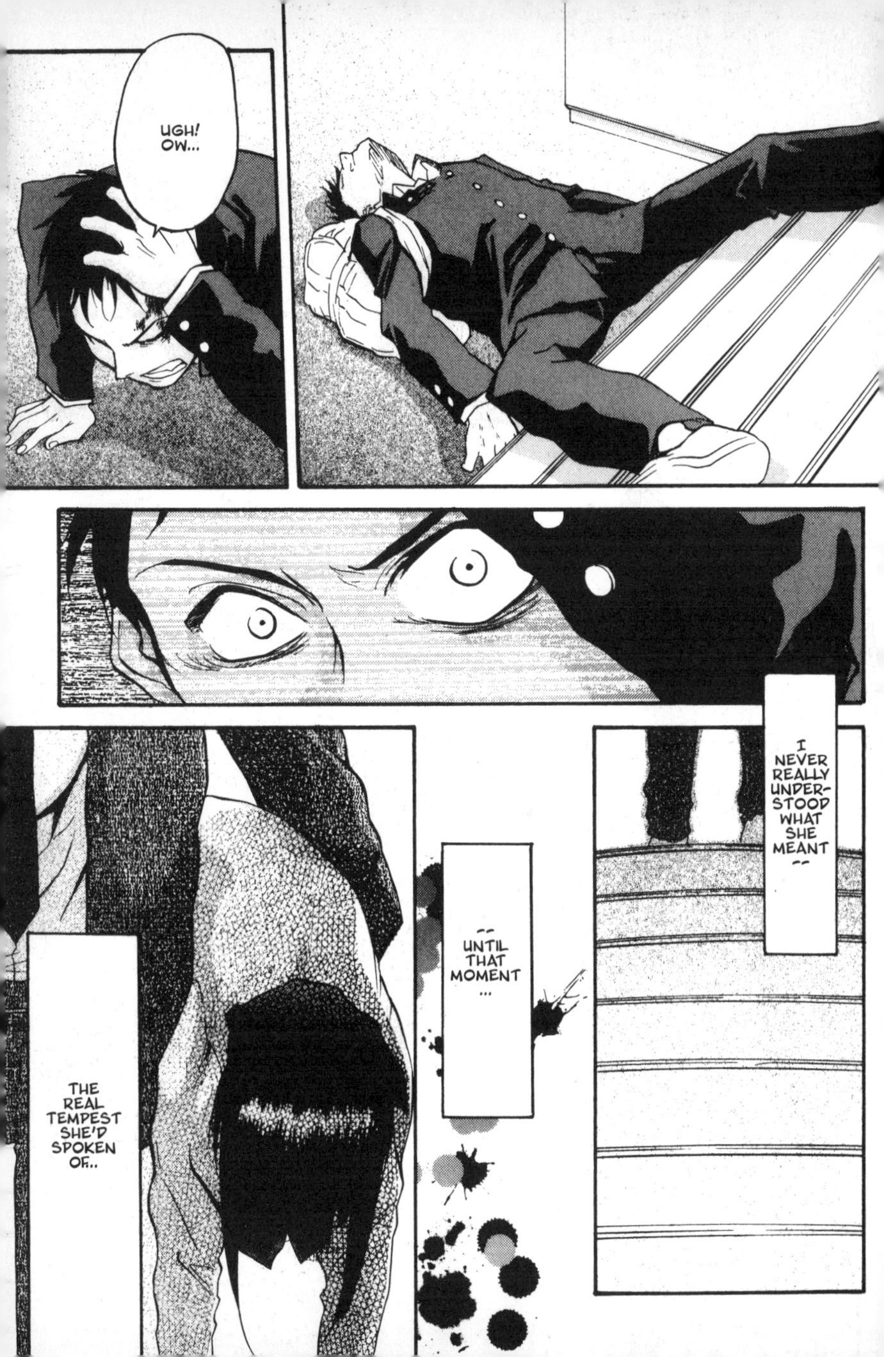
UGH! OW...
I NEVER REALLY UNDER-STOOD WHAT SHE MEANT --
-- UNTIL THAT MOMENT ...
THE REAL TEMPEST SHE'D SPOKEN OF..

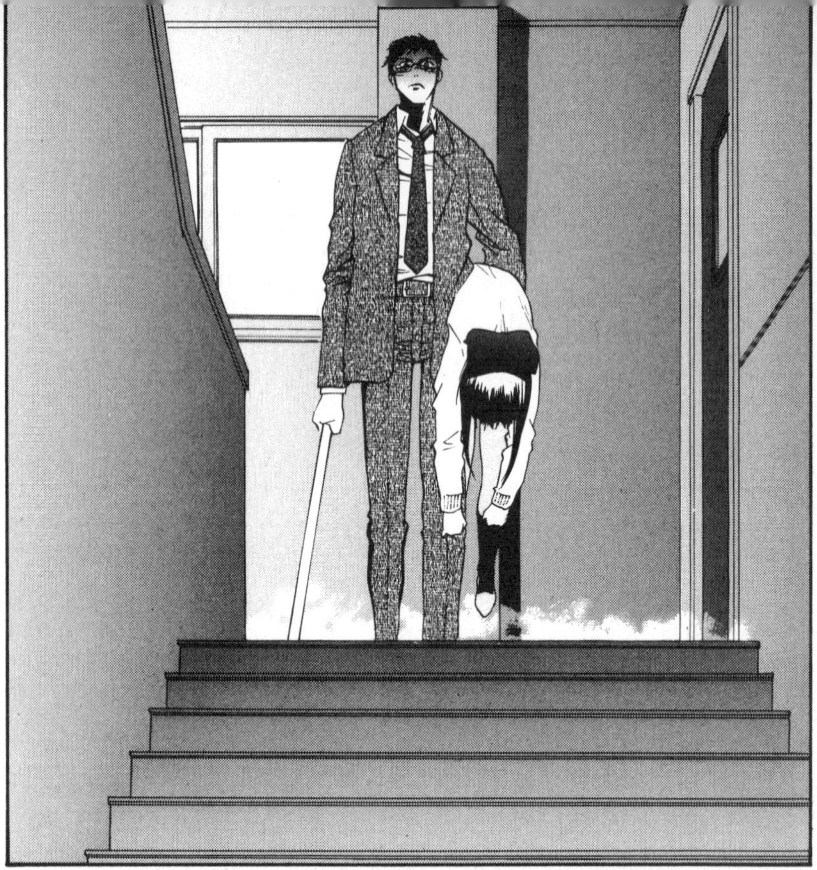

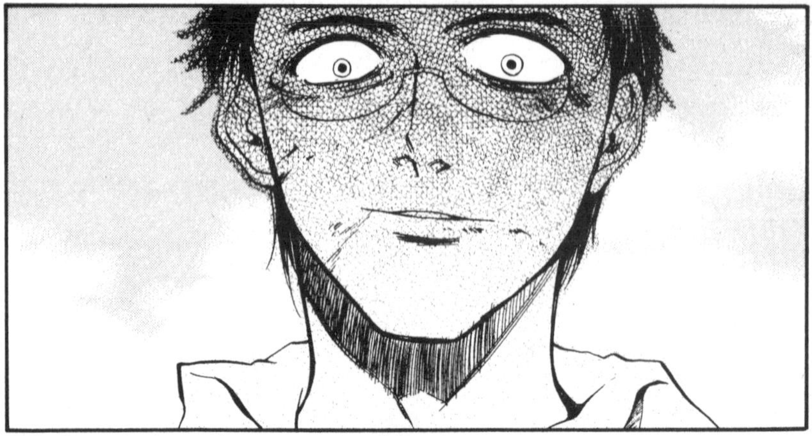

#4. The Quickening...and... / END

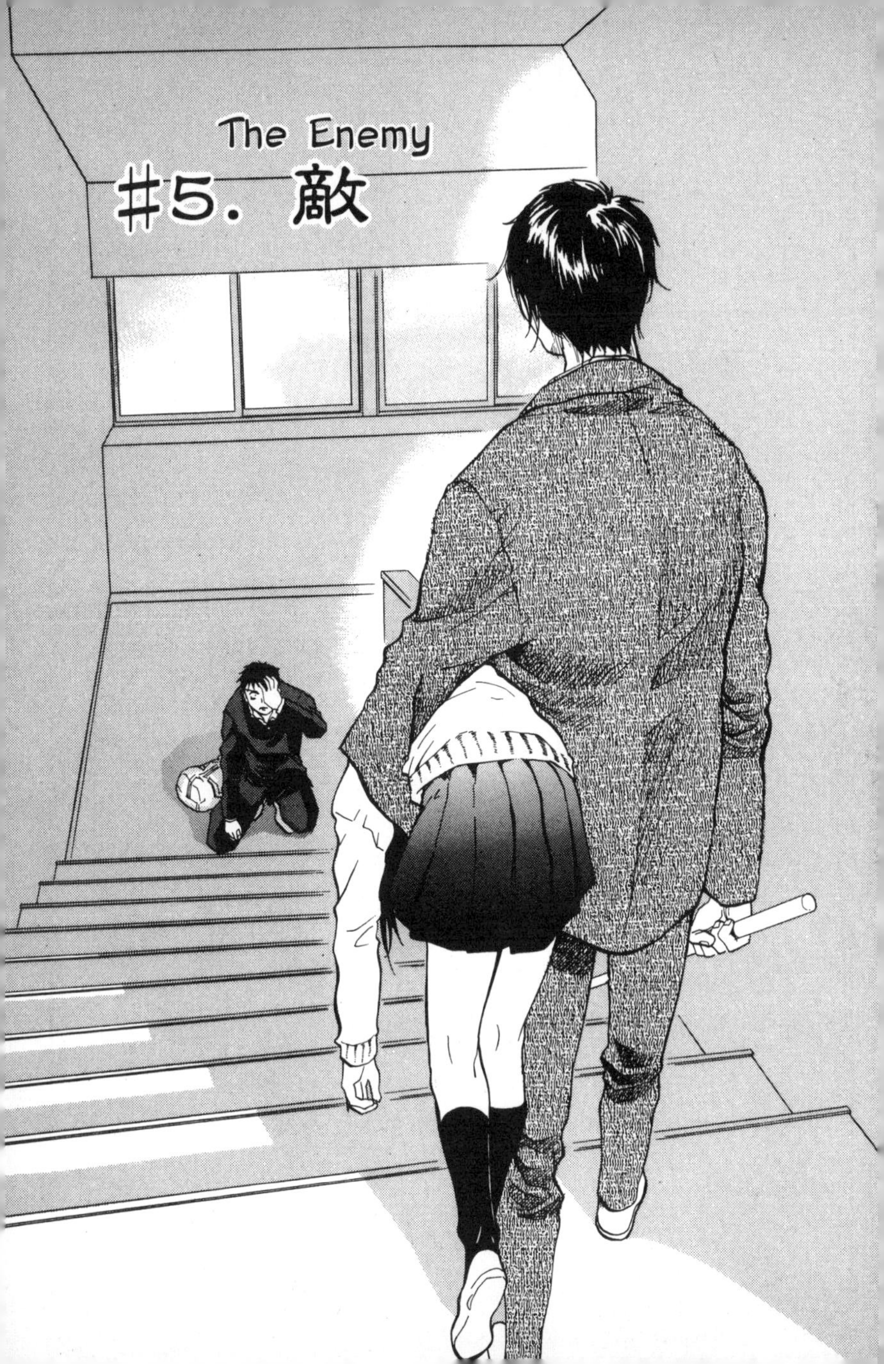
The Enemy
#5. 敵

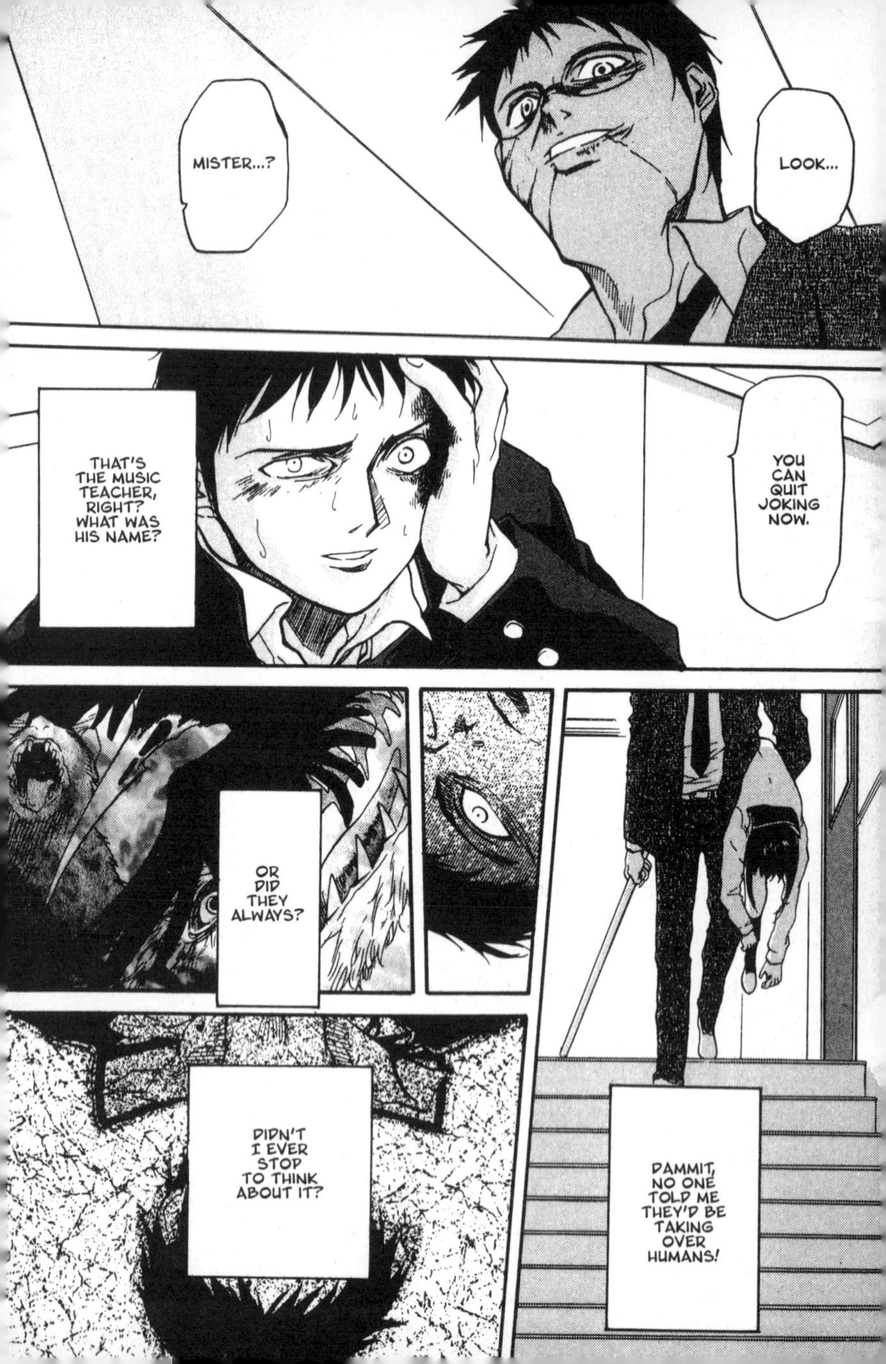
LOOK...
MISTER...?
YOU CAN QUIT JOKING NOW.
THAT'S THE MUSIC TEACHER, RIGHT? WHAT WAS HIS NAME?
DAMMIT, NO ONE TOLD ME THEY'D BE TAKING OVER HUMANS!
OR DID THEY ALWAYS?
DIDN'T I EVER STOP TO THINK ABOUT IT?

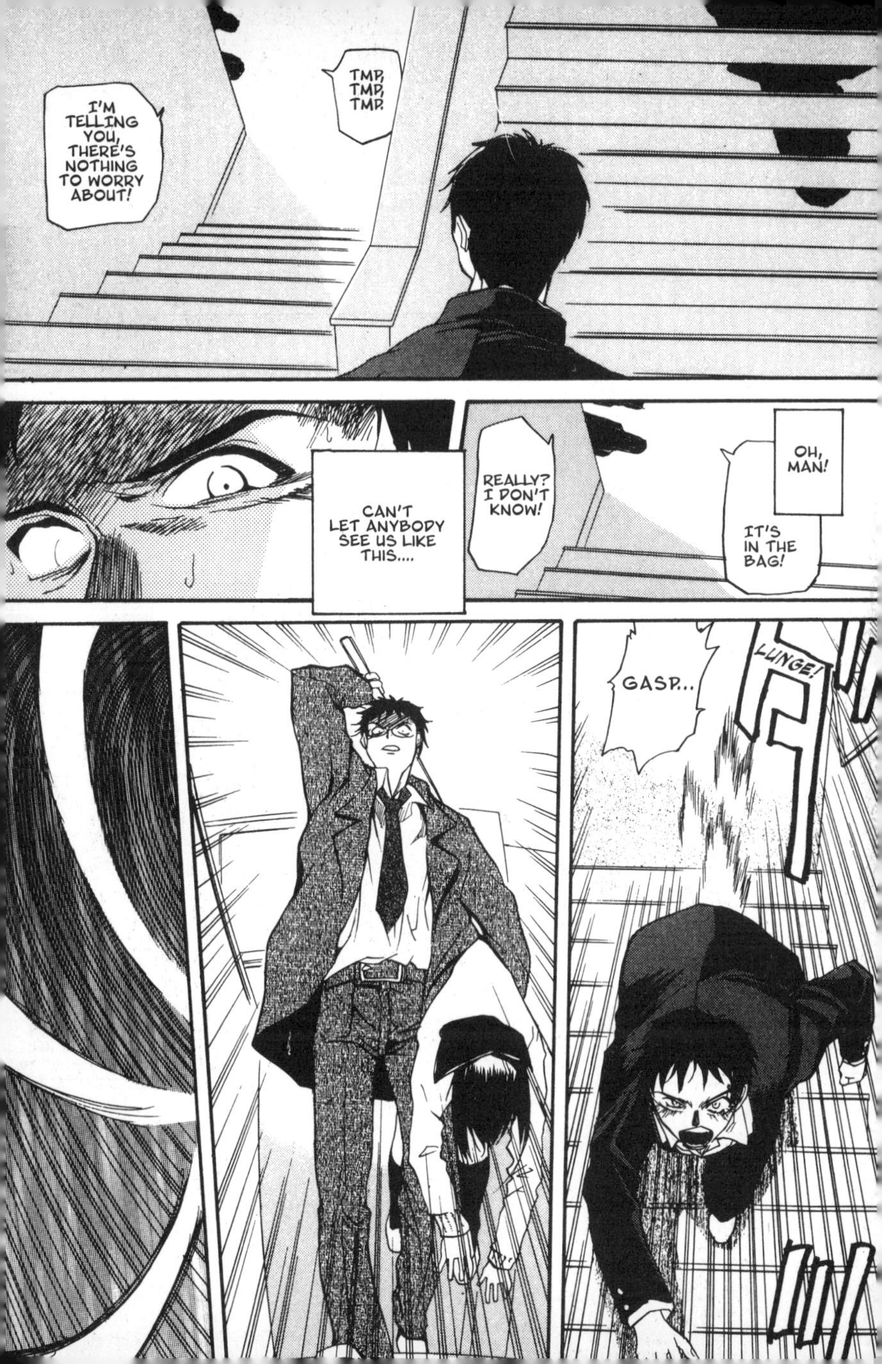
TMP, TMP, TMP.
I'M TELLING YOU, THERE'S NOTHING TO WORRY ABOUT!
OH, MAN!
IT'S IN THE BAG!
REALLY? I DON'T KNOW!
CAN'T LET ANYBODY SEE US LIKE THIS....
LUNGE!
GASP...

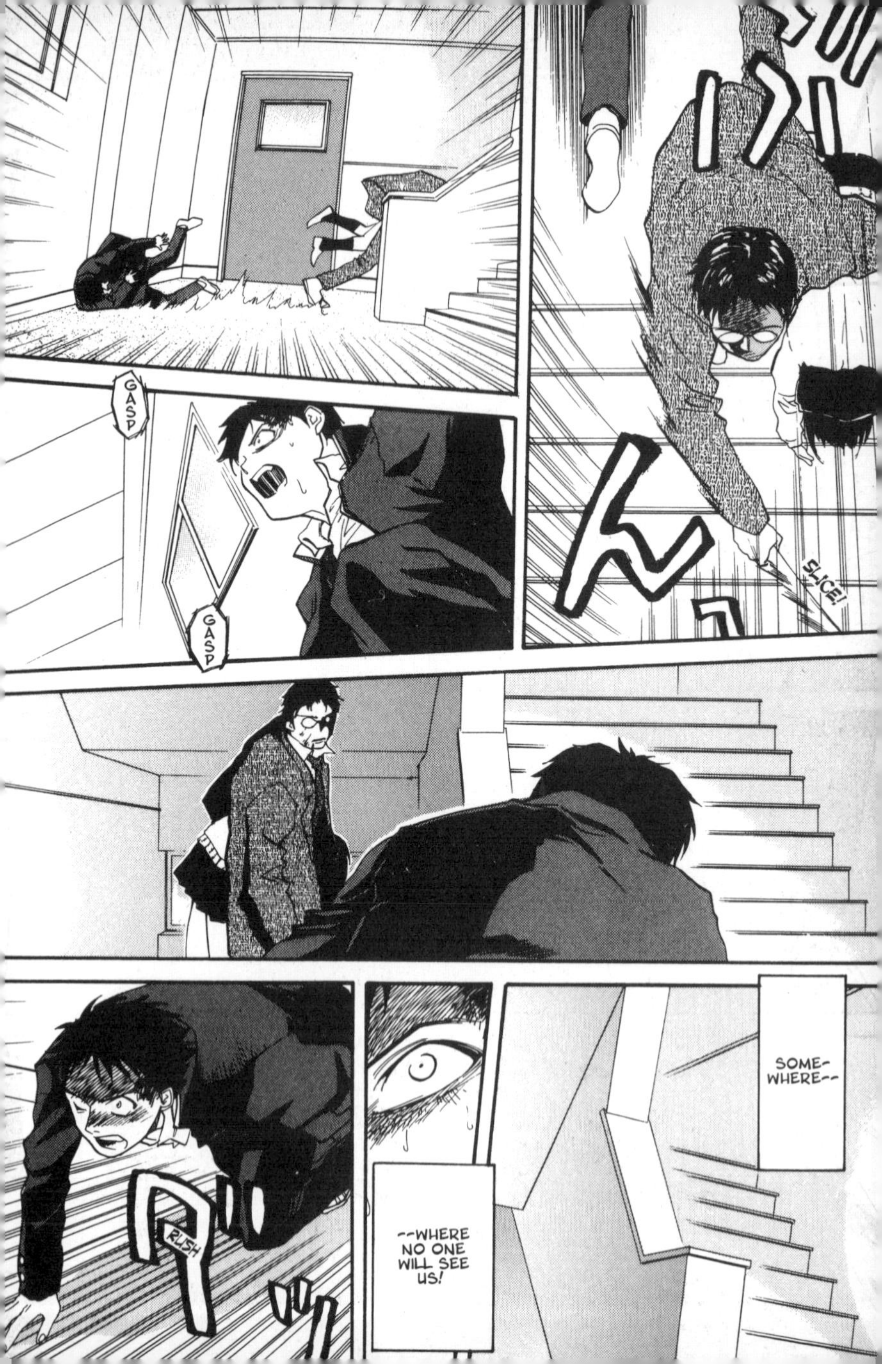
SLICE!
GASP
GASP
SOME-WHERE--
--WHERE NO ONE WILL SEE US!
RUSH

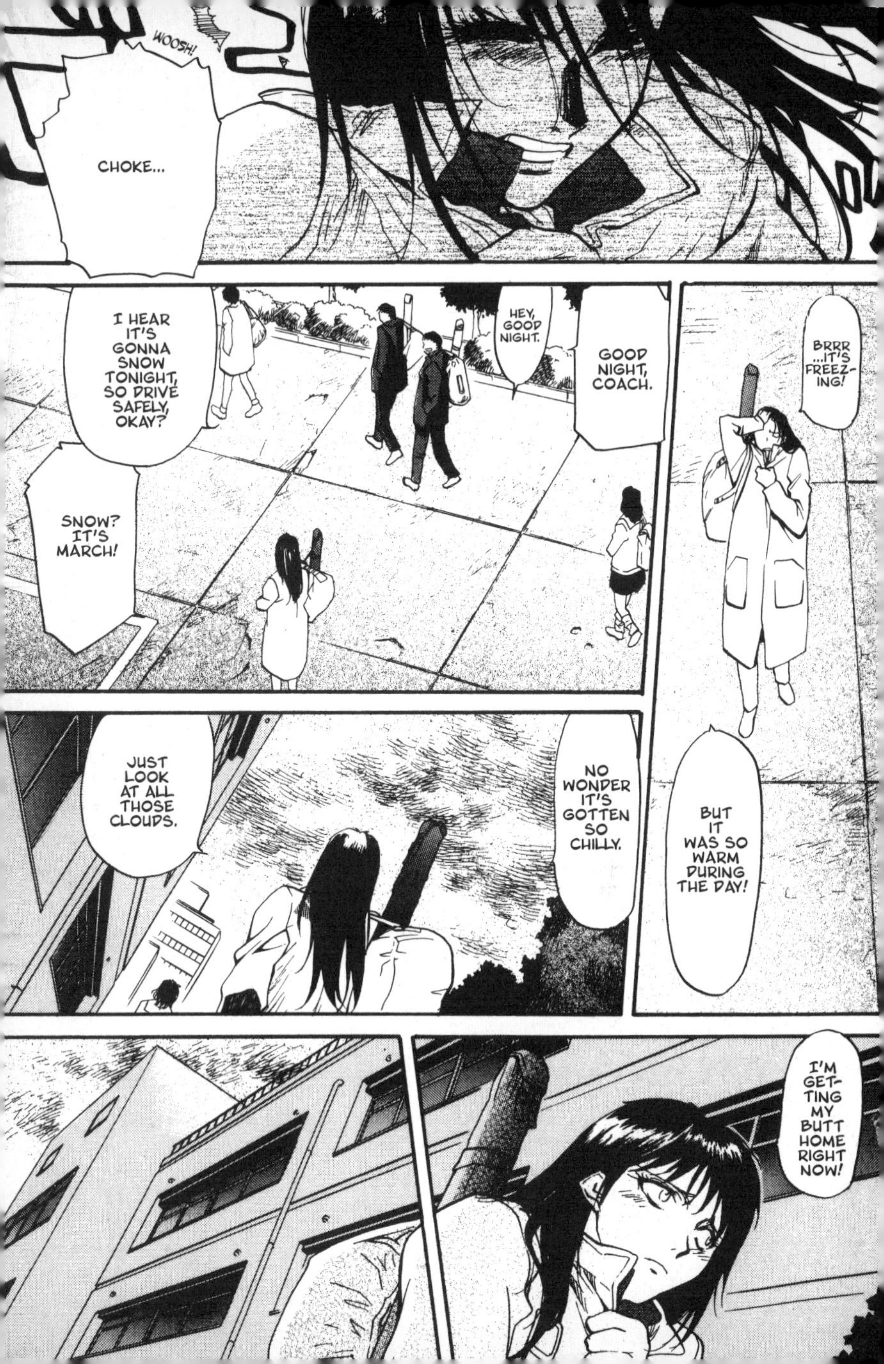
WOOSH!
CHOKE...
BRRR ...IT'S FREEZ-ING!
BUT IT WAS SO WARM DURING THE DAY!
GOOD NIGHT, COACH.
HEY, GOOD NIGHT.
I HEAR IT'S GONNA SNOW TONIGHT, SO DRIVE SAFELY, OKAY?
SNOW? IT'S MARCH!
NO WONDER IT'S GOTTEN SO CHILLY.
JUST LOOK AT ALL THOSE CLOUDS.
I'M GET-TING MY BUTT HOME RIGHT NOW!

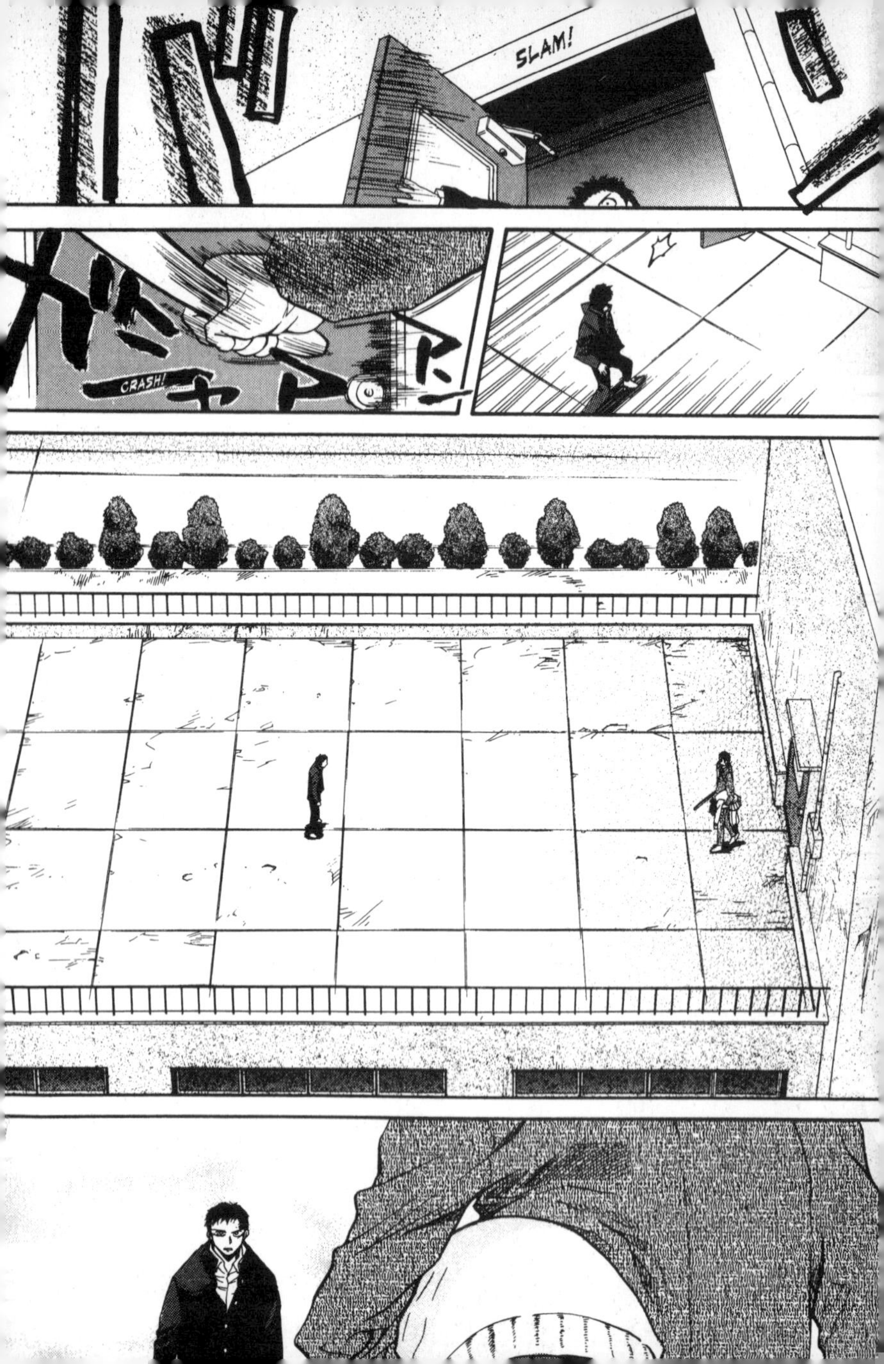
SLAM!
CRASH!

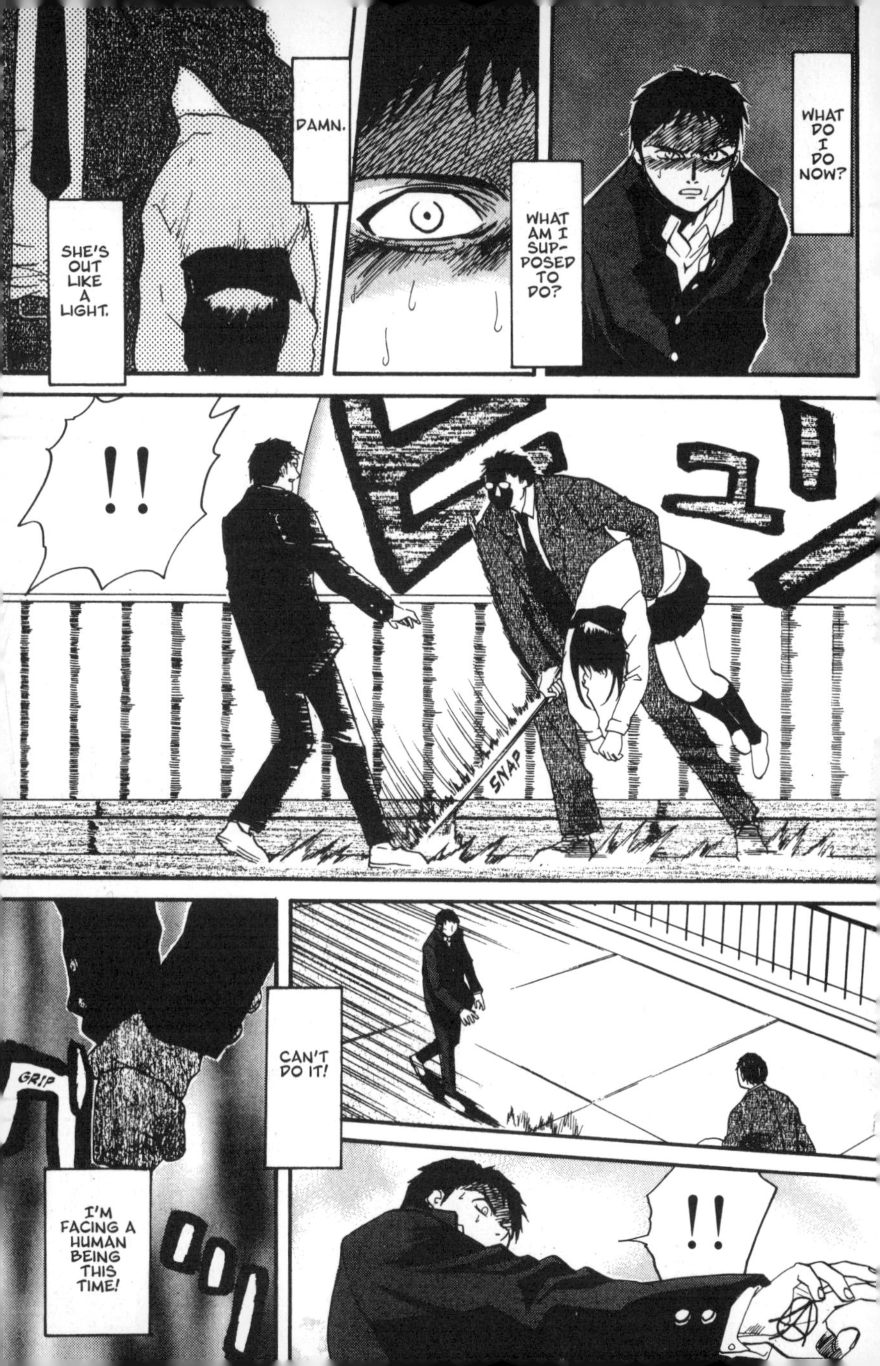
WHAT DO I DO NOW?
WHAT AM I SUP-POSED TO DO?
DAMN.
SHE'S OUT LIKE A LIGHT.
!!
SNAP
CAN'T DO IT!
!!
GRIP
I'M FACING A HUMAN BEING THIS TIME!

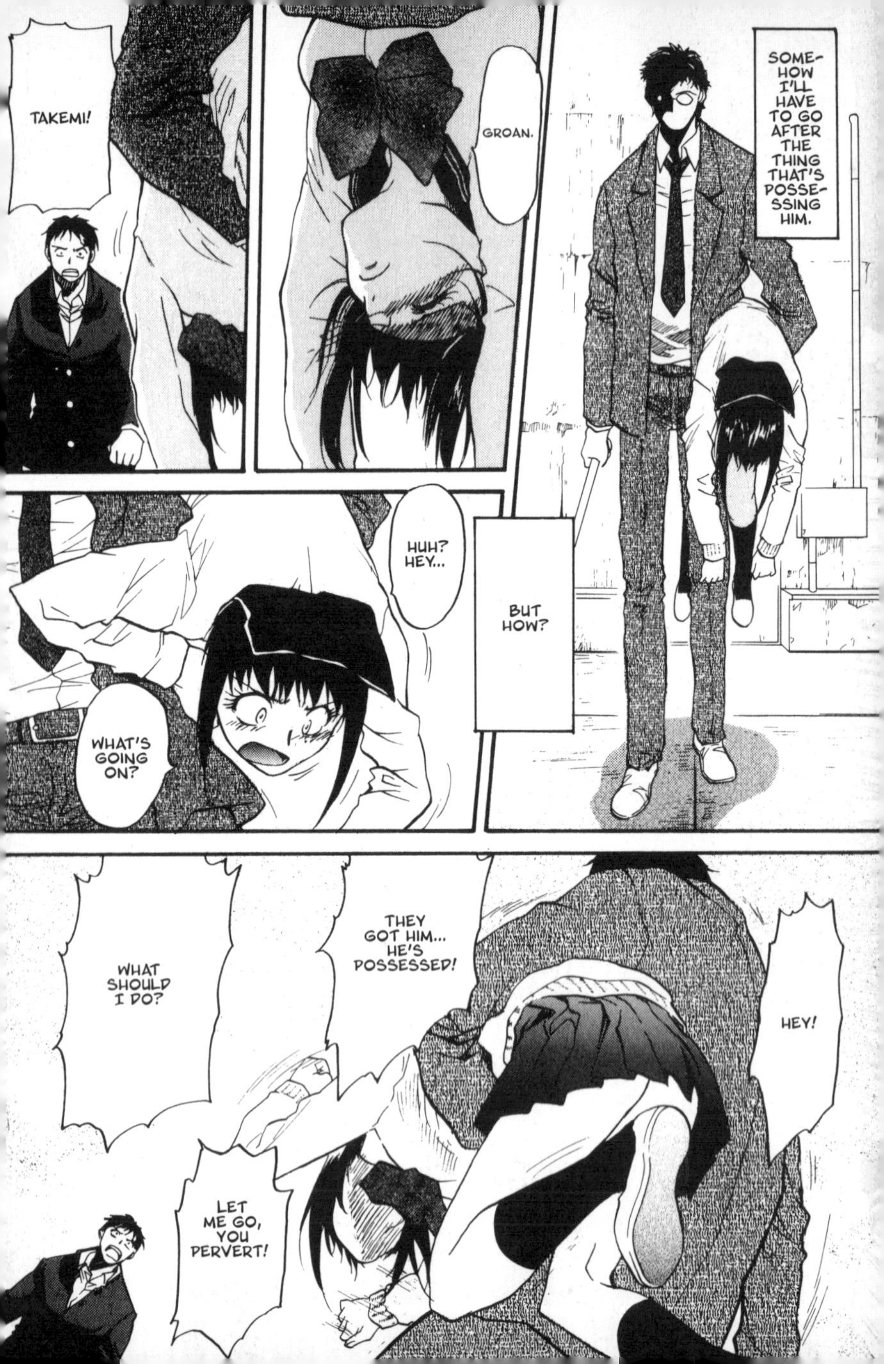
SOMEHOW I'LL HAVE TO GO AFTER THE THING THAT'S POSSESSING HIM.
BUT HOW?
GROAN.
TAKEMI!
HUH? HEY...
WHAT'S GOING ON?
HEY!
THEY GOT HIM... HE'S POSSESSED!
WHAT SHOULD I DO?
LET ME GO, YOU PERVERT!

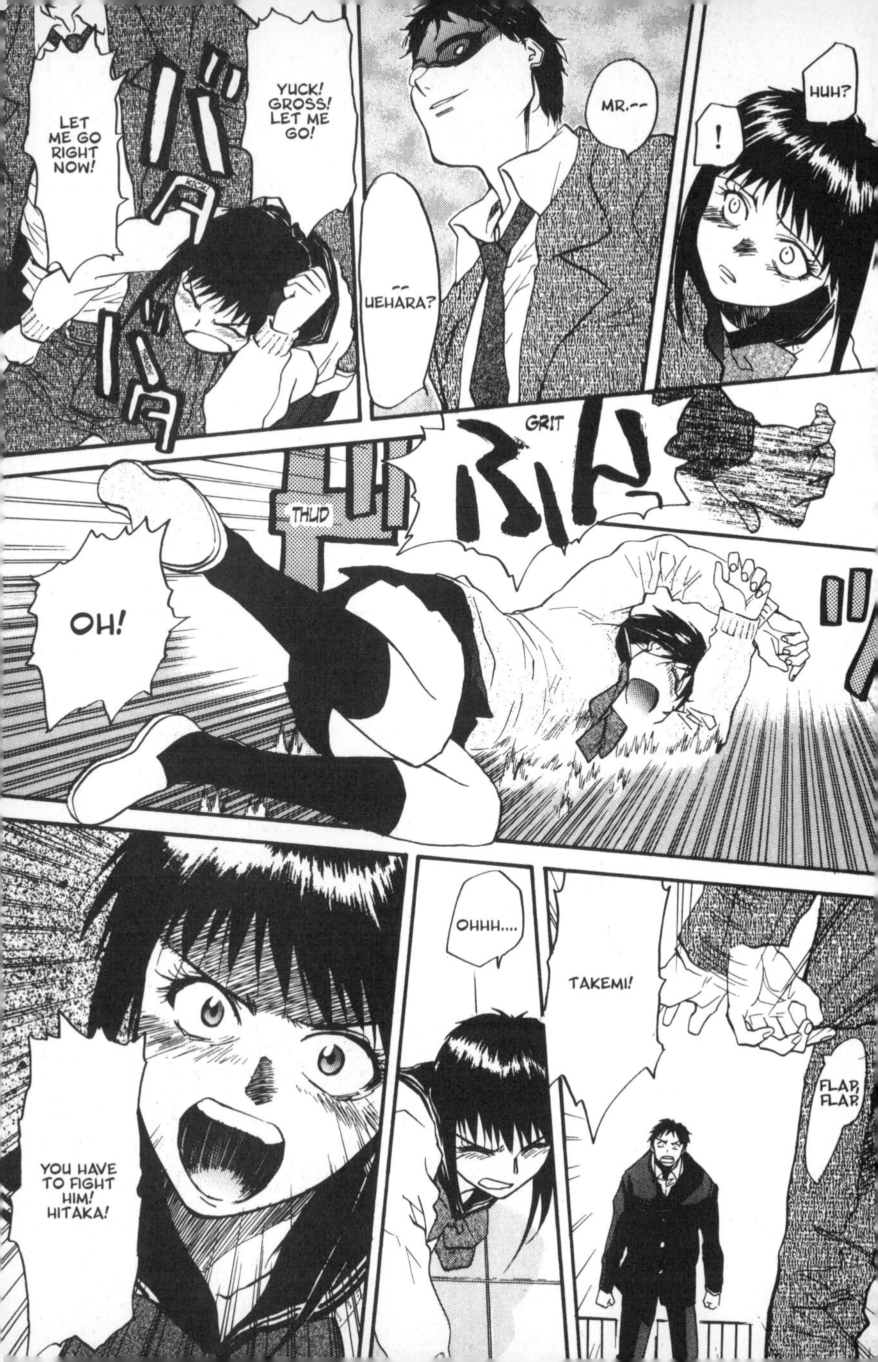
HUH?
!
MR.--
--UEHARA?
YUCK! GROSS! LET ME GO!
LET ME GO RIGHT NOW!
KICK!
GRIT
THUD
OH!
FLAP, FLAP.
OHHH....
TAKEMI!
YOU HAVE TO FIGHT HIM! HITAKA!

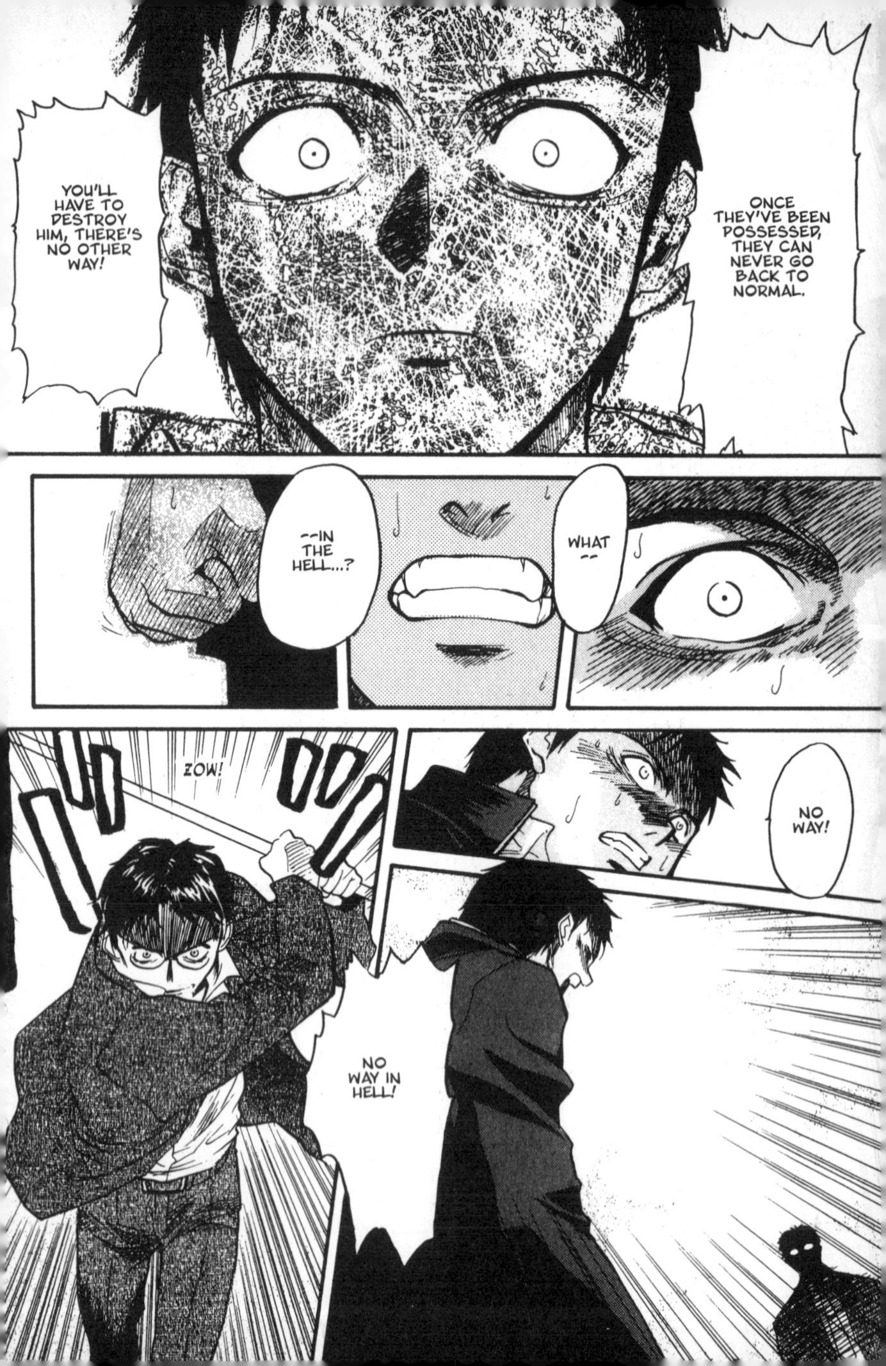
ONCE THEY'VE BEEN POSSESSED, THEY CAN NEVER GO BACK TO NORMAL.
YOU'LL HAVE TO DESTROY HIM, THERE'S NO OTHER WAY!
WHAT --
--IN THE HELL...?
NO WAY!
ZOW!
NO WAY IN HELL!

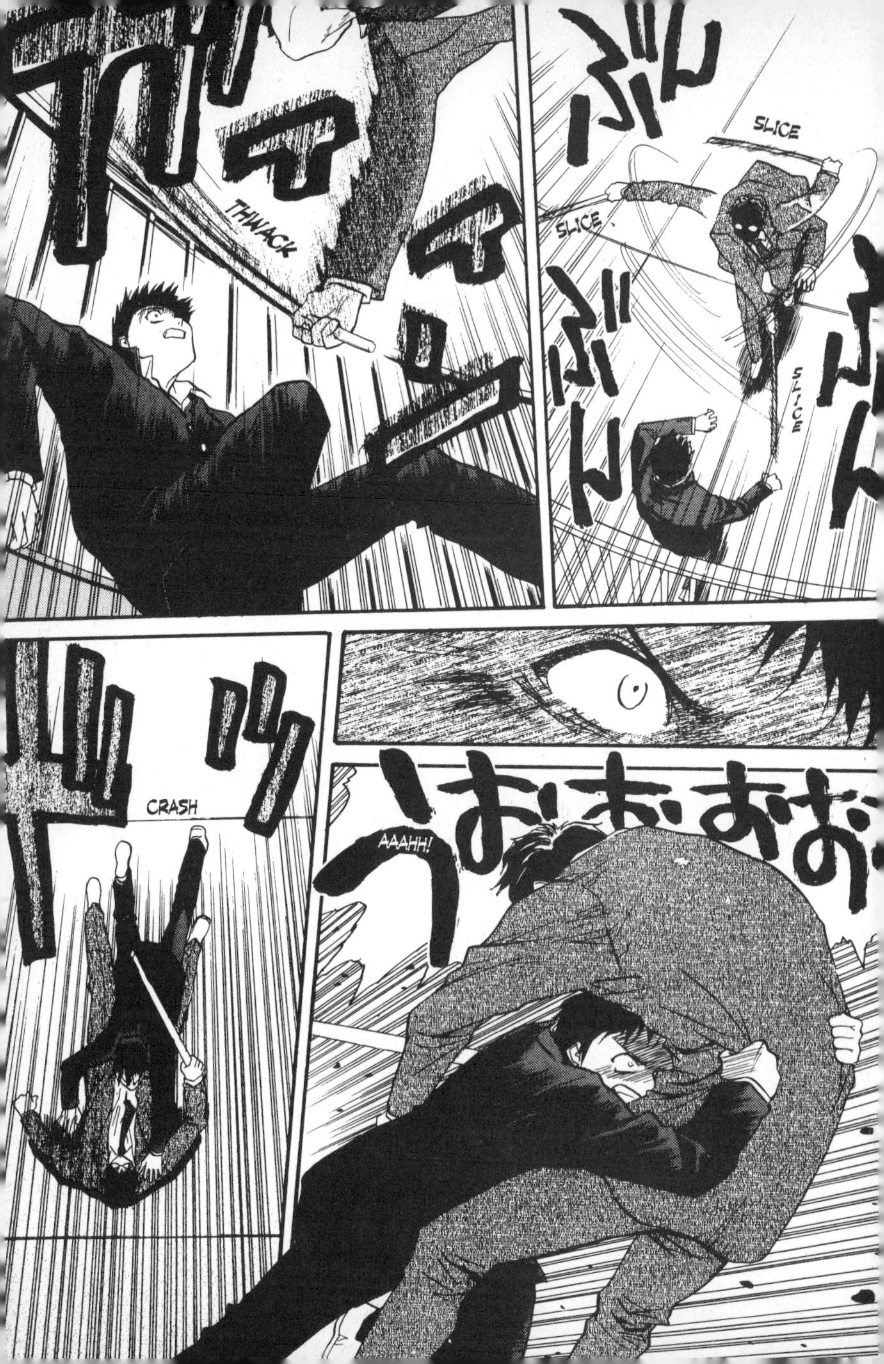
SLICE
SLICE
SLICE
THWACK
AAAHH!
CRASH

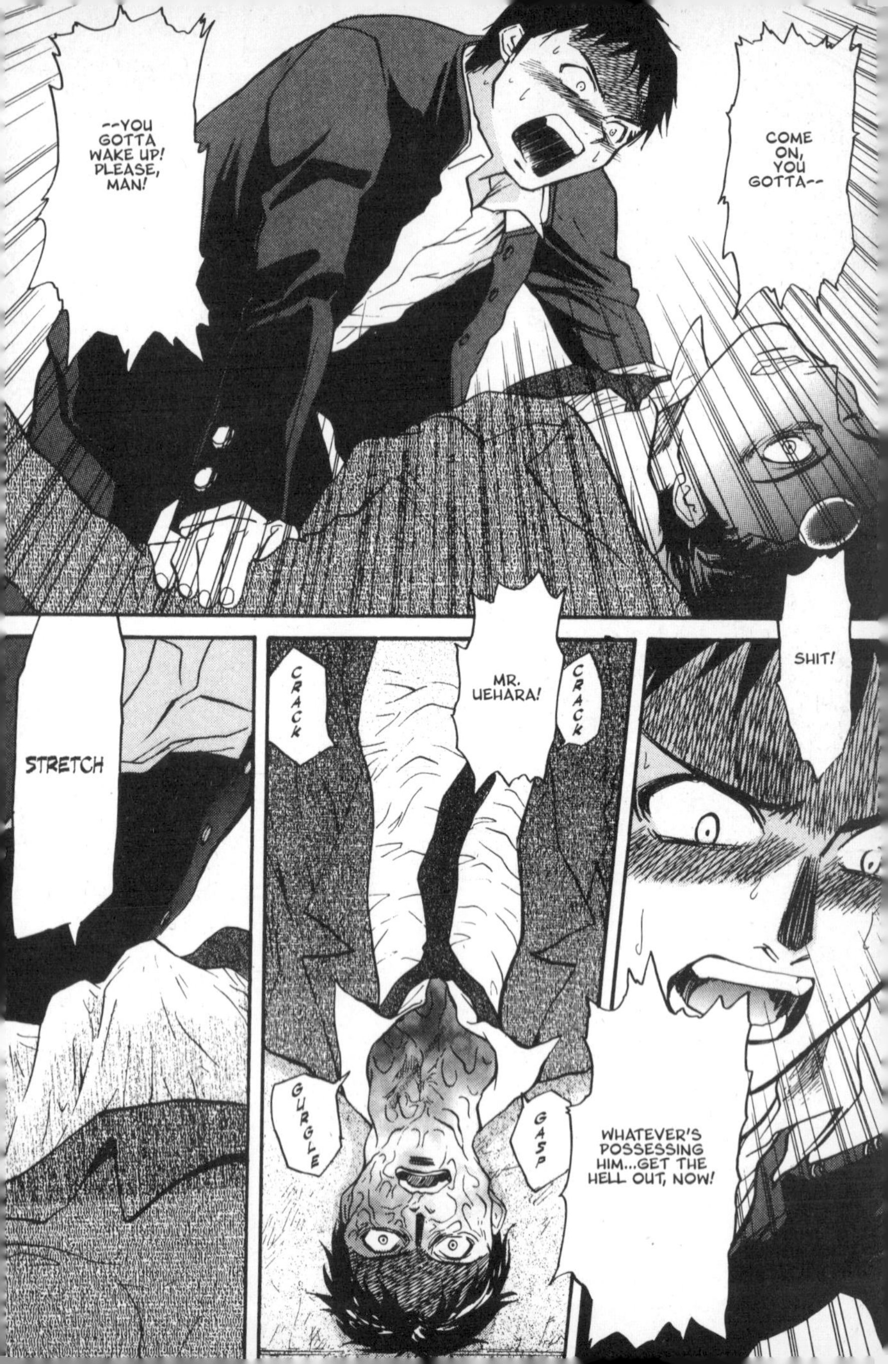
COME ON, YOU GOTTA--
--YOU GOTTA WAKE UP! PLEASE, MAN!
SHIT!
WHATEVER'S POSSESSING HIM...GET THE HELL OUT, NOW!
CRACK
MR. UEHARA!
CRACK
GASP
GURGLE
STRETCH

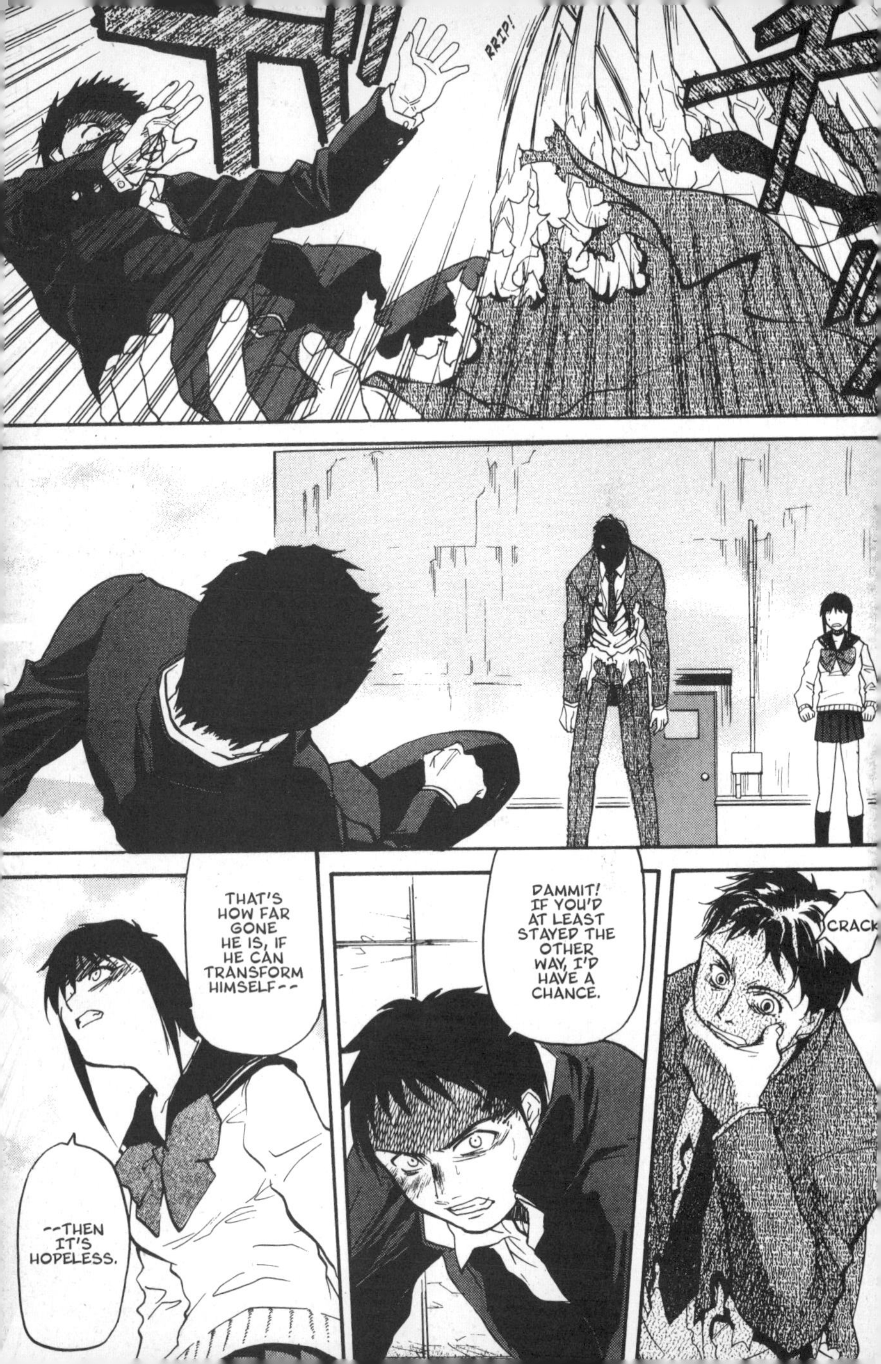
RRIP!
CRACK
DAMMIT! IF YOU'D AT LEAST STAYED THE OTHER WAY, I'D HAVE A CHANCE.
THAT'S HOW FAR GONE HE IS, IF HE CAN TRANSFORM HIMSELF--
--THEN IT'S HOPELESS.

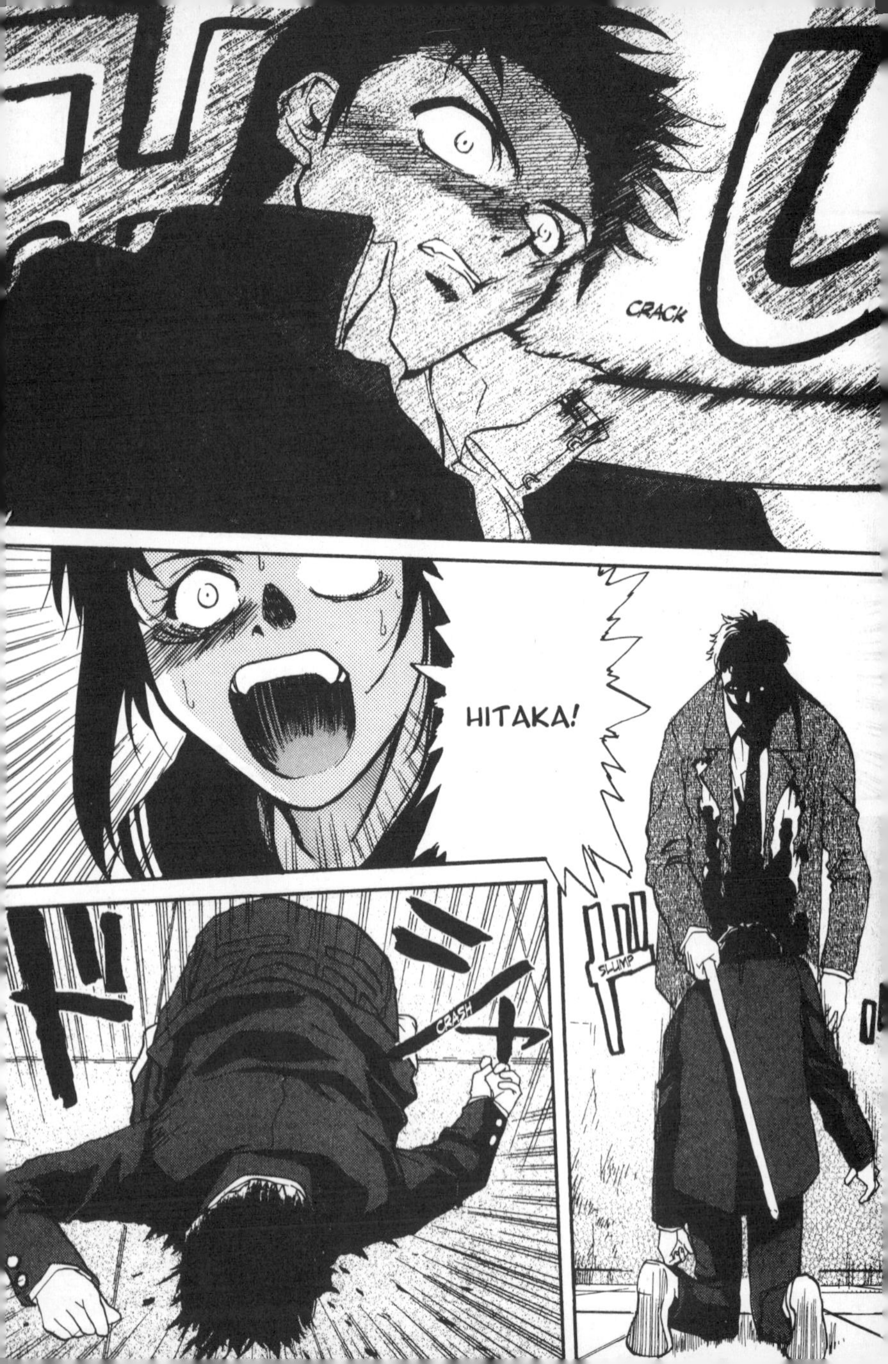
CRACK
HITAKA!
SLUMP
CRASH

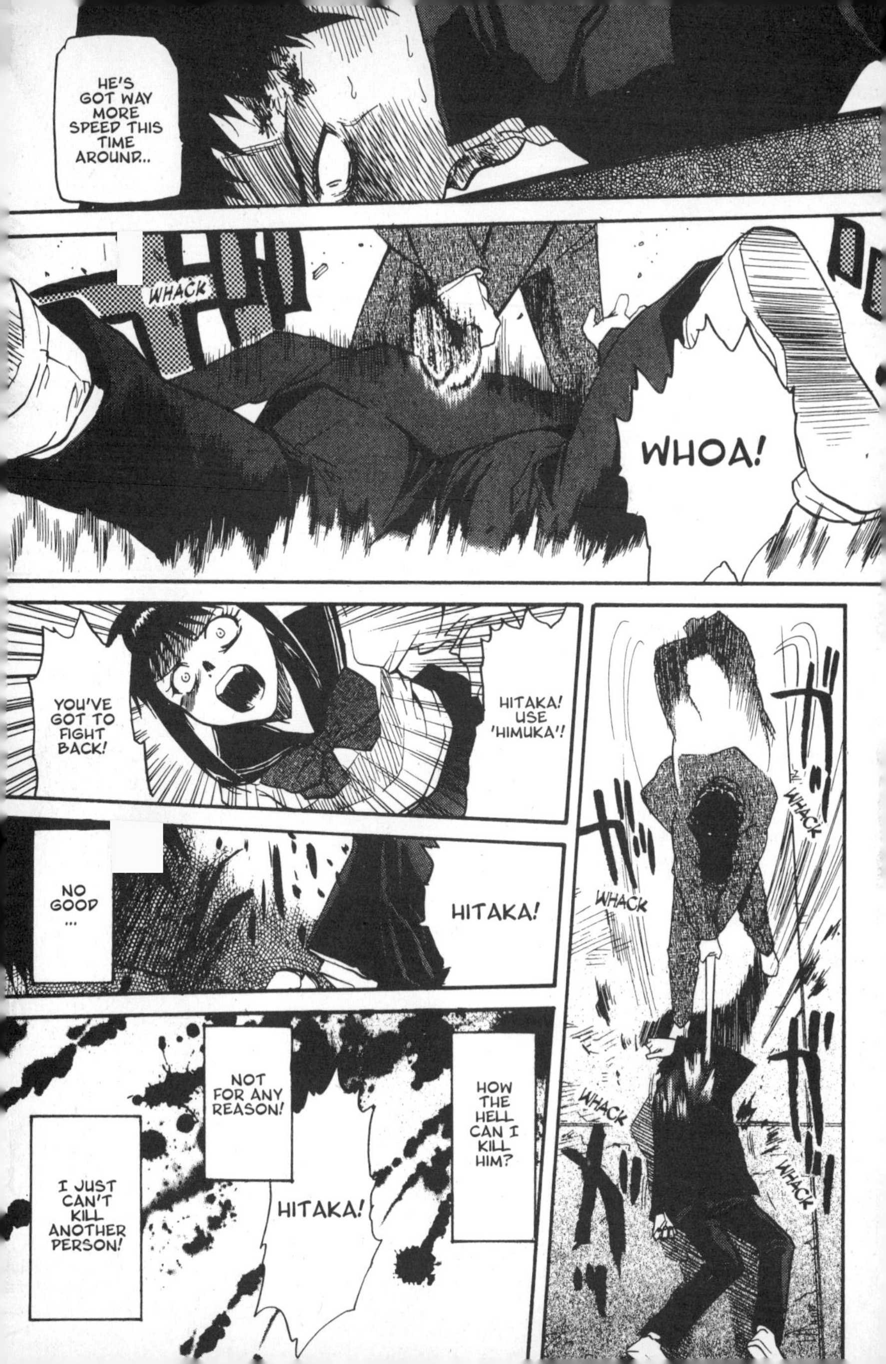
HE'S GOT WAY MORE SPEED THIS TIME AROUND...
WHOA!
WHACK
WHACK
WHACK
WHACK
WHACK
HITAKA! USE 'HIMUKA'!
YOU'VE GOT TO FIGHT BACK!
HITAKA!
NO GOOD ...
HOW THE HELL CAN I KILL HIM?
NOT FOR ANY REASON!
HITAKA!
I JUST CAN'T KILL ANOTHER PERSON!

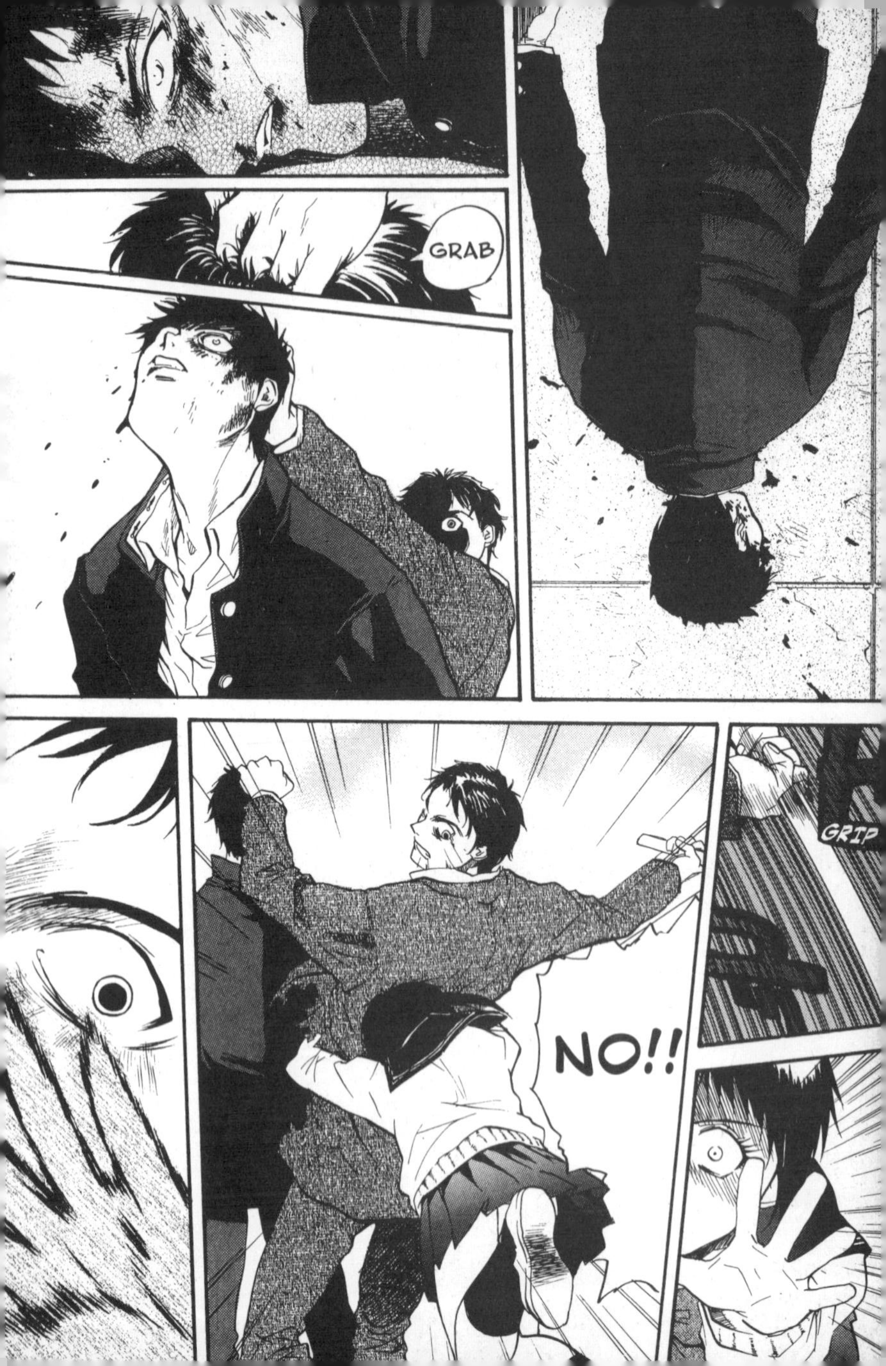
GRAB
GRIP
NO!!

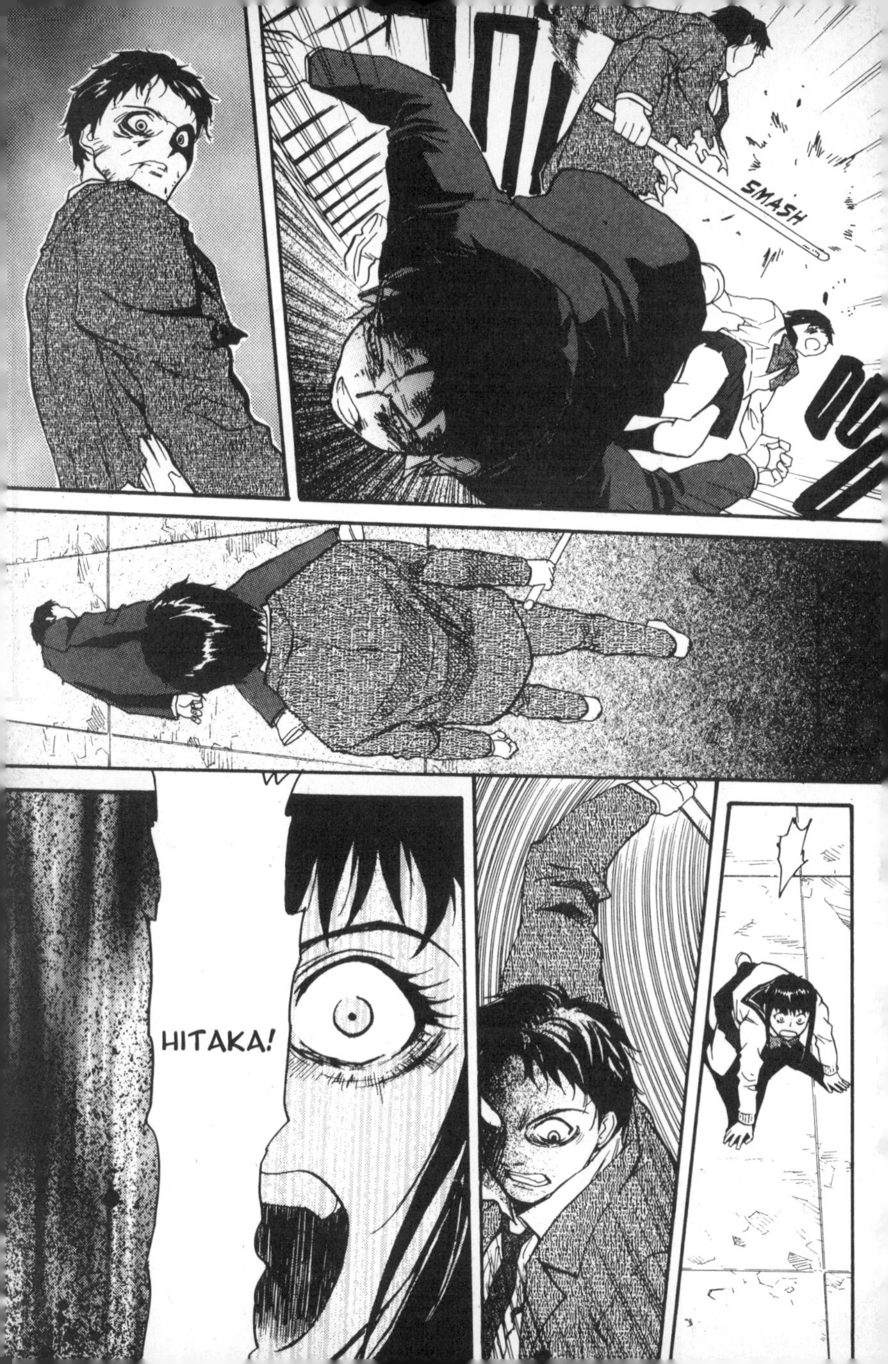
SMASH
HITAKA!

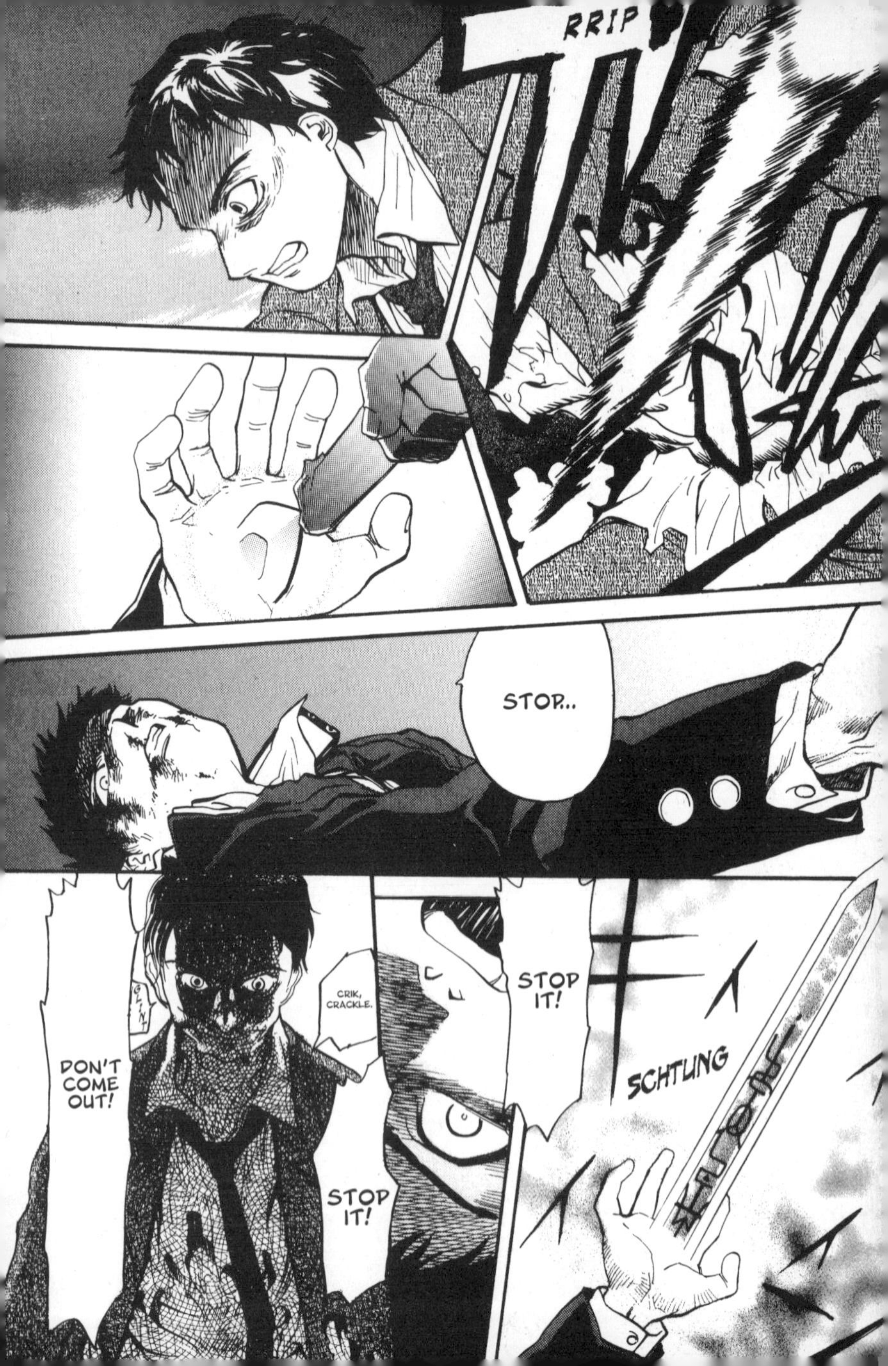
RRIP
STOP...
SCHTUNG
STOP IT!
CRIK, CRACKLE.
GLINT
DON'T COME OUT!
STOP IT!

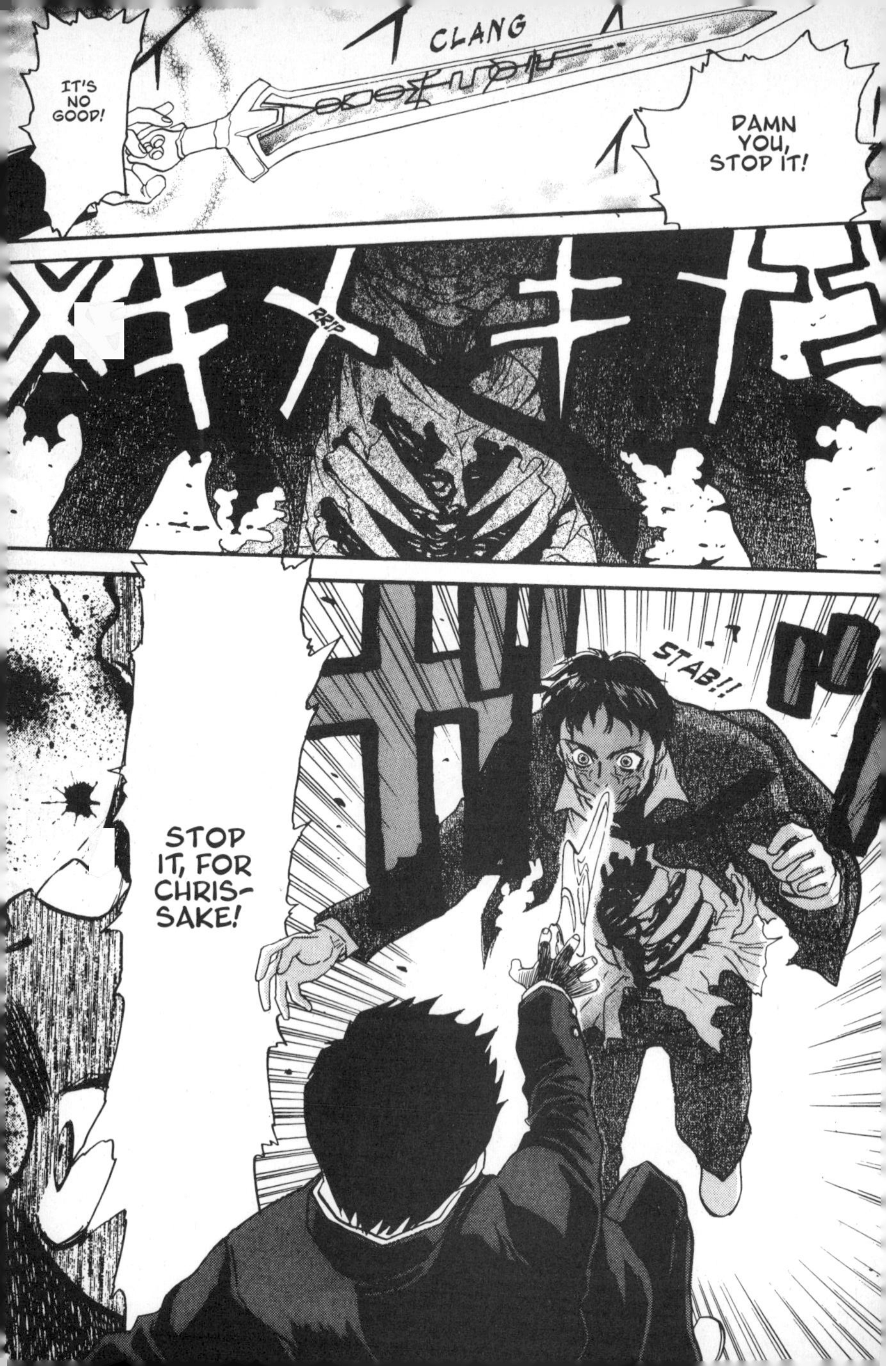
DAMN YOU, STOP IT!
CLANG
IT'S NO GOOD!
RRIP
STAB!!
STOP IT, FOR CHRIS-SAKE!

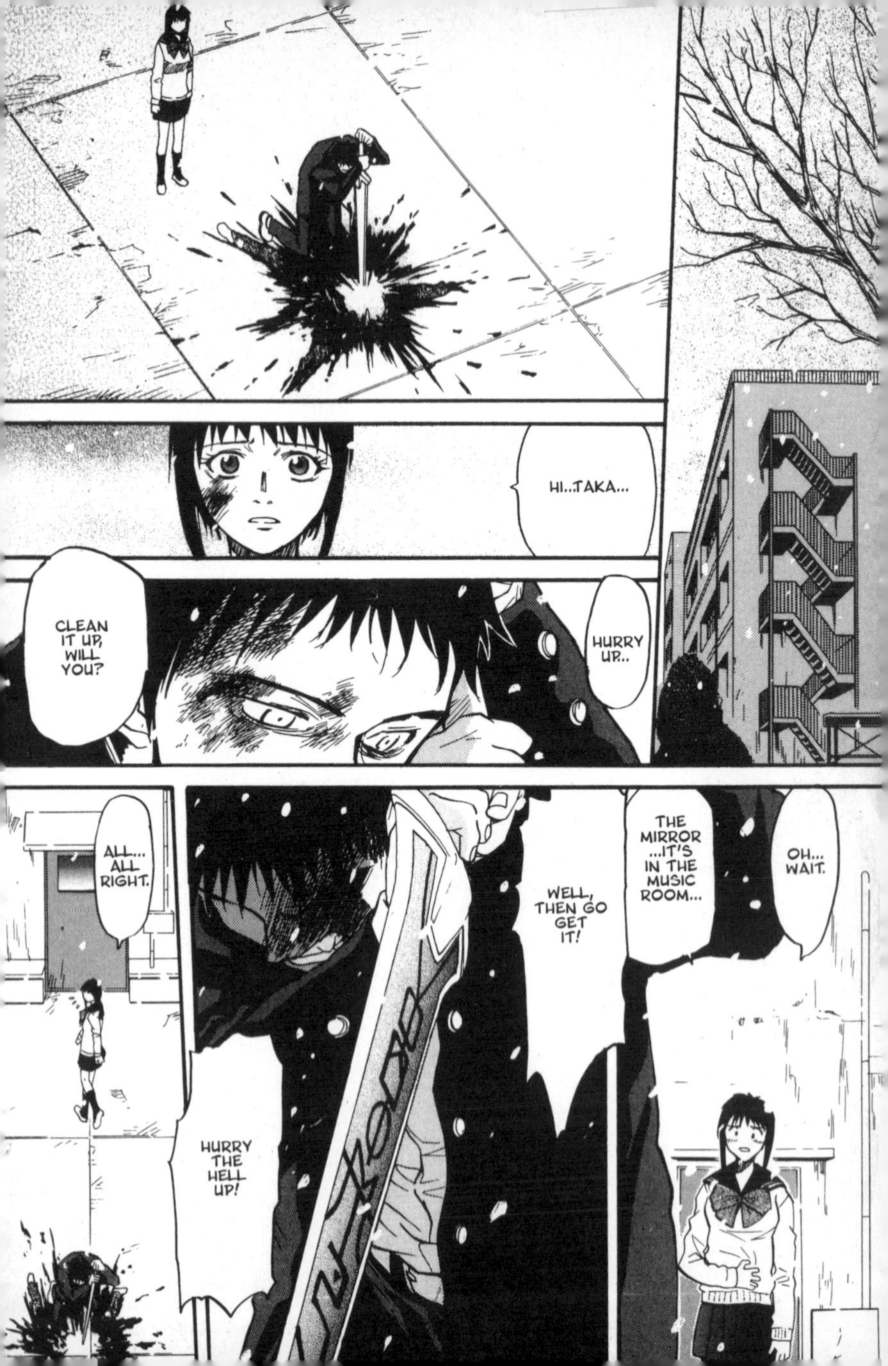
HI...TAKA...
HURRY UP...
CLEAN IT UP, WILL YOU?
OH... WAIT.
THE MIRROR ...IT'S IN THE MUSIC ROOM...
WELL, THEN GO GET IT!
HURRY THE HELL UP!
ALL... ALL RIGHT.

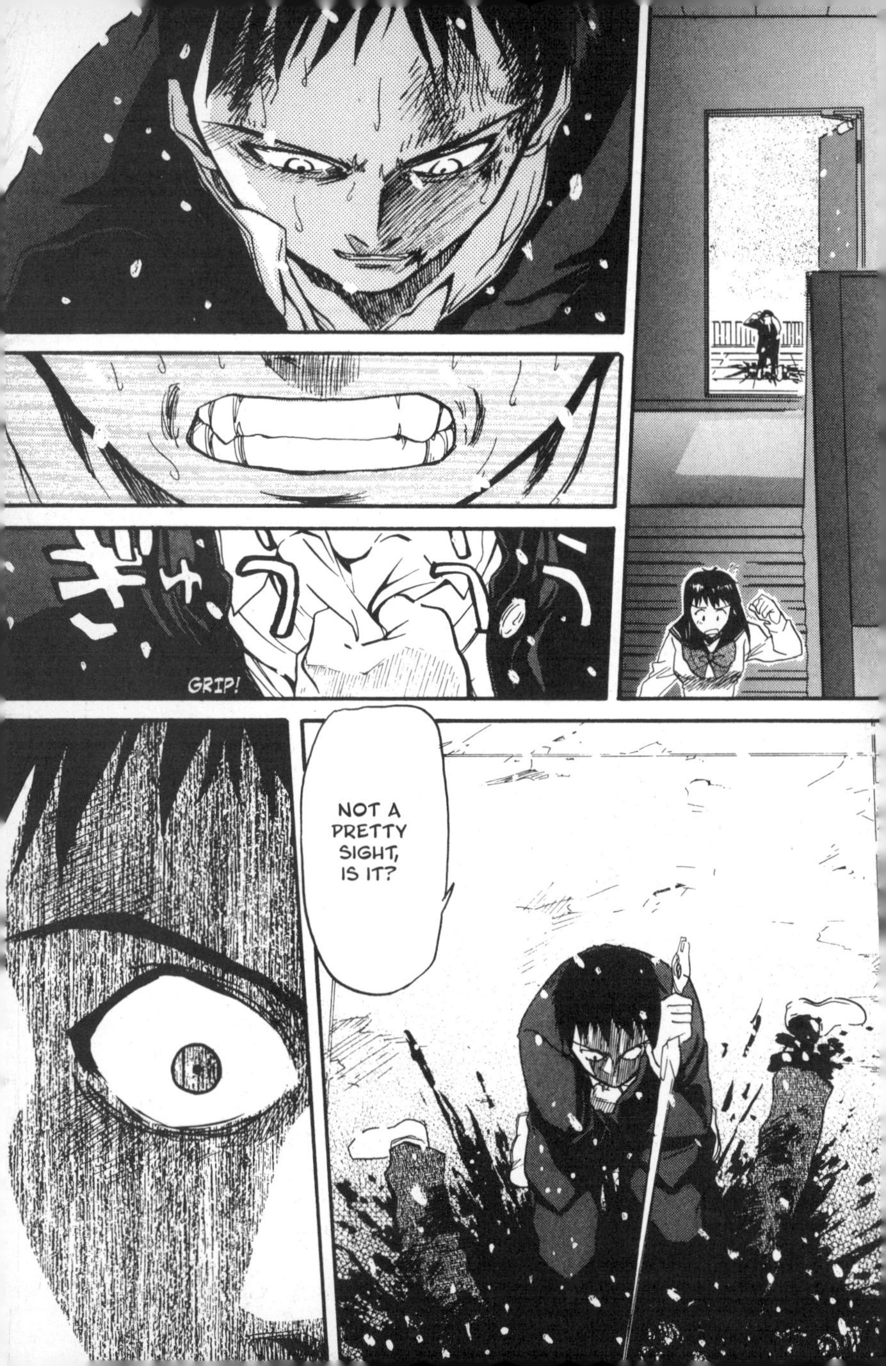
ぎゅ
GRIP!
NOT A PRETTY SIGHT, IS IT?

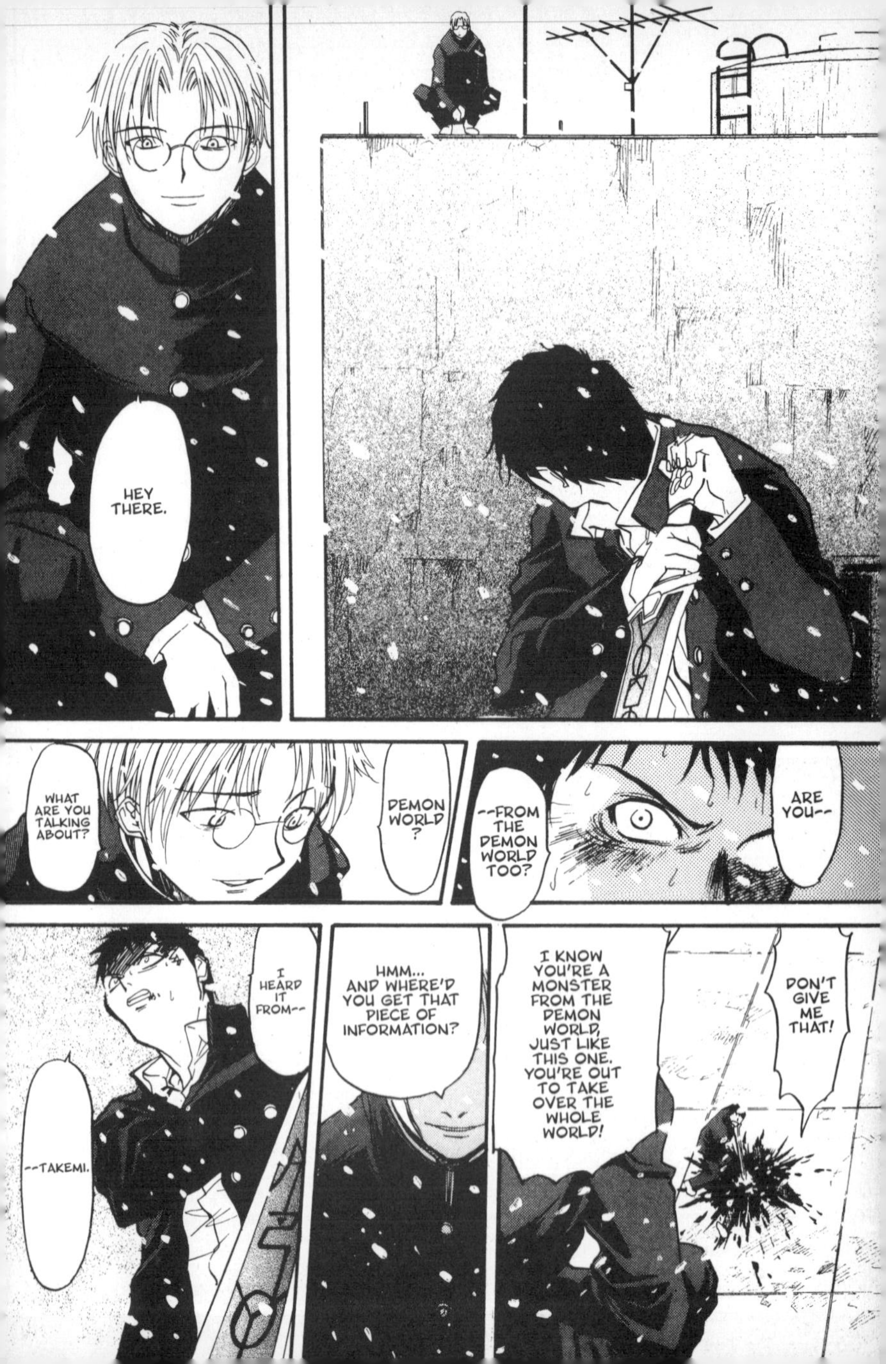
HEY THERE.
ARE YOU--
--FROM THE DEMON WORLD TOO?
DEMON WORLD?
WHAT ARE YOU TALKING ABOUT?
DON'T GIVE ME THAT!
I KNOW YOU'RE A MONSTER FROM THE DEMON WORLD, JUST LIKE THIS ONE. YOU'RE OUT TO TAKE OVER THE WHOLE WORLD!
HMM... AND WHERE'D YOU GET THAT PIECE OF INFORMATION?
I HEARD IT FROM--
--TAKEMI.

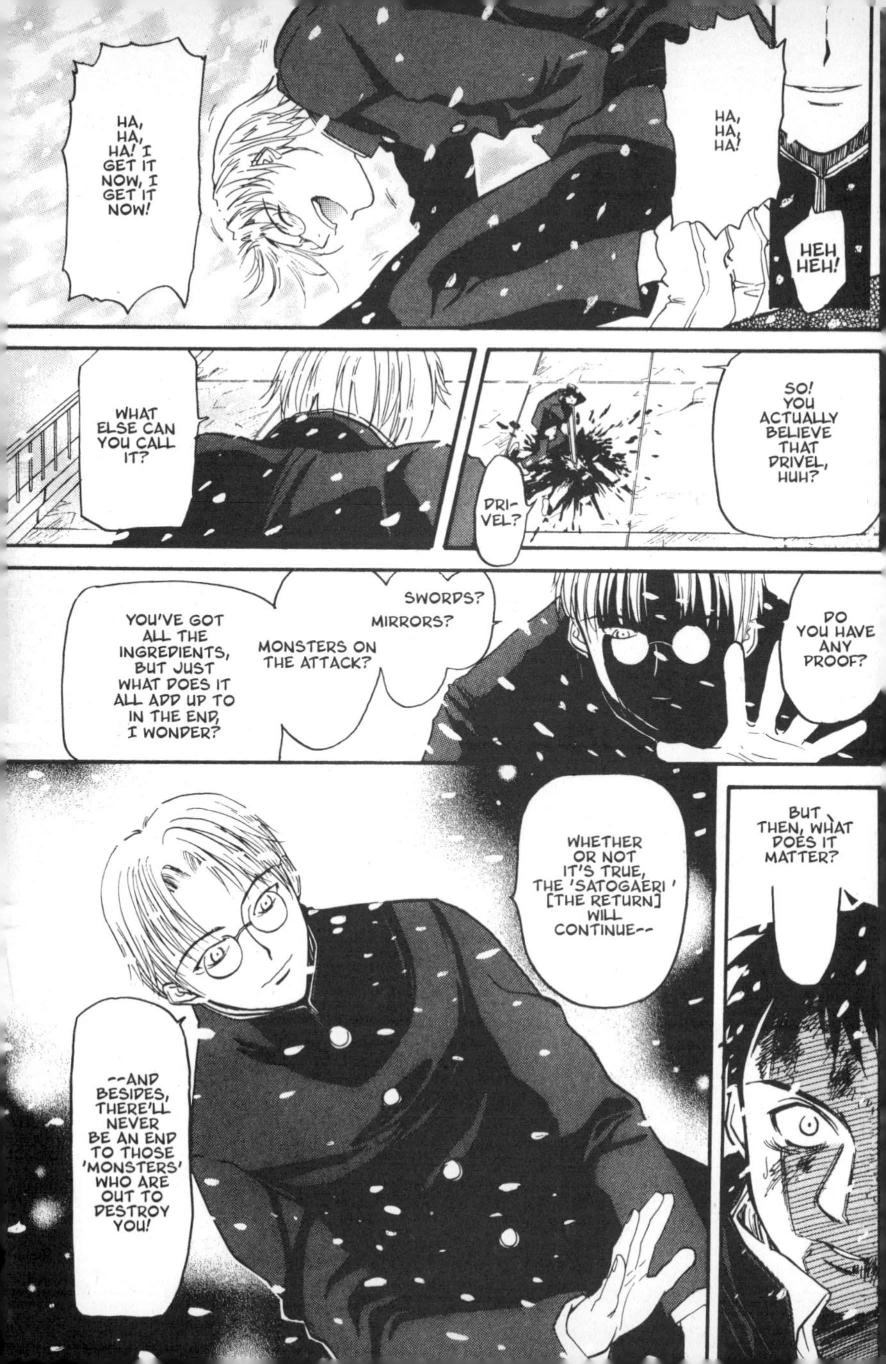
HA, HA, HA!
HEH HEH!
HA, HA, HA! I GET IT NOW, I GET IT NOW!
SO! YOU ACTUALLY BELIEVE THAT DRIVEL, HUH?
DRI-VEL?
WHAT ELSE CAN YOU CALL IT?
DO YOU HAVE ANY PROOF?
SWORDS? MIRRORS? MONSTERS ON THE ATTACK?
YOU'VE GOT ALL THE INGREDIENTS, BUT JUST WHAT DOES IT ALL ADD UP TO IN THE END, I WONDER?
BUT THEN, WHAT DOES IT MATTER?
WHETHER OR NOT IT'S TRUE, THE 'SATOGAERI' [THE RETURN] WILL CONTINUE--
--AND BESIDES, THERE'LL NEVER BE AN END TO THOSE 'MONSTERS' WHO ARE OUT TO DESTROY YOU!

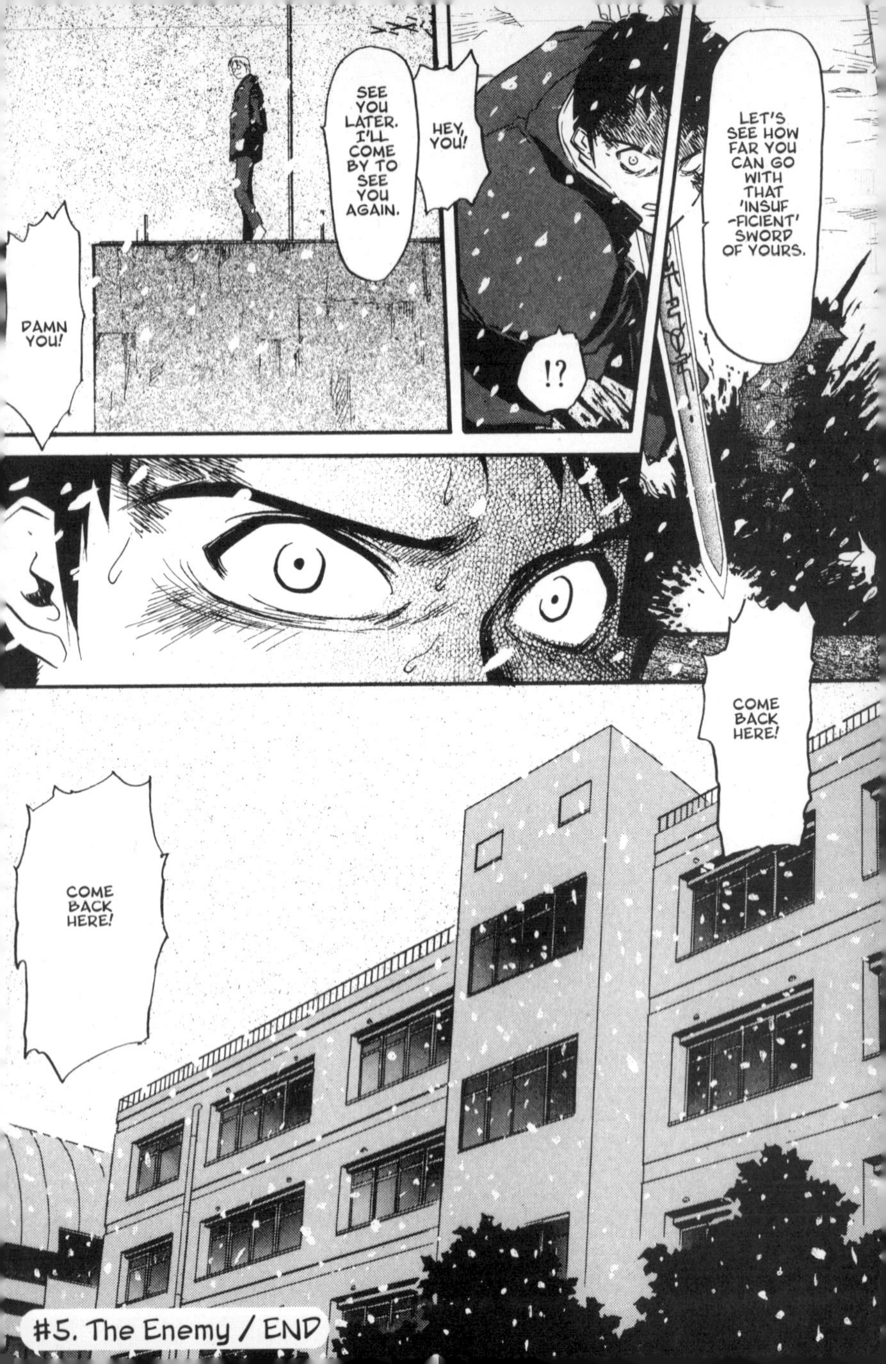
LET'S SEE HOW FAR YOU CAN GO WITH THAT 'INSUF -FICIENT' SWORD OF YOURS.
!?
HEY, YOU!
SEE YOU LATER. I'LL COME BY TO SEE YOU AGAIN.
DAMN YOU!
COME BACK HERE!
COME BACK HERE!
#5. The Enemy / END

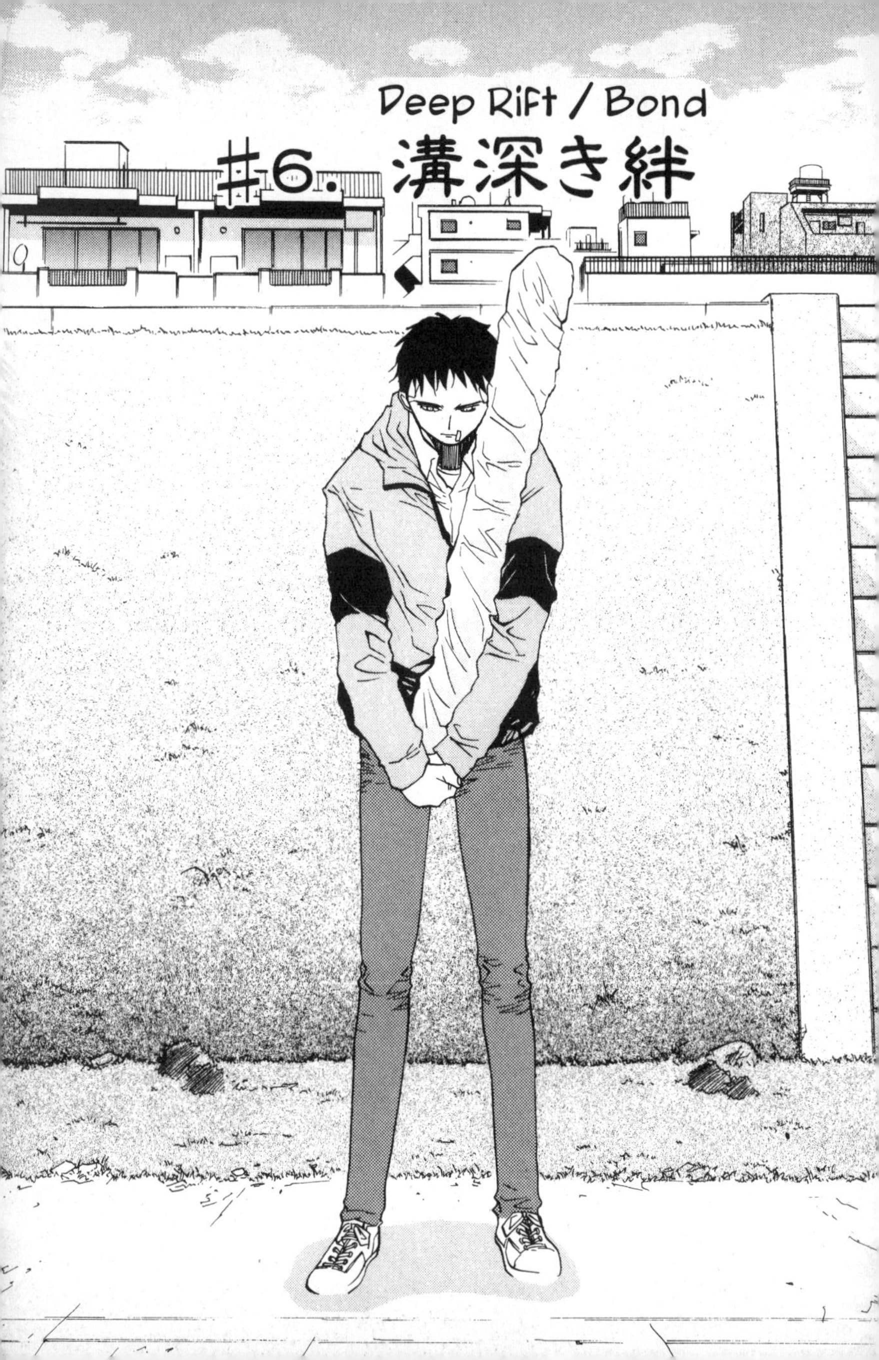
Deep Rift / Bond
#6. 溝深き絆

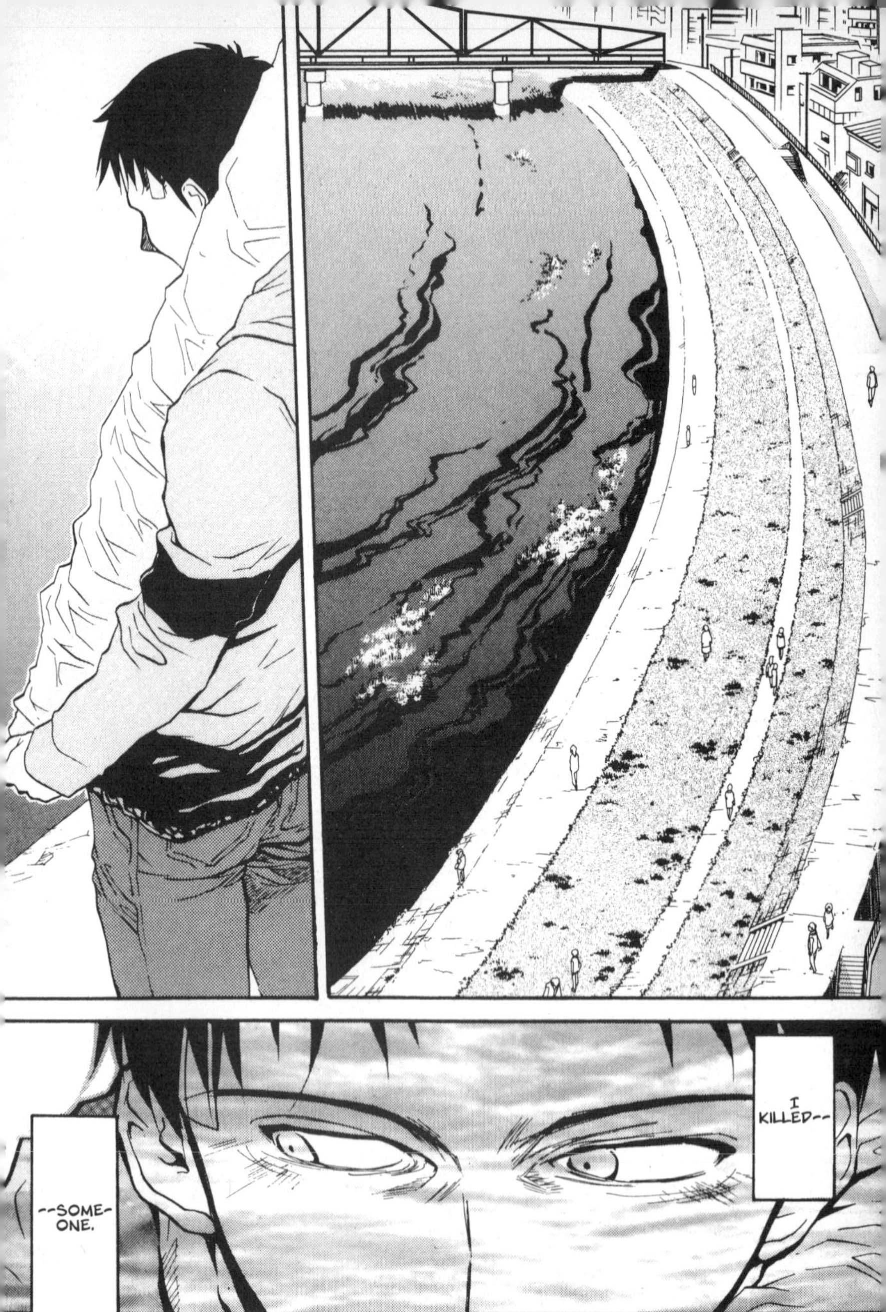
I KILLED--
--SOME-ONE.

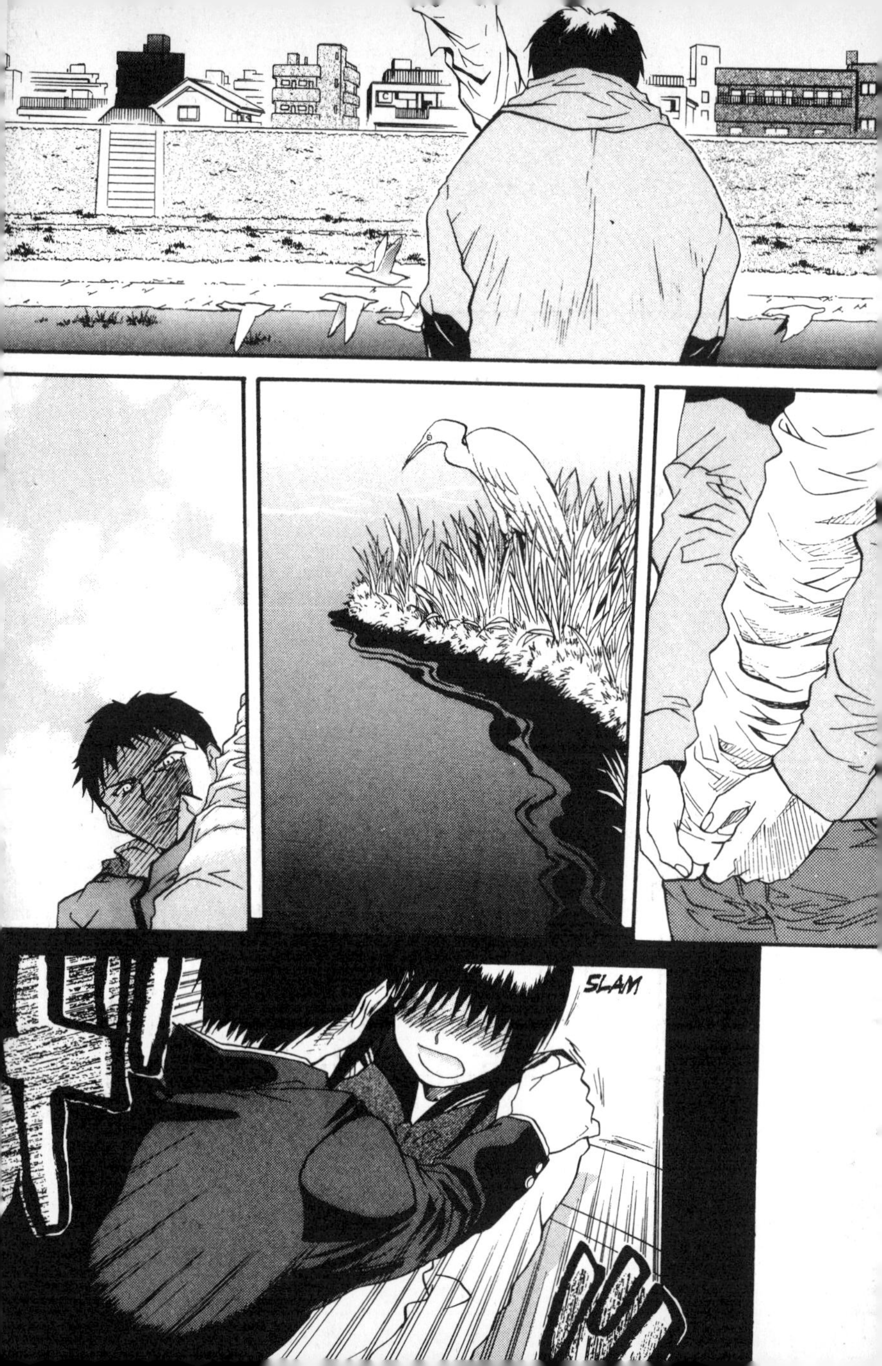
SLAM

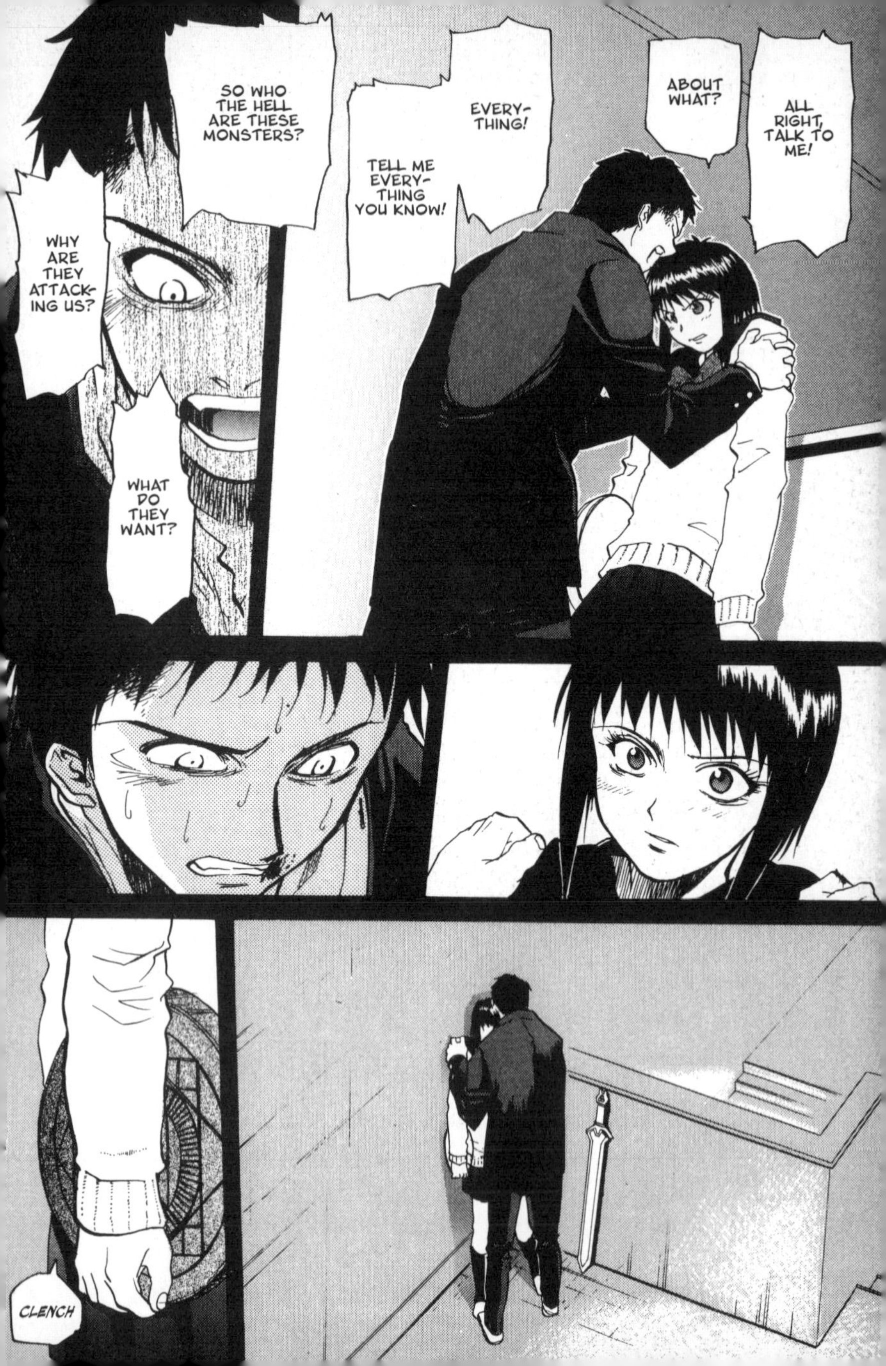
ALL RIGHT, TALK TO ME!
ABOUT WHAT?
EVERY-THING!
TELL ME EVERY-THING YOU KNOW!
SO WHO THE HELL ARE THESE MONSTERS?
WHY ARE THEY ATTACK-ING US?
WHAT DO THEY WANT?
CLENCH

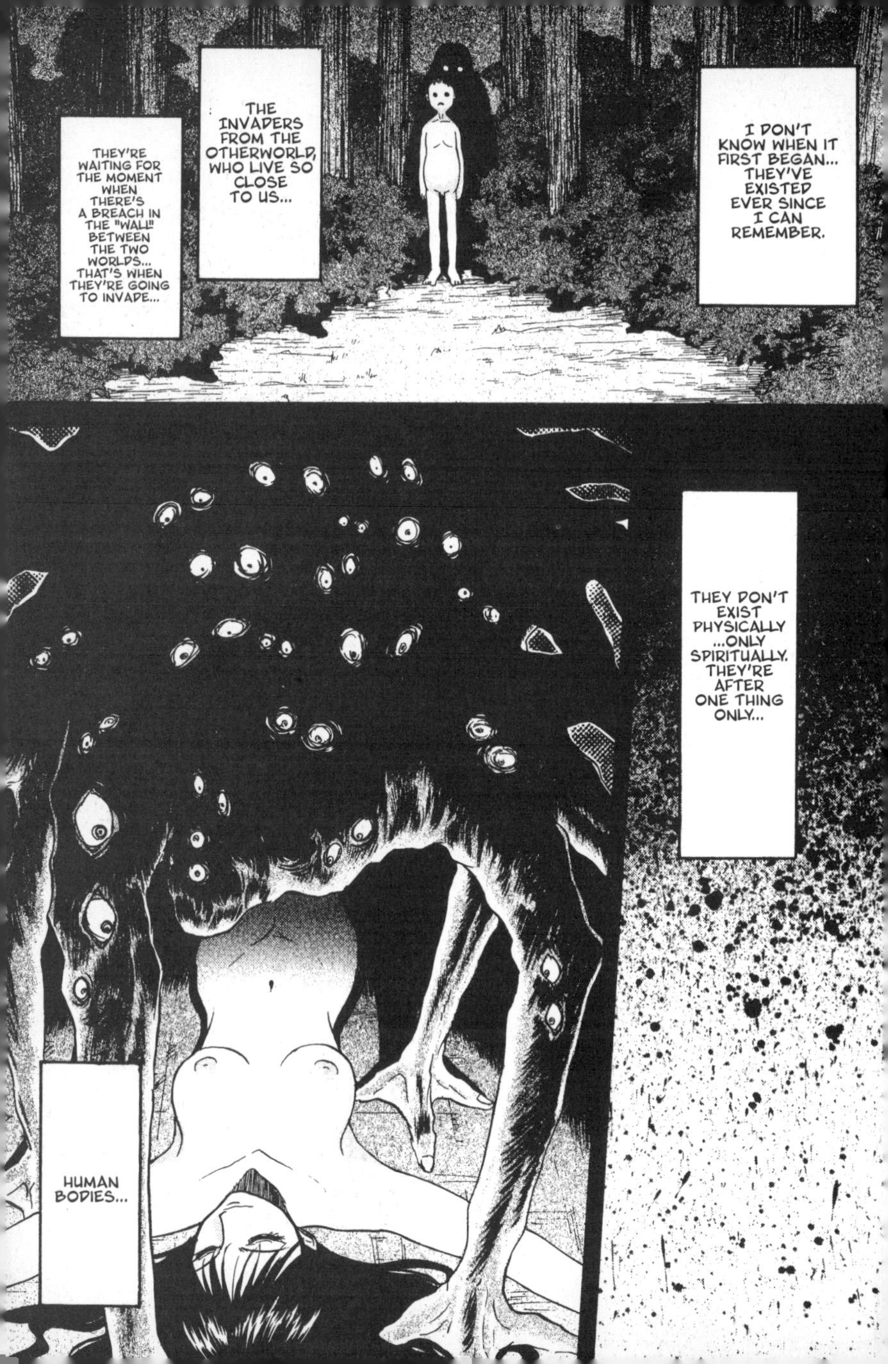
I DON'T KNOW WHEN IT FIRST BEGAN... THEY'VE EXISTED EVER SINCE I CAN REMEMBER.
THE INVADERS FROM THE OTHERWORLD, WHO LIVE SO CLOSE TO US...
THEY'RE WAITING FOR THE MOMENT WHEN THERE'S A BREACH IN THE "WALL" BETWEEN THE TWO WORLDS... THAT'S WHEN THEY'RE GOING TO INVADE...
THEY DON'T EXIST PHYSICALLY ...ONLY SPIRITUALLY. THEY'RE AFTER ONE THING ONLY...
HUMAN BODIES...

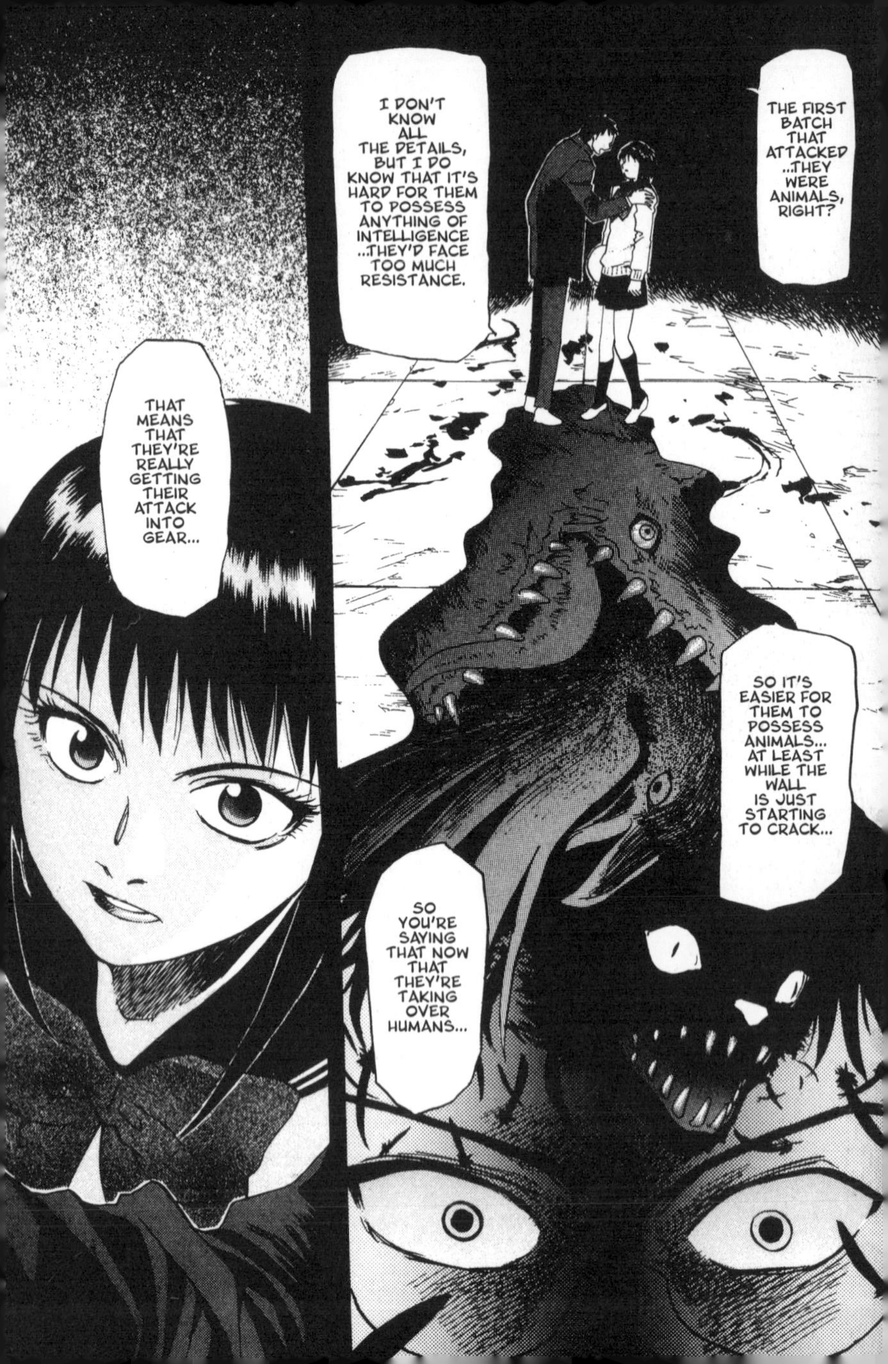
THE FIRST BATCH THAT ATTACKED ...THEY WERE ANIMALS, RIGHT?
I DON'T KNOW ALL THE DETAILS, BUT I DO KNOW THAT IT'S HARD FOR THEM TO POSSESS ANYTHING OF INTELLIGENCE ...THEY'D FACE TOO MUCH RESISTANCE.
SO IT'S EASIER FOR THEM TO POSSESS ANIMALS... AT LEAST WHILE THE WALL IS JUST STARTING TO CRACK...
SO YOU'RE SAYING THAT NOW THAT THEY'RE TAKING OVER HUMANS...
THAT MEANS THAT THEY'RE REALLY GETTING THEIR ATTACK INTO GEAR...

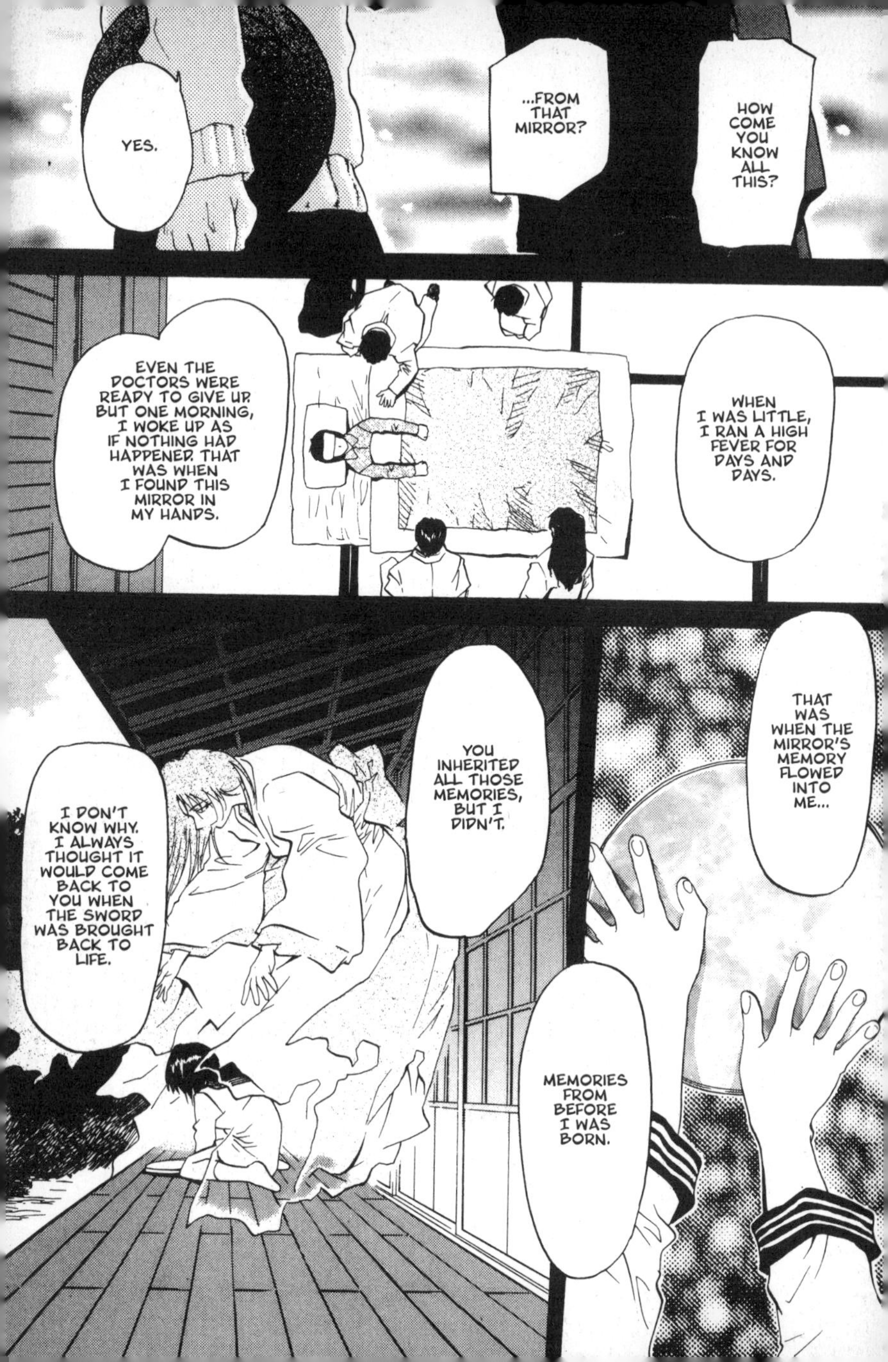
HOW COME YOU KNOW ALL THIS?
...FROM THAT MIRROR?
YES.
WHEN I WAS LITTLE, I RAN A HIGH FEVER FOR DAYS AND DAYS.
EVEN THE DOCTORS WERE READY TO GIVE UP. BUT ONE MORNING, I WOKE UP AS IF NOTHING HAD HAPPENED. THAT WAS WHEN I FOUND THIS MIRROR IN MY HANDS.
THAT WAS WHEN THE MIRROR'S MEMORY FLOWED INTO ME...
MEMORIES FROM BEFORE I WAS BORN.
YOU INHERITED ALL THOSE MEMORIES, BUT I DIDN'T.
I DON'T KNOW WHY. I ALWAYS THOUGHT IT WOULD COME BACK TO YOU WHEN THE SWORD WAS BROUGHT BACK TO LIFE.

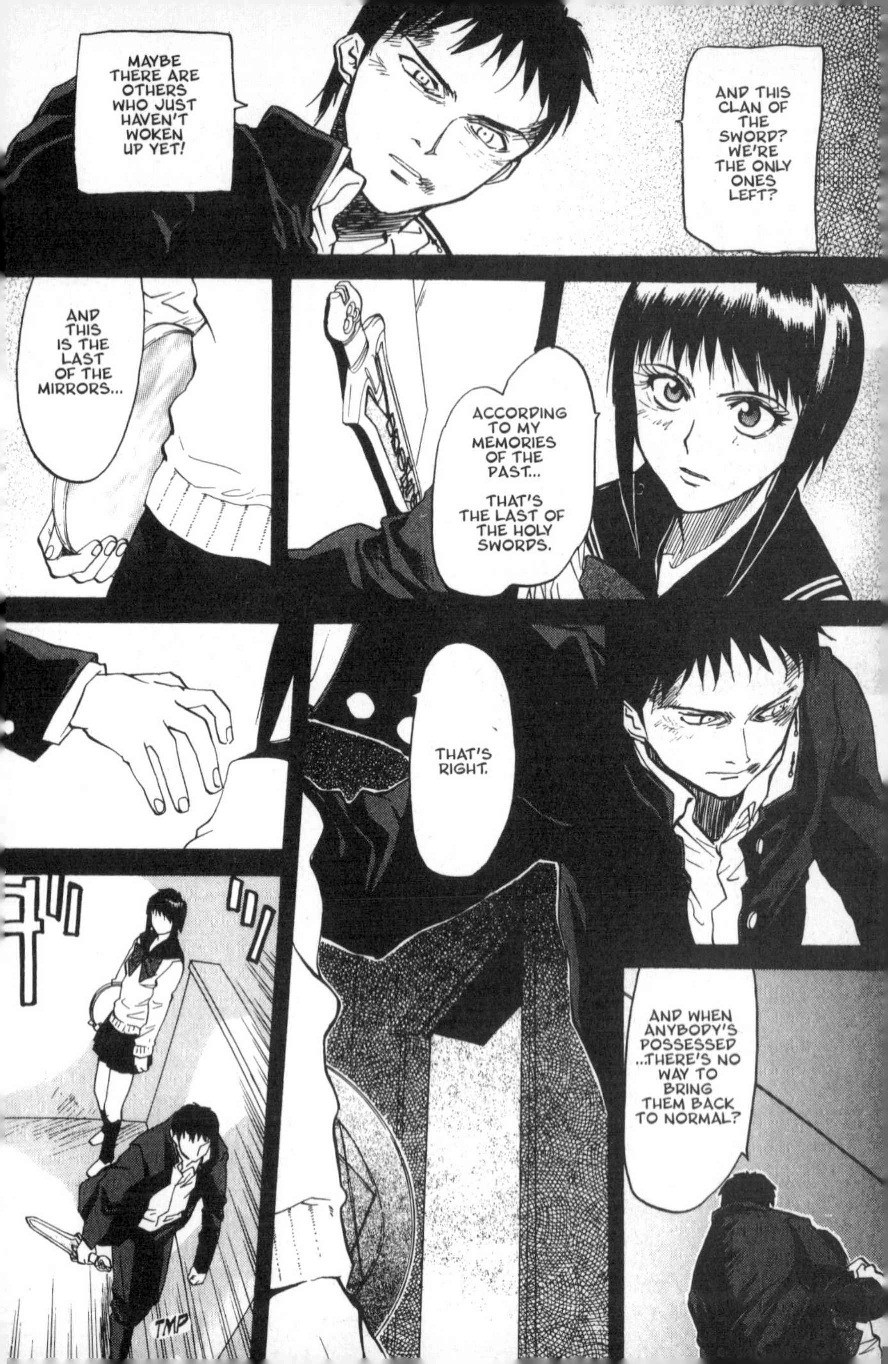
AND THIS CLAN OF THE SWORD? WE'RE THE ONLY ONES LEFT?
MAYBE THERE ARE OTHERS WHO JUST HAVEN'T WOKEN UP YET!
ACCORDING TO MY MEMORIES OF THE PAST... THAT'S THE LAST OF THE HOLY SWORDS.
AND THIS IS THE LAST OF THE MIRRORS...
AND WHEN ANYBODY'S POSSESSED ...THERE'S NO WAY TO BRING THEM BACK TO NORMAL?
THAT'S RIGHT.
TMP

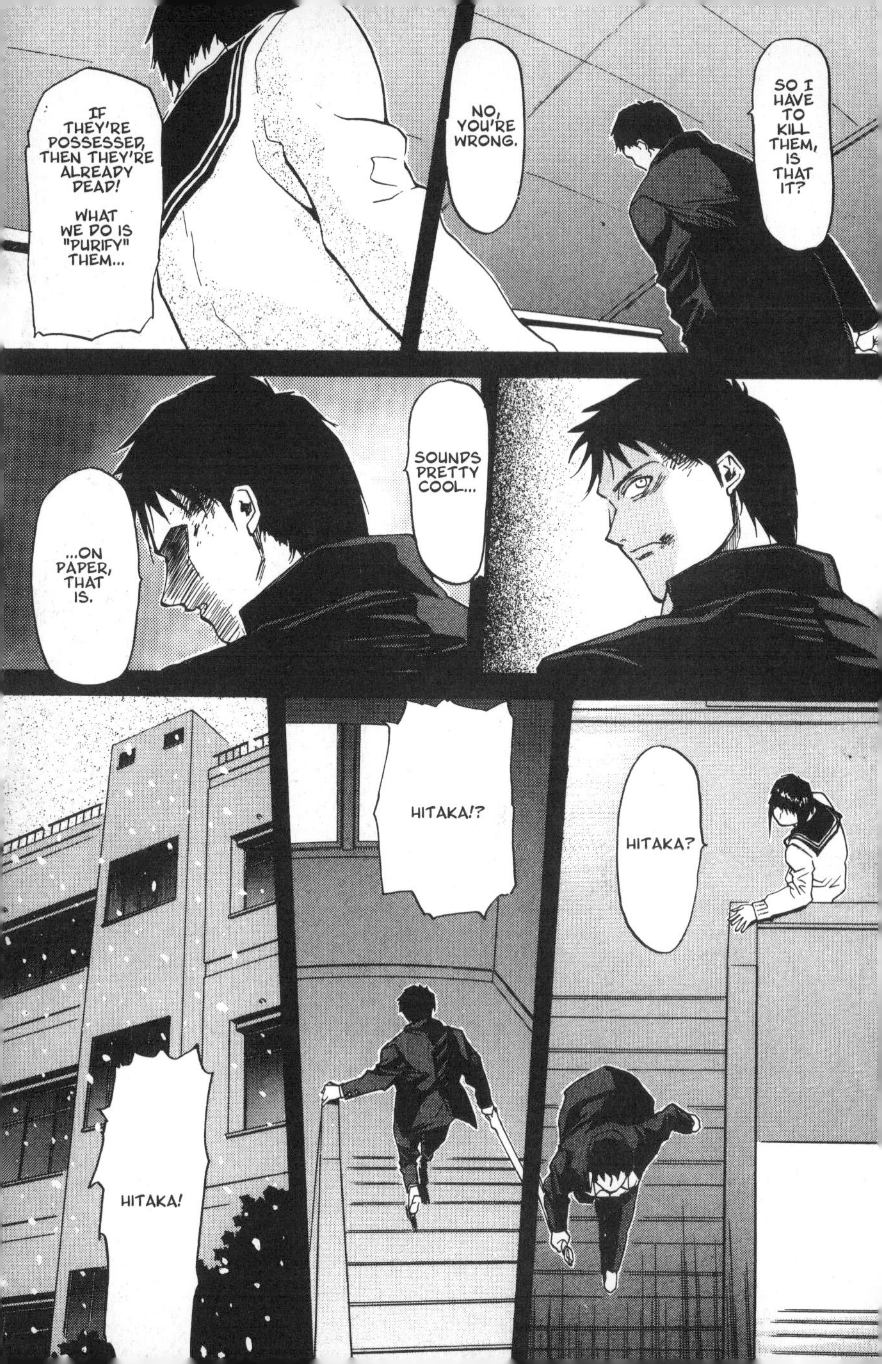
SO I HAVE TO KILL THEM, IS THAT IT?
NO, YOU'RE WRONG.
IF THEY'RE POSSESSED, THEN THEY'RE ALREADY DEAD!
WHAT WE DO IS "PURIFY" THEM...
SOUNDS PRETTY COOL...
...ON PAPER, THAT IS.
HITAKA?
HITAKA!?
HITAKA!

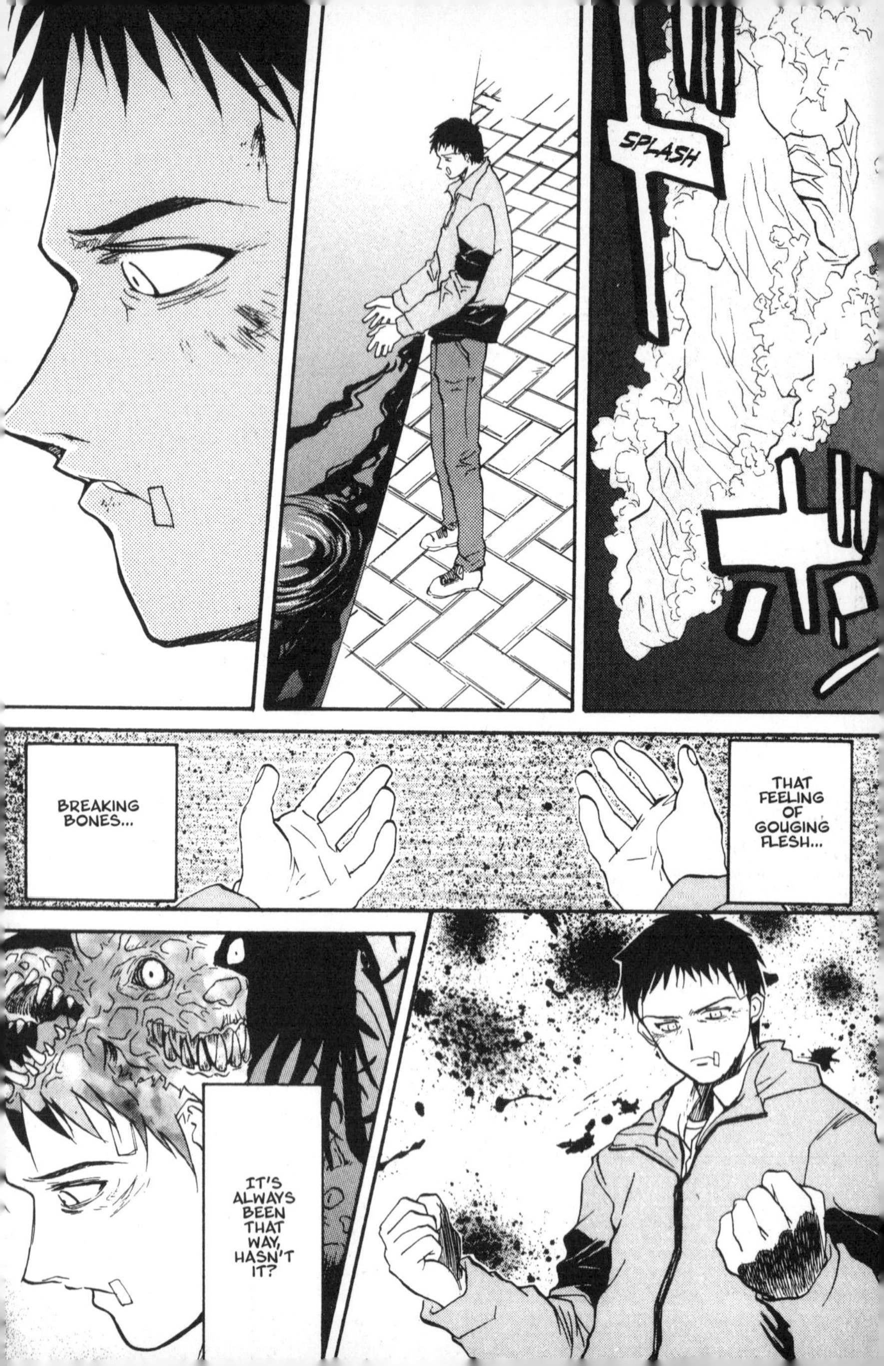
SPLASH
THAT FEELING OF GOUGING FLESH...
BREAKING BONES...
IT'S ALWAYS BEEN THAT WAY, HASN'T IT?

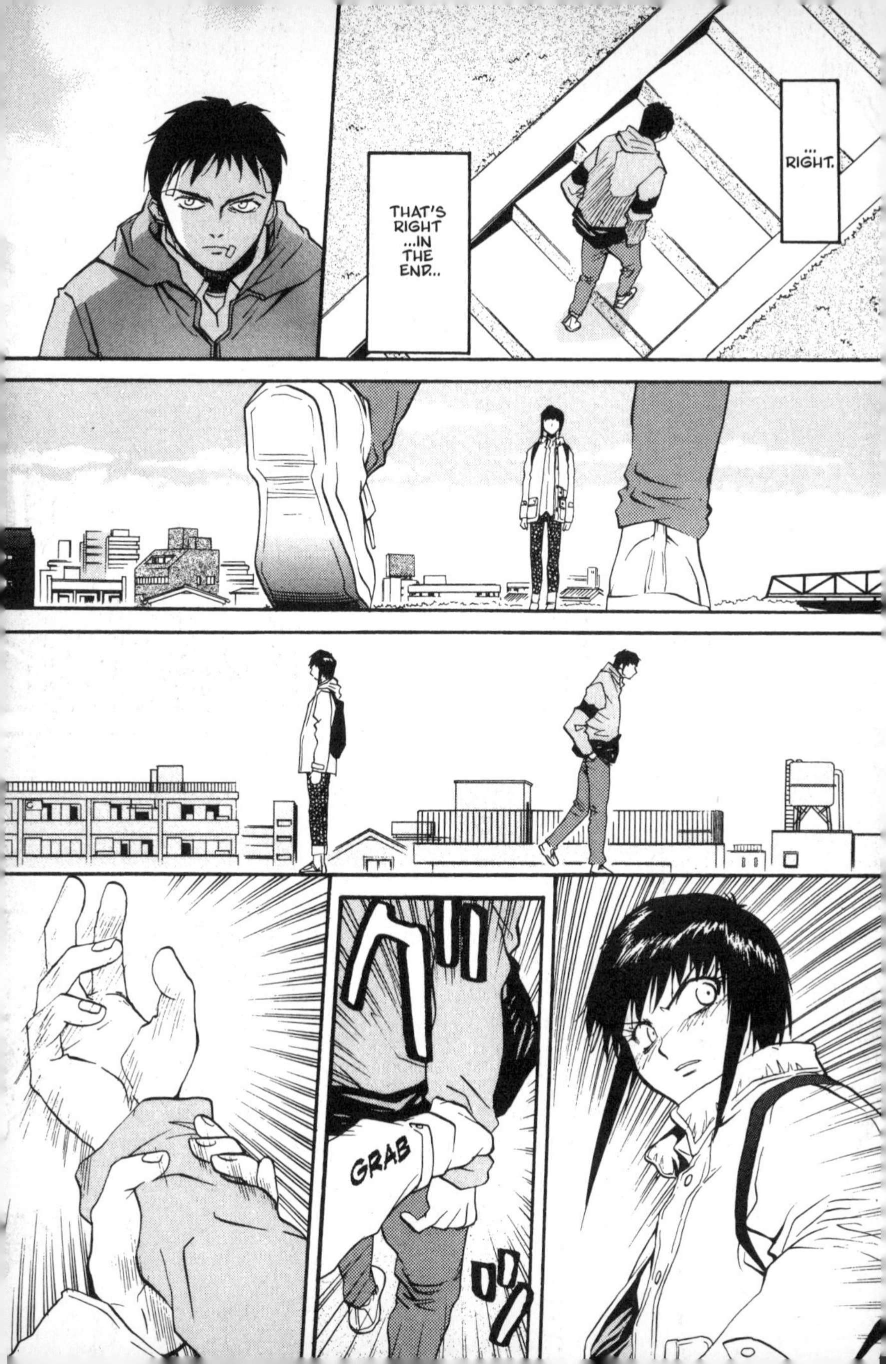

... RIGHT.
THAT'S RIGHT ...IN THE END...
GRAB

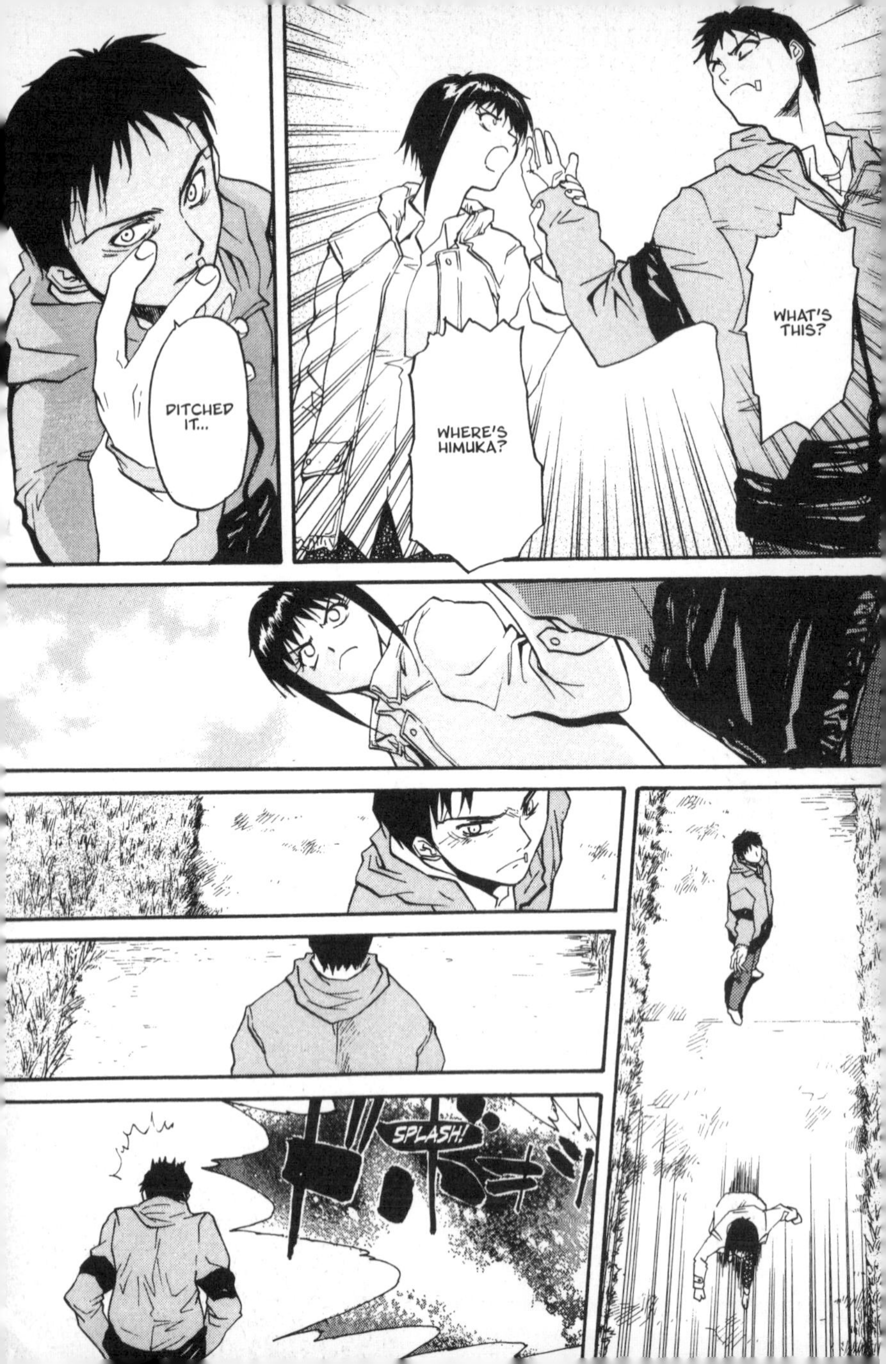
WHAT'S THIS?
WHERE'S HIMUKA?
DITCHED IT...
SPLASH!

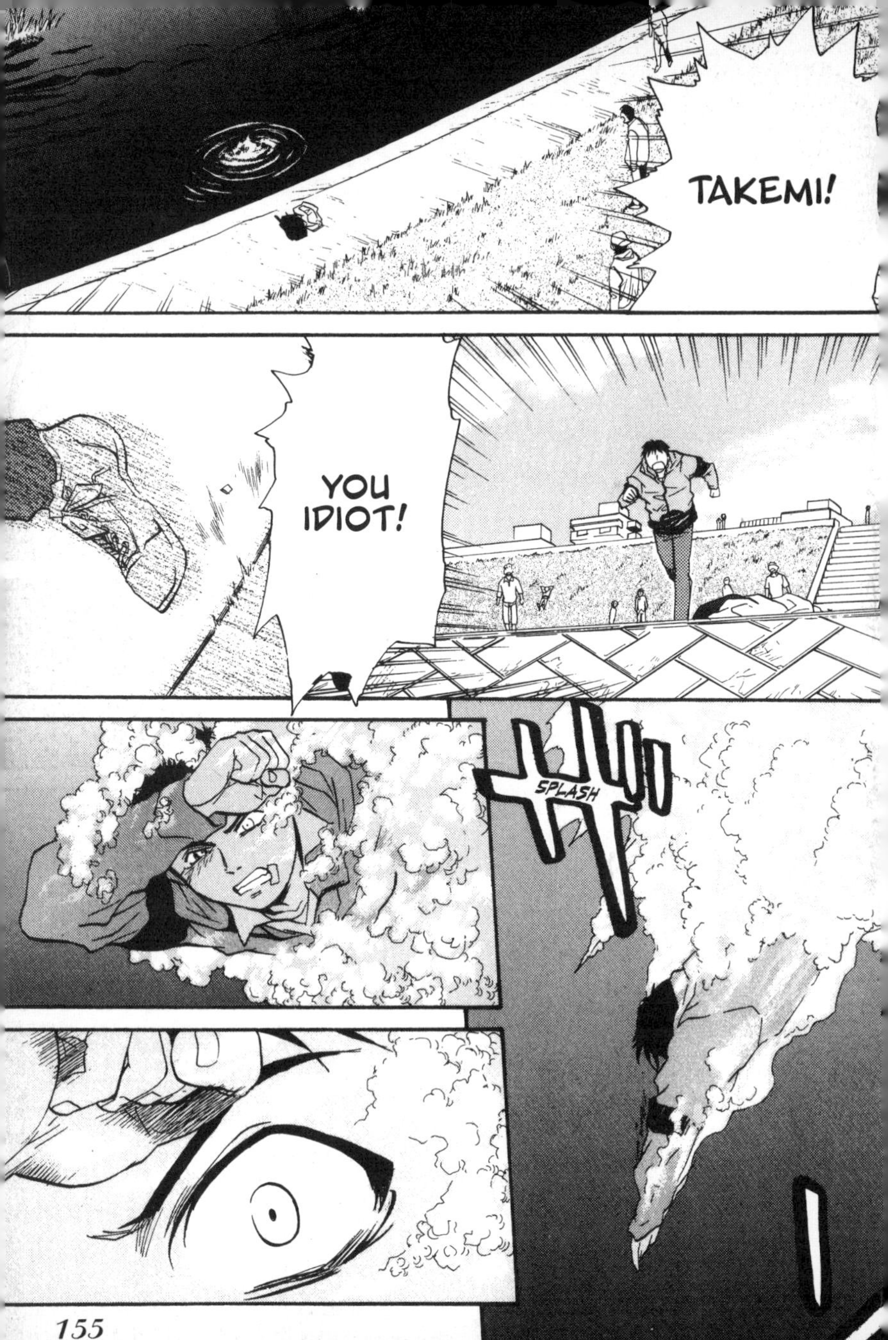

TAKEMI!
YOU IDIOT!
SPLASH

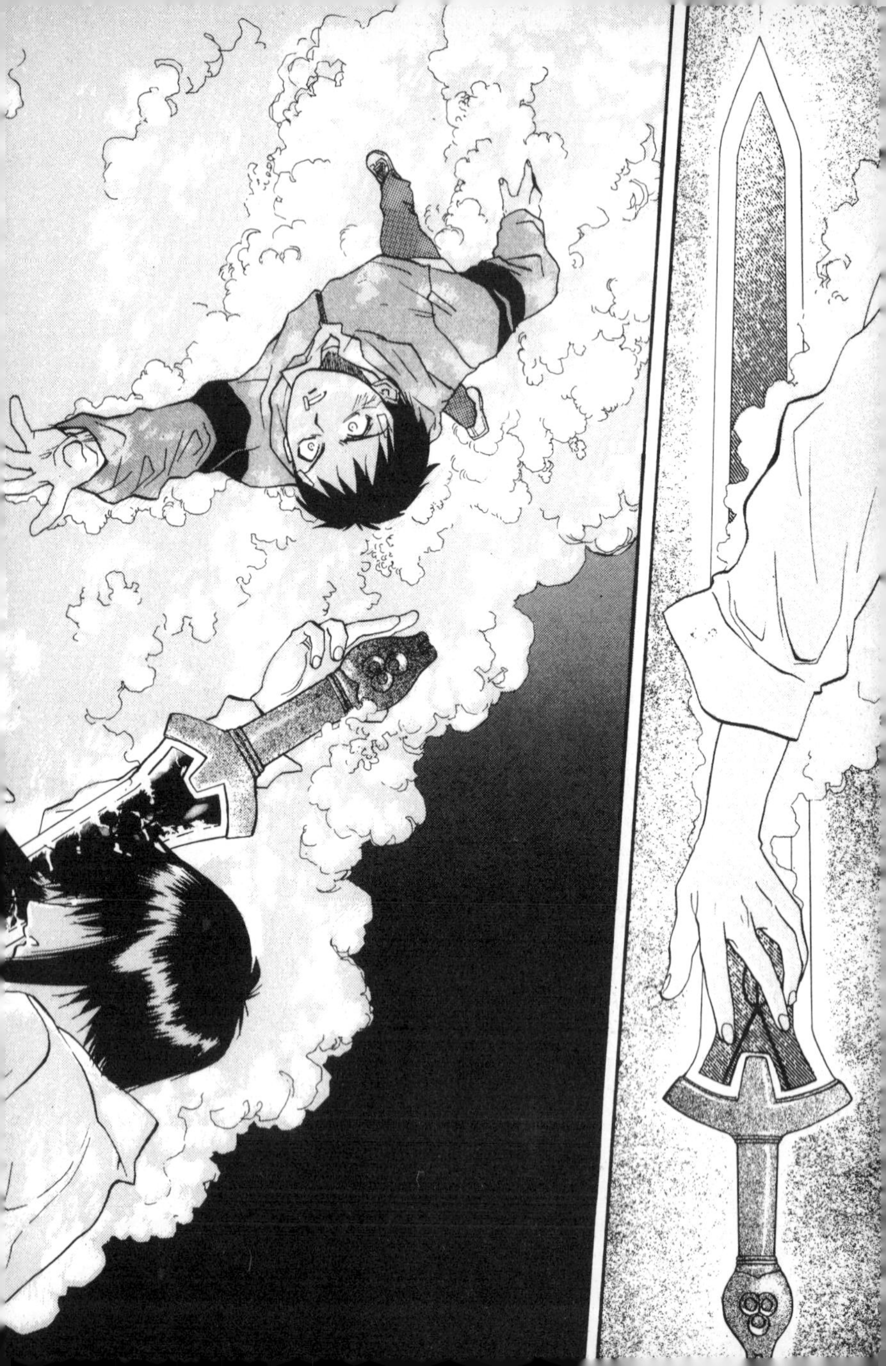

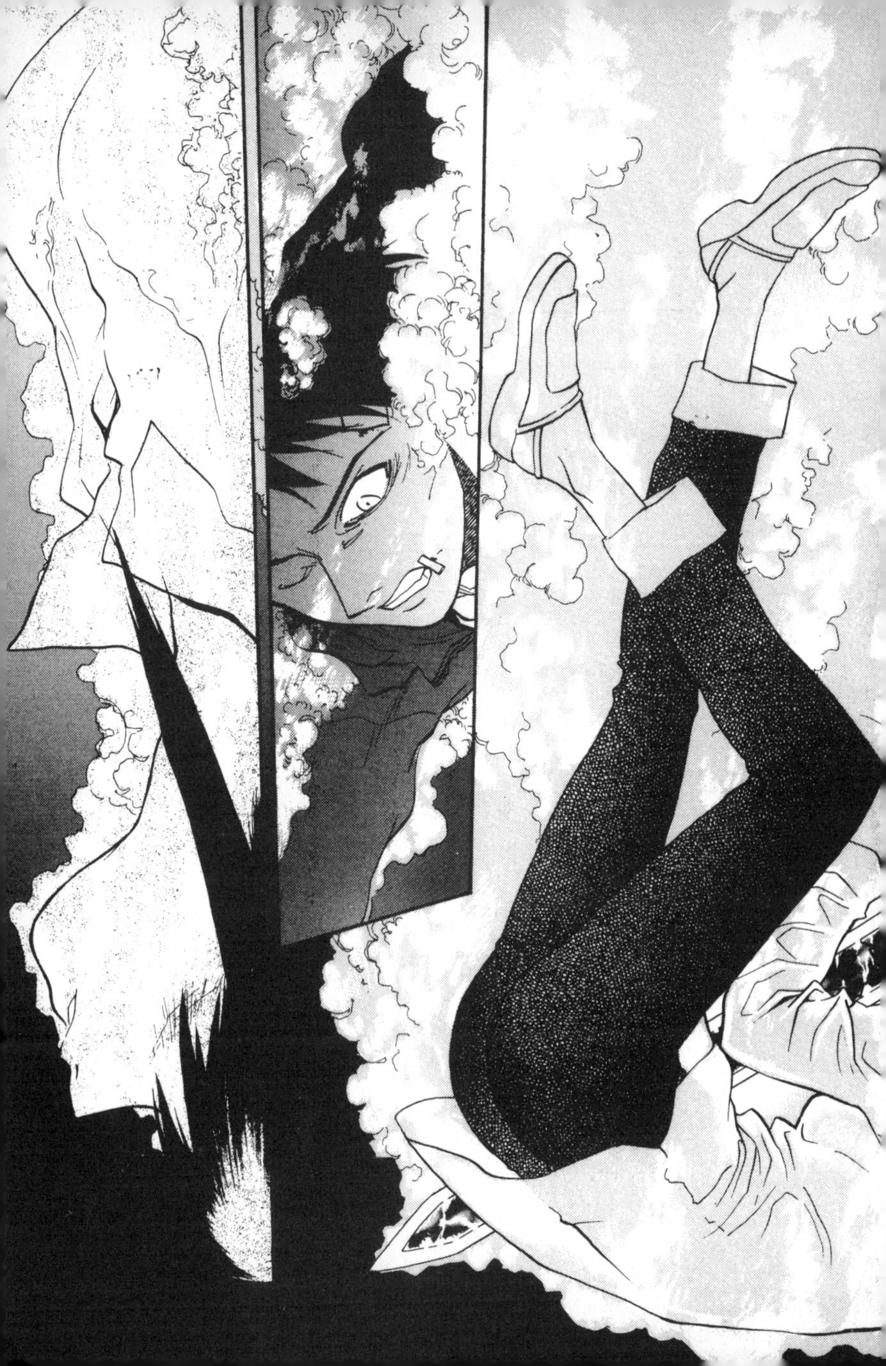

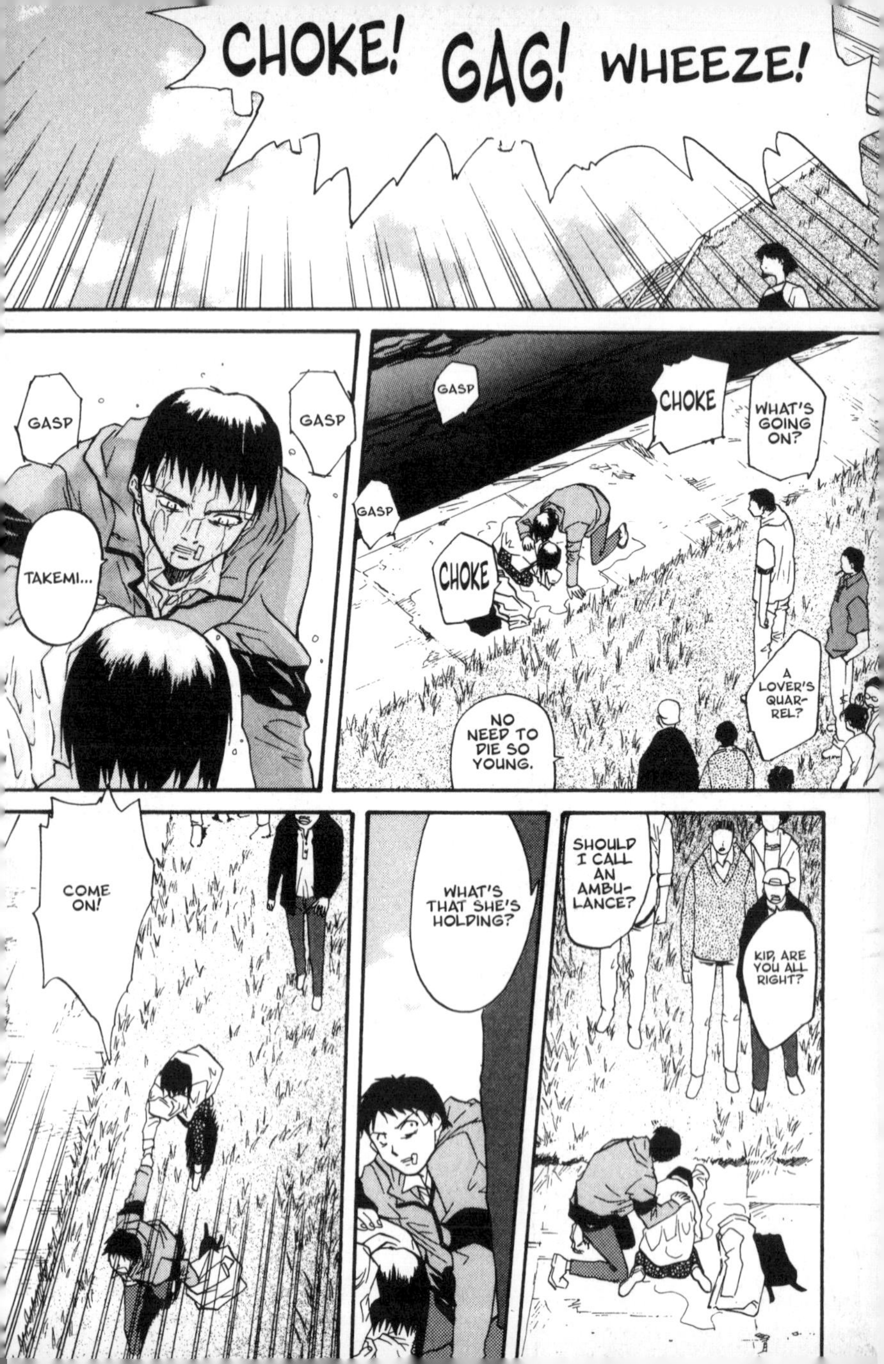
CHOKE!
GAG!
WHEEZE!
WHAT'S GOING ON?
CHOKE
GASP
GASP
CHOKE
A LOVER'S QUARREL?
NO NEED TO DIE SO YOUNG.
GASP
GASP
TAKEMI...
SHOULD I CALL AN AMBULANCE?
KID, ARE YOU ALL RIGHT?
WHAT'S THAT SHE'S HOLDING?
COME ON!

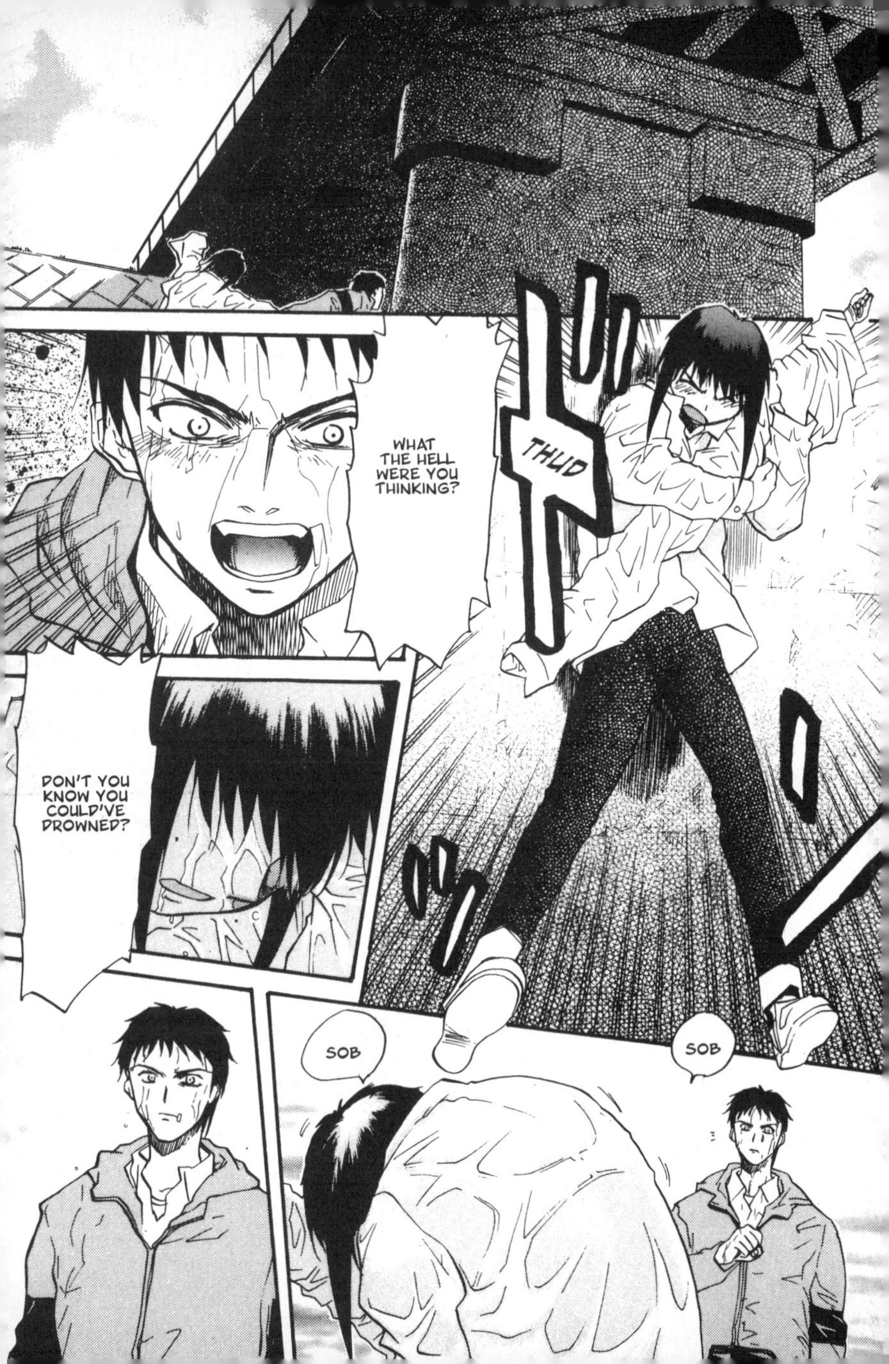
THUD
WHAT THE HELL WERE YOU THINKING?
DON'T YOU KNOW YOU COULD'VE DROWNED?
SOB
SOB

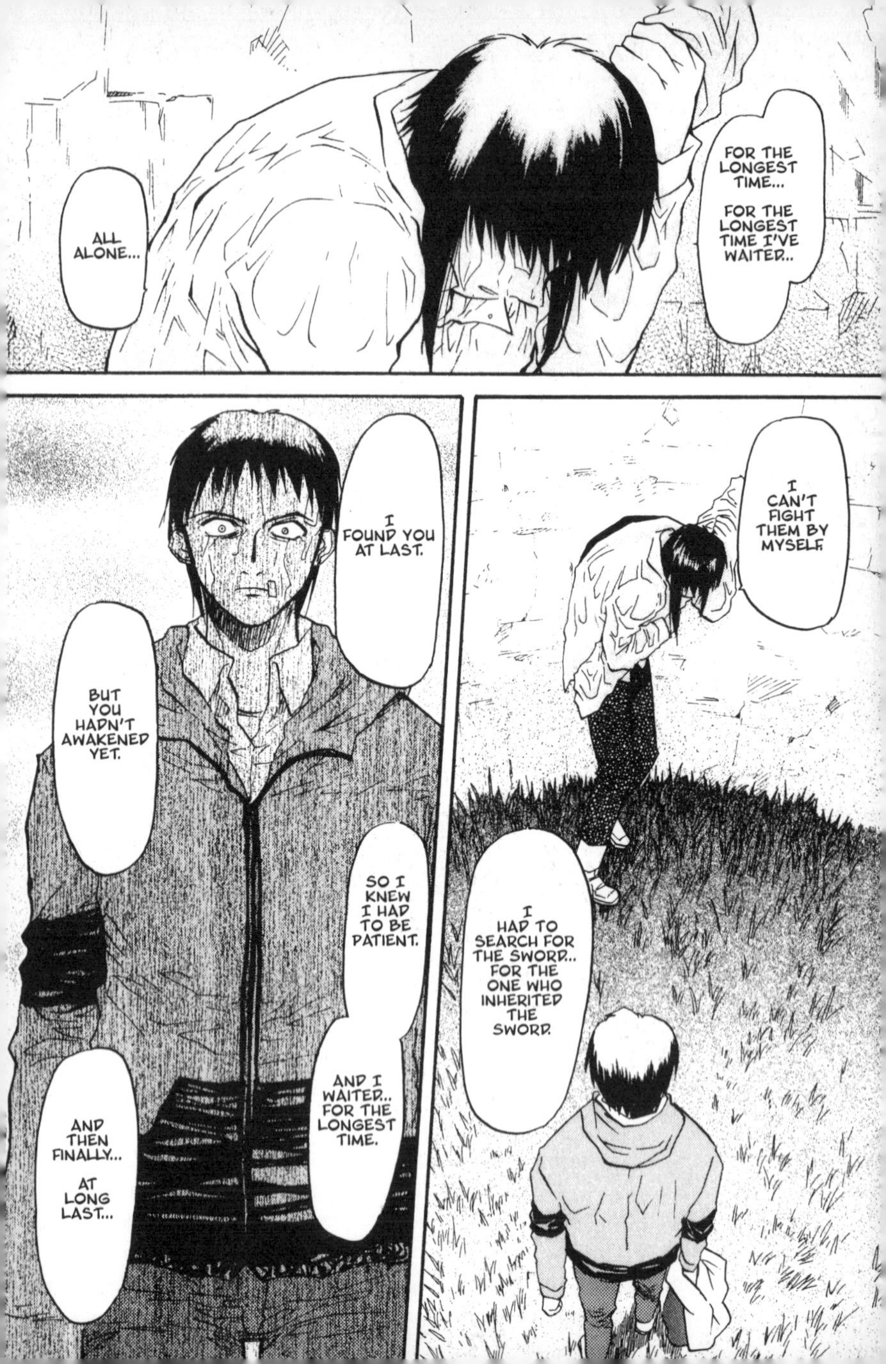
FOR THE LONGEST TIME... FOR THE LONGEST TIME I'VE WAITED...
ALL ALONE...
I CAN'T FIGHT THEM BY MYSELF.
I HAD TO SEARCH FOR THE SWORD... FOR THE ONE WHO INHERITED THE SWORD.
I FOUND YOU AT LAST.
BUT YOU HADN'T AWAKENED YET.
SO I KNEW I HAD TO BE PATIENT.
AND I WAITED... FOR THE LONGEST TIME.
AND THEN FINALLY... AT LONG LAST...

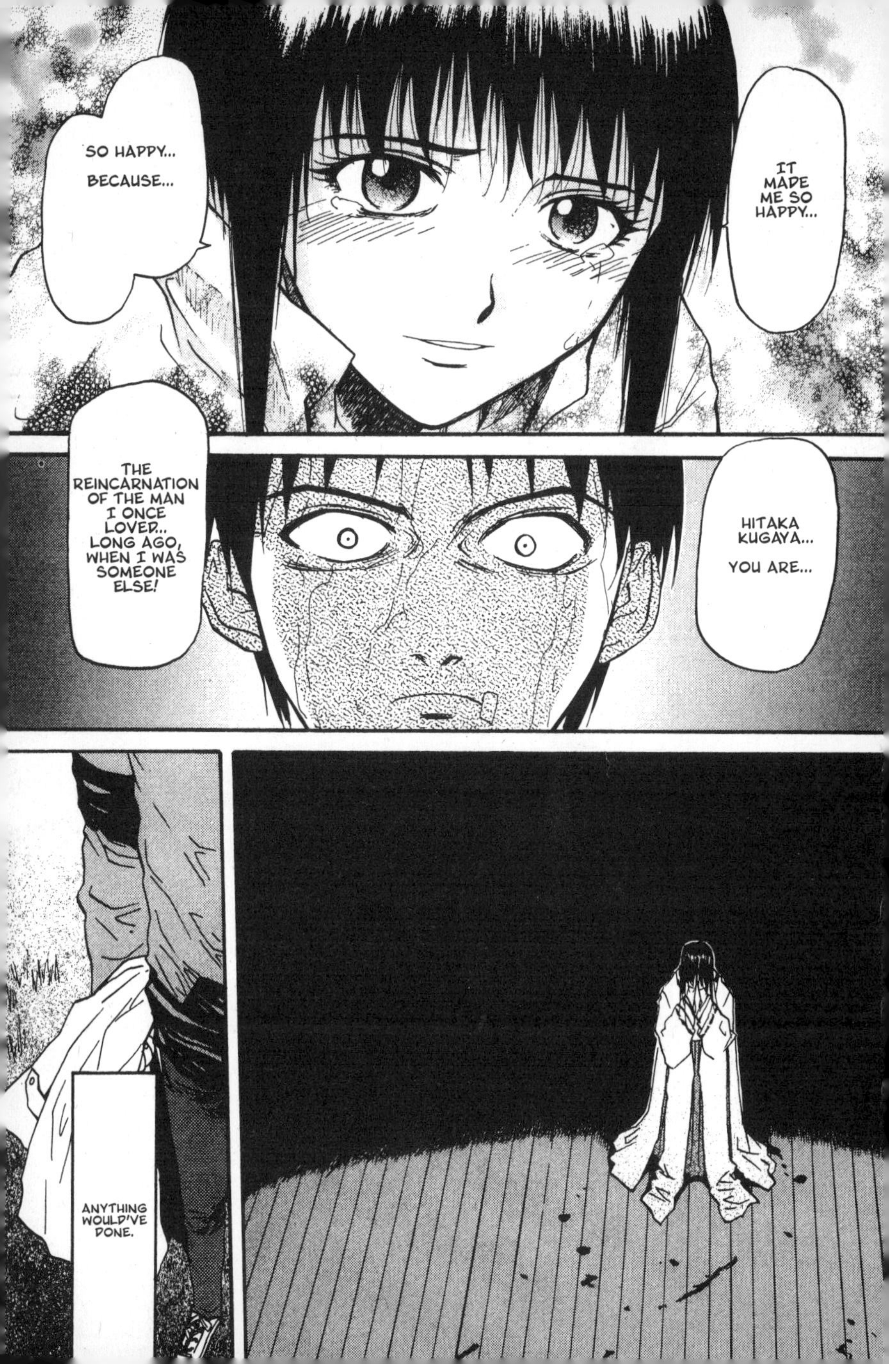
IT MADE ME SO HAPPY...
SO HAPPY... BECAUSE...
HITAKA KUGAYA... YOU ARE...
THE REINCARNATION OF THE MAN I ONCE LOVED... LONG AGO, WHEN I WAS SOMEONE ELSE!
ANYTHING WOULD'VE DONE.

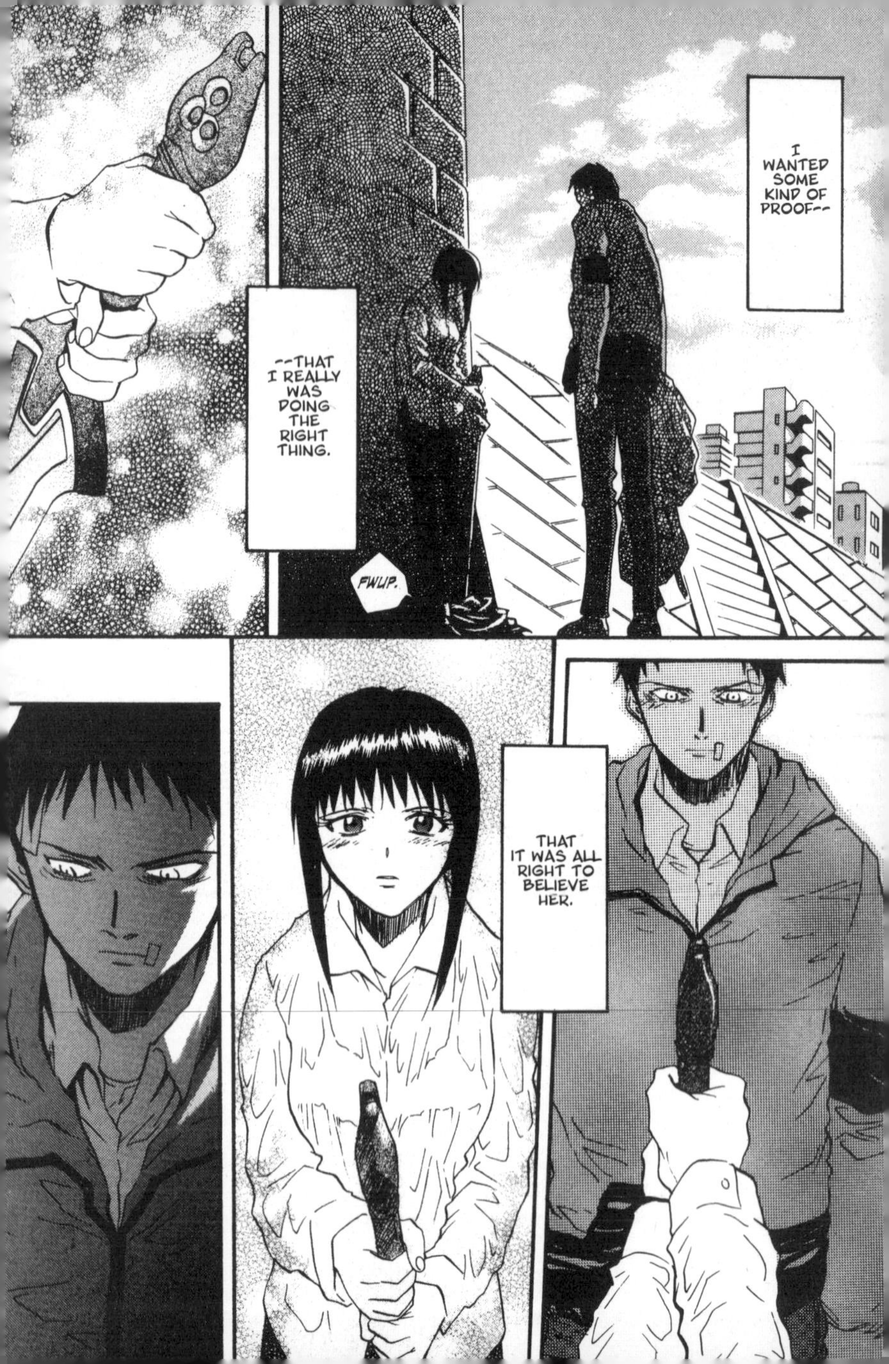
I WANTED SOME KIND OF PROOF--
--THAT I REALLY WAS DOING THE RIGHT THING.
FWUP.
THAT IT WAS ALL RIGHT TO BELIEVE HER.

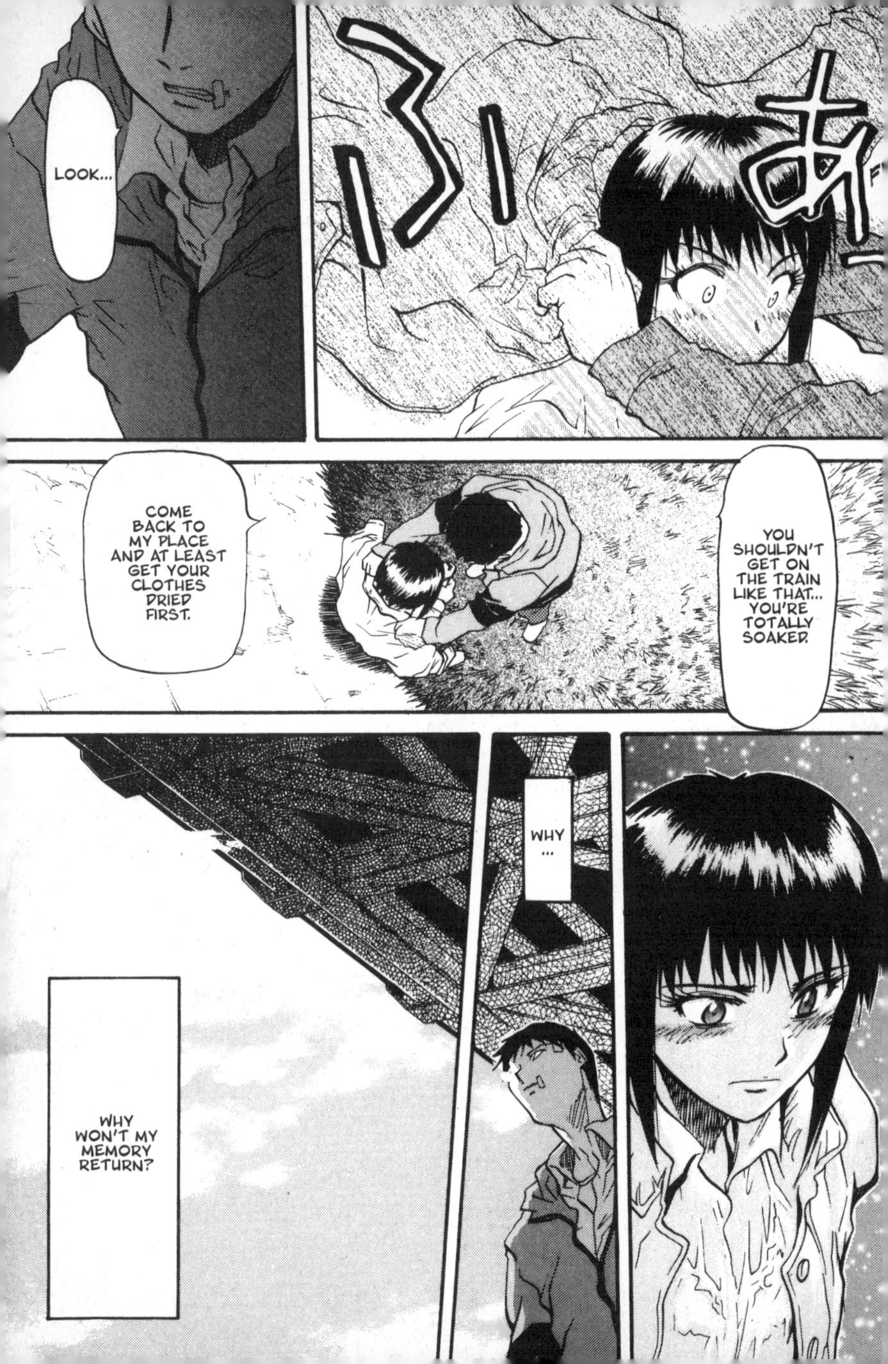
LOOK...
YOU SHOULDN'T GET ON THE TRAIN LIKE THAT... YOU'RE TOTALLY SOAKED.
COME BACK TO MY PLACE AND AT LEAST GET YOUR CLOTHES DRIED FIRST.
WHY ...
WHY WON'T MY MEMORY RETURN?

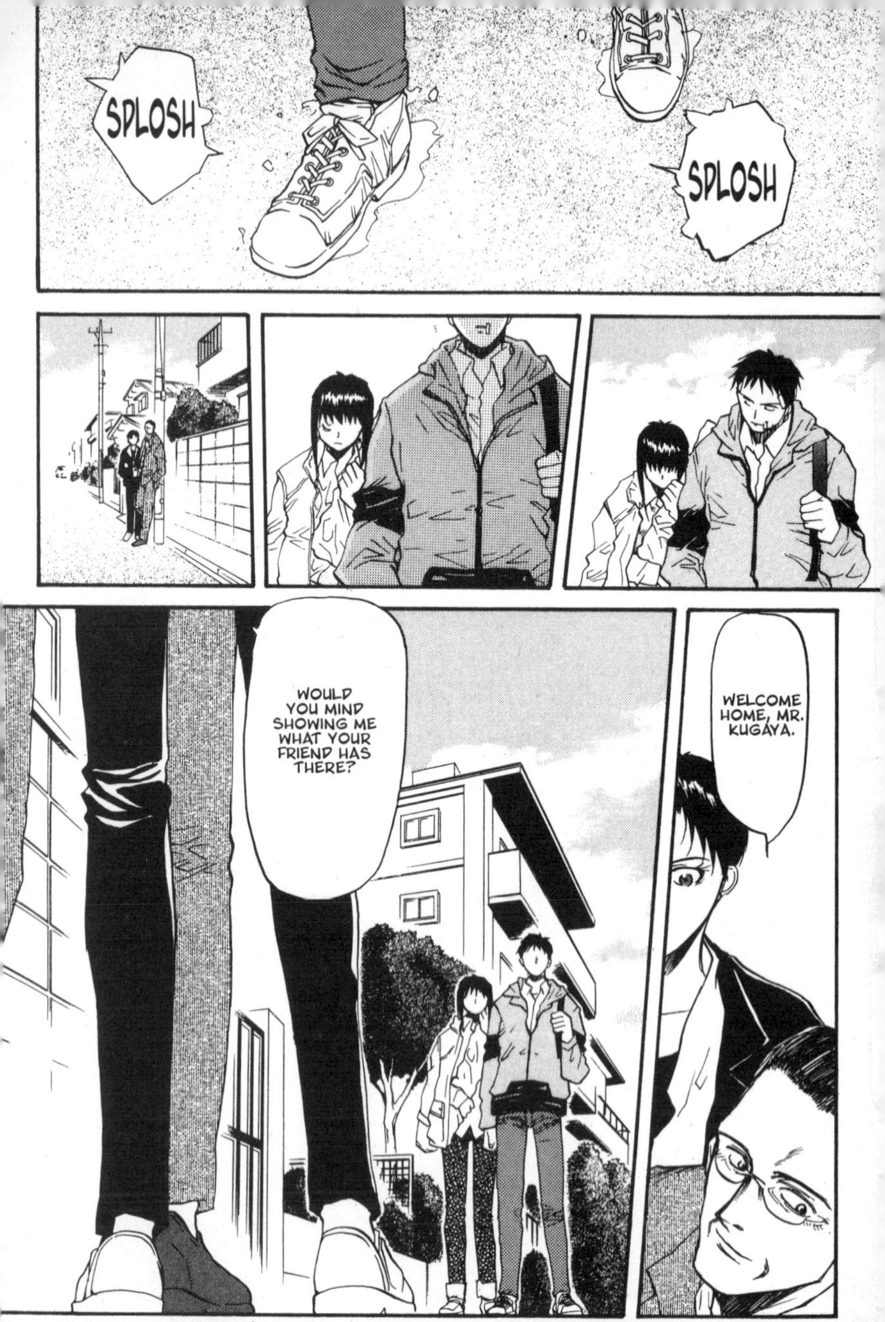
SPLOSH
SPLOSH
WELCOME HOME, MR. KUGAYA.
WOULD YOU MIND SHOWING ME WHAT YOUR FRIEND HAS THERE?

#6. Deep Rift/Bond / END

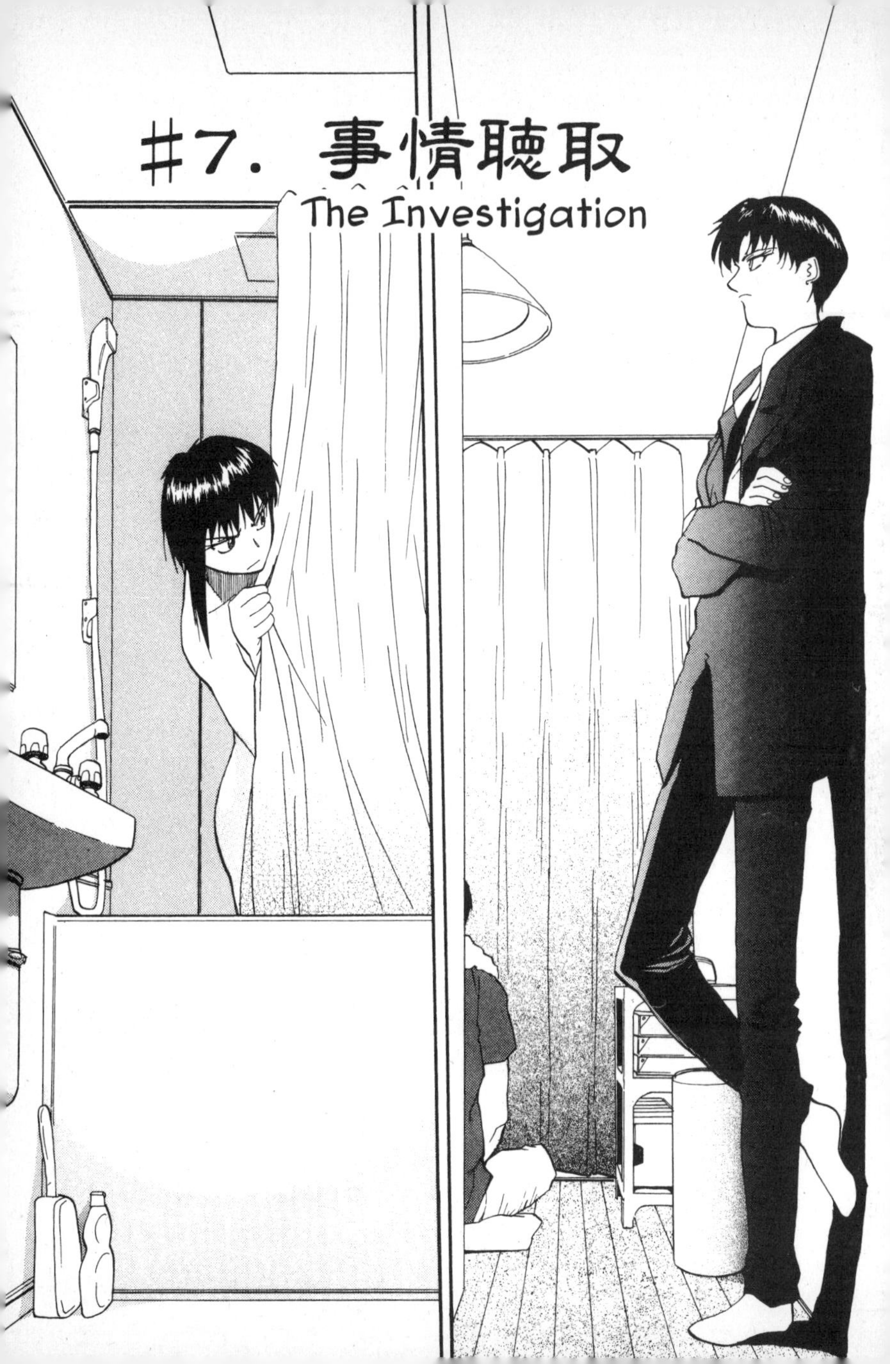
#7. 事情聴取
The Investigation

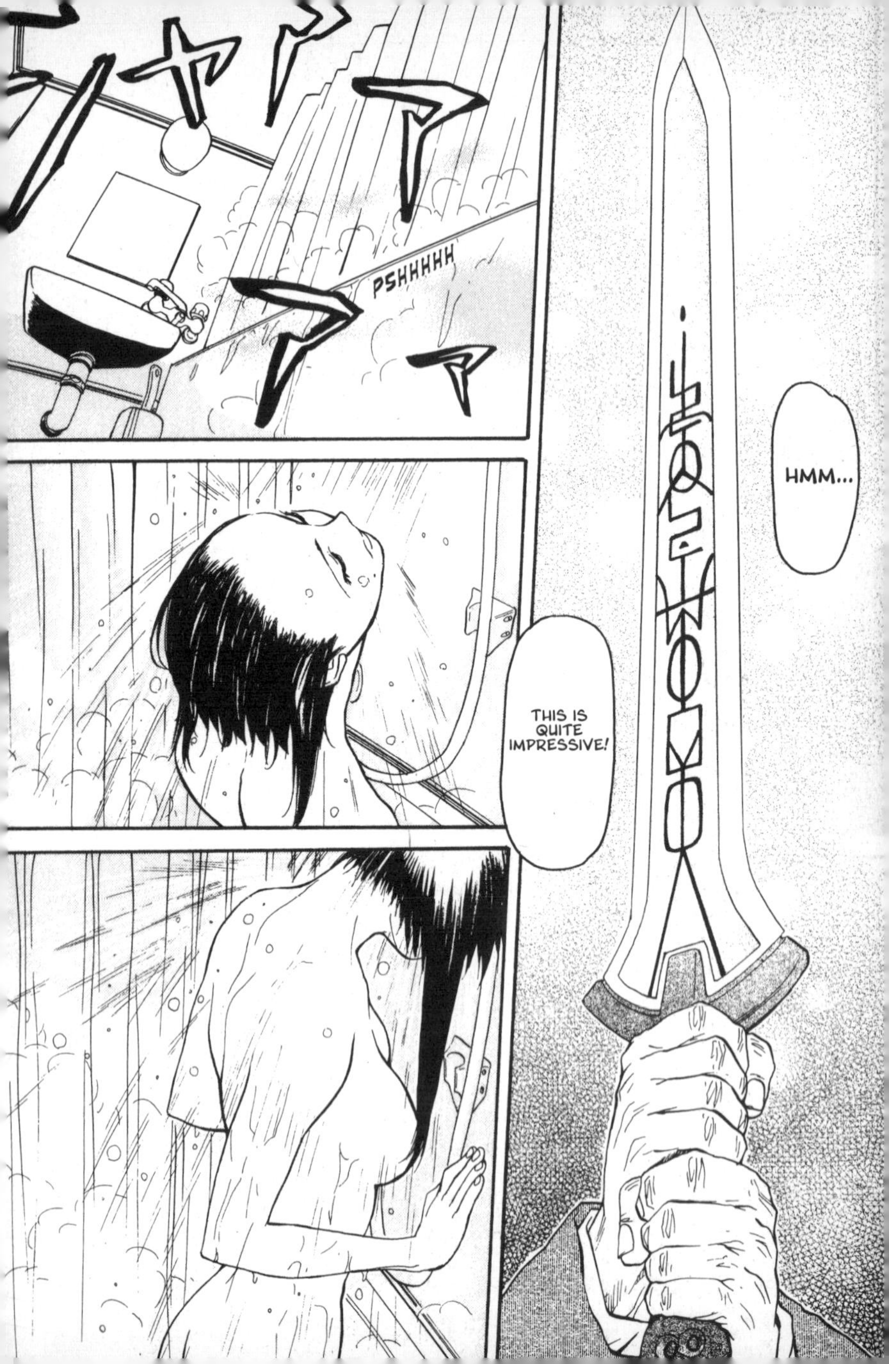
HMM...
THIS IS QUITE IMPRESSIVE!
シャアアアァ
PSHHHHH

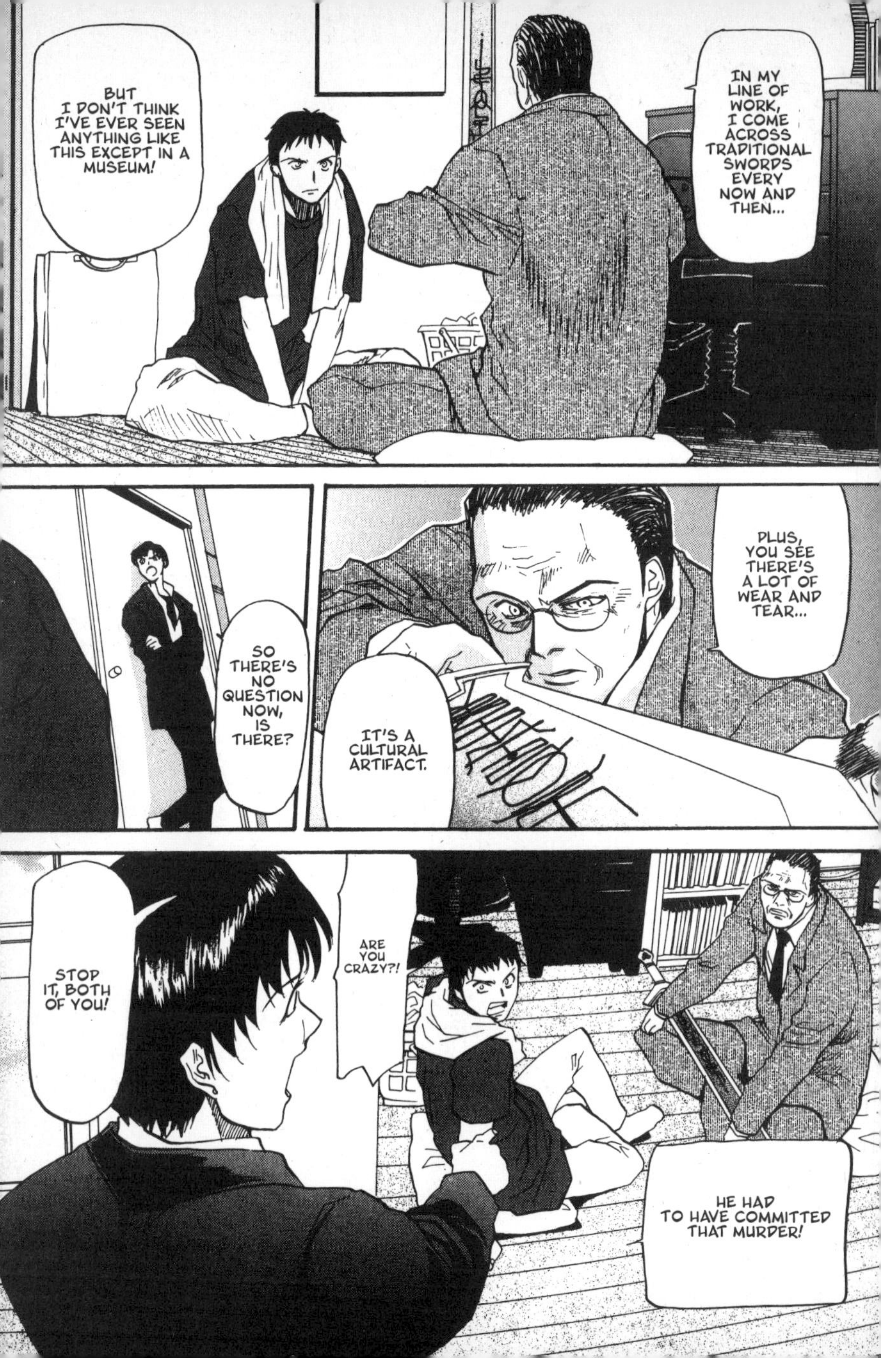
IN MY LINE OF WORK, I COME ACROSS TRADITIONAL SWORDS EVERY NOW AND THEN...
BUT I DON'T THINK I'VE EVER SEEN ANYTHING LIKE THIS EXCEPT IN A MUSEUM!
PLUS, YOU SEE THERE'S A LOT OF WEAR AND TEAR...
IT'S A CULTURAL ARTIFACT.
SO THERE'S NO QUESTION NOW, IS THERE?
HE HAD TO HAVE COMMITTED THAT MURDER!
ARE YOU CRAZY?!
STOP IT, BOTH OF YOU!

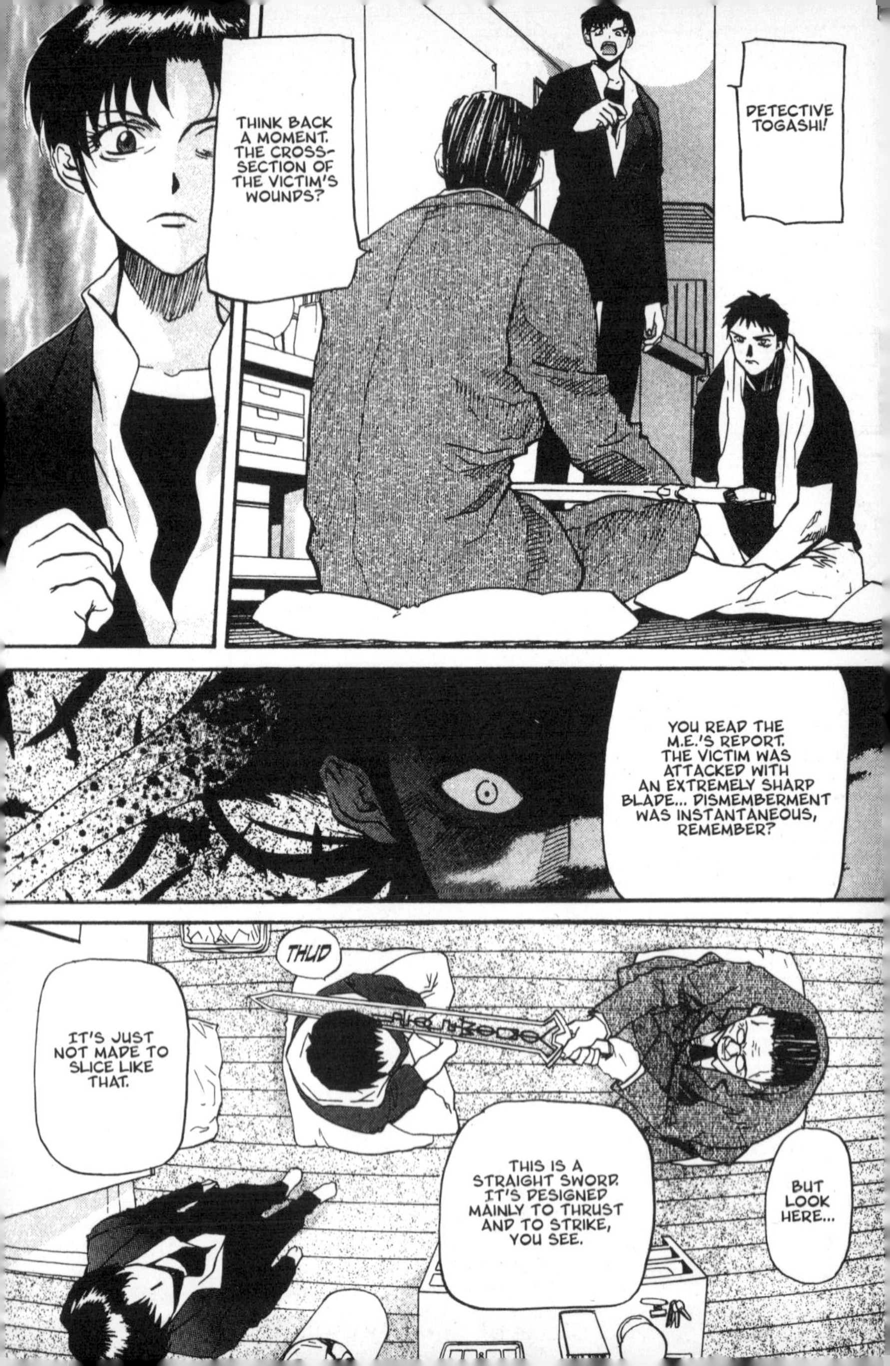

DETECTIVE TOGASHI!
THINK BACK A MOMENT. THE CROSS-SECTION OF THE VICTIM'S WOUNDS?
YOU READ THE M.E.'S REPORT. THE VICTIM WAS ATTACKED WITH AN EXTREMELY SHARP BLADE... DISMEMBERMENT WAS INSTANTANEOUS, REMEMBER?
THUD
BUT LOOK HERE...
THIS IS A STRAIGHT SWORD. IT'S DESIGNED MAINLY TO THRUST AND TO STRIKE, YOU SEE.
IT'S JUST NOT MADE TO SLICE LIKE THAT.

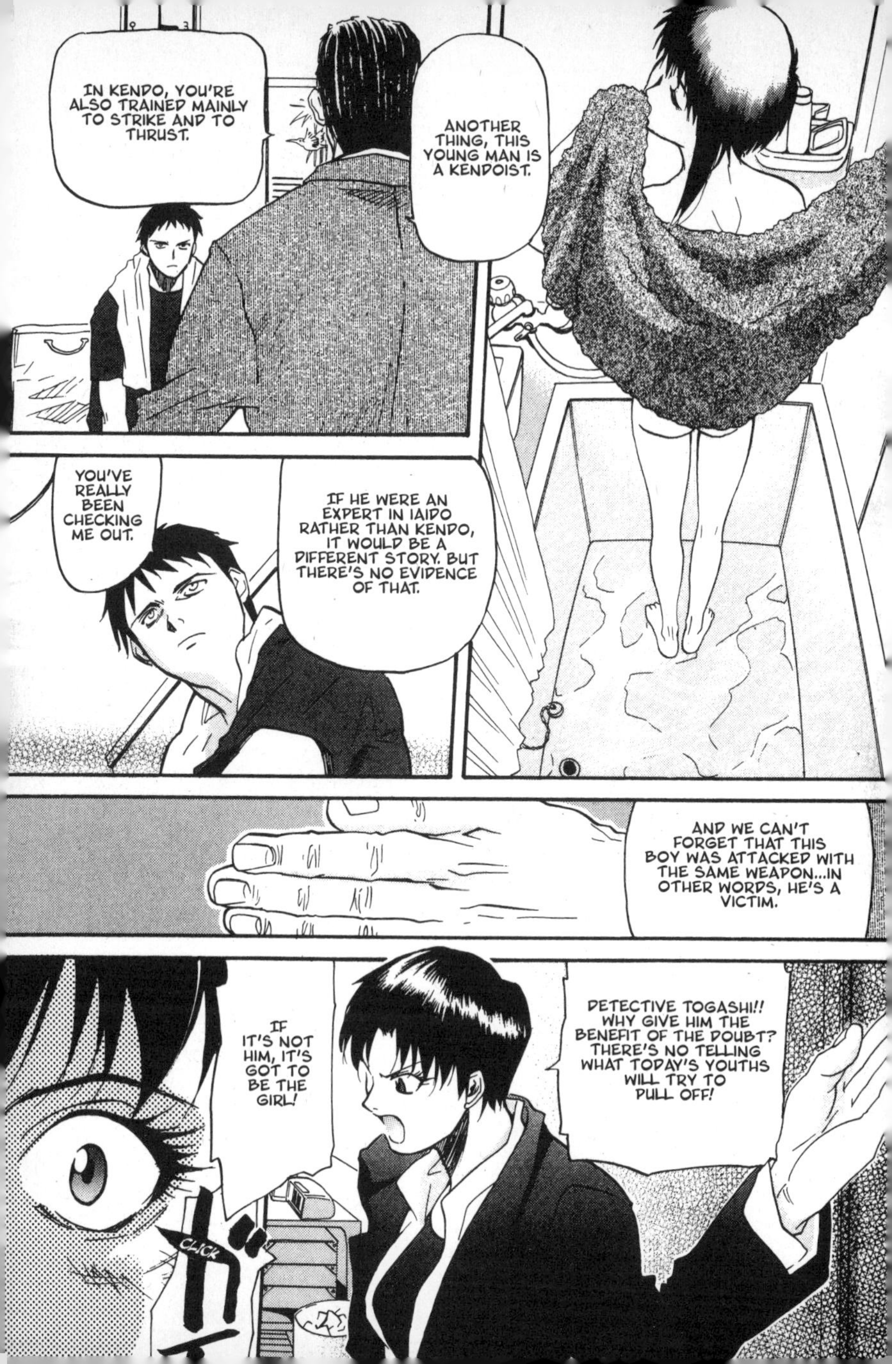
ANOTHER THING, THIS YOUNG MAN IS A KENDOIST.
IN KENDO, YOU'RE ALSO TRAINED MAINLY TO STRIKE AND TO THRUST.
IF HE WERE AN EXPERT IN IAIDO RATHER THAN KENDO, IT WOULD BE A DIFFERENT STORY. BUT THERE'S NO EVIDENCE OF THAT.
YOU'VE REALLY BEEN CHECKING ME OUT.
AND WE CAN'T FORGET THAT THIS BOY WAS ATTACKED WITH THE SAME WEAPON...IN OTHER WORDS, HE'S A VICTIM.
DETECTIVE TOGASHI!! WHY GIVE HIM THE BENEFIT OF THE DOUBT? THERE'S NO TELLING WHAT TODAY'S YOUTHS WILL TRY TO PULL OFF!
IF IT'S NOT HIM, IT'S GOT TO BE THE GIRL!
CLICK

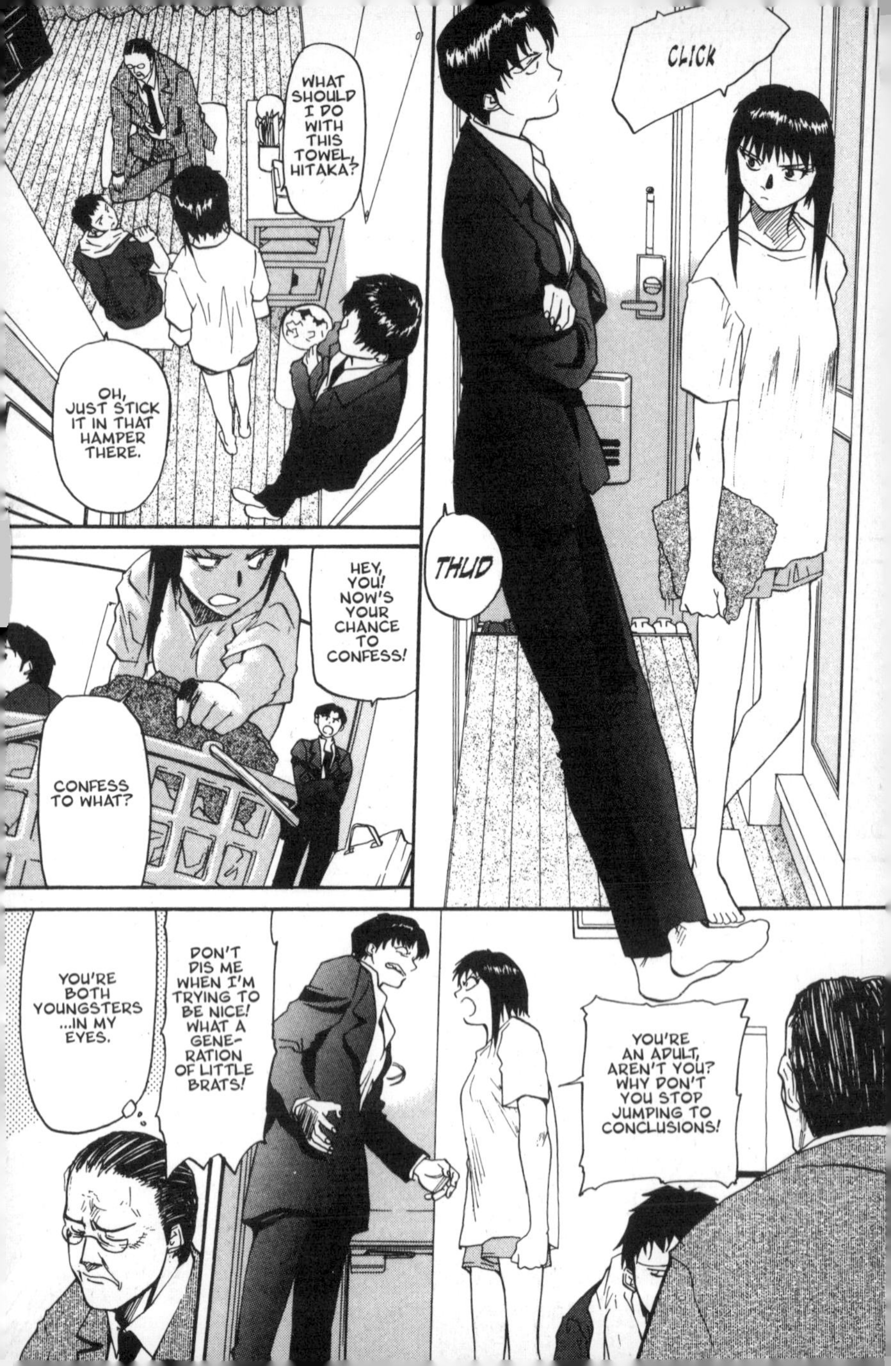
CLICK
THUD
WHAT SHOULD I DO WITH THIS TOWEL, HITAKA?
OH, JUST STICK IT IN THAT HAMPER THERE.
HEY, YOU! NOW'S YOUR CHANCE TO CONFESS!
CONFESS TO WHAT?
YOU'RE AN ADULT, AREN'T YOU? WHY DON'T YOU STOP JUMPING TO CONCLUSIONS!
DON'T DIS ME WHEN I'M TRYING TO BE NICE! WHAT A GENERATION OF LITTLE BRATS!
YOU'RE BOTH YOUNGSTERS ...IN MY EYES.

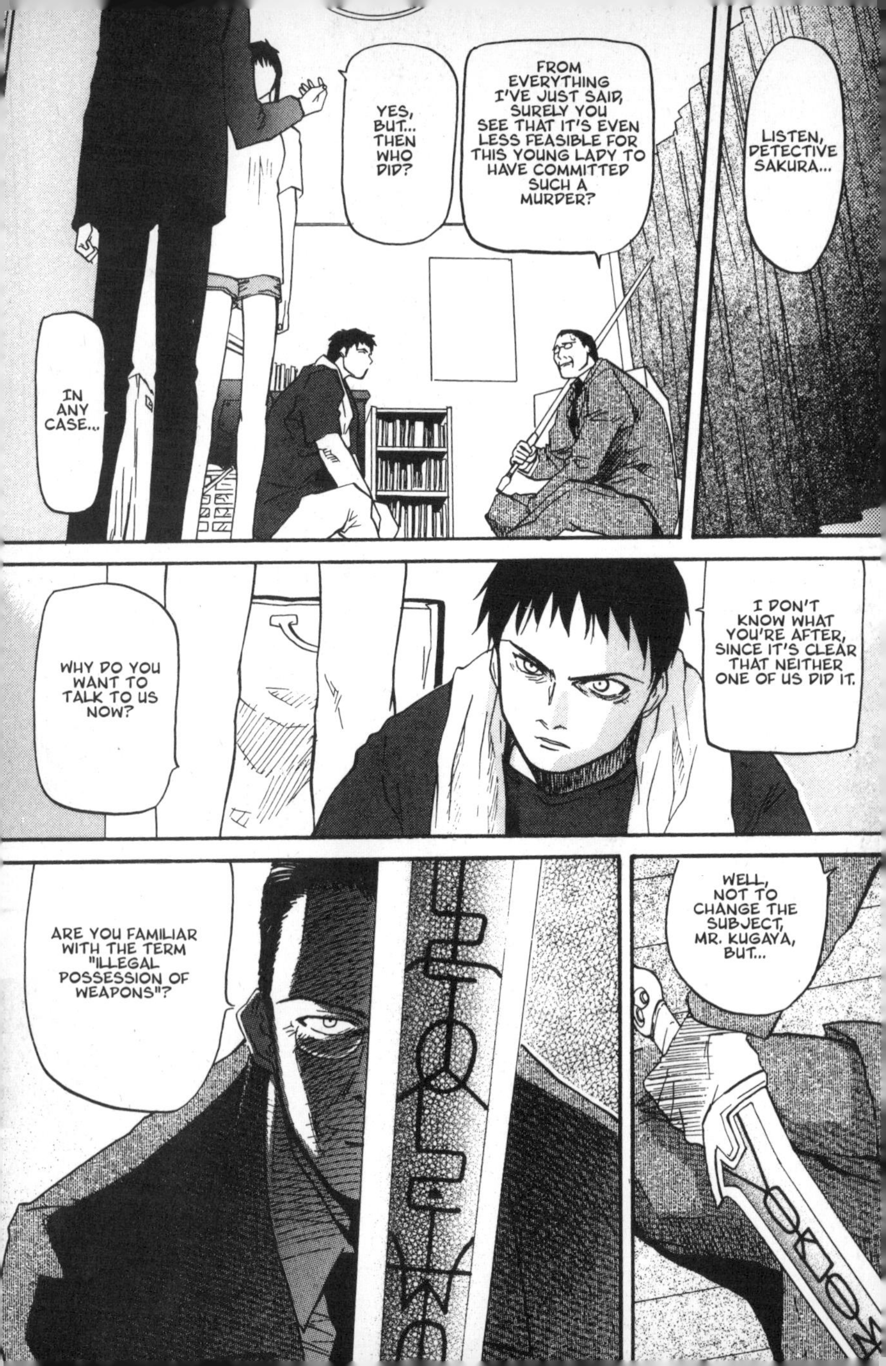
LISTEN, DETECTIVE SAKURA...
FROM EVERYTHING I'VE JUST SAID, SURELY YOU SEE THAT IT'S EVEN LESS FEASIBLE FOR THIS YOUNG LADY TO HAVE COMMITTED SUCH A MURDER?
YES, BUT... THEN WHO DID?
IN ANY CASE...
I DON'T KNOW WHAT YOU'RE AFTER, SINCE IT'S CLEAR THAT NEITHER ONE OF US DID IT.
WHY DO YOU WANT TO TALK TO US NOW?
WELL, NOT TO CHANGE THE SUBJECT, MR. KUGAYA, BUT...
ARE YOU FAMILIAR WITH THE TERM "ILLEGAL POSSESSION OF WEAPONS"?

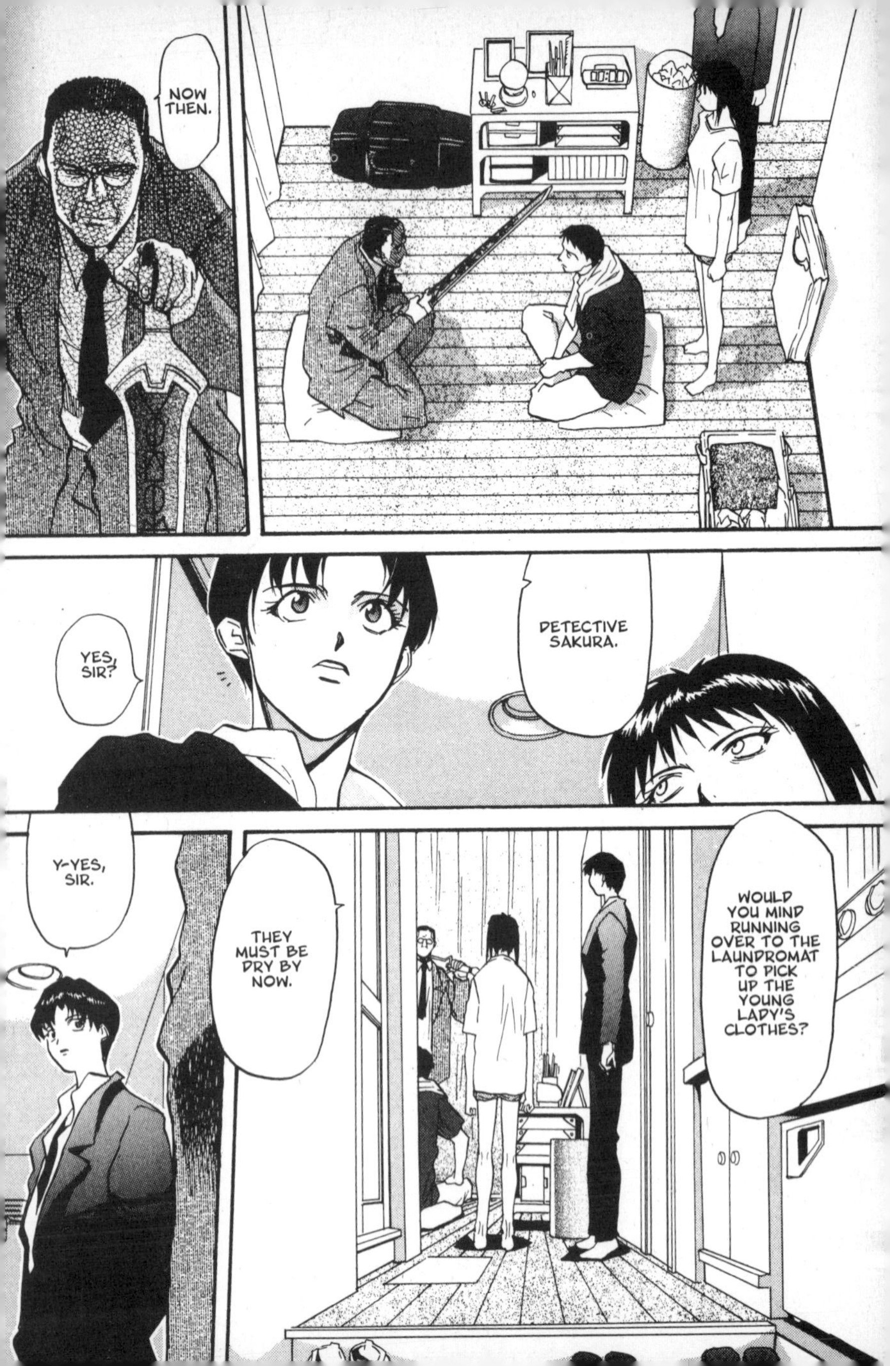
NOW THEN.
DETECTIVE SAKURA.
YES, SIR?
WOULD YOU MIND RUNNING OVER TO THE LAUNDROMAT TO PICK UP THE YOUNG LADY'S CLOTHES?
THEY MUST BE DRY BY NOW.
Y-YES, SIR.

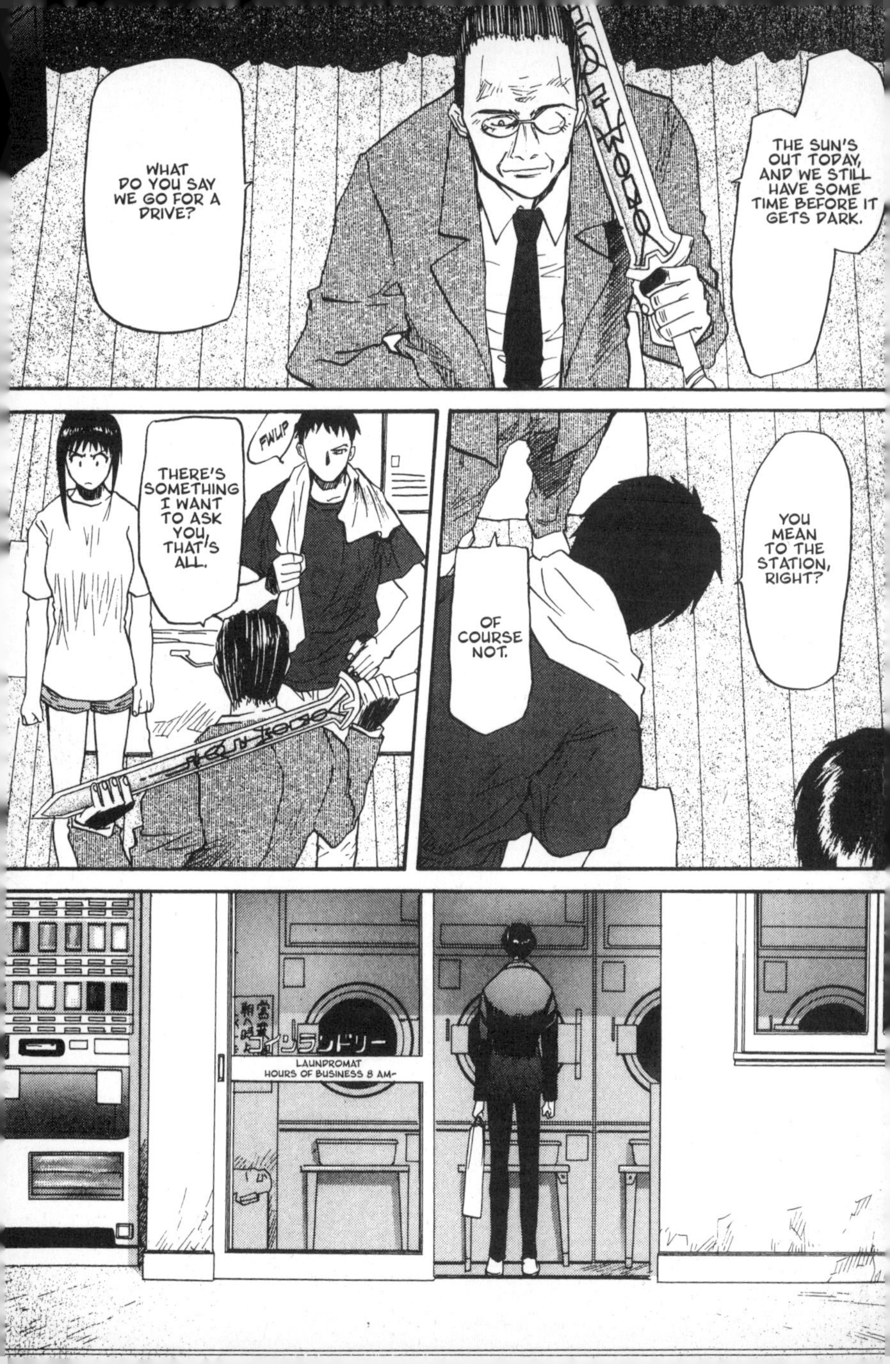
THE SUN'S OUT TODAY, AND WE STILL HAVE SOME TIME BEFORE IT GETS DARK.
WHAT DO YOU SAY WE GO FOR A DRIVE?
YOU MEAN TO THE STATION, RIGHT?
OF COURSE NOT.
FWUP
THERE'S SOMETHING I WANT TO ASK YOU, THAT'S ALL.
コインランドリー
LAUNDROMAT
HOURS OF BUSINESS 8 AM-

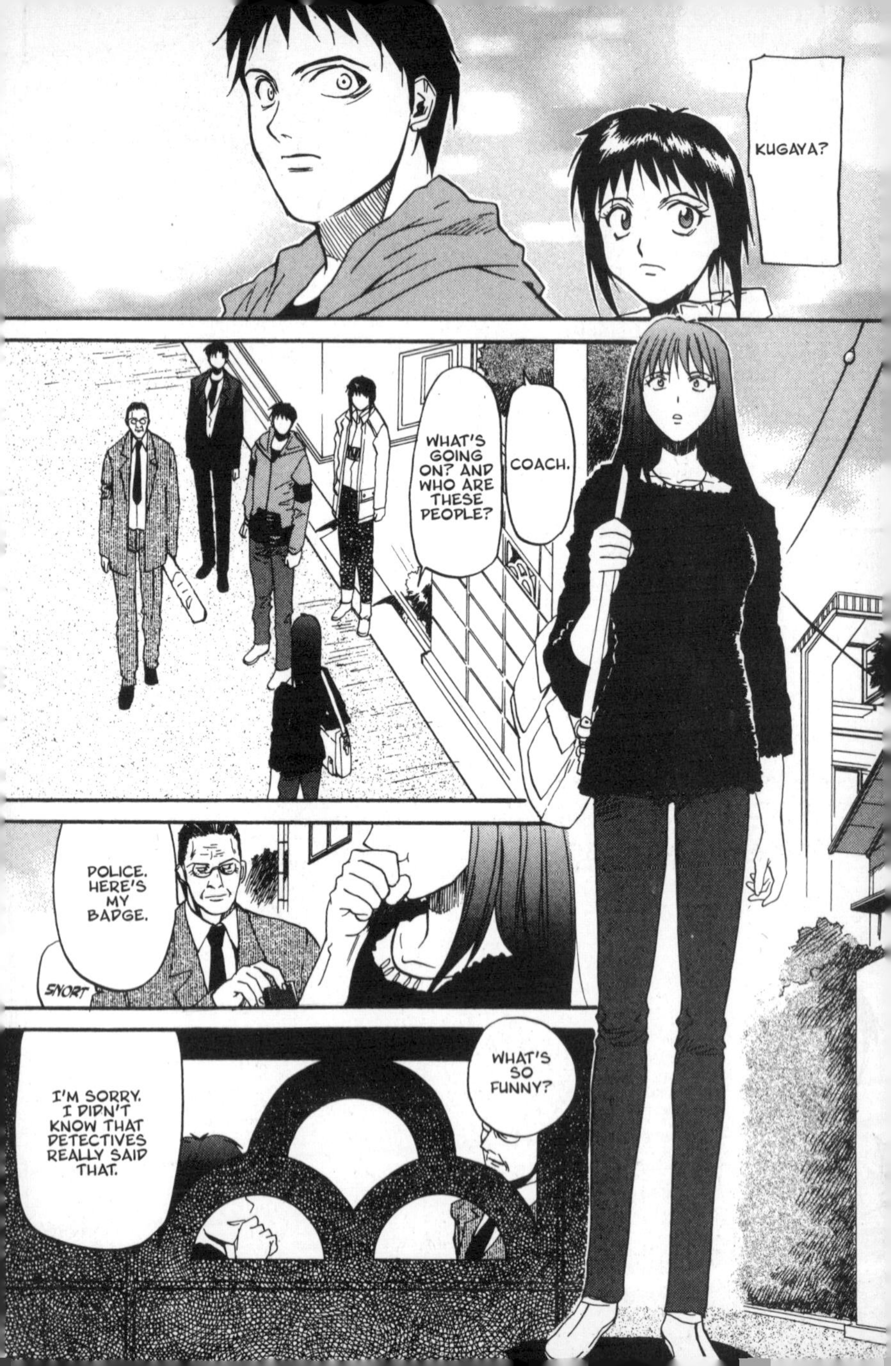
KUGAYA?
COACH.
WHAT'S GOING ON? AND WHO ARE THESE PEOPLE?
POLICE. HERE'S MY BADGE.
SNORT
WHAT'S SO FUNNY?
I'M SORRY. I DIDN'T KNOW THAT DETECTIVES REALLY SAID THAT.

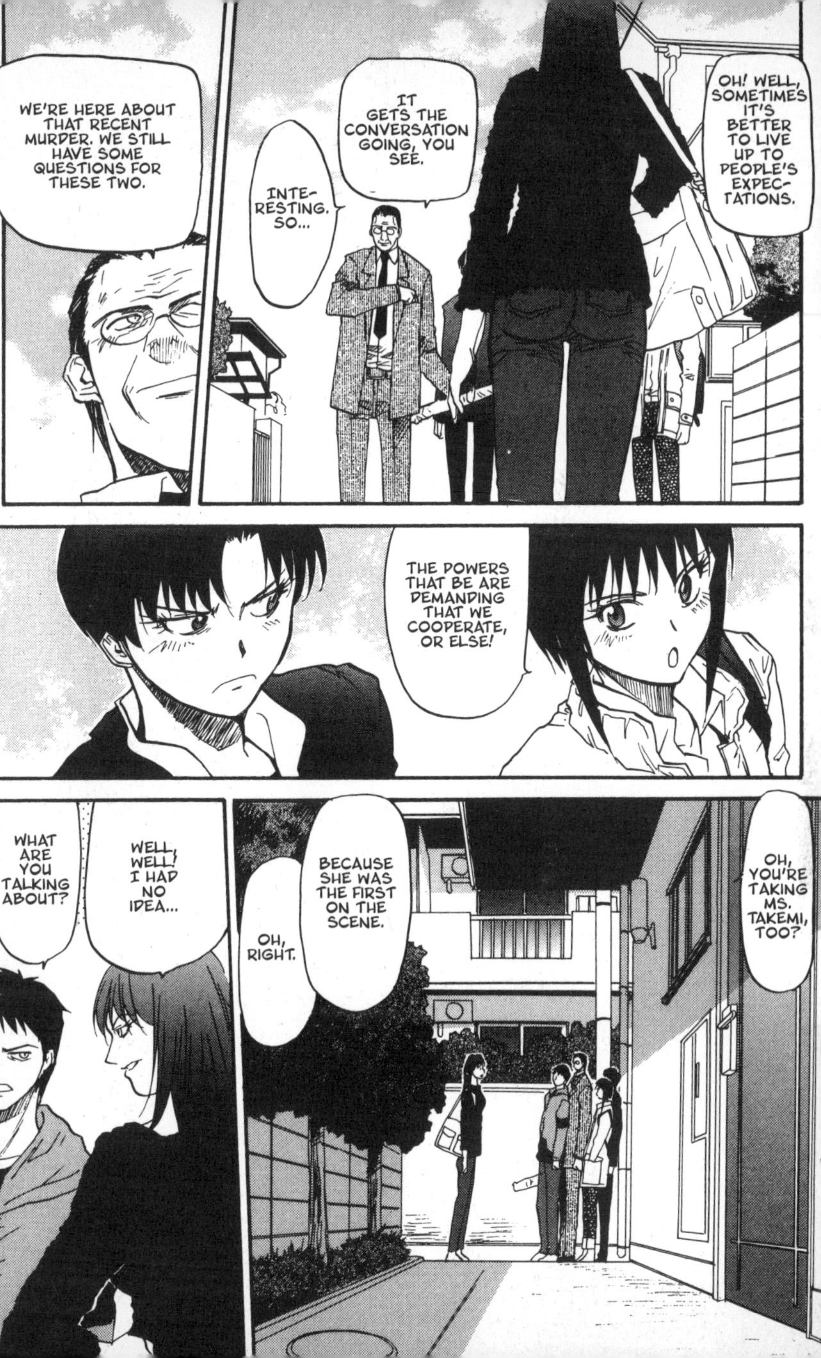
OH! WELL, SOMETIMES IT'S BETTER TO LIVE UP TO PEOPLE'S EXPECTATIONS.
IT GETS THE CONVERSATION GOING, YOU SEE.
INTERESTING. SO...
WE'RE HERE ABOUT THAT RECENT MURDER. WE STILL HAVE SOME QUESTIONS FOR THESE TWO.
THE POWERS THAT BE ARE DEMANDING THAT WE COOPERATE, OR ELSE!
OH, YOU'RE TAKING MS. TAKEMI, TOO?
BECAUSE SHE WAS THE FIRST ON THE SCENE.
OH, RIGHT.
WELL, WELL! I HAD NO IDEA...
WHAT ARE YOU TALKING ABOUT?

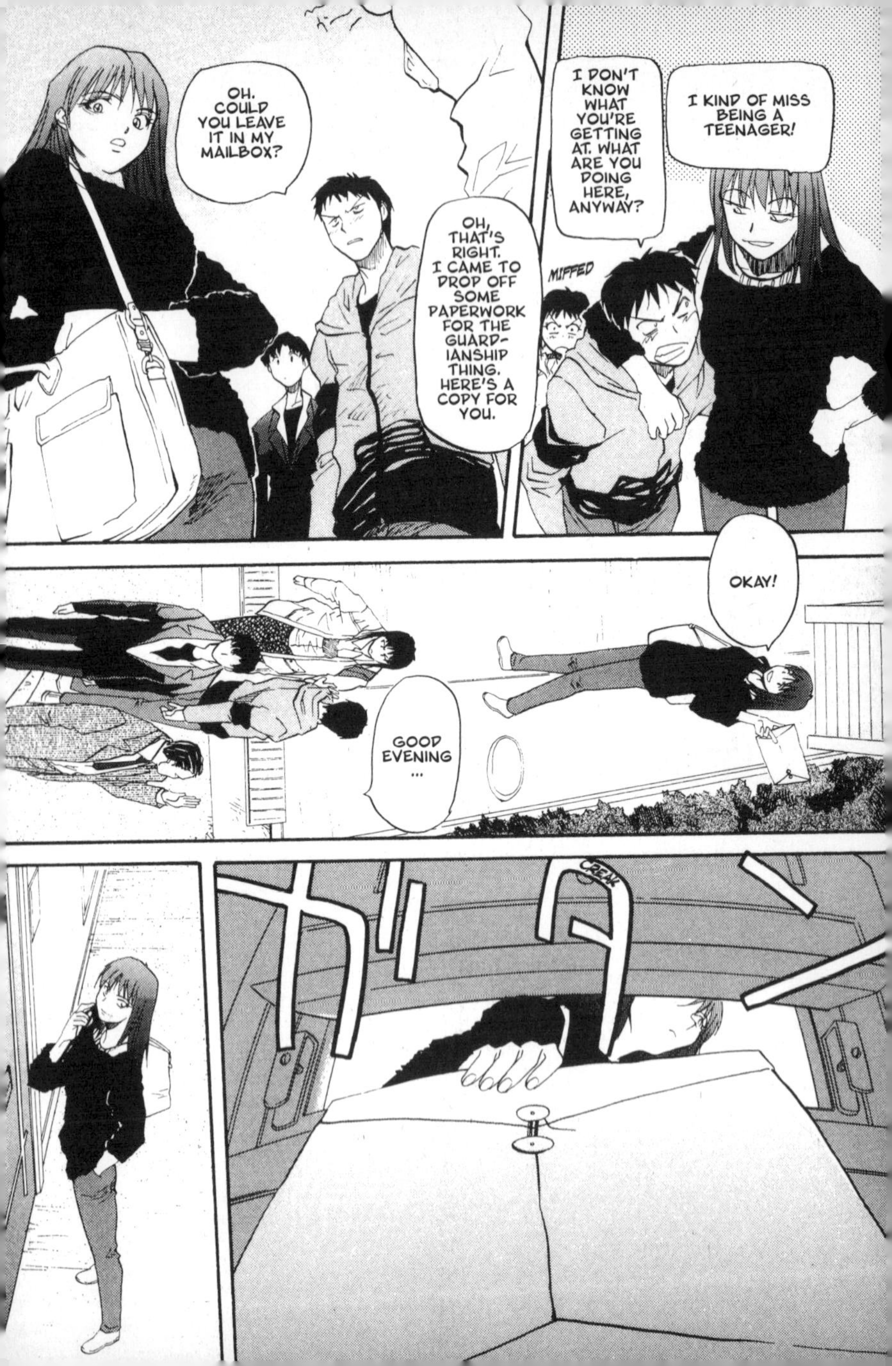

I KIND OF MISS BEING A TEENAGER!
I DON'T KNOW WHAT YOU'RE GETTING AT. WHAT ARE YOU DOING HERE, ANYWAY?
MIFFED
OH, THAT'S RIGHT. I CAME TO DROP OFF SOME PAPERWORK FOR THE GUARDIANSHIP THING. HERE'S A COPY FOR YOU.
OH. COULD YOU LEAVE IT IN MY MAILBOX?
OKAY!
GOOD EVENING ...
CREAK

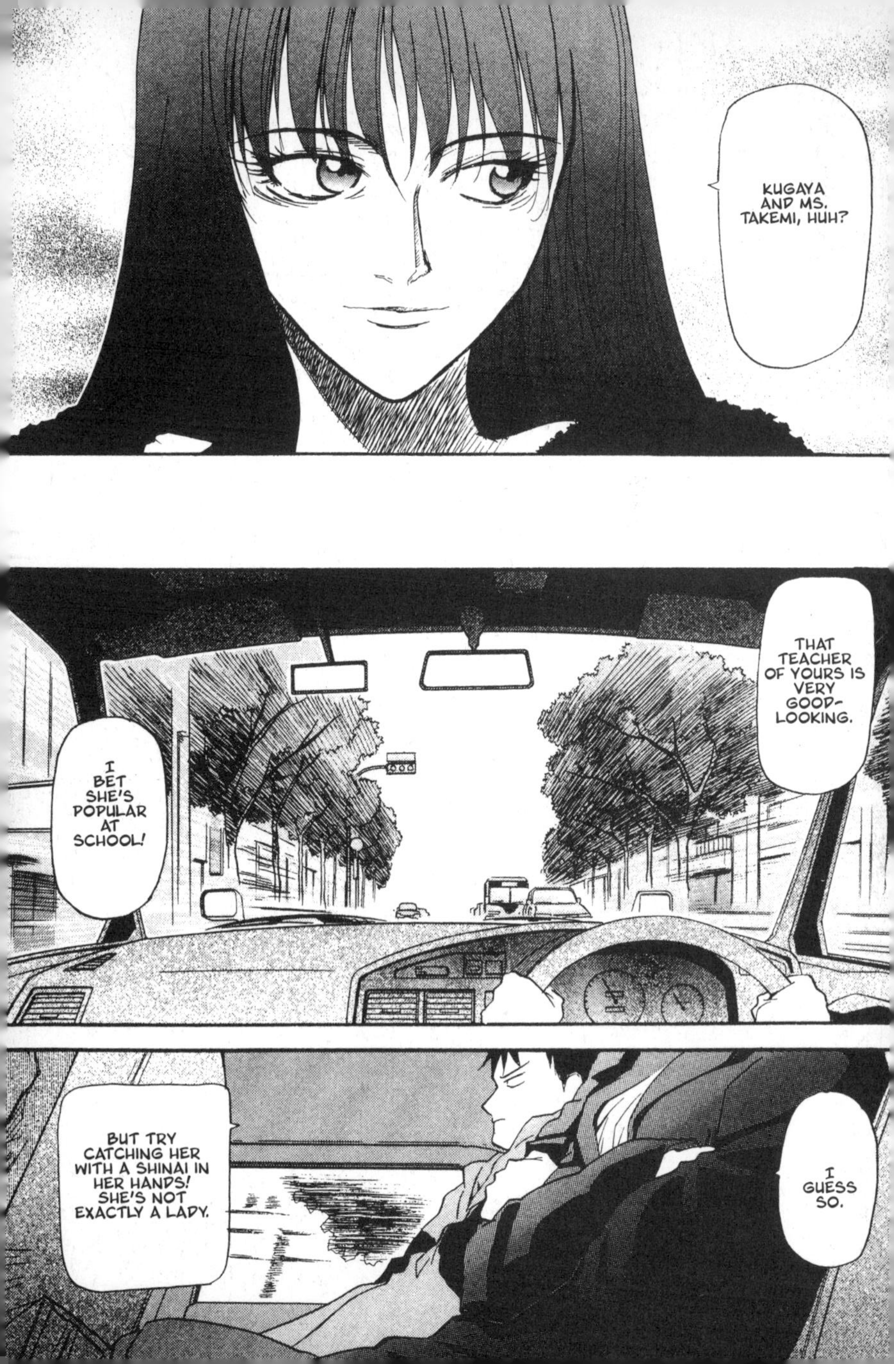
KUGAYA AND MS. TAKEMI, HUH?
THAT TEACHER OF YOURS IS VERY GOOD-LOOKING.
I BET SHE'S POPULAR AT SCHOOL!
I GUESS SO.
BUT TRY CATCHING HER WITH A SHINAI IN HER HANDS! SHE'S NOT EXACTLY A LADY.

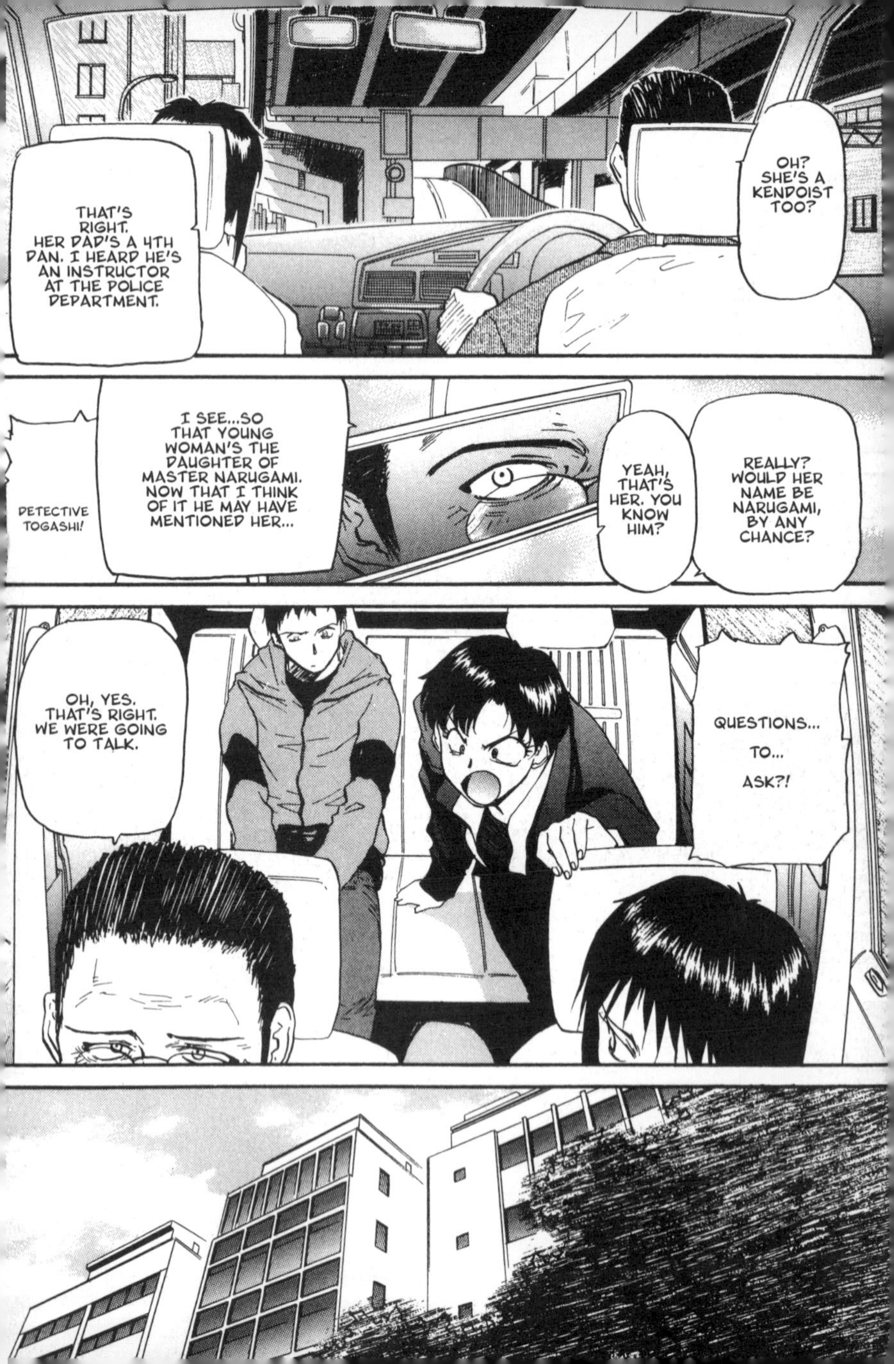
OH? SHE'S A KENDOIST TOO?
THAT'S RIGHT. HER DAD'S A 4TH DAN. I HEARD HE'S AN INSTRUCTOR AT THE POLICE DEPARTMENT.
REALLY? WOULD HER NAME BE NARUGAMI, BY ANY CHANCE?
YEAH, THAT'S HER. YOU KNOW HIM?
I SEE...SO THAT YOUNG WOMAN'S THE DAUGHTER OF MASTER NARUGAMI. NOW THAT I THINK OF IT HE MAY HAVE MENTIONED HER...
DETECTIVE TOGASHI!
QUESTIONS... TO... ASK?!
OH, YES. THAT'S RIGHT. WE WERE GOING TO TALK.

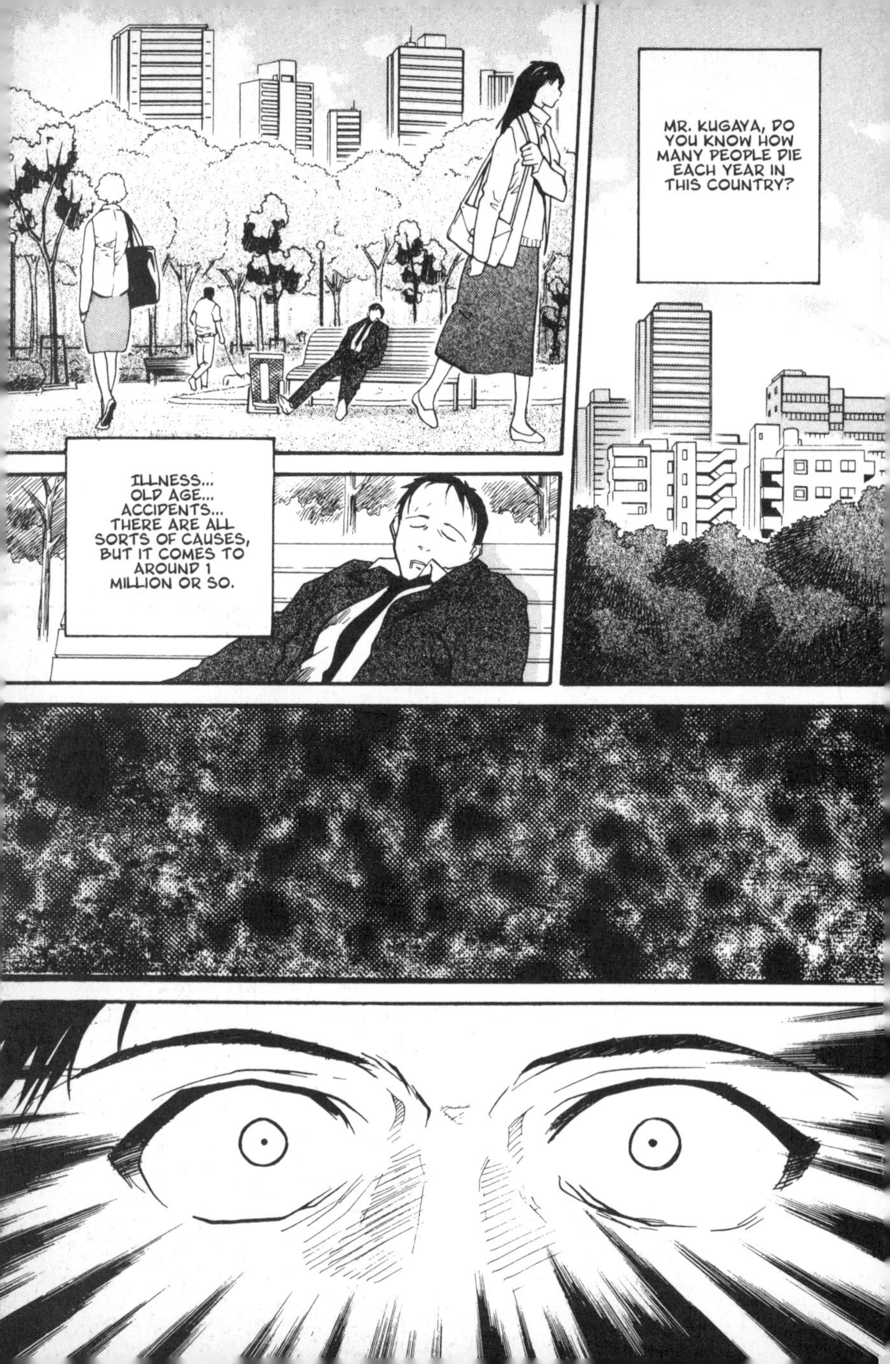
MR. KUGAYA, DO YOU KNOW HOW MANY PEOPLE DIE EACH YEAR IN THIS COUNTRY?
ILLNESS... OLD AGE... ACCIDENTS... THERE ARE ALL SORTS OF CAUSES, BUT IT COMES TO AROUND 1 MILLION OR SO.

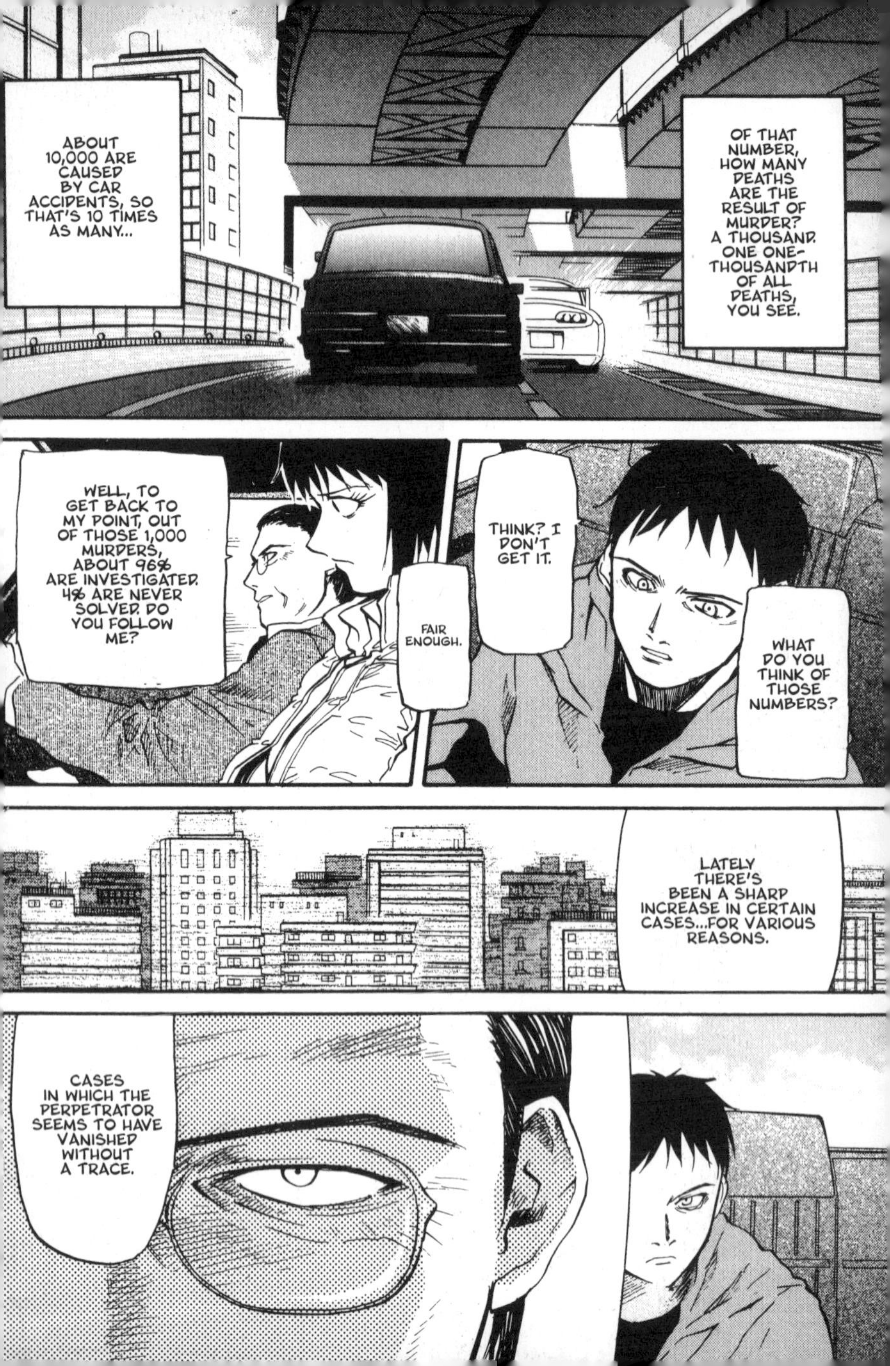
OF THAT NUMBER, HOW MANY DEATHS ARE THE RESULT OF MURDER? A THOUSAND. ONE ONE-THOUSANDTH OF ALL DEATHS, YOU SEE.
ABOUT 10,000 ARE CAUSED BY CAR ACCIDENTS, SO THAT'S 10 TIMES AS MANY...
WHAT DO YOU THINK OF THOSE NUMBERS?
THINK? I DON'T GET IT.
FAIR ENOUGH.
WELL, TO GET BACK TO MY POINT, OUT OF THOSE 1,000 MURDERS, ABOUT 96% ARE INVESTIGATED. 4% ARE NEVER SOLVED. DO YOU FOLLOW ME?
LATELY THERE'S BEEN A SHARP INCREASE IN CERTAIN CASES...FOR VARIOUS REASONS.
CASES IN WHICH THE PERPETRATOR SEEMS TO HAVE VANISHED WITHOUT A TRACE.

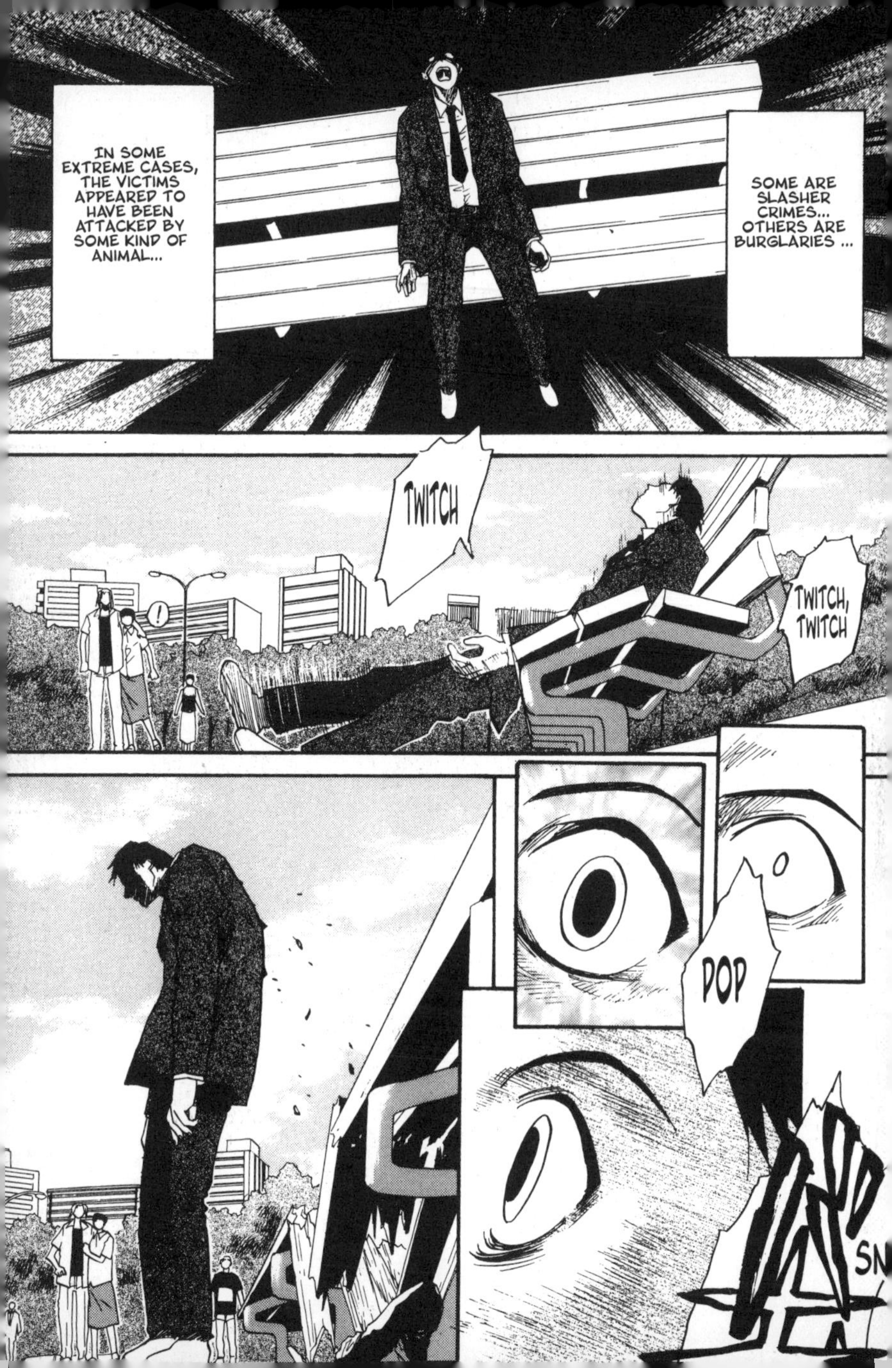
SOME ARE SLASHER CRIMES... OTHERS ARE BURGLARIES ...
IN SOME EXTREME CASES, THE VICTIMS APPEARED TO HAVE BEEN ATTACKED BY SOME KIND OF ANIMAL...
TWITCH, TWITCH
TWITCH
!
POP
SN

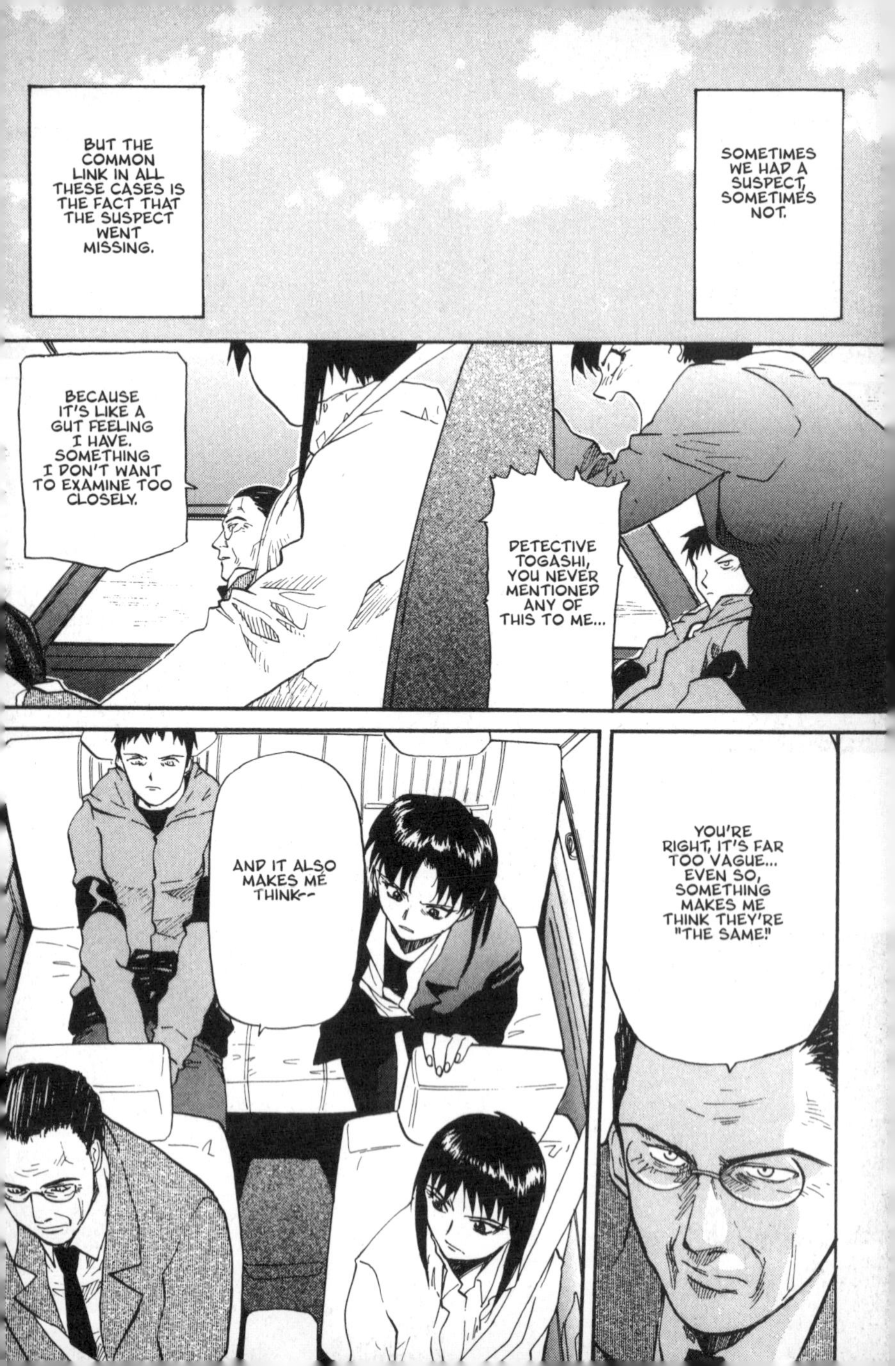
SOMETIMES WE HAD A SUSPECT, SOMETIMES NOT.
BUT THE COMMON LINK IN ALL THESE CASES IS THE FACT THAT THE SUSPECT WENT MISSING.
DETECTIVE TOGASHI, YOU NEVER MENTIONED ANY OF THIS TO ME...
BECAUSE IT'S LIKE A GUT FEELING I HAVE. SOMETHING I DON'T WANT TO EXAMINE TOO CLOSELY.
YOU'RE RIGHT, IT'S FAR TOO VAGUE... EVEN SO, SOMETHING MAKES ME THINK THEY'RE "THE SAME!"
AND IT ALSO MAKES ME THINK--

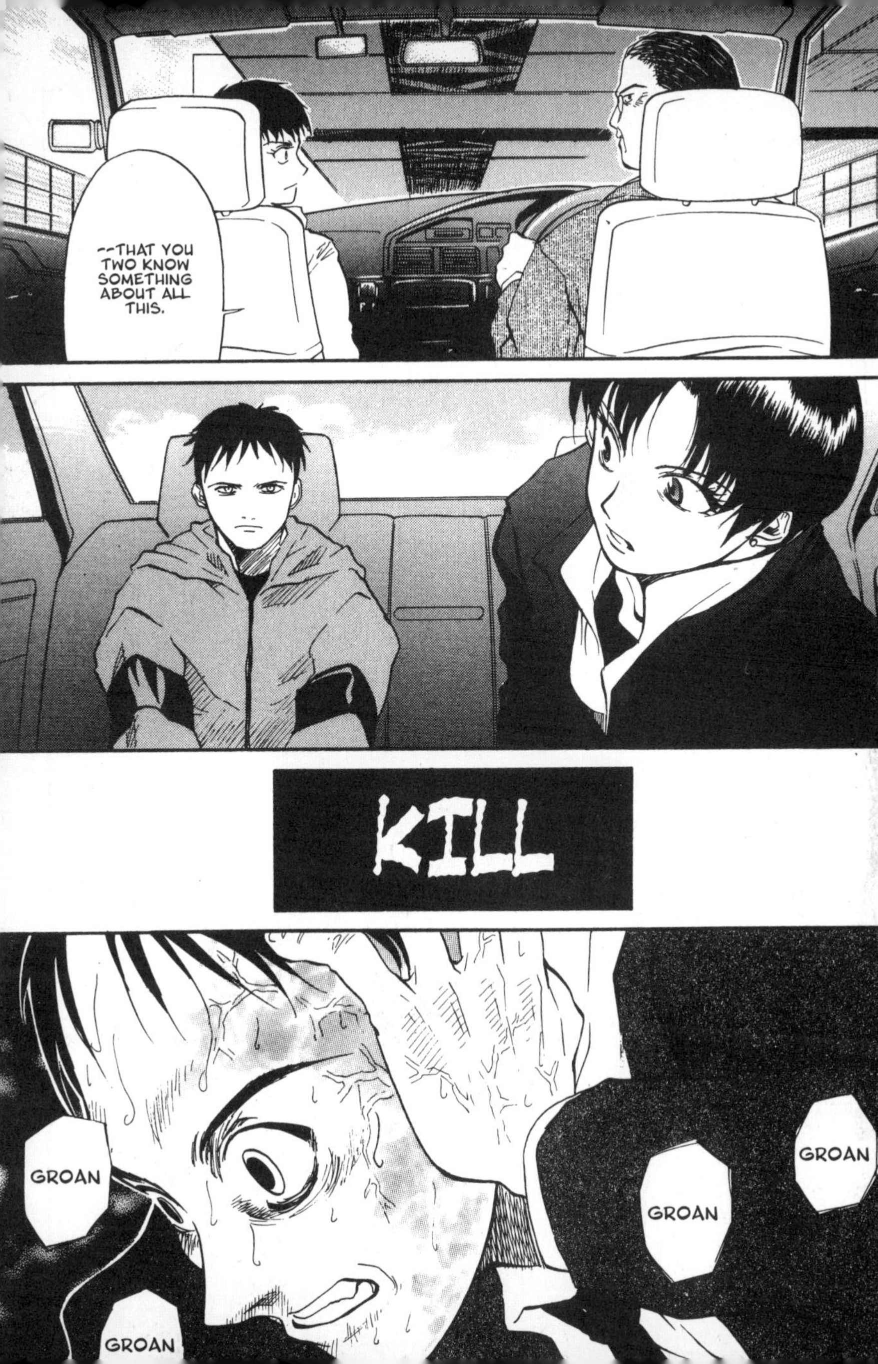
--THAT YOU TWO KNOW SOMETHING ABOUT ALL THIS.
KILL
GROAN
GROAN
GROAN
GROAN

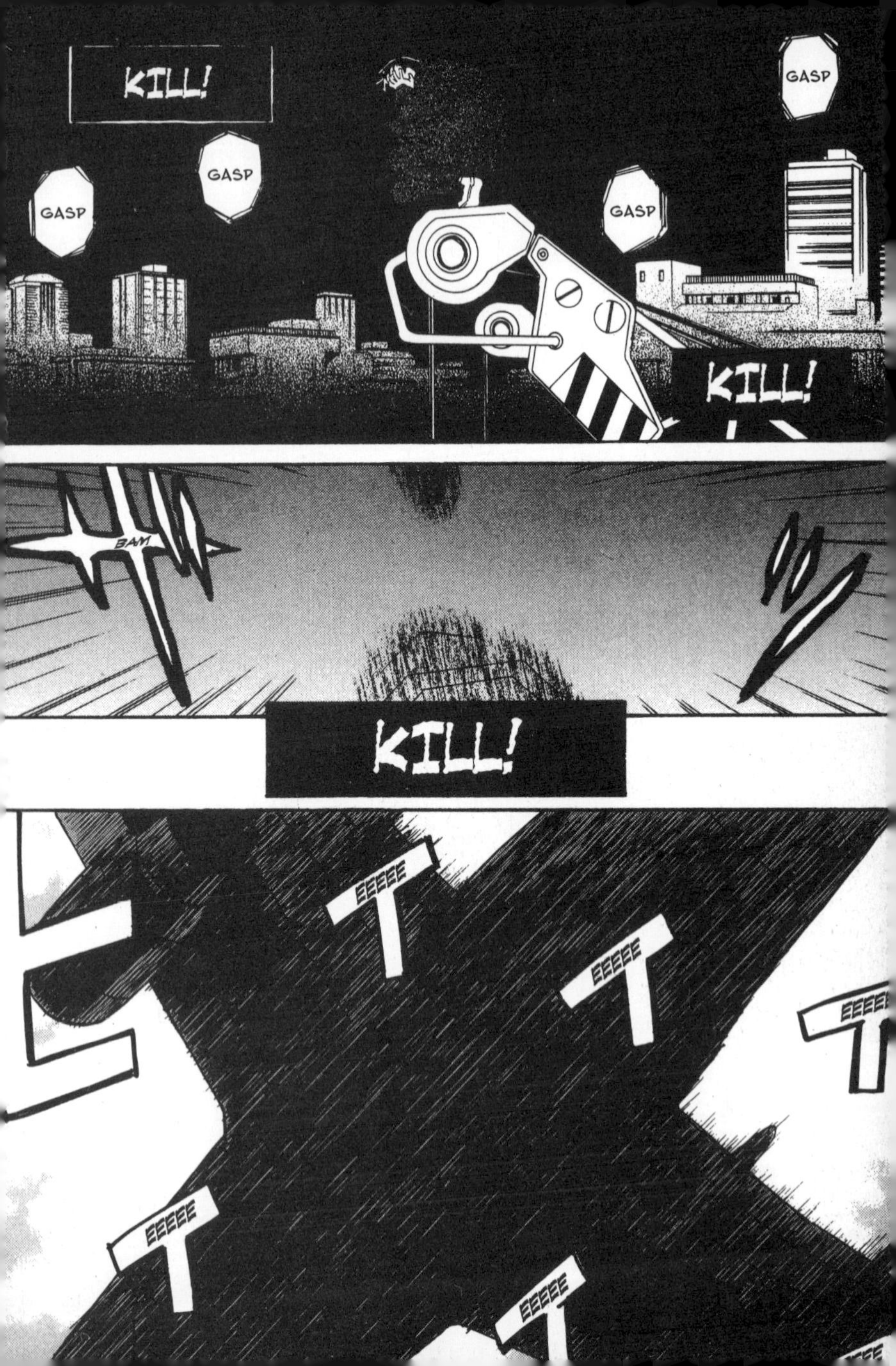
GASP
KILL!
GASP
GASP
GASP
KILL!
BAM
KILL!
EEEEE
EEEEE
EEEEE
EEEEE
EEEEE
EEEEE

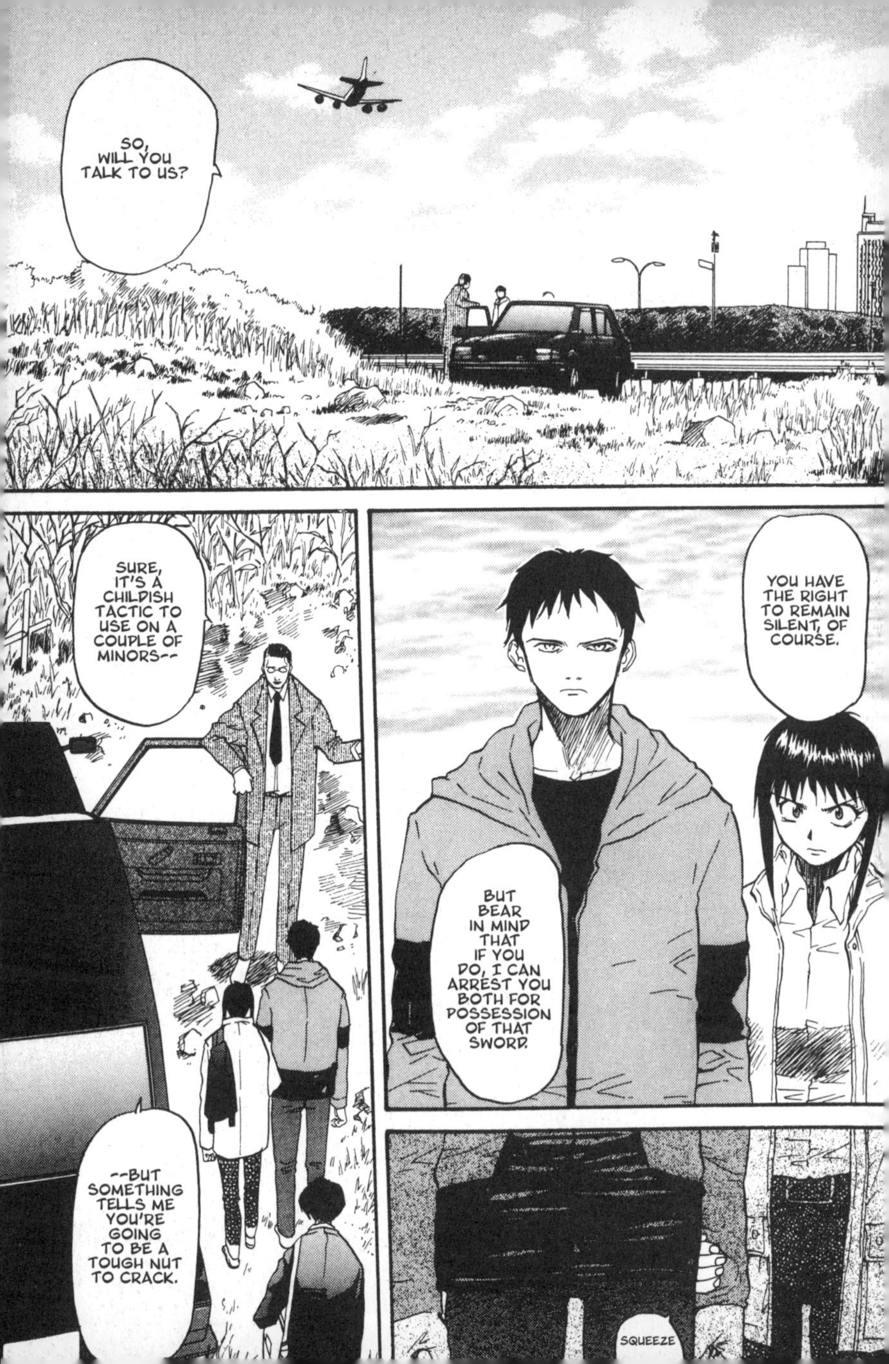
SO, WILL YOU TALK TO US?
YOU HAVE THE RIGHT TO REMAIN SILENT, OF COURSE.
BUT BEAR IN MIND THAT IF YOU DO, I CAN ARREST YOU BOTH FOR POSSESSION OF THAT SWORD.
SQUEEZE
SURE, IT'S A CHILDISH TACTIC TO USE ON A COUPLE OF MINORS--
--BUT SOMETHING TELLS ME YOU'RE GOING TO BE A TOUGH NUT TO CRACK.

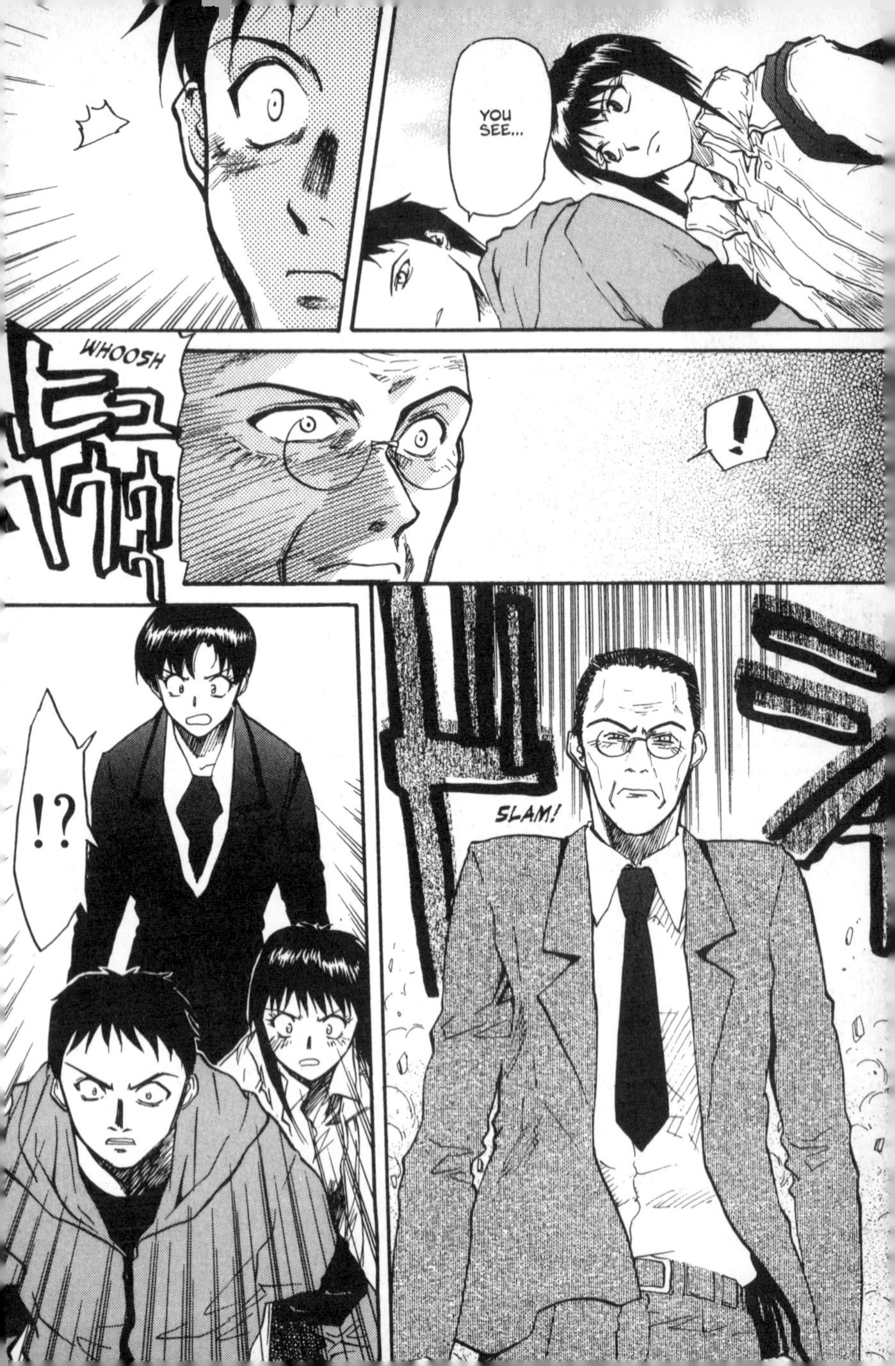
YOU SEE...
WHOOSH
!
SLAM!
!?

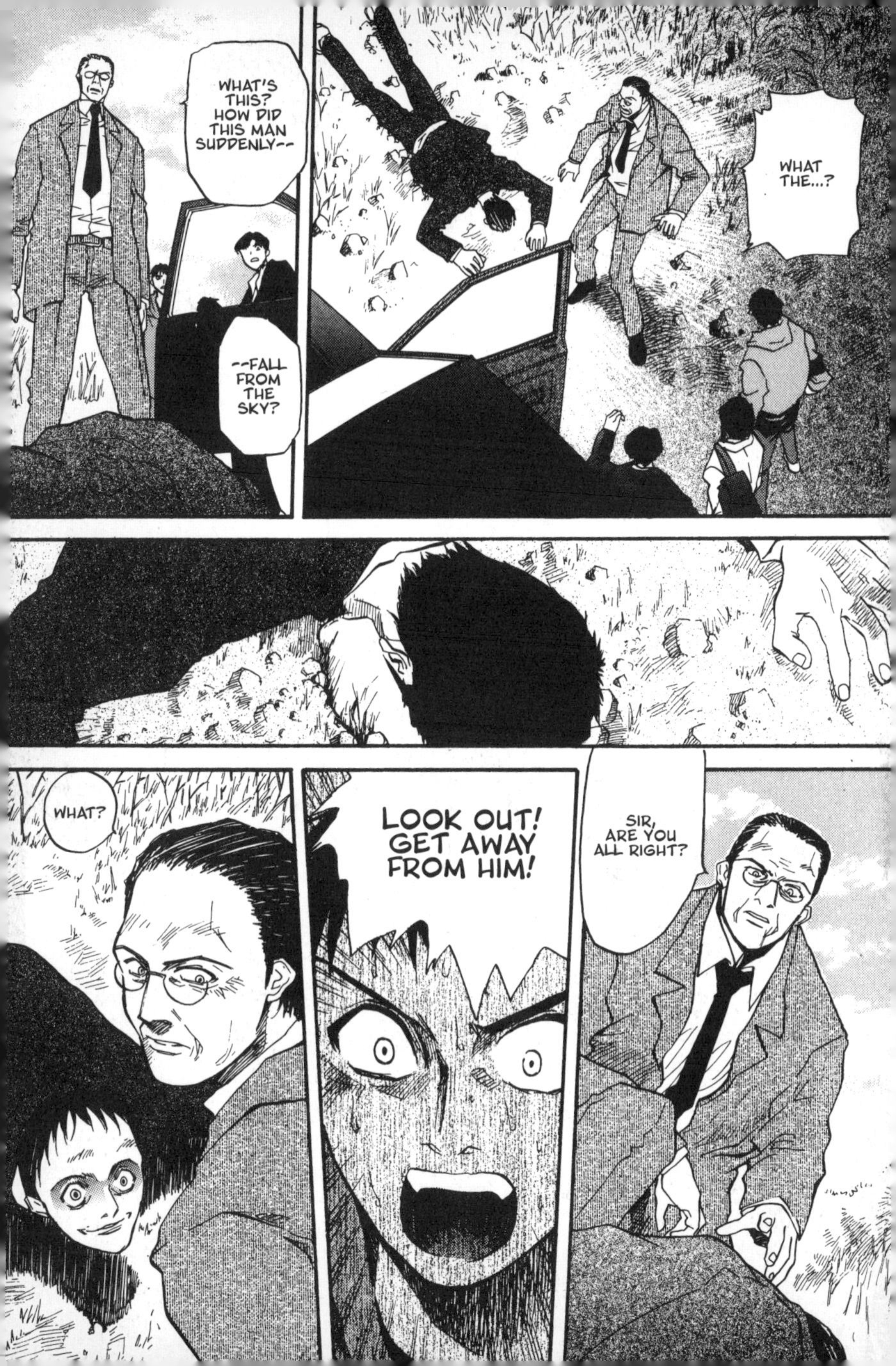
WHAT THE...?
WHAT'S THIS? HOW DID THIS MAN SUDDENLY--
--FALL FROM THE SKY?
SIR, ARE YOU ALL RIGHT?
LOOK OUT! GET AWAY FROM HIM!
WHAT?

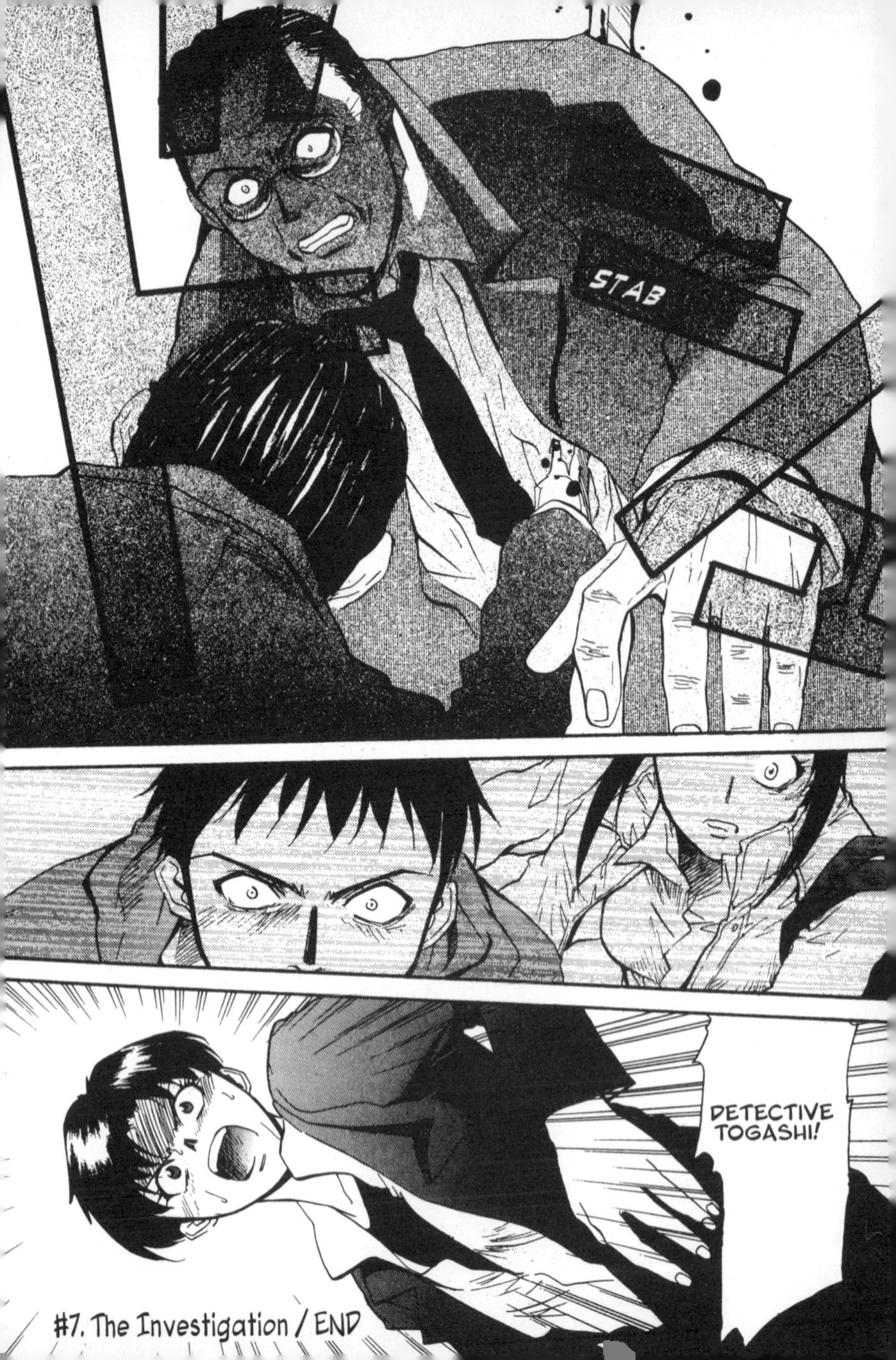
STAB
DETECTIVE TOGASHI!
#7. The Investigation / END

1ST PRINTING/YK OURS JAN '00—JUL'00

KAMUNAGARA
Inheriting the Sword

カムナガラ
～剣を継ぐもの～

Vol. 1 / END

To be continued in Vol. 2

ASSISTANTS: ASAAKI KANEKO, KEI TOKINO

(16)
YOSHINO MIHAMA
KANATA'S CLASSMATE

(16)
YUKA KAWAUCHI
KANATA'S CLASSMATE

(35)
SAKURI OGAWA
HITAKA'S AUNT

(48)
KIJU TOGASHI
METROPOLITAN POLICE DEPT.
INVESTIGATION UNIT #1
(POLICE INSPECTOR)
LIKES CAFÉ AU LAIT. SMOKER.

▲ **ASAMI SAKURA (25)**
(METROPOLITAN POLICE DEPT. INVESTIGATION UNIT #1
(ASSISTANT POLICE INSPECTOR)

(16)
SHINJI TOMARI
HITAKA'S CLASSMATE

(16)
KIYONOBU
KASHIWAZAKI
HITAKA'S CLASSMATE

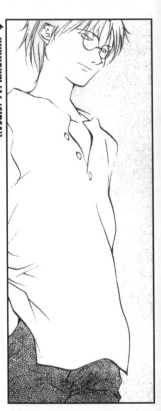

▶ **UNKNOWN [16 (CIRCA)]**
HEIGHT: 5'5" WEIGHT: 112 LBS SHOE SIZE: 8 JEANS SIZE:27" (CHANNELS MYSTERIOUS RADIO WAVES)

CHARACTER INDEX

YAMAMURA HAJIME

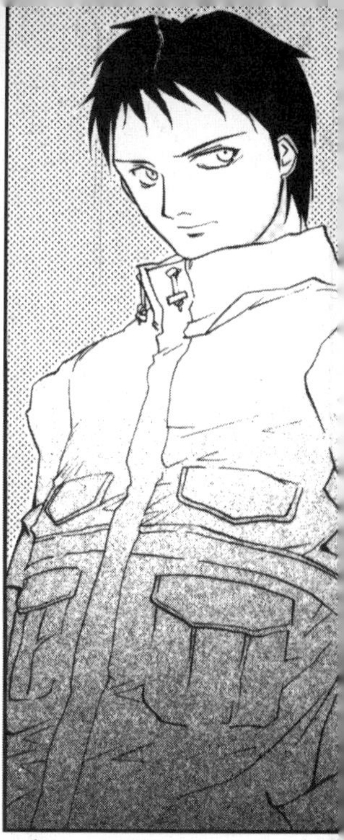

▲ **HITAKA KUGAYA (16)**

HIRO HIGH SCHOOL STUDENT
SCION OF THE CLAN OF THE SWORD
(ENGAGED IN AN EONS-OLD BATTLE
WITH INVADERS FROM THE OTHERWORLD)

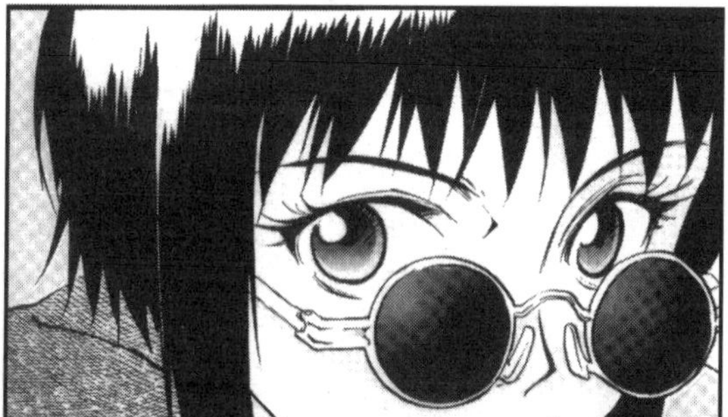

▲ **KANATA TAKEMI (16)**

HIRO HIGH SCHOOL STUDENT
SCION OF THE CLAN OF THE SWORD
BEARER OF
THE MIRROR OF CONTAINMENT

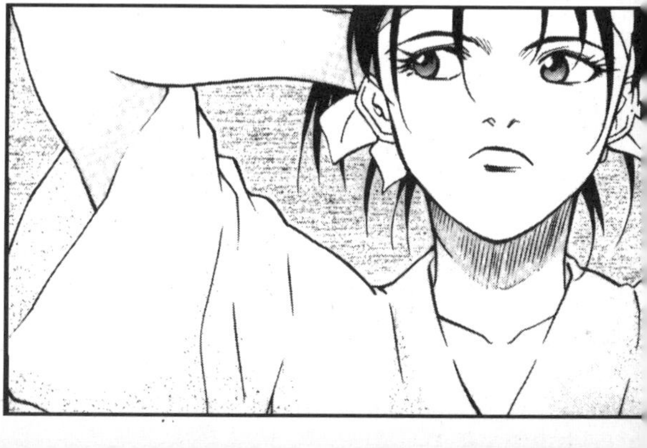

▶ **HARUKA NARUGAMI (26)**

P.E. INSTRUCTOR, HIRO HIGH SCHOOL
KENDO COACH

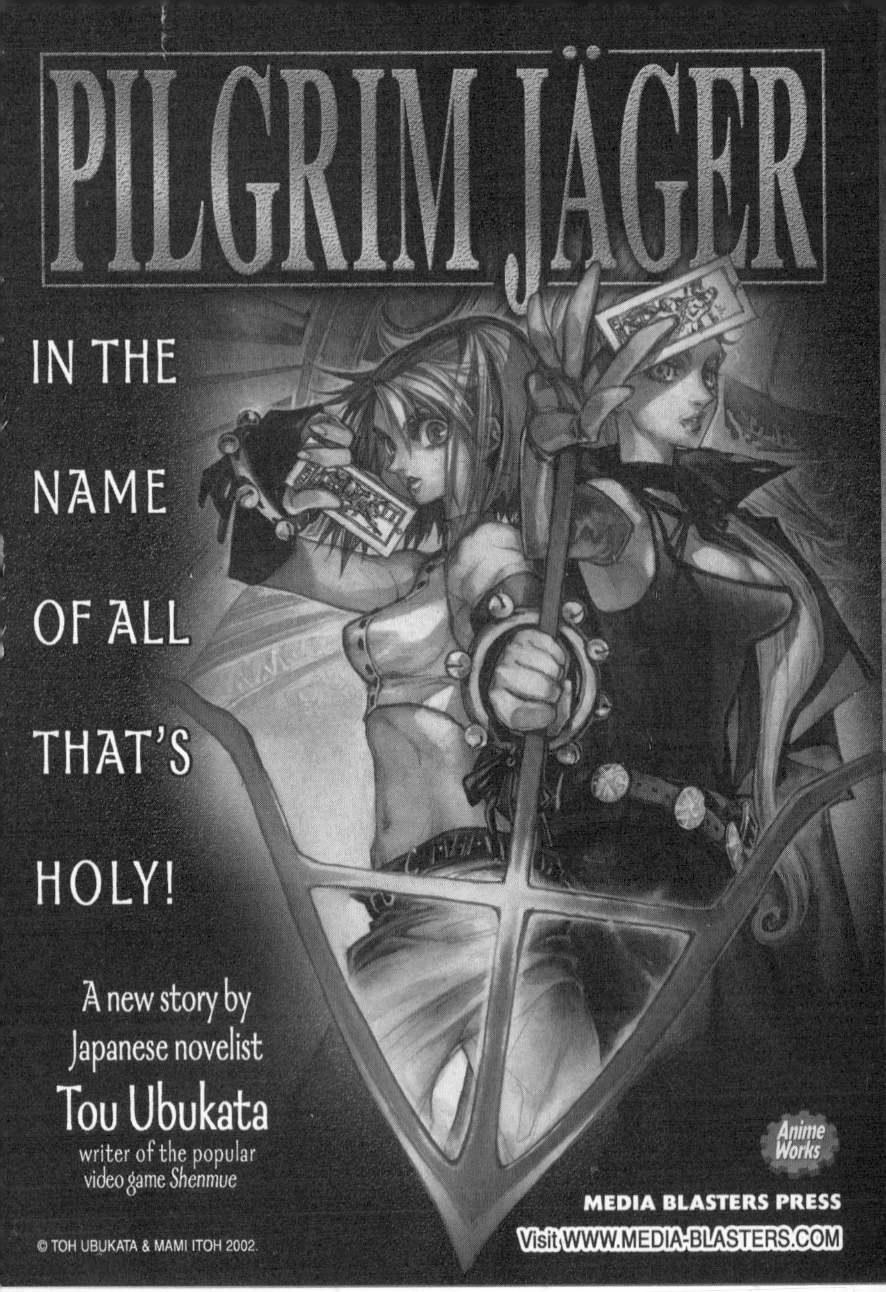
PILGRIM JÄGER
IN THE NAME OF ALL THAT'S HOLY!
A new story by Japanese novelist
Tou Ubukata
writer of the popular video game Shenmue
Anime Works
MEDIA BLASTERS PRESS
Visit WWW.MEDIA-BLASTERS.COM
© TOH UBUKATA & MAMI ITOH 2002.